the gravity of birds

TRACY GUZEMAN

HARPER

Harper
An imprint of HarperCollins*Publishers*
77–85 Fulham Palace Road,
Hammersmith, London W6 8JB

www.harpercollins.co.uk

Published by Harper 2013

1

'No Voyage' by Mary Oliver copyright © 1965, 1976 by Mary Oliver
Reprinted by kind permission of the Charlotte Sheedy Literary Agency

A catalogue record for this book
is available from the British Library

ISBN: 978-0-00-748839-1

Set in Meridien by FMG using Atomik ePublisher from Easypress

Printed and bound in Great Britain by
Clays Ltd, St Ives plc

For my parents, Jane and Dean and my sisters,
Jill and Marnie—voracious readers, all

I wake earlier, now that the birds have come
And sing in the unfailing trees.
On a cot by an open window
I lie like land used up, while spring unfolds.

Now of all voyagers I remember, who among them
Did not board ship with grief among their maps? —
Till it seemed men never go somewhere, they only leave
Wherever they are, when the dying begins.

For myself, I find my wanting life
Implores no novelty and no disguise of distance;
Where, in what country, might I put down these thoughts,
Who still am citizen of this fallen city?

On a cot by an open window, I lie and remember
While the birds in the trees sing of the circle of time.
Let the dying go on, and let me, if I can,
Inherit from disaster before I move.

Oh, I go to see the great ships ride from harbor,
And my wounds leap with impatience; yet I turn back
To sort the weeping ruins of my house:
Here or nowhere I will make peace with the fact.

Mary Oliver, 'No Voyage,' 1963

ONE
AUGUST 1963

Alice haunted the mossy edge of the woods, lingering in patches of shade. She was waiting to hear his Austin-Healey throttle back when he careened down the utility road separating the state park from the cabins rimming the lake, but only the whistled conversation of buntings echoed in the branches above. The vibrant blue males darted deeper into the trees when she blew her own *sweet-sweet chew-chew sweet-sweet* up to theirs. Pine seedlings brushed against her pants as she pushed through the understory, their green heads vivid beneath the canopy. She had dressed to fade into the forest; her hair was bundled up under a long-billed cap, her clothes drab and inconspicuous. When at last she heard his car, she crouched behind a clump of birch and made herself as small as possible, settling into a shallow depression of ferns and leaf litter. Balancing her birding diary and a book of poetry in her lap, she peeled spirals of parchment from the trunks and watched as he wheeled into the graveled parking space at the head of his property.

He shut off the engine but stayed in the convertible and lit a cigarette, smoking it slowly, his eyes closed for so long she wondered if he had fallen asleep or maybe drifted into one of his moody trances. When he finally unfolded himself from the cramped front seat, he was as straight and narrow as the trunks behind him, the dark, even mass of them swallowing his shadow. Alice twitched, her left foot gone to pins and needles. The crunch of brush beneath her caused no more disturbance than a small animal, but he immediately turned to where she was hidden and stared at a spot directly above her head while she held her breath.

'Alice,' he whispered into the warm air. She could just hear the hiss of it, could barely see his lips moving. But she was sure he had said her name. They had that in common, the two of them; they were both observers, though of different sorts.

He lifted a single paper bag from the passenger seat, cradling it close to his chest, almost lovingly. Bottles, she decided, thinking of her father and his many trips back and forth between the car and their own cabin, carefully ferrying the liquor he'd brought, enough for a month's worth of toasts and nightcaps and morning-after hair-of-the-dogs. *Damn locals mark their inventory up at the first sign of summer people*, her father had said. *Why should I pay twice for something I'm only going to drink once?* No one was going to get the better of him. So there'd been bottles of red and white wine, champagne, Galliano and orange juice for her mother's Wallbangers, vodka and gin, an assortment of mixers, one choice bottle of whiskey, and several cases of beer. All of which had been cautiously transported in the same fashion Thomas Bayber now employed.

She waited until he'd navigated the short flight of flagstone steps and the screen door banged shut behind him before she moved, choosing a soft mound of earth pillowed with needles. She scratched at a mosquito bite and opened the book of poetry to read it again. Mrs. Phelan, the librarian, had set it aside for her when it first came in.

'Mary Oliver. *No Voyage and Other Poems*. My sister sent it to me from London, Alice. I thought you might like to be the first to read it.' Mrs. Phelan fanned the pages recklessly, winking at Alice as though they were conspirators. 'It still has that new book smell.'

Alice had saved the book for the lake, not wanting to read any of the poems until she was in exactly the right surroundings. On the dock that morning, she'd grabbed a towel, still faintly damp and smelling of algae, and stretched out on her stomach, resting on her elbows as she thumbed through the book. The glare of sunlight off the crisp pages gave her a headache, but she stayed where she was, letting the heat paint her skin a tender pink. She kept reading, holding her breath after each stanza, focusing on the language, on the precise meaning of the words, regretting that she could only imagine what had been meant, as opposed to knowing with any certainty. Now the page with the poem 'No Voyage' was wrinkled, pocked from specks of sand, its corner imprinted with the damp mark of Alice's thumb. *I lie like land used up . . .* There were secrets in the lines she couldn't puzzle out.

If she asked, Thomas would decipher the poem for her, without resorting to the coddling speech adults so often used, choosing vague words and pretending confusion. The two of them had fallen into the habit of bartering knowledge whenever she visited. He schooled her in jazz, in bebop and exotic bossa nova, playing his favorites for her while he painted—Slim Gaillard, Rita Reys, King Pleasure, and Jimmy Giuffre—stabbing the air with his brush when there was a particular passage he wanted her to note. In turn, she showed him the latest additions to her birding diary—her sketches of the short-eared owl and American wigeon, the cedar waxwing and late warblers. She explained how the innocent-looking loggerhead shrike killed its prey by biting it in the back of the neck, severing the spinal cord before impaling the victim on thorns or barbed wire and tearing it apart.

'Good grief,' he'd said, shuddering. 'I'm in the clutches of an avian Vincent Price.'

She suspected their conversations only provided him with reasons to procrastinate, but she made him laugh with her descriptions of the people in town: Tamara Philson, who wore her long strand of pearls everywhere, even to the beach, after reading of a burglary in the neighboring town; the Sidbey twins, whose parents dressed them in matching clothes, down to the barrettes in their hair and the laces in their sneakers, the only distinguishable difference between the two being a purple dot Mr. Sidbey had penned onto the earlobe of one. *You, Alice,* Thomas said, *are my most reliable antidote to boredom.*

She peered through the birch trunks toward the back of the house. If she waited too long before knocking, he might start working, and then she risked interrupting him. His manner would be brisk, his sentences clipped. He was like a feral animal that way, like the cats at home she tried to entice from behind the woodpile and capture. She would never have gone over without an invitation—one had been extended, after all, in general terms—but even so, she had found it best to approach him cautiously.

Come over and visit, he'd said to her family that first day, introducing himself on the dock the properties shared, appearing from the woods to retrieve the frenzied dog that circled his feet. But introductions weren't necessary—at least not on his part. They knew exactly who he was.

* * *

'That artist' was the way her father referred to him, the same way he might say 'that ditch digger' or 'that ax murderer.' She'd staked out a listening post at the top of the stairs at home long before they'd ever driven to the lake, eavesdropping on her parents' conversation.

'Myrna says he's gifted,' her mother had said.

'Well, I imagine she would know, what with her expertise in the field of . . . what is it he does?' Her father's voice had the exasperated tone he often used when confronted with Myrna Reston's expertise in a myriad of subjects.

'You know perfectly well what he does. He's a painter. She says he's received a scholarship to the Royal Academy.'

Her father snorted, unimpressed. 'A painter. So people pay him to drink their booze and make eyes at their daughters and sit in a chair sucking on the end of a paintbrush. Nice work if you can get it.' Alice pictured her father rolling his eyes.

'There's no need for sarcasm, Niels.'

'I'm not being sarcastic. I just don't want anyone in my family fawning over some artist. We've already had more than we can handle with . . .' There was a pause, the whispers became inaudible, and Alice knew they were discussing Natalie. Her father's voice boomed again and startled her on the step where she perched. 'Why now, after all these summers of the house being deserted? Better it should stay that way—'

Her mother interrupted. 'Whether or not they use the house is no business of ours. You're only annoyed because if he's there, you won't be able to keep one of the boats tied up to the Baybers' side of the dock. You can hardly blame the young man for that.'

Her father exhaled loudly—his sigh of defeat. 'I can certainly try.'

The four of them had arrived on a Saturday evening three weeks ago: Alice, her parents, and her older sister, Natalie, all of them sweaty and road-weary, wrinkled and wretched from the long drive. When she woke the next morning the first things she saw were their suitcases lying open-jawed on the bedroom floor, spilling things yet to be unpacked. The swimsuit she grabbed from the clothesline and tugged onto her body after breakfast pulled like rubber against her skin, still damp from their ritual swim at dusk the night before. In spite of her father's wild laughter as he splashed Alice and her mother, and her mother's dramatic squeals in response, Natalie had refused to join in, and remained on the shore in the fading light, just watching them; her arms crossed and her face fixed with a cold violence, an expression she'd mastered since returning from her time away. Alice couldn't account for Natalie's sudden and intense dislike of the three of them. *Why are you being such a pill?* she'd whispered in the backseat of the car on the drive up, deliberately choosing a word Natalie often directed at her, then elbowing her sister when she refused to reply. *You're going to make them unhappy. You're going to ruin everything.*

When Alice was younger, her father had fashioned a rough mask from evergreen needles and lake grass glued to a rotten shell of pine bark, shed like a skin. He secured it to the end of their canoe with heavy yellow cord, telling Alice their ancient Dutch relatives believed water fairies lived in the figureheads of ships, protecting the vessels and their sailors from all manner of ills—storms, narrow and treacherous passageways, fevers, and bad luck. *Kaboutermannekes* he called them. If the ship ran aground, or even worse, if it sank, the *Kaboutermannekes* would guide the seafarers' souls to the Land of the Dead. Without a water fairy to guide him, a sailor's soul would be lost at sea forever. Natalie, locked in place on the rocky shore, did not look like she would protect any of them from anything.

Alice lounged on the dock that first morning, listening to her parents talk about all the things they might do with the day. They never moved from their chairs, only shifted from one hip to the other, their skin smeared white with contrails of suntan lotion, their eyes invisible behind dark glasses, their fingers intertwined until they traded sections of newspaper or reached for their Bloody Marys. When the dog suddenly appeared on the dock, a low growl deep in its throat, Alice's mother drew her feet up onto the chair, alarmed. They heard a voice coming from the deep part of the woods, calling sharply, 'Neela. Neela, come here right now.'

'She's really harmless, just suffers from 'small dog complex' is all' was what he said. She was tempted to say in return, 'You're not what I expected,' but held her tongue.

She stopped at the back door to Thomas's cabin, the books tight in her hand, and took a deep breath, brushing the forest from her feet: a stain of pitch, the powdery dust of dry leaves, a citron smear of moss. It wasn't as though she hadn't visited him before, but her parents had always known exactly where she was, had waved and shouted after her, *Don't be a bother and don't overstay your welcome*. In that moment she realized what it was to be Natalie, to know what you shouldn't do, and to do it anyway.

The paint on the door was tired brown fading to gray, cracked and buckled as alligator hide, chunky flakes of it falling to the ground as she brushed against it. She folded up the right sleeve of her shirt to hide the damp cuff she'd let dangle in the lake while reading. The wet of it soaked through, cooling a patch of her skin, but the rest of her body felt like a thing on fire, all twitchy and skittering. She rocked on her heels, holding her books to her chest. When she touched the doorknob it felt electric in her hand, hot from a shaft of sunlight slicing between the pines. She held on to it, letting it burn against her palm.

A breeze shifted across the lake, carrying with it the echo of gulls and the pungent smell of alewives rotting onshore after last night's storm. Alice looked up through the maze of branches knotted overhead, to the bright washed sky. Her head swam, and she held the doorknob more firmly in her hand.

Feel free to visit whenever you like, he'd said. At the time of the invitation her mother nodded hesitantly, eyeing Bayber's dog as the animal sniffed and scratched its way from plank to plank. Her father pulled himself up from the weathered Adirondack, causing the dock to sway slightly beneath them. With that unexpected movement something shifted, and Alice felt they were suddenly different people from the family they'd been only moments before.

'Felicity Kessler,' her mother said, offering her hand. 'This is my husband, Niels. We rent the Restons' cabin every August. You must know Myrna, Mrs. Reston?'

'My family doesn't let me out very often.' He winked at her mother, and Alice was appalled to see her mother's cheeks color. 'Myrna's—Mrs. Reston's—name may have come up in conversation, but I haven't yet had the pleasure.'

'Lucky you, on that count,' her father said.

'Niels!'

'I'm only joking, of course. As my wife will tell you, Mr. Bayber, it can be useful to have the acquaintance of someone so . . . well-informed.'

'Please, I only answer to Thomas.' He was wearing a dark sweater unraveling at the cuffs with a white button-down beneath it and paint-spattered khakis. A wicker basket piled with grapes swayed in one of his hands. 'Here,' he said, handing the basket to her father. 'Our property's thick with them. It seems criminal to let them go to waste when they're ripe.'

When no one replied, he forged on, undeterred by the guarded look on her father's face.

'Consider them a peace offering. An apology for Neela, here. She and I have a great deal in common, chief being that, according to my mother, we're both completely untrainable.'

That was the moment Alice liked him. Up until then she'd merely thought him strange, with his paint-spotted clothes, unruly hair, and eyes the same gray as the morning lake. Too sure of himself and too tall. And he stared at them—something her mother constantly admonished her not to do—but nonetheless there he was, staring at them quite deliberately and making no attempt to hide it, as if he could see past their fleshy outlines and deep inside them, into the places where they hid their weaknesses and embarrassments.

She wasn't used to people speaking so directly, especially not at the lake, where adult conversations were burdened with enthusiasm and insincerity. *We must get together while you're here! You must come over for cocktails! What charming, attractive children you have! I'll call soon!* With August stretched out before her, she'd been sure her only excitement would be found in the books she'd brought. Living next door to someone completely untrainable sounded like salvation.

'I'm Alice,' she said, reaching down to pat Neela's head. 'What sort of dog is she?'

He towered over her. His eyelashes were black and as long as a girl's and his hair was black and long as well, curling up around the pointed ends of his collar.

'Alice. Pleased to meet you. Well, no one seems sure of her parentage. I have my suspicions, but, being a gentleman, one hesitates to make accusations. There's a border collie and a Yorkie we usually see sitting on the porch of the market in town. Neela starts up with an earsplitting racket whenever we drive past. I'm quite sure they must be relatives of hers.'

Alice shielded her eyes from the sun in an attempt to get a better look at him. 'So you and Neela come here often?'

He laughed, but it was a dry, cracked sound without a trace of happiness. 'Lord, no. My parents have owned this property for decades, but have too much leisure time on their hands to actually vacation. Relaxation is very hard for the rich. There's always something that needs to be watched, some event requiring an appearance.' He glanced at her mother before adding, 'Mrs. Reston may have mentioned they're quite wealthy.'

Alice watched her mother's throat work as she swallowed slowly and looked down to examine the planks of the dock. Her father choked on his Bloody Mary before laughing and slapping Thomas Bayber on the back. 'And you said you'd never met the woman. Ha!'

Thomas smiled. 'Up until now circumstances have prevented me from spending any time in this tranquil community.' He gazed out across the lake. 'But *now* arrived earlier this year, in no uncertain terms, speaking in an emphatic voice that sounded amazingly like my father's. So I've been here since June, using their summer house as a studio. I paint, as you may be able to tell.' He gestured toward his clothes and shrugged. 'Not something my father considers a suitable occupation.'

He took a step back and squinted, studying them with his chin down, his arms folded. Alice wondered what they looked like to a stranger. Common enough, she imagined, like any cluster of people you'd see getting off of a train or passing you on the street, with only the vaguest hints that they somehow belonged to each other: the way they smoothed their hair with the palms of their hands; the determined set of their shoulders; the pale skin, easily freckled; a feature echoed here or there—her mother's pert nose on Natalie, her father's pale blue eyes repeated in her own face. The sister who was lovely; the other who was smart; a father with an expression grown increasingly somber through the years; a mother who knew how to achieve a certain degree of balance among all of them. They could be any family she knew.

Thomas nodded, his expression thoughtful. 'Your arrival provides me with an opportunity. I wonder, would you let me sketch you? All of you together, I mean.'

'Well, I'm not really sure—'

Thomas cut her father off. 'You'd be doing me a favor, sir, I assure you. I can only paint this idyllic scenery so many times. Birches, hemlocks, the gulls and woodcocks, boats tacking back and forth across the lake. Frankly, I'm losing my mind.'

Her mother laughed, interrupting before Alice's father could demur. 'We'd be delighted. It's very kind of you to ask. How exciting!'

'You could keep the sketch. Who knows? Someday it might be worth something. Of course, it's equally possible that someday it will be worth absolutely nothing.'

Alice could see her father weighing his options, one of which was likely four weeks of her mother's wrath if he declined Bayber's invitation. She wondered why he hesitated.

'I suppose if it's all of us together, it would be all right,' he finally offered. 'You've already met Alice, our amateur ornithologist. She's fourteen, and starting ninth grade in the fall. And this is Natalie, our oldest. She'll be a junior at Walker Academy next month.'

Alice realized then that her sister hadn't looked up from the dock once, seemingly enthralled with a book she was reading. Odd, considering Natalie was long accustomed to being the center of attention. She had the shiny, polished look of a new toy. Her appearance drew gawky young men to their front porch in droves, each of them hoping to be favored with a task: fetching lemonade if Natalie was warm, retrieving a sweater if she felt a chill, swatting at bugs drawn too close to her dizzying gravity. Alice had less immunity to Natalie than any of them, practicing her sister's mannerisms in the mirror when she was alone; accepting her hand-me-downs with secret delight; wishing for even a small measure of Natalie's unapologetic impulsiveness. There was power associated with her sister's prettiness. Even now, listless and drawn from some bug she'd caught after weeks spent away looking at colleges, Natalie was still the bright sun, the star around which the rest of them orbited. Her failure to attempt to charm, or even acknowledge Thomas Bayber was surprising. Even more surprising was the fact that neither of her parents admonished Natalie for her rude behavior or insisted she say hello. And Thomas Bayber, for his part, seemed equally unaware of Natalie.

'Hello. Thomas, are you there? It's Alice.' She knocked louder; the slick doorknob turned in her hand and the door creaked open.

'Thomas?'

Her father was on the skiff, halfway across the lake; Natalie had shunned her invitation to skip rocks, and instead put on her swimsuit, packed a lunch, and said she was going to the beach near town and didn't want company. Her mother was meeting summer friends for a game of bridge.

'Thomas?'

There was a scrambling sort of noise, and there he was, looming in front of her, blocking out the light. He looked as though he'd been sleeping—sloe-eyed, one side of his cheek creased with little half-moon impressions, his dark hair knotted—though she'd watched him carry the paper bags into the house not quite half an hour ago.

'You look a fright,' she said.

He smiled at her and ran a hand through his hair. 'Alice. What an unexpected surprise.'

'Is it all right?'

'Of course. Why wouldn't it be?'

'Where's Neela?' She'd grown attached to the little dog, carrying table scraps with her in case of a chance encounter. Natalie, on the other hand, referred to Neela as the *vicious little cur*.

'She'll bite you if you're not careful,' she'd told Alice.

'She will not. You're jealous because she likes me.'

'That didn't stop her from taking a bite out of Thomas, and he's her owner.'

'I don't believe you.'

'You should.' Natalie had smirked. 'I've seen the scar.'

Thomas turned and walked into the main room of the cabin. 'Neela's out visiting friends, I imagine.' His bare feet left marks in a fine dust on the floor, and Alice trailed in after him.

'Damn chalk dust,' he said. 'It gets over everything.'

'What are you working on? Can I see?'

'I'm not sure it's ready for public consumption, but if you

insist, I suppose you can have a preview. Stay there.' He sorted through canvases stacked on an easel facing the bank of windows overlooking the lake. Settling on one, he picked it up by the edges and walked back across the room, sitting on an old velvet sofa, patting the cushion next to him.

The sofa was the color of dark chocolate, the fabric stained and threadbare in places, with big tapestry pillows stuffed into the corners. In spite of its condition, a shadow of elegance clung to it. That same shadow cloaked everything in the room. Beautiful books with tattered covers and pages plumped by mildew, a grandfather clock with a cracked cabinet door and a sonorous chime that sounded on the quarter hour, expensive-looking Oriental carpets with patchy fringe—all of it near to ruin, yet perfect in the way that something is exactly as you imagine it should be. The Restons' cabin, by comparison, was a third the size and designed to look as though its owners were sportsmen, though nothing could be further from the truth. This place was like Thomas, Alice decided: flawed and sad, yet perfectly true.

She settled on the sofa next to him, folding her legs underneath her. He turned the canvas so she could see. It was a chalk sketch of the beach near town, sadly without birds. She recognized the silhouette of hemlock trees against the sky and the lip of shoreline that curled back toward itself after the point. But even though she knew the location, the way Thomas had depicted it made it unfamiliar. The pier was drawn in dark, violent slashes; the trees were leafless, charred spires; and the water looked angry, foaming against rocks and railing against the beach.

'Why did you draw it that way? It scares me to look at it.'

'I should thank you for preparing me for the critics. It's supposed to do that, Alice.'

'That stretch of beach is beautiful. It doesn't look anything like this.'

'But you recognized it.'

'Yes.'

'You recognized it even though it frightens you, even though you find it dark and ugly. So maybe those qualities are inherent, but you choose to overlook them. You don't see the ugliness because you don't want to. That's the job of an artist: to make people look at things—not just at things, but at people and at places—in a way other than they normally would. To expose what's hidden below the surface.'

Alice followed the line of a tree trunk, the tip of her finger hovering just above the paper. When she realized he was looking at her hands, she tucked them under her legs.

'Why are you hiding them?' His voice was patient, but firm. 'Let me see.'

She wavered before offering them up for inspection. He took both of them in his own, his palms warm and smooth as a stone. He examined them carefully, turning over first the right, then the left. He ran his own fingers slowly down each of hers, circling her knuckles and rubbing the skin there as if trying to erase something, watching her face the whole time. Alice bit the inside of her cheek and tried not to wince, but the pain was sharp and she pulled away.

'Be still. Why are you fidgeting?'

'It hurts.'

'I can see that.' He let go of her hands, got up from the sofa, and walked to the window, resting his sketch again on the easel. 'Have you told anyone?'

'No.'

'Not your parents?'

She shook her head.

He shrugged. 'I'm not a doctor. I'm barely an artist to

some people's way of thinking. But if something hurts you, you should tell someone.'

'I've told you, haven't I?'

Thomas laughed. 'I hardly qualify as a responsible party.'

She knew something was wrong; she'd known for a while now. She limped when she got out of bed in the morning, not every morning, but often enough that she wouldn't be able to blame it on something random much longer: a twisted ankle, a stone bruise, a blister. Fevers came on like sudden storms at night, leaving her flushed and dizzy, then vanished by the time she got up and went to the medicine cabinet for an aspirin. Rashes dotted her trunk and disappeared along with the fevers. Her joints warred with the rest of her body, using tactics that were simple but effective: flaming the skin around her knees to an unappealing red, conjuring a steady, unpleasant warming that annoyed like an itch. She'd never been blessed with Natalie's natural grace, but lately she was wooden and clumsy. Balls, pencils, the handles of bags—all fell from her fingers as if trying to escape. She stumbled over her own feet, even when staring at them. At night, time slowed to the point of stopping, each tick of the clock's minute hand stretching longer as she tried to distract herself from the pain in her joints.

She'd said something to her mother, but only in the vaguest of terms, making every effort to sound unconcerned. Her mother's reactions tended toward the extreme and Alice had no interest in finding herself confined for the entire summer. But her mother, who'd been getting ready for a dinner party at the time, had answered absently, 'Growing pains. They'll pass. You'll see.'

'Sometimes my hands shake,' she told Thomas.

'Sometimes my hands shake, too. That's when a little whiskey comes in handy.'

She couldn't help smiling. 'I don't think my parents would approve of that.'

'Hmm. I imagine you're right. Do you think you could sit still for a bit?'

'I suppose so. Why?'

'I just want to do a quick sketch. That is, if you don't mind.'

'You already did the drawing of all of us.'

'I know. But now I just want to sketch you. Is it all right or not?'

'As long as you don't draw my hands.'

He rolled up his shirtsleeves and shook his head. 'Don't start hating parts of yourself already, Alice; you're too young. I won't sketch your hands if you don't want me to, but they're lovely. Hold them up. See? Your fingers are perfectly tapered. You could hold a brush or play a musical instrument more easily than most people because of the distance from the middle joint of your finger to the tip. Ideal proportions.'

He picked up a pencil and sharpened it against a small square of sandpaper. 'Why do we lack the capacity to celebrate small bits of perfection? Unless it's obvious on a grand scale, it's not worth acknowledging. I find that extremely tiresome.'

'Birds are perfect. Yet most people completely overlook them.'

'Well, if birds are perfect, then you are as well. And I can't imagine anyone failing to notice you, Alice. Now, hold up your hand. I want you to study it.'

She was suddenly self-conscious, aware of her unruly hair, her dirty feet. She held up one hand and stared at the back of it, wondering what it was she was supposed to see, while Thomas went to the phonograph in the corner of the room and thumbed through a stack of albums before taking one from its sleeve. He set the needle down on the record, then poured himself a drink and lit a cigarette. The voice that filled the room was French and mournful, the singer entirely alone in the world.

'Are you concentrating on your hand? Do you see that river of blue running just beneath your skin? It's a path begging to be followed, or a stream running over a crest of bone before dipping into a valley. Now sit still and let me sketch you. I'll be quick.'

'Who is that?'

'Edith Piaf.'

'She doesn't sound happy.'

He sighed. 'You're going to have to stop talking. Your expression keeps changing. She's called the Little Sparrow— ah, something bird-related! If she doesn't sound happy it's because she hasn't had reason to be. Married young. Got pregnant. Had to leave her child in the care of prostitutes while she worked.' He paused and looked up from his easel. 'Am I shocking you?'

She shook her head, secretly alarmed over the woman's circumstances, but thrilled with the image that formed: an insignificant brown-gray bird with a stubby beak breaking forth into magnificent, sorrowful tones.

'The little girl died when she was just two years old from meningitis. Piaf was injured in a car accident and became a morphine addict. Her one true love died in a plane crash. She's quite a tragic figure. But her history flavors her music, don't you think? She's haunted. You hear it in her voice.' He hummed along, apparently pleased with his macabre story.

'You're not happy. Are you haunted?'

He peered at her from the side of his sketch pad before

setting the pencil down on the easel tray. He was scowling, but one corner of his mouth curved up, as if she'd amused him. 'What makes you think I'm unhappy?'

It was a fault of hers, telling people exactly what was on her mind. *You should practice the art of subtlety*, Natalie had told her once.

'I shouldn't have said anything.'

'Alice.'

She bit the inside of her cheek before answering him. 'Unhappiness is easy to see. People try so hard to hide it.'

'Very astute. Continue.'

'Maybe you hide it by the way you look at people. You only focus on their bits and pieces. Like you don't want to get to know them as a whole person. Or maybe you just don't want them to get to know you. Maybe you're afraid they won't like you very much.'

He stiffened at the last. 'I'm finished. I told you I'd be quick. It's an interesting theory, especially coming from a fourteen-year-old.'

'You're angry.'

'With someone as precocious as you? That would be dangerous.'

'Don't call me that.'

'You don't like it? It's meant as a compliment.'

'It's not a compliment.' A flush of heat swept her cheeks and her eyes started to tear. She was miserable realizing she'd said the wrong thing. 'It only means you know more than adults think you should, and that you make them uncomfortable. They're not sure what they can and can't say around you. Besides, it sounds too much like *precious*. I hate that word.'

He walked over to the sofa and offered her a handkerchief crusted with paint, but she pushed it back toward him, blinking in an effort not to cry. Thomas chuckled. The thought that he was laughing at her made her furious, and she started stammering until he put a finger under her chin and turned her face up to his.

The air in the room grew warm. The sound of her own heart startled her, the racing thump of it so obvious, so loud in her ears. How could he not hear? It drowned out the Little Sparrow, roaring over her words, her melancholy cry. The contents of the room twisted and Alice's mouth went dry. She couldn't get enough air into her lungs. Soon she'd be gasping to breathe, a fish flailing in shallow water. Her eyes darted from his feet, to the cuff of his sleeve, to the needle of the phonograph, gently bobbing along the surface of the record. Her skin tingled. There was no help for it. She had to look at him and, when she did, his expression changed from mock remorse, to concern, and then to understanding. Her face burned.

He dropped his hand and stepped back, studying the floor for a moment before looking at her again. 'Fine. From this point forward, I will eliminate both *precocious* and *precious* from my vocabulary. Am I forgiven?' He made a face and pressed his hands together, as if praying.

He was making fun of her in a kind way, or else trying to make her laugh. The world righted itself as quickly as it had been thrown off its axis. He was sorry he'd hurt her feelings. He wanted to be forgiven. A small current of power coursed through her.

'Yes. I forgive you. Besides, I'll bet if I asked your parents, they'd say you weren't very mature yourself. You can't be that much older than I am, Thomas.'

This time he didn't smile. 'Subterfuge doesn't suit you, Alice, and I hope it's not something you'll grow into. If you want to know how old I am, just ask. Although I wouldn't recommend it as a common practice. Most people would take offense. Fortunately, I am not most people.' He bowed at the waist. 'I'm twenty-eight. Worlds older than you. Ancient.'

'You don't seem ancient.'

'Well, I am. I was born old. My mother told me once that I looked like a grumpy old man from the moment I was born—wrinkled, pruney face, rheumy eyes. You've heard the expression *an old soul*? I was born with a head full of someone else's failed dreams and a heart full of someone else's memories. There's nothing to do for it, I suppose, although if I knew I was going to turn out this way, I would have preferred to choose whose memories and heartbreaks I'd be saddled with.' He looked at her. 'And you? I suppose, like most people your age, you're anxious to be older.'

She ignored the pointed *people your age*. She didn't want to admit that whatever serious plans she'd made for herself changed depending on the day of the week, or on the book she'd just read, or whether she felt strong from a full night of sleep or weak from a fevered one. The future was a dark cave yawning just ahead, beckoning her to enter.

'Not anxious. You get older, whether you want to or not.' She shrugged. 'Maybe we'll all be blown up and it won't matter.'

'What? You mean by the Communists? I shouldn't think so.'

'Why not?'

'I don't suppose the majority of them want to blow us up any more than they'd want us blowing them up.'

Alice nodded, remembering other conversations she'd overheard. 'Mutual assured destruction.'

'I'm shocked at the knowledge you possess. At your tender age I think it might be healthier for you to be less well-informed. At the very least, it would make for better sleeping. You'll grow up fast enough as it is. One becomes jaded and cynical so quickly.' He tore a filmy piece of vellum from a roll, placing it over the sketch and rolling the pieces into a tube.

'Maybe *one* should try harder not to be so jaded and cynical.'

Thomas laughed and poured himself another drink. 'A toast to you, Alice. You're a young lady wise beyond your years. Wise beyond mine, as well. May nothing, and no one, disappoint you. Now take your drawing and go. I've got work to do.'

'Can I come again tomorrow?'

'I'll likely go mad if you don't. And as you kindly indicated, I need help improving my perspective.'

She was almost all the way down the drive and back to the Restons' cabin before she realized she'd left her books sitting on the end table next to the sofa. She hadn't even asked him about the poem. *Tomorrow*, she thought. But there was a sketch she wanted to finish—the domino-marked bufflehead she'd spotted scooting through the lake's shallows that morning—and other poems waiting to be read. So she retraced her steps.

The wind picked up. A flock of grackles darkened the sky overhead, their raucous chatter filling the air like the swing of rusty gates. There was another storm coming in and if she wasn't quick she'd be drenched, even though the walk back was no more than five minutes. She left the door to the cabin ajar when she went in, calling his name softly, but there was no answer. *Work to do* most likely meant sleep, she imagined, seeing his empty glass. She hurried into the main room. The doors leading to other parts of the house were closed and everything was quiet. The cabin itself seemed to have stopped breathing, its creaks and settlings absent in spite of the wind outside. She could still see his footprints in the chalk dust on the floor, like a ghost's, leading to and away from his easel.

A gust swept into the room and sent the pile of drawings resting on the easel flying. Why hadn't she thought to close the door? She started to pick them up, intending to put them back before he noticed anything was out of place, but stopped when she glanced at the first piece of paper she touched, a colored pencil sketch. Her breath caught in the back of her throat and her skin turned clammy. She sank to her knees, unable to breathe.

Even if she hadn't looked at the face, she would have known it was Natalie. Those were her sister's arms and legs flung so casually across the sofa, the pale thread of a scar just below her knee from a skiing accident two years prior. That was Natalie's hair, mussed and wild, like caramelized sand, one long curl wrapped around a finger. That was the necklace from her latest boyfriend, the tiny pearls glowing against the skin of her neck. The tan line crossing the slope of her breasts, the small whorl of her belly button, the pale skin stretched taut between her hip bones, all the secret, private pink of her. And, erasing any hope or possible doubt, Natalie's knowing smile.

TWO

OCTOBER 2007

Finch groped for the belt of his raincoat as he got out of the cab, holding his arm up in an attempt to shield his bare head from the late October rain. He crossed the sidewalk in two steps and took the steep flight of stairs, steering clear of the refuse and odors percolating on either side of him, but landing squarely in the puddles that had formed in the centers of the treads. The wet seeped into his socks as he watched the cab disappear. Stranded. He briefly considered calling a car service and returning to his own apartment, a warmly lit, tidy brownstone in Prospect Heights, where, thanks to his daughter, the refrigerator would be well-stocked with whole-some if uninteresting food. *Your blood pressure,* she would say. *Your heart. Your knees.* He would ask, *How are prunes going to help my knees?,* wondering if he had remembered to hide his pipe, and she would simply shrug and smile at him and in that smile he would see for the briefest of moments his wife's mouth, and his entire perfect world, all as it had once been.

When he'd arranged for the Williamsburg apartment for Thomas Bayber five years ago, the neighborhood was in what the smiling real estate agent termed 'a period of transi-tion.' Finch had considered it an investment, optimistically assuming it would transition for the better, but gentrification had yet to make its way this far south. He peered through a grimy, cracked pane of glass. He could barely open the front door, swollen from all the rain, and when he pressed the buzzer for 7A there was, as always, a comedic interlude when *buzzer* and *buzzee* could not coordinate their efforts and Finch yanked impatiently at the elevator door several times, always managing to turn the knob just as the lock reengaged. After three thwarted attempts and much cursing under his breath, he turned down the hall and headed toward the stairs.

He made it as far as the fifth-floor landing before he stopped, sitting down on a step and rubbing his throbbing knees. These persistent fissures in the machinery presented themselves with stunning diligence. His head ached, whether from guilt or anger, he couldn't be sure. He only knew he didn't enjoy being summoned. There was a time he might have chalked this visit up to a responsibility of friendship, stretching the very definition of the word. But he had moved beyond the requirement of an explanation and now saw things for what they were. He was useful to Thomas at times, less so at others. It was as simple as that.

His wife would not have wanted him here. Claire might even have surprised him by voicing the words she'd kept tied beneath her tongue for so many years. *Enough is enough, Denny.* She would have been right. Even the elaborate funeral spray Thomas had sent to the church—Finch couldn't help but wonder whether he'd paid for that expression of Thomas's largesse as well—wouldn't have appeased Claire. Nor had it been of any particular comfort to him. Thomas, or things regarding Thomas, had consumed too many of their hours together to be balanced by one obscene display of orchids. A wave of grief washed over Finch, and he was overcome with her absence. Eleven months was not long—he still found the occasional sympathy card in his mailbox—but time had expanded and slowed. His days swelled with the monotony of hours, piling up in colossal heaps before and after him, the used the same as the new.

He shuddered to his feet and grabbed the stair rail, reminding himself to be thankful for this diversion. Would he have otherwise left the house today? This week? It was far more likely he'd have barricaded himself in the brown-stone, surrounded by dissertations and examinations, half-listening to Vaughan Williams's Tallis Fantasia and allowing a sharp red pencil to float just above the surface of a paper. The text would waver in front of his eyes and he would lose interest in whatever thought his student had been struggling to express, instead becoming maudlin and drifting in and out of sleep, his head snapping to attention before sinking again to his chest.

Even the small distraction of teaching might soon be behind him. Dean Hamilton had strongly suggested a sabbat-ical at the beginning of the new term next year, a suggestion Finch had opted not to share with his daughter or anyone else. 'Take some time, Dennis,' Hamilton had said to him, smiling as he stuffed wristbands and racquetball goggles into a shiny gym bag. It was all Finch could do not to throttle the man. Time. There was too damn much of it. If only he could wish it away.

When he was younger, he had often wondered about the kind of old man he was likely to become. His father had been a well-grounded person, amiable and easygoing with strangers, though rigorous with his own son. Finch assumed when he reached his own waning years he'd likely be the same, perhaps slightly more reserved. But in the void left by Claire, he found himself morphing into someone less agreeable. It was apparent to him that while they'd been together, he'd viewed people through his wife's far more generous lens. The neighbors she'd always insisted were thoughtful, he now found prying and meddlesome, cocking their heads with an expression of concern whenever he passed, clucking noises of pity escaping from their mouths. The woman across the street, for whom Claire had cooked unsettled, custardy things, seemed helpless and completely incapable of the smallest task, calling on Finch whenever she needed a lightbulb changed or her stoop swept. As if he were a houseman. The general rudeness, the lack of civility, the poor manners—all of humanity appeared to be crashing in on itself, exhibiting nothing but bad behavior.

Reaching the sixth floor, he realized it was easy enough to shift all the blame to Thomas. The man made himself an obvious target. But with each step, he recalled some slight, some other way he himself had no doubt hurt his wife over the years. The gallery openings and the parties, any occasion where Thomas held court, his arm snug around the waist of a lovely young thing. The girl would be draped in fabric that clung to her sylphlike frame; hair polished and floating about her shoulders, buoyant with light; lips stained dark and in a perpetual pout, close to Thomas's ear. These were the girls who looked off to a point just beyond Finch's shoulder, never at his face, never interested enough to pretend to commit anything about him to memory. In spite of these offhanded dismissals, how many times had he casually unlaced his fingers from Claire's or let his arm slide, almost unbidden, from her waist to his side? How many times had he taken a half step in front of her? Created a meaningful wedge of distance by gently grasping her elbow and turning her in the direction of the bar or the nearest waiter? As if she wasn't quite enough, not in this situation, not with these people. His head throbbed and a slow burn flickered and ignited somewhere near the base of his spine as he forced himself up the final flight of stairs. She had been more real than anything else in those carefully ornamented rooms, the chill so prevalent he could almost see his own breath.

There was something more he alone bore responsibility for, the thing he knew must have cut her to the quick. It was the way he'd inferred that Thomas's talent was beyond her understanding, that to be in the presence of such a rare thing was reason enough to allow oneself to be subjugated, to play the lesser role. He'd struggled against using the very words *you just don't understand* on more than one occasion. But she'd understood well enough. She knew this was as close as he was ever going to get to adulation and success on a grand scale and he'd done more than just succumb to the temptation. He dove in, headfirst, with a great splash, causing a swell that threatened to upend everything, and everyone, in his life.

Forty years ago, Finch was teaching art history and struggling to support his young family on what the college considered generous recompense for someone of his age and limited experience. A colleague suggested he pad his meager funds by writing reviews for exhibition catalogs, which in turn led to his writing newspaper articles on various gallery shows. He was fair and open-minded in his appreciations, a stance that engendered neither an ardent following nor vocal detractors, but kept the work coming his way. He was temperate with his praise, anxious to encourage interest in an artist he felt deserved it, but never overly enthusiastic, staying well back from the precipitous edge of fawning. Then, a simple request from a friend in the English Department. A young man, quite gifted she'd heard, had a small showing at a gallery uptown. Would he stop by? The father was wealthy and well-connected, had contributed generously to the college. Could he just take a look? Finch mumbled under his breath before reluctantly agreeing. Days later, halfway home before he remembered his promise, he turned around in a disagreeable state and made his way to the gallery.

At first he'd thought Thomas was the gallery owner. He was too well-dressed for a young artist, not nearly as nervous as Finch would have expected for someone giving his first solo show. He stood in a corner, towering a head above the tight circle of women surrounding him. Occasionally one would sacrifice her spot to fetch another glass of wine or a plate of cheese, returning only to find her place taken. Finch noted with humor the jostling for position. These women were all purposeful elbows and withering glances. When he parted the waters and forced a hand into the circle to introduce himself, Thomas barely smiled but grasped his hand firmly and pulled himself toward Finch as if he'd been thrown a life preserver.

'How long do I have to stay, do you suppose?' he asked. He pushed a dark curl away from his face, and Finch gauged that they were of a similar age, while acknowledging this was the only physical quality they shared. Thomas would certainly have been thought of as striking: his thin nose, unsettling gray eyes, and skin with the same pallor as a blank canvas. His shoes were tasseled and uncreased, as if purchased just for this occasion. His clothing looked flawlessly tailored and expensive, and made Finch immediately conscious of the haphazard nature of his own appearance— slightly rumpled verging on disheveled.

He shook his head, not understanding. 'I beg your pardon?'

'Here, I mean. Do I stay until the drink is gone or until the people are? I certainly know what my preference would be.'

Finch smiled, disarmed by the man's honesty. 'You're not the gallery owner.'

'Afraid not. I'm the one with all the stuff on the walls. Thomas Bayber.'

'Dennis Finch. Happy to meet you. Don't take this the wrong way, but I should probably excuse myself.'

'Ah. Critic, heh?'

'Afraid so.'

'Oh, nothing to be afraid of, I'm sure. Everyone seems to think I'm quite brilliant.' He motioned to a passing waiter for a drink and holding up two fingers, tilted his head toward Finch. 'I'll look forward to reading your review. *The Times?*'

Finch liked him a little less. 'For a first show, that would be unlikely, Mr. Bayber.'

'Please. Call me Thomas. No one ever calls me Mr. Bayber, thank God.' He put an arm around Finch's shoulder as if they were conspirators. 'Perhaps at our next meeting we will both be in slightly more elevated positions.' Thomas pointed in the direction of a group of canvases. 'As I said, I look forward to your review.'

It was as close as Finch had come to deliberately disliking something before seeing it. *Criticism with malice*, he thought, as he made his way across the room. Hubris was a quality he found hard to stomach; respectful deference had been drilled into him by both his parents. But standing in front of the work, it was impossible not to see the talent behind it, and not to be shocked. The series of surrealistic portraits was unlike anything Finch had seen, managing to look new at a time when most said the movement was dying down. There was boldness in the way Bayber used color—it made Finch feel as if he were being shouted at—and an intimacy that made him almost ashamed to study the canvas closely. People pressed in all around him, stunned into collective silence. He felt the need for air. He tried taking notes, but quickly scratched out the few words he put to paper, unable to adequately describe what he was seeing. Something pricked at his skin, tightened in his throat. He turned. Bayber was staring at him with a smile.

At the seventh floor Finch paused and wiped his face and the back of his neck with a handkerchief. Four o'clock in the afternoon and he was exhausted. He stood outside Thomas's apartment and wondered why he hadn't bothered to inquire as to the purpose of this visit. When he knocked on the door, it opened. The curtains were drawn and what little afternoon light filtered into the room was filled with swirling motes of dust. The ceiling was the same pale ivory as always, but in the year and a half since his last visit the walls had been painted a deep shade of pomegranate. Finch looked more closely and realized the paint had been applied directly onto the wallpaper, already flaked and bubbling in spots. Chairs were everywhere, turning the space into an obstacle course. As his eyes adjusted to the dim, he noticed Thomas sitting in an overstuffed wing chair against the east wall, spiraling remnants of wallpaper cascading down on either side of him. Thomas's eyes opened and closed slowly, those of a lizard king in a drugstore comic. He was dressed entirely in black except for the scarf around his neck, a plaid of dirty colors, and though Finch was used to his appearance, today it stuck in his craw. Damned annoying affectation. It certainly wasn't cold in the room; the heat and smells of liquor and sweat washed over him in waves, and he looked for someplace to sit down.

'Denny! Come in. Make yourself comfortable, why don't you? Don't hover in the doorway like some sort of salesman.' Thomas's eyes narrowed and he leaned forward in his chair as if trying to satisfy himself of something. 'You don't look well.'

'I'm fine. Couldn't be better. But I can't stay long, I'm afraid. I'm having dinner with Lydia. Some new bistro she and my son-in-law have discovered.' Finch despised lying in others as much as in himself, but he offered this up without a pang of remorse. Much easier to lay the ground-work for taking his leave sooner rather than later. He chose one of the small chairs and instantly regretted it, first hearing the squeak of springs and then feeling an uncomfortable pressure against his backside.

'How is your daughter?'

'Lydia is fine, thank you, although she fusses over me to no end. It's almost like having a babysitter.' He paused, realizing how disloyal he sounded. 'I'm lucky to have her.'

'Indeed you are. I question whether anyone really knows their own good fortune before it's too late.' Thomas gave Finch a rueful smile. 'Too late to enjoy it or exploit it, one of the two.'

Thomas appeared at odds with himself. His hands worried the fabric at the ends of the chair arms, and Finch found himself growing nervous. He couldn't remember the artist ever seeming so distracted, so undone. Thomas muttered something under his breath and looked up at Finch, as though surprised to see him still standing there.

'Tell me the truth, Denny. You've envied me my solitude at times, no doubt. No more than I have envied you the companionship of a daughter. And the bosom of family to rest your weary head upon, eh?' He gave a barely perceptible wave of his hand, before frowning. 'Well, what's to be done about it at this point?'

Had he ever wished for Thomas's solitary life? Finch tried to imagine his home of so many years void of its past activity, absent its sounds and smells of family, the briefly lingering childhood traumas, their daily interactions that had turned, almost unnoted, into habits. His wife brushing his daughter's hair in the afternoon at the kitchen table, her hand following flat behind the brush, smoothing any errant hair into place. The three of them, a family of readers, curled into small pieces of furniture on Sunday mornings, faces half-hidden behind a newspaper or a book. Claire tucked up next to him in bed, her body a sweet comma pressed against his. Lydia in his study in the evenings, her cinnamon breath warming his neck as she leaned over his shoulder and asked about the work he was studying. This and so much more had been his life. He could not bring to mind a moment when he had wished any of it away.

'You know, Denny, the older we get, the better I like you and the less fond I become of myself.'

'You're sounding positively maudlin. You must be out of gin.'

'I'm serious.'

'In that case you've proven what I've always surmised. The most successful artists are filled with self-loathing. This revelation on your part must indicate you're entering a new period of productivity, my friend.'

A thin smile broke across Thomas's lips and he closed his eyes briefly before responding. 'We both know I'll never paint anything again.' He rose from the chair and walked over to the credenza to pick up a decanter. 'Join me in a drink?'

Finch patted his coat pocket. 'I'll stick with my pipe, if you don't mind.'

'Each to his own agent of destruction.'

Finch could feel his mood deteriorating from its already low state. The atmosphere in the room was oppressively dismal. 'So, Thomas. Something is on your mind.'

Thomas laughed, a dry rattle that turned to a cough and reverberated across the room. 'Always one to dispense with the niceties, Denny. I appreciate that. Yes, there is something on my mind.' He hesitated, and Finch drummed his fingers against the worn fabric on the arm of the chair. 'What would you say if I told you I had a painting I wanted you to see?'

'An artist you're interested in?'

'The artist I've always been most interested in, of course. It's one of mine.'

Finch was certain he'd misheard. 'I've seen everything you've done, Thomas. You know I'm one of your most ardent admirers, but you haven't picked up a brush in twenty years. You told me so yourself.'

'Twenty years. Time passes so slowly and then suddenly it doesn't. At which point one becomes aware of how much of it's been squandered. Twenty years. Yes, that's true.' He walked back to the chair and stood behind it, as if for protection. 'What if this wasn't something new?'

Finch felt his tongue thicken as his mouth went dry. 'But all of your work is cataloged in my books. And in the catalogue raisonné. Every one of your paintings, Thomas, examined in minute detail.'

'Perhaps not every one.' Thomas emptied his glass and drew an unsteady hand across his chin. 'I know what a perfectionist you are. How thorough in your work and research. I had my reasons for holding back. And now, well, I wanted you to see it first. I owe you that, don't I?'

His voice took on a hypnotic note, and Finch's head began to swim. Another Bayber. It simply wasn't possible. Anger flashed warm in his veins and he dug his nails into the flesh of his palms, recalling the years he'd spent working on the catalogue raisonné. The hours away from Claire and Lydia, locked up in his cramped study, his neck angled stiffly over one photograph or another, deciphering the meaning in a brushstroke, assigning reason to a choice of color. The envy he barely tamped down at the recognition that this prodigious amount of talent had all been dumped into the hands, into the mind, into the soul of just one person. One insulated, selfish person. And now, another Bayber? This withholding seemed untenable, especially in light of the years they had known each other; the presumed friendship; the insinuation of trust, of favored status. The rent Finch paid out of his own pocket, the small monthly allowances sent to Thomas to keep him fed, although it was far more likely the money was keeping him well-lubricated. An omission such as this made his position all too clear.

Thomas cleared his throat. 'There's something else, Denny. The reason I've called you here, obviously.'

'Obviously?'

'I want you to arrange to sell it for me.'

'Me? Forgive me, Thomas, if I find this insulting.' Finch stood up and paced the circumference of the room, marking a path free from furniture. 'Why me? You could just as easily call Stark, or any one of a hundred dealers for that matter.'

'I have my reasons. I don't want this sold through a dealer or through a gallery. Besides, my arrangements with Stark ended a long time ago.' Thomas walked over to Finch, putting a hand on his shoulder. 'I want this to go straight to auction. You still have connections, Denny. You can arrange that for me, can't you? It needs to be done quickly.'

Finch's head was on fire. The pain that had started in his back spread across his body. He could torch the entire room simply by laying a finger to it.

'You could have asked me to do this years ago.' Finch could feel steam rising off his skin. 'Look at you. Look at the way you live. This isn't just a quirk or some strange artistic temperament. You live in squalor. And I've paid for a good deal of it. Why now?'

'You're angry. Of course you are. I should have expected that. I know things haven't been easy for you lately.' Thomas drew himself up and took his hand away from Finch's shoulder. He walked across the room to one of the large floor-to-ceiling windows hidden behind heavy drapes and pushed the curtain aside with his finger. 'Would it be so strange I would want back what I once had, just as you do?'

'You're the one who stopped painting. You let your reputation slide away, you didn't lose it. Kindly don't patronize me. And don't make assumptions about my life.'

'I don't expect you to understand.'

The words stung his ears with their familiarity, and a wretched knife turned in his gut. *I don't expect you to understand.* So this was what Claire had felt. This was how he'd hurt her.

Thomas studied his fingers, then turned from the window. 'In truth, Denny, I was thinking of you. It will be worth so much more now than it would have been when I painted it. I'll be able to pay you back tenfold, don't you see?' He emptied his glass and walked to the credenza again, pouring himself another. He raised the glass in Finch's direction. 'Just imagine the publicity.'

Unfortunately, Finch could imagine it quite easily. That shameful desire he was unable to submerge, the longing that persisted on the fringe of his consciousness, the unspoken wish for a speck of what Thomas had frittered away: the money, the swagger, and the talent; his ability to transport those who saw his work to a place they hadn't known existed. Finch had almost convinced himself the books were purely for scholarship. Other than insubstantial royalties, there was no personal gain. He was not the artist after all. He was an art history professor and a critic. He could pretend to understand what he saw, to divine the artist's meaning, but his was the paltry contribution. A frayed dream rose up and swirled in his head. The first to see another Bayber, to discover it, after twenty years. His disappointment in finding himself tempted was as palpable as his wife's voice in his head, their conversations continuing, unabated, since her death. *Enough is enough, Denny*. He pushed Claire away, shutting out those same melodic tones he struggled to summon each day, letting her be silenced by his racing thoughts. His pulse quickened. He rubbed his hands together, feeling a chill.

'Let's see it.'

The sly smile. As if he was so easily read, so quickly persuaded.

'Not just yet, Denny.'

'What do you mean? I can't very well talk about something I haven't seen.'

'Oh, I imagine if you put the word out, there will be the appropriate level of required interest, sight unseen. And I don't have the painting here, of course.'

Thomas's body may have been in some state of disrepair, but his ego was as healthy as ever. 'Until I see it,' Finch said, 'I'm not making any calls.'

Thomas appeared not to have heard him. 'I was thinking you might ask Jameson's son to take a look at it. Pass judgment on its authenticity. He's at Murchison, isn't he? And struggling a bit since Dylan died, from what I hear.'

'Stephen? Stephen Jameson? Surely you're joking.'

'Why?'

Was it Finch's imagination or did Thomas seem insulted his suggestion was met with so little enthusiasm? 'The young man has a brilliant mind—frighteningly so, really. He's certainly gifted, providing one manages to overlook his . . . quirks, shall we say? But they'd never send him. Cranston wouldn't let him out alone. Not to see you.'

Thomas interpreted his emotions with little more than a passing glance. 'You feel sorry for him.' He smiled. 'You're right about Cranston, of course, wretched piece of puffery that he is. But if you called Jameson, Denny. If you gave him the opportunity . . .'

How could Thomas have known? Dylan Jameson had been a longtime acquaintance, someone Finch liked and respected, the sort of friend artists long for: a champion of the unknown and overlooked, a man whose gallery was warm with the sound of laughter and kind praise, and whose opinion was delivered thoughtfully and with great seriousness. When he was alive, he'd run interference for his son, softening Stephen's spells of verbosity, tempering the impatience and the arrogance others perceived in him. As people were genuinely fond of the father, a degree of latitude was afforded the son. Stephen was in his early thirties now, drifting since his father's death, an odd duck, socially inhibited and overly sensitive. He possessed a near-photographic memory as far as Finch could tell, and an encyclopedic bank of knowledge. If rumors were to be believed, he had squandered his opportunities with an unfortunate affair.

Finch had taken Stephen out a few times after his father died, repaying old debts, he told himself, but the truth was he enjoyed having something penciled in his agenda. The man's company could be invigorating in spite of the fact that he often vacillated between morose and brooding, or became obsessive when arguing a point. After a glass or two of Bushmills, Stephen would wax rhapsodic over something he'd seen in Europe, or goad Finch into a debate on the merits of restoration versus conservation.

'Look at India. Those laws hamstringing resources in the private sector. It's obvious public projects require talent unavailable to them. The work can only be done in-house, yet most institutions don't have the necessary resources, so their art languishes in museum basements,' Stephen had said, slamming his glass on the bar and pulling his hands through his hair. 'The humidity, the poor storage facilities, all the pieces I've seen with tears and pigment damage. It's criminal. As good as treason. I can't understand why they won't move forward.'

'I'm sure they'll be happy to take your opinions under advisement, Stephen, especially considering the benign manner in which they're offered.'

Their confrontations rarely ended in consensus, as that would have required compromise and the younger Jameson seemed overly fond of his own opinions. But Finch relished their exchanges nonetheless. His meetings with Stephen kept him on his toes; they also gave him a reason to get out of the apartment, shoring up the remains of his dignity by allowing him to turn down a few mothering visits from Lydia without having to invent assignations.

How Thomas would have gotten wind of any of this was beyond Finch. He assumed little in the way of a social life for the artist, imagining him confined twenty-four hours a day to the dark, brooding apartment from which Finch now longed to escape.

'Jameson doesn't have the authority to take the piece. You know that.'

'Yes.'

'Then why involve him?'

'I've heard he's good at what he does.' Thomas turned his back to Finch and asked, 'Or should I be using the past tense?'

'You already know the answer, or you wouldn't have suggested him. Why don't you just deal with Cranston directly if you're committed to selling the piece? And why Murchison & Dunne? What aren't you telling me, Thomas? I'm not in the mood for games.'

'I want a party who will devote the appropriate amount of attention to the work. And who can be completely impartial.'

It was Thomas's questioning of his impartiality that drove Finch to the door. What a relief it would be to be done with all this, to finally put this chapter of his life behind him, where it belonged, and move on to something else. But Thomas trailed after him.

'You aren't looking at this objectively, Denny. Wouldn't it seem strange if after all this time, what with my living conditions being as they are, you were the one to 'find' another painting? If you were the one to authenticate it, after resolutely documenting my life's work?'

'All your work I knew of.'

'Precisely my point. This way no one can question your motives, cast aspersions on your reputation. I'll be the guilty party for a change, Denny. We both know I've had too much practice and taken too little credit in that department.' Thomas's hand rested on his upper arm, the weight of it light, tentative. 'I've long ago depleted my bank of favors. Whether you believe me now or not, I wouldn't trust this to anyone else. I need your help.'

Claire would have cautioned him. *It's not that you're gullible,*

Denny; you just prefer to trust the best part of a person, no matter how small. Even when there may not be any best part left to merit your trust.

Finch was exhausted, every one of his sixty-eight years weighing on him. He had never heard Thomas sound so nakedly in need of something. He looked at the man, the sucked-in hollows of his cheeks, the rattle with each inhale of breath, and capitulated. 'Fine.'

'Your word?'

Finch nodded. 'I'll call Jameson. But if this isn't legitimate, Thomas, you won't be doing him any favors. There'd be plenty of people happy to see him fall and not get back up.'

'Burned some bridges, has he?'

'Socially, he's a bloody bull in a china shop. Cranston hasn't made it easy for him, not that he's obliged to. He did give him a job, after all.'

Thomas sniffed, as if he'd gotten wind of a noxious aroma. 'I imagine that fool's getting more than his money's worth. But I wouldn't want to cause the young man further difficulties. Tell him to bring Cranston along. And thank you, Denny, for your promise to help. I'm indebted to you, more so than I ever intended.'

Finch squirmed under the word *promise,* a string of unease threading itself into his skin.

Thomas seemed to sense his discomfort, and smiled. 'The best way to slow the march of time, Denny, perhaps the only way, is to throw something unexpected in its path. I believe it will be a most interesting meeting. For all of us.' And with that, Thomas Bayber shuffled back into his bedroom, laughing.

THREE

Stephen Jameson shook the rain from his umbrella, stepped into the ancient elevator, and punched the button for the twenty-second floor with his elbow while carrying a thermos cup of coffee, his briefcase, and several manila folders. The doors closed, and he was enveloped in humid, clotted air, thick with the smells of mold and other people's body odor and a trace of something sweet and slightly alcoholic, like a rum drink. The car lurched. As it headed up, he gazed wistfully at the button marked '57,' where the executive offices of *Murchison & Dunne, Auctioneers and Appraisers of Fine Art and Antiques*, were located.

His office—the only one on the twenty-second floor—was directly adjacent to the elevator shaft, which meant the hours of his day were punctuated by the creaks and groans of transportation, as the elevator ferried those individuals more highly prized than himself to higher floors. Clutching his briefcase against his chest, he fumbled with the knob while pushing the warped office door open with a thrust of his hip. He elbowed the light switch on and glanced around the room on the off chance that some miraculous transformation might have happened overnight. No, it was all still there, exactly as he'd left it the night before. A rope of twisted phone wire emerged from a small hole in the upper front corner of the room and exited through a slightly larger hole that had been gouged in the drywall at the upper back corner; popcorn-colored insulation puffed out from one of the acoustic ceiling tiles; and there was the small but constant puddle of stale-smelling water on the floor next to the radiator.

Framed diplomas, awarding him graduate degrees in art history and chemistry, hung on the wall opposite a walnut desk, the varnish of which had peeled off in large patches. There was a catalog wedged beneath one of the desk legs where a ball foot was missing. His attempts at decoration were limited to a 'Go Wolverines!' pennant he had pilfered from a neighboring student's wall following a 42–3 blowout between Michigan and the University of Minnesota's Golden Gophers, and a crisp philodendron entombed in a pot of cement-like soil, its skeletal leaves papery against the side of the file cabinet.

He dropped the folders on top of the cabinet and plopped himself behind his desk, the leather of the chair cracked and pinching beneath him. The message light on his desk phone blinked frenetically and his cell vibrated in his pocket. He ran the tip of his finger over each button on the desk phone three times, left to right, right to left, then left to right again, but made no attempt to retrieve his messages. Instead he chewed on a hangnail as he opened his bottom drawer. From there he retrieved a bottle of Maker's Mark, generously dosed his coffee, and loosened his tie before folding his arms on the desk. He buried his head. God, he was miserable.

His eighteen-year-old self had imagined a far different future for the man of thirty-one he was now. There should have been a wife by this point. Some children would have been appropriate, to say nothing of several milestones illuminating the trajectory of his career. He pinched the bridge of his nose between thumb and forefinger to ward off a sneeze. The air ducts delivered a steady stream of dust and other noxious particles into his office, and in the two and a half years he'd been at Murchison & Dunne, he'd developed full-blown allergies as well as occasional migraines. A tickle haunted the back of his throat, giving him a hesitant intonation as he tried not to wheeze.

His desk phone rang, and after glaring at it with an intemperate eye, he mustered what remaining energy he had and raised his head.

'Stephen?'

'Speaking.'

'It's Sylvia. I left a voice mail for you earlier. Didn't you get it?'

He sat up in the chair and straightened his tie, as if Cranston's executive assistant was scrutinizing him from the opposite side of a two-way mirror instead of speaking to him from thirty-five floors above. Sylvia Dillon took a perverse delight in making his already wretched existence more so. She was a small-mouthed, crab-faced, M & D lifer with wispy blond hair that did little to cover her patchy pink scalp. As executive assistant to the president, she controlled all access to Cranston, giving her an unfortunate amount of power and an imagined degree of authority, the latter of which she did not hesitate to exercise. Her typical expression was crafted from suspicion, disdain, and disgust, and she favored Stephen with it often. Unless she was speaking with Cranston, she ended her phone conversations by abruptly hanging up on whomever she was talking to, minus the standard offering of *good-bye*, *thanks*, or even *ta*.

Those in the know made efforts to stay in her good graces: obsequious compliments, elaborately wrapped boxes of candy at the holidays, even the occasional potted plant. Stephen had silently mocked them for being stupid and toadying but now wondered if his lack of deference caused her to single him out. Either that, or it was a not-so-subtle reminder that she, like everyone else, knew exactly why he'd left his previous position four years ago.

'Sylvia. I just walked in. Just now. I stopped to look at a painting. On my way in, that is.'

'What painting was that?'

Bloody St. Christopher. Why hadn't he offered up a dental appointment or a traffic delay due to some minor smashup involving a pedestrian? He'd never been a good liar. A good lie called for a degree of calmness, a quality he did not seem to possess. He pictured Sylvia sitting behind her desk, her shoulders pinched toward each other with a military discipline, shaping her nails into talons with calculated strokes of an emery board.

'Bankruptcy case. I mean, insurance claim. Around a bankruptcy case. I wanted to have another look before putting a final valuation to the piece. Now about your message . . .'

She sighed loudly, as if their brief interchange had already exhausted her. 'Mr. Cranston would like to know if you've finished the appraisals for the Eaton estate.'

Eaton. Eaton. He rubbed his forehead and worked his way backward as was his habit. Eaton rhymed with Seton. Seton Hall. Seton Hall was in New Jersey. New Jersey was the Garden State. His favorite gardens were at Blenheim Palace. Palace Place—4250 Palace Place. The Eatons' address! The image he reeled in from the corner of his brain was of a withered eighty-seven-year-old, propelling his wheelchair down a marble-floored gallery, gesturing with a frozen finger at one painting, then another. He remembered the man's bald pate, the fascinating birthmark in the shape of Brazil that covered most of his head. Unfortunately, this Eaton was the same man foolish enough to believe his twenty-eight-year-old, third wife had married him for love. Now he was gone and she was wasting no time liquidating the estate's assets.

There was nothing extraordinary about the collection save for some Motherwell lithographs and an acrylic by Mangold that would bring a fair price at auction. Some nice furniture, most of it Louis XIV: a pair of inlaid marquetry side tables, an oak *bonnetière,* a Boulle-style, burl mahogany bronze clock that might bring fifty thousand. But most of the pieces were of lesser quality, collectibles purchased by a wealthy, bored man whose primary interest was in one-upping his neighbors.

Stephen remembered inventorying and photographing the collection more than eight months ago. The camera flash bouncing off all that blinding white—the walls, the marble floor, the sheer curtains in the gallery's Palladian windows—had given him a throbbing headache. But when had Cranston asked for the appraisals? And where had he put the file? Nothing had been transferred to his computer yet; a quick glance at his directory showed an empty folder marked 'Eaton.' He pushed his chair back and flipped through the folders on top of his desk, on top of the filing cabinet, on top of the bookcase. Nothing. If he couldn't locate it, he was done for. Cranston wouldn't be inclined to give him another chance.

'Stephen?'

'Yes, Sylvia?'

'The Eaton estate?'

'Right. Just finishing up with it.'

'Good. He wants to see you at four this afternoon to go over the paperwork.'

'Uh, that would be difficult. I already have an appointment at four.'

'I checked your online schedule. It doesn't show you being out today.'

The woman was practically purring. He pictured himself tearing the phone out of the wall and hammering her with it until pieces of her chipped off, then reconstructing her à la Picasso: an ear attached to her hip, an arm shooting out from her head, lips springing from her big toe.

'In fact, Stephen, I don't show you with anything on the books for the next several days.'

'My fault, I suppose,' he said, sifting through a stack of conservation reports and greasy sandwich wrappers on the corner of his desk. 'I haven't synced my calendar. I was planning to do it this morning. So today would be difficult.'

'He really needs this done.'

Stephen tried to visualize Cranston standing in front of her making this plea. *I really need this done, Sylvia.* Unlikely. Maybe she'd taken it upon herself to put this on Cranston's agenda in an attempt to undermine his credibility. But Stephen detected a distracted quality in her tone that indicated her attention was flagging. Perhaps another unfortunate had crept into her field of vision. Please, please, please, shit, please. He bit down hard on his lower lip, drawing blood.

'If there's no way you can do it today, I suppose I could fit you in tomorrow morning.'

'Let me just check.' He flipped through the empty pages of his agenda. 'Yes, that would be better for me, Sylvia. I'll plan to see him then. Good-bye.' He hung up the phone, waiting for a second before taking the receiver off the hook and stuffing it in his top desk drawer. He penciled a brief note on the legal pad on his desk: 'Buy potted plant.'

Four years paying for a mistake that had taken him less than a minute to make. Stephen had obliterated his oh-so-promising career single-handedly. Perhaps not single-handedly. He hadn't known Chloe was married; at least, he hadn't allowed himself to dwell on the possibility. He certainly hadn't known who she was married to. She hadn't acted like a married person, though looking back he wasn't sure how he'd thought a married person would act, aside from the obvious assumption of fidelity. *Rather an unhappy omission,* he'd told her on his cell phone, standing outside of his ex-office building waiting for a cab, his possessions crammed into a cardboard box.

He'd been in her husband's office—her husband being the recently appointed head of acquisitions for Foyle's New York, as well as his new boss—flipping through a portfolio containing photos of the material slated for the coming week's auction, when he'd looked up from an image of a pair of Sèvres blue-ground vases, circa 1770, to see Chloe's face regarding him sternly from a framed photo on the credenza.

That's Chloe, he'd said.

You know her? the man had asked.

She's my girlfriend, he'd responded automatically, unable to contain the satisfied smile that followed. At the man's astonished stare, he'd ignored the nagging buzz in the back of his brain and fumbled on, unknowingly digging the trench deeper. He had assumed it was not the image but the frame that was the treasure—a Romantic Revival, circa 1850; brilliant gold leaf over gray bole; an oval of flowers and leaves with a deep scoop and a concave outside edge; in immaculate condition aside from one hairline crack in the scoop. A piece he might covet if not for the fact he already had what lay inside the frame. So he'd opened his mouth and sealed his fate.

Seeing the picture of Chloe had made him understand both the necessity of the superlative and the fateful pride associated with acquiring something of beauty. He could feel the soft swell of her cheek under his thumb, brush a finger over the freckles dotting her nose. He could smell the exotic scent she wore, frangipani, which made him slightly queasy, like being at sea. *In Australia, they call it 'Dead Man's Finger,'* she'd told him once, before pressing her body against him under the starched hotel sheet that skimmed their shoulders. He'd shivered at the sweep of her dark hair across his chest. How had he defined happiness before her?

He'd watched other men's eyes follow her when they made their way to a table in a restaurant, had seen the subtle turn of a head on the street, followed by the gaze sizing him up. They were wondering how he'd gotten so lucky. He'd wondered himself. When he'd asked her why she was with him, she'd simply said, 'You're smarter.' If he'd thought to ask, 'Than whom?' he'd just as quickly squelched the idea, not caring to know whether the 'whom' in question was generic or specific. It was enough to be with her. He became more attractive by proxy.

But when they were apart, the feeling dogging him was a murky stew of incredulity, suspicion, and the numbing sensation of being struck dumb by his good fortune. So struck, or so dumb, his first thought hadn't been to wonder why Chloe's picture was on his boss's credenza.

'How the hell could you?' she'd demanded, in a tone that alarmed him.

'How could *I*? Can I just remind you, of the two of us, you're the one who's evidently married here? The man asked me a question. Was I supposed to lie? Besides, you're missing the more important point. I've been let go. Fired. Three years building my reputation at one of the best auction houses in the country, gone.'

'No, you're the one who's missing the point. Of course you were supposed to lie. *Anyone* else would have known that. How could you tell him I was your girlfriend?'

'Well, clearly I didn't realize who I was saying it to, for one thing. But now he knows. Is that a terrible thing? I hate to point out the obvious, but you are, after all, my girlfriend.'

The silence before she'd answered provided him horrible clarity. 'Don't you understand what you've done, Stephen? How could you be so unbelievably thick?'

At least that was explainable. His entire life he'd been blessed with an exceptional gift for misunderstanding, especially when women were involved—their desires, their needs, their way of thinking. Even his mother, on more than one occasion, had given him a studied look, as if he wasn't her child but an alien species deposited in her house. 'Why in the world would you think I meant that?' she'd ask. Those were the times he wished for a sister instead of being an only child, longing for someone who might help him to decode the inexplicable language of women.

He dismissed the whispers that trailed after him, hissed at a decibel just loud enough to be heard—*Used him. Knew someone like that would humiliate her husband. She was getting even*—and focused on those memories that couldn't be warped, in hindsight, into calculated, duplicitous acts: Chloe weaving her fingers through his as they walked in Central Park at midnight; Chloe biting down on her lower lip as she straightened his tie, a look that ruined him every time; Chloe stuffing his pockets with throat lozenges before they went into the movie theater, sequestering themselves in the back row, where his hand could wander across the top of her thigh, unseen.

The sacking (as he had come to refer to it) and subsequent breakup were followed by an equally humiliating nine-month period when he looked for work wholeheartedly, then halfheartedly, then not at all. As a patron of the arts, of local politicos and any cause célèbre, Chloe's husband had no problem calling in favors. Stephen quickly found himself blacklisted from any job, or any future, he might have deemed worthy. There would be no significant curatorial position at a major museum, nor would he be overseeing acquisitions for any Fortune 500 company. There would be no managing of conservation personnel, no addresses delivered to the American Institute for Conservation of Historic and Artistic Works. And though he could not picture himself lecturing behind a podium considering his general dislike of people in groups numbering more than five, his academic prospects were equally dim. Worst of all, he no longer worked at the most prestigious auction house in the city, at least, the most prestigious since scandal had tarnished the reputation of both Christie's and Sotheby's.

Giving up his apartment, he camped out on the futons of various colleagues, quickly wearing out his welcome and exposing those relationships for what they were—the shallowest of acquaintances, not durable enough to withstand the weight of one party polishing off whatever alcoholic beverage was in the refrigerator, even if it was a wine cooler, leaving chip crumbs to gather in the crevices of the sofa cushions, and bemoaning his future state in a tone that vacillated between whining and suicidal.

When nothing materialized in the way of gainful employment, he took to brooding at his father's gallery, shuffling invoices from one pile to another to pass the time. He might have worked there—Dylan had offered— but Stephen assumed the offer was motivated more by pity than by any real desire for his company. The gallery was already being managed by someone genial and sincere, with more enthusiasm than Stephen could have summoned, and had he accepted the offer, he would not have been the gallery's owner, or even co-owner, but an assistant to the manager. If the lack of a title hadn't been enough to dissuade him, his father's near-palpable disappointment was.

'Best get back on the horse, boyo, and stop muckin' around feeling sorry for yourself. You're not the first man to make such a colossal blunder.'

'This is an odd pep talk.' Stephen sorted through flyers, unable to meet his father's eye.

'People forget, son, but you'd make it easier for them if you were just a little less . . .'

'A little less what?'

His father only shook his head. 'Never mind. You're today's news, but that won't last forever. Some other poor unfortunate will take your place soon enough, and he'll likely have less talent than you have, Stephen. Thank God, talent doesn't go away just because you got caught with your pants down. Though, geezus, I wish it hadn't been with somebody else's wife.'

'Dad.'

'I only mean I wish it had been with somebody you could've brought home to meet your mother.' Stephen felt the weight of his father's hand hovering just above his shoulder. He prayed for it to come down and rest there, but it did not. He looked up, and the pain and disappointment he saw in his father's face worked on him like a slow-acting poison.

His father took a step back. 'You think I'm being hard on you?'

The distance between them seemed cavernous. 'Was it my fault Chloe kept her marriage a secret? No. Am I to blame for the unhappiness in their relationship? Hardly. Yet I'm the one who's being punished here.'

His father studied his knuckles. 'Really? And what about her husband? You think he's not been punished?'

The way his father asked gave Stephen a twinge of panic. He sensed Dylan knew more about such a situation than Stephen wanted to imagine.

'She should have left him,' Stephen said. Meaning *she shouldn't have left me*.

'People who are married learn to make accommodations,' his father said. 'That's the only way they manage to *stay* married.'

Stephen looked squarely at him, suddenly seeing an old man. Age had turned his father's face into a study in tectonics—deep valleys and soft folds of skin butting up against each other, shallow divots, old scars, a peppering of brown spots; the tallies of crosshatched skin at the corners of his eyes, his frizzled, electric brows; the mouth that had become thin and pickled, losing some of its enthusiasm as well as its definition.

'Honestly, I don't care about his feelings.'

'I hope you don't mean that.'

Stephen turned away. He couldn't stand to think of the situation any longer, or his part in it. 'Yes,' he said. 'I really do.'

Stephen tipped more whiskey into what was left of his coffee and reached for a tissue as he sneezed, then blotted at the papers strewn across the top of his desk. It had been a comeuppance of near-biblical proportions. When he was still a rising star at Foyle's, his days had been spent traveling across Europe on the company's dime, and oh, what days! He visited auction houses, private homes, and museums. He marveled at Old Masters and contemporary giants, advised on the restoration project at Lascaux, skimmed his fingers across Aubusson tapestries from the hands of Flemish weavers, examined expertly crafted furniture, even humbly proffered his opinion as to the value of a Meissen thimble decorated with the coat of arms of an Irish aristocrat. Now, four years later, he was trapped at Murchison & Dunne, occupying the lowest rung on the ladder, doing nothing but appraisals while interest piled up on his credit cards, his rent crept steadily upward, and his position grew increasingly precarious.

It was no coincidence they'd stuck him here, on the twenty-second floor. Simon Hapsend, the employee who'd previously had the office, was responsible for developing the company's website and promoting the firm's capabilities for forensic valuation work, an assortment of services running the gamut from expert witness testimony and valuations for insurance purposes to prenuptial assessments, bankruptcies, and trust and estate work.

But Simon had been abruptly fired when an FBI task force traced attempts to hack into the systems of several major financial institutions back to his computer. That the task force's computer evidence had itself been hacked and could not be located was the only thing that kept Simon from an orange jumpsuit and a new address at Rikers. So Stephen inherited the office, along with the odd remnants of Simon he stumbled across: lists of passwords and user names stuffed into a gap at the back of a drawer, e-mails from an unknown sender requesting that Stephen delete the files that mysteriously appeared on his computer, and an olive drab T-shirt, the source of a rank smell, with a picture of a snake and the word *Python* in black script that was finally, and fortunately, discovered wadded up behind the file cabinet.

Stephen stared at the wall, wondering how long he could subsist on ramen noodles and beer. His confidence regarding his talent was receding at the same rate as his bank account. He studied his wavering reflection in the stainless-steel thermos. It seemed unlikely he'd age well. His black hair was already dashed with white around the temples. At six-three he'd been blessed with height in spite of having two parents of less than average stature, but a doughy paunch hugged his middle, the gym membership having been one of the first things to go. His eyes were bloodshot from a lack of sleep and an excess of bourbon; his skin had acquired the grayish tinge of a soiled dishrag. And he was sadly aware the primary reason he was kept on was his father's reputation.

Dylan Jameson had owned the small gallery in SoHo for most of his life. Stephen's childhood was spent running through those beautifully lit rooms, hiding behind oversize canvases; his playthings had been panel clips and L brackets, and exhibition catalogs that he stacked like pillars. He learned about perspective sitting astride Dylan's shoulders as his father walked closer to, then farther away from the paintings in the gallery, introducing Stephen to a mathematical vocabulary: vanishing points and horizon lines, degrees and axes and curvilinear variants. His fingertips followed the flat sections of paint on a canvas, the channels where firm brushstrokes had tongued out the heavy oil, lipping it to one side or the other. He peered through a magnifying glass as his father quizzed him: glazing or scumbling? Alla prima or underpainting? Wet into wet or fat over lean?

But in spite of his father's offer, working at the gallery, regardless of the lack of title, would have been a mistake. The airy rooms were colored with disillusion, the cheerful demeanor of the gallery manager an insidious reminder of his own lacking personality. Instead, at the beginning of the summer, Stephen had taken his meager savings and fled to Europe in a state of disgrace, slumming his way across the Continent, staying in fleabag hotels and cheap pensions, scooping the hard rolls and bits of sausage remaining from his breakfast into his knapsack for lunch, drinking cheap wine that gave him a headache, and smoking cigarettes that stained the tips of his fingers yellow. Everywhere, he imagined Chloe beside him. The steady pressure of her fingernails against his palm when she wanted him to stop talking and kiss her. The sound of her heels, pacing, as he studied Titian's *Sacred and Profane Love* in the Galleria Borghese. Her fleeting look of disappointment once she'd drained the last from a glass of pinot in a sidewalk café. And the rare expression he caught before she had the chance to substitute it with one more pleasing—a calculating hardness that froze him in his place.

In Rome, he hadn't bothered answering the call from his mother when he'd seen the number displayed, certain she was calling with her wheedling voice, attempting to lure him back. He'd turned his phone off. Four months in Europe and there were still plenty of wounds to be licked. Then, days later, he'd turned his phone back on and seen the number of messages that had accumulated. It was late autumn, everything already skeletal and bleak, when he flew home for his father's funeral. There he was, back in

New York, more miserable than when he'd left; a pair of his father's cuff links his most concrete evidence of ever having been Dylan Jameson's son.

His father's knowledge had been coupled with a poet's soul, a deep appreciation for beauty in all its guises. Dylan's understanding of what an artist hoped to convey, matched by a genuine desire for that artist's success, won him legions of fans—new artists whose work had yet to be seen, established artists coming off a bad show or hammered by negative press, auctioneers who knew his father would have the inside track, appraisers who valued a second opinion.

Stephen, on the other hand, was intrigued only by methodology. What drove someone to create didn't interest him, but the techniques used, and the idea that skill could be taught and passed on, did. How to distinguish between teacher and exacting pupil, to tell the true from the false? Establishing a work's provenance was crucial to authentication, and often difficult to achieve. When absolute provenance could not be established, there were other avenues available, and this was where Stephen's talent lay. He had the broad knowledge of an art historian combined with the hunger of an authenticator to prove the unprovable.

He was happiest engaged in solitary activities: studying pigments, performing Wood's lamp tests, conducting graphology analyses. Hours sped away from him while he hunched over the signature on a painting, relishing the beauty in the pattern of ascenders and descenders; scrutinizing bold, heavy strokes as carefully as faint, trailing meanderings; deciphering that final touch of brush to canvas. Had it meant pride? Triumph? Or, as he often suspected, merely relief at having finally finished?

It was nothing more than coincidence that he'd been standing next to Cranston at an estate sale two and a half years ago; nothing beyond a fluke that they'd both been staring at the same unattributed painting. And when Stephen started talking, the words that came forth were meant for no one but himself; it was a habit too difficult to break, this reciting of facts as he divined them. The work always gave the artist away, no different than the tell of a gambler. But when the call came from Cranston with the offer of a job, Stephen knew it was not providence but the hand of his father, prodding him to pick up the pieces of his life and move on.

The phone buzzed from where he'd hidden it in the desk drawer. He hesitated, imagining Sylvia's abrasive voice again insulting his eardrum. But when he looked at the display, he saw the call wasn't internal. It was Professor Finch.

The last thing he wanted was an evening out with Finch, though Stephen's options for companionship were few. Finch had limited contacts outside the world of academia, but he made up for it with his general knowledge of art history, and his very specific knowledge on one particular subject: Thomas Bayber. In addition to heading the committee who had authored Bayber's catalogue raisonné, the professor had written two volumes on Bayber's work, both lauded and favorably received. Stephen had met him years ago, at one of his father's gallery parties. No one else at Murchison & Dunne was willing to parcel out the time to listen to Finch's stories or take him out for the occasional Bushmills, to endure the pipe smoke and the dribble of brown spittle that inevitably formed in the corner of the professor's mouth. But Stephen had to admit he found the professor's company enjoyable.

'Stephen Jameson.'

'Stephen, it's Dennis Finch.'

'Professor Finch, I can't talk just now. On my way out the door to a meeting. An appointment. An appointment for a meeting, I mean. Another time?'

'Of course, Stephen. Although, if you could get back to me at your earliest convenience, I'd appreciate it. I wanted to speak with you about another Bayber.'

The air around him grew heavy. Stephen no longer heard the elevator as it groaned past his office, or the hiss of the radiator. Everything was still.

'You said another Bayber?'

'I did. I was wondering if you might be interested in authenticating the piece.'

Thomas Bayber was a recluse who had stopped painting twenty years ago and one of the most brilliant artists alive. One hundred and fifty-eight cataloged works, all in museums except for three in a private collection in Spain, one in Russia, and four others privately owned by parties in the United States. The possibility he might be the one to authenticate another caused Stephen's hands to tremble. A find like this would all but erase any past mistakes. There would be interviews and promotions, expensive restaurants; he'd be taking the elevator to the top floor, if only to offer his resignation. The myriad possibilities caused him to break out in a sweat, and his nose ran. Then doubt began swirling in his head. Of all people, Finch would know whether a Bayber was authentic; he'd devoted his life to studying the artist's work. Why not call Christie's or Sotheby's? A sour germ of suspicion curdled Stephen's insides. Someone was setting him up. His tattered reputation would not survive a second humiliation.

'Why me?' he asked flatly.

'Thomas asked for you, specifically. Since I've already compiled the catalogue raisonné and this is a piece unknown to me, he feels it would be better for someone less—shall we say, prejudiced?—to examine the work.'

'He's afraid you'd be inclined to denounce it, since it wasn't included earlier?'

There was a pause. 'I'm not certain of his reasoning, Stephen, but I agree with him. Having someone other than myself look at the piece would be best.' The professor's voice sounded strained. 'There's something else. Assuming you confirm the work as Bayber's, Thomas wants it put up for auction immediately. He wants Murchison & Dunne to handle the sale. You may need to bring Cranston along.'

Stephen didn't relish the idea of involving the president of Murchison & Dunne without first knowing the situation. On the other hand, if Cranston found out he'd examined the work on his own, he'd suspect Stephen of acting as his own agent instead of in the best interests of the firm. Better to talk to Cranston right away. If they both saw the piece at the same time and it was a fake, Stephen could expose it as such, saving Murchison & Dunne any humiliation. If the piece was a Bayber, it would not be lost on Cranston that Thomas Bayber himself had asked Stephen to authenticate it.

'When?'

'I was hoping tomorrow afternoon. If you can make yourself available, that is.'

Stephen ignored Finch's rather pointed dig. 'We can be available.' They set a time, and Stephen copied the address on a scrap of paper before hanging up the phone. His hands shook as he punched in the numbers of Sylvia's extension, and he wiped his palms on his trousers while waiting for her to pick up the phone.

'Sylvia.' His voice reverberated with strange authority. 'I will meet with Cranston this afternoon, but not in regards to the Eaton estate. We'll be discussing something else. Something confidential. Book a conference room.' He hung up without saying anything more, and pictured Sylvia's shocked expression, her mouth like that of a beached fish, opening and closing in a stunned, breathless sort of O.

FOUR

The following afternoon at exactly 1:15, Stephen found Cranston pacing the marble floor of the lobby, the heft of his belly riding over his belt, his hands stuffed into the pockets of his camel's hair coat. Beyond Cranston's grousing about the rain, little conversation was exchanged during the car ride, for which Stephen was grateful. Cranston had made it clear the previous afternoon he thought it unlikely anything would come from this meeting, but on the slim chance Bayber and Finch weren't attempting to pull off some sort of scam, the firm had an obligation to assess the situation before contacting the authorities and reporting the two of them for attempted fraud. Despite his declarations to the contrary, Stephen could see Cranston was imagining the possibilities should there be any truth to the story. Murchison & Dunne had never played at this level; the thought of what an acquisition like this would do for the firm's reputation, for future business, and for the guaranteed good fortune of Mr. Cranston himself was not lost on the man.

'Before we go any further, let's be clear. I'll do the talking, Mr. Jameson. I'm still not sure I understand why the query came directly to you, but since it has, I feel it only fair you be there. Strictly in the capacity of an observer, of course.' The car pulled over. The sidewalk was obscured by several bags of trash and the shell of an old television set. Cranston sniffed. 'Let us hope for your sake, Mr. Jameson, this turns out well.'

Stephen groaned inwardly and nodded. Cranston's tone made clear his tenuous position. Since Finch's call yesterday, Stephen had suspected something was up, wondering if he heard the catch of deception in Finch's halting speech. But even this wariness couldn't dampen his enthusiasm for meeting Bayber. That the two of them would be in the same room at the same time had guaranteed him a giddy, sleepless night.

They picked their way up the front stairs, avoiding the bits of garbage twisted around the bases of the stair railings, and were buzzed in promptly when they rang the bell; no one asked for their identity. The elevator was tiny, and Stephen, holding his tool case to his chest, was forced to stand between Cranston and a stooped woman carrying a thinly furred cat, a long leash dangling from the collar around its neck.

Finch answered the door while Stephen was still knocking. The professor grabbed his hand before Cranston's, shaking it firmly and pulling him across the threshold.

'Come in, but mind where you walk. Thomas keeps it dark in here. I rolled over a pencil earlier and saw my life flash before my eyes.'

There was a quick nod of acknowledgment to Cranston as he shuffled in, then Finch closed the door behind them, striding across the room and claiming his spot—a badly frayed bergère with a high back and sagging cushion.

Stephen looked around in astonishment. It was like a

movie set, a strange splicing of horror film with twentieth-century period piece. Heavy, floor-length curtains shut out most of the light. The walls were a dull blood red with strips of paper spiraling away from the corners as if trying to escape, the ceiling moldings flocked in dust. The air blowing from the register ferried smells of old food and whiskey. Chairs were scattered around the room in no discernible arrangement, and Oriental carpets, all of them frayed and worn, several with bare patches interrupting the pattern, had been laid at odd angles. It was a drunk's nightmare—an indoor field sobriety test composed of a maze of furniture and hazards at differing heights.

Bayber was nowhere to be seen, but Stephen heard repeated sounds of rustling and periodic crashes in one of the back rooms, as if an animal was trapped in too small a space. The thought that a man whose talent he had long admired could be so close, that he might actually be shaking his hand in a matter of moments, caused his throat to go dry. He tried to compose something to say by means of an introduction to indicate he had at least a modicum of intelligence when it came to the man's body of work.

'I'm glad you could join us, especially with so little advance notice,' Finch said.

'We could hardly ignore such an invitation.' Cranston gave Finch a tight smile, but Stephen could see he was on his guard. A previously unknown Bayber surfacing now, appearing to be consigned to Murchison & Dunne to dispose of, viewed in the dim light of a derelict apartment. It made no sense. Cranston had the uneasy look of someone who suspected he was the mark in a game of three-card monte.

But Stephen could barely contain his enthusiasm. No matter the outcome, the day had already surpassed any of those he'd muddled through in the past thirty months. For whatever reason, the fates were dangling an opportunity for deliverance in front of his nose.

'Is he here?' he asked Finch, gesturing toward the rooms at the back of the apartment.

'He'll join us shortly. In the meantime, can I offer you gentlemen a drink?'

Stephen clutched the glass of whiskey Finch handed him as if it were something sacred. Cranston demurred. 'Need to keep my wits about me,' he said, frowning at Stephen, who noted his superior's expression, but nonetheless downed the whiskey in short order.

'Perhaps,' Cranston started, 'while we are waiting, you could provide some background. Mr. Jameson did not seem to have many details to offer.'

Finch's face remained placid, and Stephen marveled at his calm demeanor. Surely he must be upset? On the phone, he'd claimed not to have seen the painting, nor did he know anything of its subject matter, when it had been painted, or where it had been. Stephen thought him remarkably restrained considering the catalogue raisonné he had spent years compiling was no longer complete or valid, the omission by his friend appearing to be intentional.

'I'll allow Thomas to provide additional illumination, since my knowledge pertaining to the piece is limited. I can only say that yesterday the existence of another Bayber was made known to me. Per Thomas's wishes, I contacted our colleague Mr. Jameson here.'

Cranston flashed him a quick glance and nodded slightly. Stephen was unsure whether the look was one of admiration or merely a reminder that as chief representative of the company, Cranston would do the talking.

Ignoring Finch's reticence, Cranston continued his queries.

'This piece, a study, perhaps? For a work already in the catalogue?'

Finch's eyes narrowed before he turned toward the bar to refill his glass.

'No, not a study. A rather large oil from what I understand.'

'I see.' Cranston rubbed his thumb across his chin. 'You can understand my surprise, Professor, although I hope you will not take it as any lack of interest on the part of Murchison & Dunne. Past auctions of Mr. Bayber's work have been through larger houses, and I admit to having some curiosity as to why we, alone, would be the fortunate party to be considered.'

'I imagine Thomas has his reasons. Artists. Eccentrics all of them, yes?' Finch paused and tipped his glass toward Cranston. 'You don't feel unsure of your ability to get a good price for the piece, do you?'

'Not at all. Should we decide to accept it, the auction would receive our utmost attention. No detail would be overlooked.'

Stephen bit the inside of his cheek. As if there was any question they would accept the piece.

Finch shot Cranston a hard look, unfazed by his disclaimer of caution. 'I'm sure that will set his mind at ease.'

The heavy curtains hanging from an archway leading to the back rooms parted. Stephen saw first the hand that held the drape aside—the long fingers, the speckled skin against the deep red fabric of the drapes. Then the rest of Thomas Bayber entered the room. He was as tall as Stephen, only slightly bowed with age, and he moved deliberately, not as if the act of walking required specific effort, but as though strategy was associated with each step. His eyes darted among the company gathered as he navigated his way toward a chair next to Finch. He settled into it without a word and held out a hand, into which Finch promptly placed a glass. For the first time, Stephen pitied the professor. He performed the role of lackey seamlessly, and Stephen understood that he and Cranston were witnessing behaviors finely honed from years of repetition.

The air in the room was stifling. Unable to control the tickle at the back of his throat, Stephen coughed emphatically, his face flushing as he tried to find the glass he'd set down earlier.

'Perhaps, Mr. Jameson, it would be prudent to switch to water at this point,' Cranston admonished after thumping him hard on the back.

'Yes,' Stephen said, running his thumb between his shirt collar and his neck. 'That would be prudent. My apologies.'

Finch and Bayber looked at each other and to Stephen's profound humiliation, began laughing. He felt the flush in his face deepen as whatever confidence and enthusiasm had shored him up earlier ebbed away.

'I apologize, Mr. Jameson, but it's as true now as it ever was. Another's misfortune is always the easiest way to break the ice. Regardless, I am delighted to finally meet you.'

Bayber's voice carried the resonance of a well, and in spite of Stephen's resolution to remain indifferent he was entranced by the man staring at him intently. He knew Bayber was in his early seventies and had assumed, perhaps because he'd been out of the public eye for such a long period, that the artist's physical stature would have diminished. But aside from his complexion, which was deathly pale, and a degree of hesitation in his movements, he was much as he was in the pictures Stephen had seen: tall and lean, his head erect, his hair now a thick crest of white. His manner was imperious but at the same time charming.

'I knew your mother through the gallery, Mr. Jameson, though not your father. He was a rare man, I believe, someone worth admiring. The world would be a kinder place for artists, indeed, for people in general, were there more like him. Allow me to express my sympathies.'

It was unexpected to hear his father mentioned at the precise moment Stephen was thinking of him, his fingers rubbing the cuff links he kept in his jacket pocket. His father would have been thrilled to be in such company: his friend Finch, the pompous Cranston, and Bayber, a man whose talent he had lauded in spite of the artist's renowned moral lapses. *If only he'd allowed me that much latitude*, Stephen thought, quickly ashamed of himself. Bayber was studying him. To think the man had been in his father's gallery and Stephen had never known.

Bayber cleared his throat. 'Pleasantries aside, let's get down to business, shall we, gentlemen? I have a painting I want to sell. I'm assuming it's a painting you will be happy to sell for me, yes?'

'Once we have an opportunity to examine the piece and verify its authenticity, we would be delighted,' Cranston said.

Bayber held his hands together as if in prayer, the tips of his fingers resting against his lips. Stephen realized he was attempting, poorly, to hide a smile.

'Of course, Mr. Cranston. I would expect nothing less. And here we have with us, in this very room, two men who should be able to provide you with a definitive answer as to the authenticity of the piece, do we not? Mr. Jameson, would you mind?'

Bayber gestured to the corner of the room, where a pile of tarps covered the floor. Stephen walked over and gingerly lifted a corner of the top tarp, only to find another beneath it. He rolled back five in total before the faint gleam of a gilt edge made him catch his breath.

The room was silent. Stephen shook his head and fixed himself firmly in the moment, shutting out all but the work in front of him. Fighting the desire to pull the entire tarp away from the painting, he focused initially only on the frame, and gently nudged the tarp to the side until the entire vertical edge of it was exposed.

'Little Miss Muffet, sat on a tuffet,' he recited half under his breath. He began every examination with some rhyming nonsense to quiet his mind and aid his concentration. Finch had been right, it was a large piece. The frame itself was a thing of beauty: a cassetta frame in the Arts and Crafts style of Prendergast, featuring a hand-carved cap with a gently coved panel and reeded ogee lip, furnished in water-gilt, twenty-two-karat, genuine gold leaf.

'Eating her curds and whey. Along came a spider . . .' The gold had been agate burnished over dark brown bole on the cap and lip and left matte over green bole on the panel. The corners of the frame were punched and incised with an acanthus leaf motif, and the gilding had been given a light rub to expose the bole. The joinery appeared solid, and the overall condition of the frame was good. With its size, the frame might be worth ten to fifteen thousand or more.

He glanced over his shoulder. The other three watched him intently. He pushed the tarp away from the painting and pulled a pair of cotton gloves from his jacket pocket. After removing his watch, he waved a second pair toward Cranston, saying, 'Your watch will need to come off, and your cuff links, as well.' He looked up at Bayber.

'Where?'

'Here, I think. Against the wall.'

Cranston nodded at Stephen, and the two of them lifted

the painting cautiously and carried it to the far wall, where a small bit of sun spilled into the room. They gingerly rested the painting there, then stepped back and stood alongside Finch, and Bayber, who had risen and was clutching the back of the chair. Stephen wondered if he felt any anxiety, or if insecurity had long ago left him. But the man looked more pained than anxious, as if his memories of the piece were not happy ones. The three of them looked at the painting and with raised brows, looked at Bayber, studying him quickly before turning to look at the painting again.

A tarnished plate on the bottom edge of the frame read, 'Kessler Sisters.' The scene was of a living room in what appeared to be a large cabin—rough-paneled walls, wood floors, a high ceiling with a sleeping loft. A late summer afternoon. Open windows ran across the back of the room, and the curtains had been painted to suggest a breeze. Stephen could almost feel the breath of it on his neck. A fringe of ivy softened the window's perimeter; a sliver of water was visible in the far distance. Diffuse light dully illuminated various surfaces: a slice of the faded Oriental carpet covering part of the floor, the face of a grandfather clock, the open pages of a book on a coffee table. The room was crowded with objects, each limned with an eerie glow, no doubt from the underpainting, as if everything carried an equal importance.

Three people anchored the center of the painting: a young man, perhaps in his late twenties, and two younger girls. Stephen's skin prickled. The young man was clearly Bayber. Whether it was the expression on his face or the way the girls were positioned next to him he couldn't decide, but Stephen felt a flare of discomfort as he studied the canvas.

The artist had captured his own youthful arrogance, rendering himself in an honest if unflattering light. In the painting, Bayber lounged on a love seat, one pale ankle balanced on the opposite knee; there were scuff marks visible on his boat shoes. He wore a white dress shirt with the sleeves rolled up past his elbows and the neck unbuttoned, and well-lived-in khakis, the wrinkles and shadows of wrinkles so expertly wrought that Stephen had to fight the urge to reach out and touch the fabric. Bayber's hair was long, with dark curls framing his face. A throw covered the top of the love seat; one of Bayber's arms stretched out across it, the other arm rested on his thigh. His expression was *certain*—that was a kind word for it; *smug*, a less kind word. He looked straight ahead, as if fascinated by the man capturing all of this.

The girls, on the other hand, were both looking at Bayber. The older of the two had a sly smile of the sort that breaks a father's heart. Stephen thought she might have been sixteen or seventeen, but her expression made her look older, a hard, knowing glint in her eyes. She was standing behind the love seat to the right of Bayber. Her blond hair was pulled back off her face into a sleek tail that cascaded over her shoulder and turned into curls. Small gold hoops in her ears caught the light but were too dressy for her costume—a pale green, sleeveless blouse and jeans. Her skin was the color of warm caramel, and he could tell at a glance she was the sort of girl things came to without her having to ask for them. *Like Chloe*, Stephen thought, remembering the pale flesh in the crook of her arm when he turned it over. One of this girl's hands rested on Bayber's shoulder, but as Stephen took a step closer to examine the painting, he realized she was firmly gripping him there. The joints of her fingers were slightly bent, the fingernails pale, the fabric of Bayber's shirt puckering just beneath them. Her other arm hung casually at her side, disappearing behind the fabric of the throw.

The younger sister sat on the love seat next to Bayber. She looked to be about thirteen, all long arms and legs, brown as an Indian, Stephen's mother would have said, her freckled limbs shooting out from frayed denim shorts and a madras shirt bunched around her waist. Stephen could almost see the downy gold hairs against the tan skin. Her legs were tucked up underneath her, the bottoms of her feet dusted with dirt and patches of shimmering sand. Her hair was loose, cascading in waves around her face, a cloud of summer blond. One of her hands rested on top of a filigree birdcage balanced on the arm of the love seat, its thin wire door ajar. Her other hand was tucked beneath Bayber's own, resting on his thigh. She had the bored look of an adolescent. The gaze she favored Bayber with was one of curiosity and tolerance, not necessarily admiration.

Stephen was speechless. There was nothing close to a formal portrait in the artist's oeuvre. He looked to Finch, who was frowning. Cranston, who was far less familiar with Bayber's body of work, glanced at Stephen and raised his eyebrows.

'Mr. Jameson? Your impression?'

'It's, er, it's . . .'

'Disturbing,' Finch said. He looked at Bayber as if he'd never seen him before.

Cranston walked closer to the painting and smiled. 'Disturbing isn't necessarily bad when it comes to art. I'm more interested in what you can tell us about the piece, Mr. Bayber.'

Bayber seemed lost in thought, unable to take his eyes from the painting. 'I don't remember much about it.' His voice came from a distance, carrying the timbre of a lie.

'I'm not sure I understand,' Cranston said.

'It was painted a long time ago. I remember little of the circumstances, although I know it's mine.' He smiled indulgently at Stephen. 'I'm counting on Mr. Jameson to verify that.'

'But when you say you remember little of the circumstances . . .' Cranston continued.

'I mean just that. The sisters—Natalie was the older of the two, Alice the younger—were neighbors of mine for a month in the summer of 1963. August, I believe. Other than that, there's not much to tell. Friends of the family, I suppose you could say.'

'They sat for this?'

'No. They did not.'

Stephen was relieved to hear it. He moved close to the painting, his fingers skimming the surface. 'Little Jack Horner sat in the corner . . .' Taking a magnifying glass from his pocket, he examined the surface, the brushstrokes, the pigments. He'd reviewed Finch's treatises on Bayber in a frenzied bout of reading last night before tackling the catalogue raisonné.

There was something unusual about the girls' outside arms, those nearest the edges of the canvas. Paint had been added to both areas. What had Bayber changed and when? He turned back from the painting and ignoring Cranston's probing look, queried Bayber uncertainly.

'The frame?'

'Yes, Mr. Jameson?'

'I need to remove it.'

Cranston started to object, but Bayber held up a hand. 'We are all of similar motive here. Mr. Jameson, you may do what is necessary.'

Cranston turned livid. 'We should remove the frame at our own facility so no damage comes to it. Jameson, you don't want to do anything to impact the integrity of the work.'

'I don't think I will. The painting appears in good condition; the paint layer is stable, no flaking or curling, only a degree of cleavage in a few areas and some minor cracking of the paint and ground layers, most likely due to environmental fluctuations.' He looked again to Bayber.

'May I ask where you've been keeping this?'

'I appreciate your concern, Mr. Jameson. The conditions may not have been ideal, but I don't believe the painting has been unduly taxed in any appreciable way.'

Stephen nodded. Cranston, sputtering, threw up his hands, abandoning any pretense of composure. Finch moved over to where Stephen was standing.

'What can I do to help?'

'My case? The tools I need will be in there.'

Stephen cleared a large space on the floor and threw down several tarps. Finch returned with the tool case, then salvaged some padded blocks that were being used as doorstops to put beneath the corners of the painting. 'Cranston, we'll need you, too,' he said.

Cranston joined them, muttering. The three of them turned the painting onto its face. Stephen ran his hands across the stretcher bars, checking to see if they had warped. All four keys were in place, the corners cleanly mitered. He noted holes that must have been for supporting hooks, although those were missing and there were no remnants of wire.

'The piece has been hung,' he said to Bayber. A statement more than a question.

'Yes. But only in my studio, Mr. Jameson. I suppose I considered it a seminal piece of work at one time. But seminal is too close to sentimental, and that never serves an artist well.'

Stephen took pliers from his case and began removing

the nails from the frame, holding his breath as he turned and pulled each one. 'Oh, the grand old Duke of York, he had ten thousand men. I need a block of wood for this last one, Finch. Something to act as a fulcrum.' Beads of sweat formed at his temples. 'He marched them up to the top of the hill, and . . .'

'Mr. Jameson, please!' Cranston was sweating as well, and huffing, obviously unused to spending much time on the floor on his hands and knees.

'He marched them down again. There.'

With the last nail out, Stephen used tweezers to coax a gap in the spline, then pulled it from the track securing the canvas. He removed the long staples holding the canvas to the frame, then rocked back on his heels, took a deep breath, and instructed Cranston to hold the frame steady. He and Finch gently pulled the canvas backward.

There was a collective sigh as the frame cleanly separated from the canvas. Finch and Cranston rested the frame against the wall while Stephen inspected the painting. Negligible frame abrasion, not enough to be of concern. Canvas stapled in the back, leaving the sides clean. The work was gallery-wrapped, the front image continued along the sides, but there were areas of crushed impasto along both vertical edges of the canvas. Stephen detected flecks of other pigments embedded in the raised strokes, as if the painting had been abraded along its sides, something pressing against it there, grinding pigment into pigment. He set the magnifying glass down and rubbed his face before turning to Bayber, staring at him.

'Well?' Cranston said.

Stephen didn't take his eyes off of Bayber. 'Where are they?' he asked.

'Where are what?' Cranston said, his voice agitated and

rising, his eyes scanning the corners of the room. 'For God's sake, Jameson, be clear. What exactly are you looking for?'

Stephen waited until Bayber gave him an almost imperceptible nod. He turned to Cranston and Finch and smiled. 'The other two pieces of the painting, of course.'

FIVE

Cranston departed in a flurry, wanting to make immediate arrangements to have the painting moved to a lab, where Stephen could use more sophisticated technology to authenticate it. 'Late for a meeting across town,' he said, tapping the face of his watch with a finger. 'You don't mind if I go ahead, do you?' He disappeared into the backseat of the waiting car and shouted out the door, 'I'll leave the two of you to your plans then. Let me know what you need, and I'll see it's taken care of.' The car's departing splash soaked Finch's shoes.

He and Stephen were left standing outside Thomas's apartment waiting for a cab in weather that had shifted from mist to drizzle. They stood uncomfortably close to each other in order to share Finch's umbrella, Finch straining to hold his arm in an awkward position over his head to accommodate the difference in their heights.

'This will make Sylvia extremely unhappy,' Stephen said, looking pleased with himself. 'She'll be forced to be civil to me.'

'Who is Sylvia?'

'Dreadful cow. Here's hoping you never meet her. Now, about these arrangements . . .'

Any semblance of calm had evaporated once Thomas confirmed the existence of two additional pieces. Cranston's normal nervous mannerisms became amplified, his fingers dancing across the air, plucking at some invisible keyboard. Stephen had begun to fidget and mutter, no doubt sensing an opportunity for redemption. Finch himself had felt an unusual level of agitation.

'All three works to Murchison & Dunne then, Mr. Bayber?' Cranston could hardly contain himself.

Thomas nodded. 'Of course, Mr. Cranston. That has always been my intention. That the work be sold in its entirety. Only in its entirety.'

'Marvelous,' Cranston said.

Finch's throat tightened. *Of course.* Never a good sign with Thomas. He felt the need to sit down, the weight of a promise he hadn't wanted to make sitting like a stone in his gut.

'So, Mr. Cranston. You will contact me with a plan, I assume?'

'A plan?' Cranston's brows arched closer to his hairline, but he smiled indulgently.

'A plan for finding the other two panels, of course.'

Finch put his hand to his forehead.

Cranston blanched, the color quickly leaving his face. 'You don't have them here?'

Thomas smiled, and shook his head.

'But you know where they are?' Stephen asked.

'Well, if he did, it's unlikely there'd be a need to find them, Mr. Jameson. Look here, Bayber . . .' Cranston's mood had abruptly sharpened, which was understandable. Finch himself was becoming less enthused by the minute.

'Please, Mr. Cranston.' Thomas opened his hands to them, as if offering the most obvious of explanations. 'Don't alarm yourself. It's a simple matter. The other two panels were sent to the Kessler sisters many years ago. I believe they'd be happy for the income the sale would presumably bring.'

'You'll call and ask them?' Stephen appeared to wait for another rebuke from Cranston, but evidently Cranston was wondering the same thing.

Thomas walked to the window, staring at the velvet curtain as if he could see through it, out onto the street and into the flat afternoon light. 'I've lost track of them, I'm afraid.'

Finch coughed. The situation was clearly getting out of hand. This wasn't anything he'd signed up for, shaky promise or not. He needed to extricate himself from the looming mess as rapidly as possible.

'Thomas,' he said, 'surely this would be better suited to an investigator of some sort? A professional person who could locate the Kessler sisters and find out whether they still have the paintings in their possession? Then Murchison & Dunne could approach the owners regarding an acquisition. And Jameson could authenticate the works. I doubt anyone in this room has the particular skills required to track down missing persons.'

'Yes,' Cranston agreed. 'That sounds quite reasonable.'

'Oh, but you have the skills,' Thomas said, pressing his fingertips together. 'Denny, I believe you and Mr. Jameson are exactly the right people for the job.'

It became alarmingly clear that Thomas had thought the whole thing out, and that Finch and Stephen had just been tasked with a quest, their fortunes now intertwined.

'If I might ask, Mr. Bayber, why is that?' Stephen appeared to be completely baffled.

'Who better to look,' Thomas said, 'than those who have a vested interest in the outcome? Financial, and otherwise.'

'So, Professor, should I make the reservations, or should you?'

'Reservations?' Finch was distracted. Drops from one of the umbrella's ribs funneled down the back of his neck. His wool socks were damp, driving the chill straight into his ankles.

'For our flights. We can get to Rochester from JFK in no time. It's probably not much of a cab ride from there.'

'I'm not entirely convinced this is the best way to go about things. Cranston shouldn't have left so quickly.'

'Is there a problem?' Stephen asked, shifting his briefcase to his other hand and waving at a taxi that slowed briefly before speeding past them. At Finch's hesitation, he blurted, 'You do believe it's his work, don't you? It was only a cursory examination, but I'm reasonably sure . . .'

'You may be only reasonably sure. I have no doubt of it.'

Finch knew it was Thomas's work the moment he saw it. Not that the portrait was like anything else Thomas had done, but Finch recognized it, nonetheless. The black, white, and yellow pigments of his verdaccio deftly knit to produce an underpainting of grayish green that toned the warm bone of the primer. He could identify Thomas's technique as easily as he could Lydia's childish scrawl on a piece of paper. Besides which, his reactions to Thomas's paintings were immediate and visceral: a sudden drop in his gut, a tingling at the tips of his fingers, a knockout punch to any prejudices he harbored regarding what defined art.

This was the gift of knowing an artist's secret language, a gift that came with age and focused study: the ability to interpret a brushstroke, to recognize colors, to identify a pattern the artist's hand created instinctually from comfort and habit. Finch could look at Thomas's work and read his pride and frustration, his delight in perfection, his obsessive desire. But he would be forced to leave it to Stephen, with his arsenal of toys and gadgets and technology, to officially christen the work a Bayber. That fact lodged in his craw like a rough crumb, making a home for itself in the darkness of his throat, refusing to be dislodged. He was an expert of one sort, Jameson of another. Money followed the word of only one of them.

'Yes, it's Bayber's work, Stephen. I'm sure a closer examination will confirm it.' Finch was furious with Thomas. The holidays were coming, the anniversary of Claire's death only a few weeks away. He didn't want to embark on some ill-defined mission. He wanted to be hibernating in his own apartment, waking only when the darkness of the months ahead had passed. But he'd given his word. That meant something to him, as Thomas well knew. He was trapped.

'You think we should start looking somewhere else then? Not go to the cabin first? Do you want to start at the house instead?'

Finch steeled himself for the inevitable abuse. 'I don't fly.'

'What?'

'I said I don't fly.'

Stephen dropped his tool case and started shaking violently until he finally bent over, hiccuping into his knees.

'I don't find it all that humorous,' Finch said.

Stephen righted himself, dabbing at his eyes with the edge of his jacket. 'Oh, but it is,' he said. 'I can't drive.'

Finch drummed his fingers on the corner of his desk, waiting for his computer screen to refresh. Once Stephen found out he didn't want to fly, he'd somehow ended up with the mundane task of handling logistics. Who, in this day and age, didn't have a driver's license? How did the man function? On the other hand, Finch could think of hundreds of people, both well-known and obscure, who chose not to fly. The laptop screen finally blinked and offered up a home page for the car rental agency; a form with questions to be answered, boxes to be ticked, numbers to be filled in, felonies to be reported; all required before they would deem him worthy to drive one of their Fiestas or Aveos. He lingered over the 'Specialty' class, tempted by the bright red of a Mustang before coming to his senses. Late fall, unseasonable weather, and Stephen Jameson. None of these screamed sporty roadster. He squinted and punched a key, squinted and punched, paused to review, then punched once more—'Submit.'

He pushed the curtain aside and looked out the window. The October sky was a gray flannel, streaked with ragged clouds. There'd be frost if the rain let up. He tapped his fingers again, waiting for confirmation of his reservation. Why this nagging sense of urgency?

The painting unsettled him. There was the age of the girls, obviously. And the expression of the older sister, disturbing in its intensity. Anger radiated from the canvas, yet her expression was contained, a quality both knowing and unnerving. *Kessler*. The name was vaguely familiar, and he racked his brain, searching for the connection.

That Thomas had inserted himself into the piece was significant. As an artist, he always maintained a certain distance. Patrons or admirers might think they knew his work, but in truth, they would only be seeing what he wanted them to. *That is the small space where I hide, Denny,* Thomas had said to him once before. *That thin line between the painting and the public persona, that's where I exist. That's what no one will ever see.*

But what made Finch most uneasy was the atmosphere of the painting. Everything artfully staged, with the exception of the emotions of the people in it. Those seemed overwhelming to Finch and painfully real. The sadness he'd felt after leaving the apartment and returning home lingered, and he shivered, wondering if there was anything he knew about Thomas with certainty, outside of the depth of his talent.

The talent he was certain of. It was confirmed time and again, most recently by the hush in the room when Stephen and Cranston first saw the painting, their expressions of awe and discomfort. He remembered his own reaction upon seeing Thomas's work for the first time, the brilliant marriage of insight and imagination with untempered physicality. The discomfort came in the emotions Thomas drew from the viewer, emotions that, for the sake of propriety, were usually cordoned off or tamped down. Scrutinizing his work left one exposed, a voyeur caught in the act. Thomas's true talent, Finch had realized long ago, was the ability to make the viewer squirm.

However, this painting made the artist uncomfortable as well. Finch had stood between them, Thomas and Stephen, the two of them dwarfing him by equal measures, and looked from one to the other—their heads tilted at the same attitude, their sharp noses fixed toward the canvas. But while Thomas's look shifted from longing to sadness, Stephen stared at the painting with an intensity that suggested he could divine what lay beneath the pigment.

Given a spread of three or four years, Finch had a good idea when the work had been done. In spite of its subject, the colors used, the intensity of brushstroke, and the level of detail in the background objects all pointed to a certain period in Thomas's work. He would leave it to Stephen to supply the finer details. What caught him off guard was the ache in the eyes of the young man in the painting. Finch had noticed that same ache in Thomas as the artist viewed his own work. There was arrogance, too, but that was not nearly so prominent as the brokenness of someone standing outside the bounds of love. It frightened Finch. In the years he'd known Thomas, he couldn't recall a time he'd ever seen him *want* after something. He'd never wondered whether there might be something desired yet missing from Thomas's life. Until now.

Finch had constructed a skeleton of Thomas's history from the few bones offered up to him. The rest was obtained through diligent research, but it was an incomplete picture, nothing Thomas had volunteered to flesh out. Finch knew Thomas's parents had been remote and disinterested. They quickly tired of what they perceived as laziness on the part of their only child—a lack of interest in contributing to the family business—and cut him off when he was twenty-eight, despite numerous accolades and his growing success, considering art no more deserving of attention than any other hobby: flower arranging, winemaking, table tennis.

Thomas was ill-equipped to deal with the world on his own. He had grown up knowing only wealth and privilege, surrounded by people his parents had hired to do things for him: feed him, transport him, educate him, work a fine grit over any inexplicable rough edges. Though his paintings sold for large sums, money circled away from him like water down a drain. Visiting his studio some fifteen or so years after their first meeting, Finch had been alarmed to find groceries lacking, the cupboards bare save for cigarettes and liquor. Noticing Thomas's gaunt frame, he'd wondered what the man subsisted on. There were stacks of unopened mail spread across the floor: long-overdue bills, personal correspondence stuffed into the same piles as advertising circulars, notices threatening the disconnection of utilities, requests for private commissions, invitations from curators hoping to mount retrospectives. Finch had waded through the detritus of monthly accountability. For Thomas, these were the peculiarities of a normal person's life, so he chose to ignore them, leaving the burgeoning collection of envelopes to form a sort of minefield he stepped across day after day.

'You should look at some of these, you know,' Finch had said, rifling through a handful of envelopes that carried a charcoal trace of footprints.

'Why would I want to do that?' Thomas had asked.

'So you aren't left in a studio with no heat, no running water, and no electricity. And before you bother with some clever retort, remember you'll have a hard time holding a brush when your fingers go numb from the cold. Besides, what if someone's trying to get ahold of you? Is there even a telephone here?'

Thomas had only smiled and asked, 'Who would possibly want to get ahold of me?'

Finch made a sweeping gesture at the floor. 'I'm guessing these people, for starters.'

Thomas shrugged and went back to painting. 'You could keep track of it for me.'

'I'm not your secretary, Thomas.'

Thomas put down his brush and stared at Finch, studying his face in a thoughtful manner Finch imagined was normally reserved for his models.

'I didn't mean to insult you, Denny. I only thought you might find it useful, while doing the catalogue, to have access to my papers. You must know I wouldn't trust anyone else with my personal correspondence.'

In the end, Finch had made arrangements for an assistant, an endearingly patient middle-aged mother of four with salt-and-pepper hair, whose familiarity with chaos made her the ideal candidate for the job. She visited Thomas's studio two days a week in an effort to bring forth order from anarchy. She seemed to take a great deal of delight in sorting, and before long Thomas's affairs were more settled than they had been in years, with the assistant, Mrs. Blankenship, leaving his letters and personal correspondence in a file for Finch, and the due notices wrapped and taped around various bottles of liquor like paper insulator jackets.

'It's the only place he'll notice them,' she'd explained to Finch, when he questioned her slightly unorthodox methods. 'And they're getting paid now, aren't they?'

It was true, and at some point Mrs. Blankenship had attempted to make inroads in Thomas's apartment as well, coming over a few times a week to collect the glasses deposited on various flat surfaces in various rooms and move them all to the sink.

'Why can't you leave him be?' Claire had asked.

'He's a friend. He doesn't have anyone else.'

'He uses you. And you let him. I don't understand why.'

How to explain it to her when he couldn't explain it to himself? He'd reached the age when his possibilities were no longer infinite; what he had now was all he was going to have. He could detach his personal satisfaction from his professional . . . what? Disappointment? Too strong a word. Averageness, perhaps? To his mind, the personal and professional were separate; one did not diminish the other. But Claire would see any discontent in him as some partial failure on her part, as if she could will him to greatness. Within these rooms, he was blessed to be the most important man in the world. Outside of them, his success had been limited.

He was not destined for accolades; there would be no super-latives conjoined to his name.

'If not for Thomas and the notoriety he's achieved, we might well be eating beans from a can, my dear, instead of . . .' He'd waved his fork over their meal, a beef tenderloin in marrow sauce, chanterelles with chestnuts, and the ruby sheen of a fine pinot noir coloring his wineglass.

'I suppose your books wrote themselves, then? That your accomplishments count for nothing?' Claire hid her face behind her napkin for a moment, and when she put the napkin back in her lap her cheeks were wet.

'What is it?' His mind entertained a score of disastrous scenarios.

'Do you feel you settled? With marriage and a child, I mean. For less than what you imagined you'd have?'

His response had been immediate. He'd shaken his head vehemently, attempting to interrupt her. He might have wished for greater success, but never at the expense of his family. If he had to choose, no choice would have been easier. She'd squeezed his arm tight and he'd let her continue.

'It's the way you are when you come home after being with him. Anxious. At odds with yourself. You look around these rooms as though something's changed in the time since you left and came back. As though everything's become smaller. More drab.'

He was stunned. 'I didn't realize I did that.'

'That makes it worse. More true.' She stared at the tines of her fork.

He brought her hands to his mouth and kissed the insides of her wrists, first one, then the other, stricken by the idea that he'd planted any doubt in her mind as to how much she meant to him. 'I didn't settle, Claire.'

'I don't believe you did. I think you are exactly what you were intended to be. A man of great value. I'm just not sure you recognize it in yourself.' She closed her eyes, then looked at him carefully. 'And Bayber? What would you say of him?'

'I would say he, too, is exactly what he was intended to be. A man of great talent.'

'He's the one who's settled, Denny. For *only* his talent. And when his time comes, he'll find himself wanting what you have more than anything else.'

He'd loved her all the more for saying it, though he doubted Thomas would be thinking of him at the end. Yet there was still a small particle in Finch, an uncontrollable element that coveted what Thomas had, not at the expense of his own bounty, but in addition to it. Thomas's talent was the cover that kept him warm at night, the meal that sustained him, the air he breathed. His talent would outlive him for generations. Finch was honest enough to admit, at least to himself, a legacy of that sort was worthy of envy. Was it so great a crime to let some of Thomas's sun fall on him? To feel just the outer rim of that warmth?

The rest, he had no desire for. The queue of women waiting for Thomas was as long as the span of time each lasted was short. When Thomas tired of an admirer's company, it was expected that the woman in question would decamp gracefully, minus the drama of a scene or hysterics, to be quickly replaced. In Thomas's opinion, no explanation was required.

But for years to go by without having the companionship of anyone of consequence? Finch tried to imagine a different life for himself, but could not. The loss of his wife had been devastating. Even now he woke in the middle of the night to find his arms stretched out to her side of the bed, encircling her missing form. Painful as this was, a life she had never been part of would have been worse. The same held true for Lydia. The lilt of her voice, the sway of her arms when she walked, the way she nibbled at the cuticle of her index finger when faced with a serious decision. All these had been imprinted on his core. Erasing them was impossible.

Sleep was also impossible. He tossed and turned for most of the night, finally giving in and getting up before sunrise. He needed to talk to Thomas alone before things went any further. He may have given his word, but he hadn't signed up to be part of a traveling sideshow. At some point in the wee hours of the morning, he decided he wasn't going anywhere with Stephen until he found out exactly what Thomas knew, and what he really wanted.

I married a wise man. Claire's voice was all the sun he needed.

'Sarcasm is wasted on those who haven't had a decent night's sleep, my darling. Be honest. You're wondering why I didn't show this much backbone years ago.'

I'm wondering what he's up to, Denny. Same as you.

He waited until after breakfast before calling Mrs. Blankenship to let her know he'd be stopping by to see Thomas. The phone rang as he reached to dial her number.

'You need to come quickly.' Mrs. Blankenship sounded as if she'd been running.

'I was just about to call you. I'm coming over to see Thomas this morning.'

'We're at the hospital, Professor. Mr. Bayber's had a stroke.'

***

He hadn't been in a hospital for almost a year. It was more grim than he remembered. All the artificial brightness, meant to be reassuring—here is order and cleanliness; surgical cure and pharmaceutical consolation; schedules kept and procedures perfected—was revealed to be otherwise by the moans issued from passing beds, by the brisk, flat-footed walk of orderlies in sneakers pushing those beds, by the janitors' high gray laundry carts and the smells of sickness and blood embedded in the linens.

Mrs. Blankenship, so capable and exacting in Thomas's apartment, had been transformed into a weepy mass of wrinkled clothing stuffed into a plastic chair in the waiting room.

'He was on the floor when I came in this morning,' she said, dabbing at her pink face with the handkerchief Finch provided. 'I called for an ambulance right away, but it took them so long to get there. I kept telling him they were on their way. I don't know whether he heard me.'

'I'm sure he did.' Finch looked for a doctor, but seeing no one, patted Mrs. Blankenship on the shoulder, then ventured over to the nurses' desk, where he found himself ignored by three different women. When repeated throat clearing proved ineffective, he picked up one of the pens with a large artificial flower attached to the end of it and in a fit of pique, stuck it behind his ear. 'Bayber,' he said. 'Thomas Bayber. I need to know what room he's in.'

The nurse nearest him gave him a withering glance and held out her hand. He returned the pen. 'Fourth floor. Turn left,' she said. 'Down to the first station on your right. They'll be taking him there from emergency. You can talk to his doctor once they get him settled.'

'And how long will that be?' he asked, but she'd already turned away. Finch collected Mrs. Blankenship, and the two of them followed the signs for the elevator, crowding on with the other sleep-deprived, wan-faced visitors, then expelled along with the masses onto a sterile floor that looked the same to him as the last.

It was two hours before Finch could talk with the doctor. A serious stroke; it was too soon to tell how much speech or movement Bayber might eventually recover. He was resting comfortably. They'd monitor him continuously; there was nothing more anyone could do for the time being. Finch called Cranston with an update and told Mrs. Blankenship to go home and rest.

'Don't come back until tomorrow,' he ordered. 'When they let you see him, I need you to tell him that Jameson and I are driving to the cabin, and to the Kesslers' old house after that. Tell him even if he's sleeping, Mrs. Blankenship. And tell him more than once. It's important.'

The shocks on the Sentra that Finch had rented were shot. The car bounced along the freeway, and Stephen bounced along with it, his head coming perilously close to the ceiling with each bump. Finch drove too fast and gestured as he talked, causing Stephen to press himself against the seat back and stare pointedly at the speedometer. An intermittent rain drummed on the roof, drowning out the classical music station that appeared and disappeared as they passed between a series of hills. Humid air from the vents targeted Stephen's neck. It was like being trapped in a mobile version of his office at Murchison & Dunne.

Finch raised his chin and sniffed the air. 'Bananas really aren't appropriate for a road trip. The fast food I can understand, but unless it's an apple, or a prune, fruit isn't the best choice.' He was secretly glad to be out of his daughter's clutches, free to enjoy a meal of fat, sodium, and limp vegetable bits with suspect nutritional value without someone chiding him about the dangers of cholesterol and high blood pressure. 'I should have gotten a bigger trash bag. How can someone as meticulous as you appear to be about certain things travel like this?'

'I'm an anomaly.'

'We'll have to get off at the next exit and find someplace to dump it.' Finch gestured toward the backseat, which had become the final resting place for Stephen's fast-food containers, banana peels, empty water bottles, used tissues, and lozenge wrappers.

'Fine.' Stephen sulked. The entire situation was ridiculous. Forced to put his life in Finch's hands for the six hours it would take to drive to the cabin, all because Finch harbored some unreasonable fear of flying. And now he was being scolded about his behavior?

'Why didn't we take your car?'

Finch pursed his lips. 'Leaky manifold gasket.'

'We could have been there by now, you know.'

'I'm aware of that.'

'Was it turbulence? Smoke in the cabin? That would be understandable, I suppose.'

Finch glared at him before turning his eyes back to the road. 'Getting one's driver's license is a simple enough thing. You might enjoy the freedom of the road.'

'And you might enjoy the freedom of the skies. I mean, how do you ever *go* anywhere?'

'We're going somewhere now.'

'That's not what I meant.'

'You don't drive because in the city you feel no need for a car. That's the gist of it?'

'Yes. And the car sickness.'

Finch looked at him uneasily and adjusted the vents,

sending more air rushing in Stephen's direction. 'Well, I live in the city and I do feel the need to have a car. A means to get out when the walls start closing in. The older I get, the less I enjoy the presence of other people. Besides, car sickness is usually alleviated when you are the one doing the driving.'

'That doesn't explain not wanting to fly. I know for a fact you've been abroad, and I doubt you swam. Bayber has a piece in the permanent collection at Palazzo Venier dei Leoni, in the Guggenheim collection. You wrote about it at length in the catalogue. And you served on the jury at the Biennale at the Chianciano Museum of Art.' Stephen left his stomach as well as his momentary feeling of satisfaction behind when the professor accelerated into a turn.

Finch was quiet for a moment before answering. 'This is a recent development. My wife died. I haven't been in an airport since.'

Stephen stared at the matted floor carpets, then out the rain-streaked window, then back at the floor carpets again. Now he'd done it. Really put his foot in it.

'I didn't know.' He watched as Finch focused on the odometer before methodically performing his check of the mirrors.

'I wouldn't have expected you to.'

'How long . . .'

'Nearly a year. I've only had one Thanksgiving, one Christmas, one Valentine's Day without her. I could almost pretend she was on vacation.' He gave Stephen a wry smile. 'Before too much longer I'll forget her minute imperfections. That's what you end up missing the most, those little faults. They burrow under your skin. Become endearing in retrospect.'

'Was there a crash? That would explain your hesitation,

though flying is the safest form of transportation. Your chance of being in an airplane crash is one in eleven million and . . .'

'Jameson.'

'Some people find knowing the odds of a certain thing happening to be comforting.'

'She wasn't on a plane. Didn't even have a ticket in her hand. She was at the airport waiting to meet her sister's flight and had a heart attack.'

The rain was coming down harder, and Finch turned the wipers on, smearing the windshield. He could have picked up his sister-in-law that day. What had been so pressing he couldn't leave it for the two hours the round trip required? No doubt it had fallen into the generic category of *work*, an excuse Claire knew was futile to rail against. If only he'd gone instead, she might have sat down on the bed and rested for a few minutes. Just a quick nap, then she'd have felt better.

'Should we pull over? You probably shouldn't drive when you're upset.'

Finch shook his head. 'I make a concerted effort to avoid the details—what moment, gone a different way, might have resulted in a different outcome. Why they hadn't been able to revive her at the airport.' He turned the wipers up a notch. 'As luck would have it, there isn't always a doctor around when you need one.'

'What's that got to do with flying?'

'It's the airport, not the flight. The endless drone of announcements, the warning beeps of carts backing up. People who look like they're traveling in their pajamas. The guards and security agents and policemen. All those trained professionals with their technical expertise, and they could only look at her on the floor and ask people to move along.' His thumb pressed against the vinyl covering on the steering wheel until the nail went bloodless. 'And I think about the shoes.'

'Of course.'

Finch stopped watching the road and looked at him, surprised.

'You understand that?'

'Well, yes.' Stephen gestured toward the windshield. 'Shouldn't you be concentrating?'

'Tell me.'

'Hundreds of people in the airport, hour after hour. So many people crossing that same spot. It would be dirty. Filthy, probably. I don't blame you for not wanting to think of her there.'

Finch eased up on the accelerator. 'Yes. I absolutely cannot stomach that part.'

'You probably have to cook for yourself, then, don't you?'

Finch stared at him, aghast, but then broke out in laughter that must have started from somewhere deep in his chest. 'I suppose you mean do I miss her? Yes. I miss her every second.'

'I can't imagine,' Stephen said.

'I would think you could.' Finch responded to the cascade of brake lights in front of them and slowed to maneuver around a mattress in the middle of the road. 'When your father died, you were in Europe, weren't you?'

Stephen squirmed. A familiar hint of bile rose in his stomach, and he smelled the banana skins in the backseat, no longer pleasantly tropical. The car steamed like a fetid jungle, the defrost faltering; warm, moist air fogged the bottoms of the windows like the breath of a ghost. 'I was in Rome. I wanted to see Caravaggio's Saint Matthew cycle, so I was on my way to the Contarelli Chapel in San Luigi dei Francesi.'

'Well?'

'I saw it.'

'That's not what I meant.'

'A wife and a father—it's not the same thing.'

'It might be.'

Stephen stared at the floor, nubby strands of carpet embedded with crumbs and mud. Heavy rain pelted the roof. 'There's an exit in another twenty miles. We can dump the trash there. I need more lozenges, anyway.'

'You certainly have the right to tell me you don't want to talk about it.'

'I don't want to talk about it.'

Finch quickly glanced in the rearview mirror, then pressed down on the gas firmly, causing the back of the car to fishtail and Stephen to throw both hands against the dashboard. Finch looked at Stephen and smiled. 'Fine with me.'

Stephen felt the blood leave his face. 'You're going to get us killed.'

'Possibly. As you pointed out, the odds would favor us meeting our demise in a car as opposed to on a plane. But you're welcome to try your hand at the wheel anytime.'

'It would serve you right if I did. I can't imagine my driving could be much worse.'

'That's debatable.'

Stephen pressed his face against the cold glass of the side window and shut his eyes. His stomach was somersaulting; a film of sweat formed above his upper lip. Traffic up ahead had slowed to a crawl and the hours of travel left stretched endlessly before him. Another flip of his gut and he contemplated leaving Finch at a rest stop and hiking the rest of the way.

He stared into the car in the lane next to them. A child with a sticky-looking mouth galloped a stuffed horse across the landscape of the side window. Stephen thought of the cave paintings at Lascaux, the Chinese horses and the Confronted Ibexes, more than seventeen thousand years old, so breathtaking in their simplicity. As adviser to the Scientific Committee in 2003, he'd donned the required biohazard suit, the booties and face mask, and made his way into the Axial Gallery, where his breathing went ragged and he cried at the persistent bloom of white mold dusting the backs of the horses. Like they'd run through a snowstorm. His father would have understood his reaction. He imagined the two of them standing in the quiet dim of the caves, in the cool, restive damp, studying the gently furred lines of manganese dioxide and ocher, of charcoal and iron oxide.

'I was a disappointment to him,' he said, turning to Finch.

Finch accelerated gently, for once keeping his eyes on the road. 'Your father was tremendously proud of your abilities.'

'My father wished I was someone else. My mother, too. Someone more ordinary. Isn't that an odd thing for a parent to wish for a child? That he would be less than what he is?'

'Wishing that your child might have done something differently isn't the same as wishing that he *was* different.' Finch stepped on the brake again, and Stephen swallowed several times in short succession.

Finch grabbed Stephen's left hand and poked it hard. 'There's a pressure point called the Joining of the Valleys on the web between your thumb and index finger. Squeeze your thumb against the base of your index finger. Look for the highest point of the bulge of the muscle, level with the end of the crease. Press down hard on it with the index finger of your other hand.'

'What's that supposed to do?'

'For one thing, keep you from throwing up in the car.'

Stephen pressed his left index finger firmly against the spot where he imagined the Joining of the Valleys might be on his right hand. He began counting backward from sixteen thousand and two hundred, the number of seconds he estimated he had left to be in the car. *Even for a Bayber no one's seen*, he thought, *this is a lot to ask of a person*. Hot air blasted against his cheek as he dozed off, and he dreamt, first of Chloe, the moist warmth of her breath as she whispered in his ear, then of Natalie Kessler as she was in the painting, her tanned arm reaching out from behind the love seat and beckoning him to join her.

SIX
OCTOBER 1971

Alice drove to the cabin alone. She didn't tell Natalie she was taking a few days off, fearing it would resurrect their ongoing argument about the cost of her education. Natalie would have insisted that if Alice wanted time away from graduate school so soon after starting, she would be better off at home, where her room and board would not chip away at their meager resources. And home, or what was left of it, was the last place Alice wanted to be.

Everything she was driving away from—school, the remnants of family, a persistent grief, and the growing shadow of her diminishment—blurred outside the windows of the car. The hum of the tires was hypnotic, pushing her toward sleep. She was driving into the sun, and warmth radiated around her; off the vinyl of the dashboard, from the wheel under her hands, through the glass. Only a thin wedge of cooler air pushed into the car from the driver's vent window, which had never closed all the way.

Somnolence. Was this what had overtaken her parents nearly two years ago? Had they felt so safe, so warm in the car with the dark night enveloping them, that they'd simply drifted off? No. She'd imagined their actions that night a thousand times, and with such clarity, that she refused to turn the radio on now, despite the fact it would keep her awake. Just putting her fingers on the knob was enough to make her flinch. Her father would have been singing along to the radio, his eager, off-key notes causing her mother to curl up in her seat with her hands over her ears, laughing. He would have turned to look at her the way he did when he thought no one else was watching, and whispered a single word, a secret language between them that had nothing to do with their daughters. Had he taken one hand from the wheel to reach out to her, to bring the back of her gloved hand to his mouth?

The officer who had come to the door that November night, pale as chalk and not much older than she was, stood with his chin to his chest, as though the weight of his news made it impossible for him to raise his head. She'd kept him standing on the doorstep in the blowing snow, under the shrouded porch light, afraid that asking him in would make whatever he'd come to tell them true. But it was true anyway, and when she'd asked him again what had happened, he would only repeat *we just don't know*.

The silence in the car became deafening. Alice talked to herself, reciting her own version of the alphabet: the common names of birds, starting with the alder flycatcher and ending with the yellowhammer. Once she finished she started over again, this time using their scientific names, *Accipiter gentilis*—northern goshawk, to *Zonotrichia leuco-phrys*—white-crowned sparrow.

She'd estimated six and a half hours between school and Seneca Lake, but hadn't accounted for the number of times she'd have to stop to rest, rubbing the stiffness from her hands. She pulled off the road when she was halfway there, parking the car in a spot where the grass had turned from supple green to crisp gold. The air in midafternoon was laced with the smell of things gone to ground. Beech leaves curled in on themselves, brushed with the dull finish of autumn; the shadbush blazed scarlet. She unkinked her body after hobbling from the car and pressed her palms against the warm hood. Whenever a twinge of pain nudged her toward panic, she reminded herself it was a relief to disappear, even if only for a while.

She'd only been at graduate school for five weeks and was still recovering from the strain of unpacking and trying to meet new people when she had a run-in with her academic adviser. Miss Pym had suggested that even with an extended schedule, it might be difficult for Alice to achieve an advanced degree in ecology and evolutionary biology given her current condition. Miss Pym's mouth dipped when she said the word *condition*, as if Alice might have something requiring a certain distance be kept.

'Rheumatoid arthritis isn't a 'condition,' Miss Pym. It's a disease. And I wasn't aware that perfect health was a prerequisite for earning a degree. As long as I can do the work . . .'

'The thing is, Miss Kessler, I'm not sure you can.'

Miss Pym's dark hair was swirled into a tight bun that pulled all expression from her face, save for the quick furrowing of her brow, which suggested a headache. Her foot tapped anxiously against her chair leg, as if she were secretly marching somewhere, away from the college, away from students who tested her patience and questioned her expertise in matters of proficiency.

'I can do the work. At Wesleyan . . .'

Miss Pym arched her eyebrows and interrupted. 'Miss Kessler, I'm aware you come to us with the appropriate credentials. I am also aware you slept through Professor Strand's midmorning lecture on avian biogeography. There were only fifteen students in the class. Your 'lack of attention' did not go unnoticed.'

Alice had argued out of sheer stubbornness, finally wearing down Miss Pym, who'd ended their conversation with the admonishment that far more care would need to be taken, before curtly dismissing her with a nod. Back in her dorm room Alice had stretched across the bed, still shaking with anger. She'd fought the urge to call Natalie, knowing the conversation she wished for would not be the conversation they would have. *The witch! You can't let her get away with that, Alice. Clearly she doesn't know what you're capable of. I can be there by nightfall. How does this sound? Miss Pym, in the teachers' lounge, with a wrench.* The Natalie who would have offered that had vanished eight years ago, replaced by an odd twin whose same sharp edge was now just as likely to be pointed in Alice's direction as toward a condescending academic adviser.

She'd watched from her second-story window as other students milled across the lawn toward a demonstration, clumping together in an amorphous blob of support: for women's rights, for racial equality, for social justice, against the war. She'd envied the ease with which they strode across campus, the way they bumped up against each other in solidarity, their confident, sympathetic embraces, any of which would have sent a wave of pain cascading across the landscape of her body.

At Wesleyan, she'd maintained a rigorous focus on getting her undergraduate degree, refusing to let herself think of anything else. She postponed her grief. She pushed away the guilt she felt about staying in school, along with her images of Natalie, alone now except for their housekeeper, Therese. She battled her way through a pharmaceutically induced fog, one of the side effects of her many medications, and made it a point not to think too far ahead. *Doctors can be wrong; new treatments are on the horizon; every case is different* became her mantras.

Coping and pushing herself were behaviours that had long ago become engrained in her DNA. When she graduated, Alice was certain sheer will and determination, combined with generous scripts from her physicians, would keep her dreams intact. She could still be the first to discover a nest as finely crafted as any architect's house; to marvel at the stippled mask of a new species of owl; to stand motionless in the Guánica forest scrub, waiting for the predawn call of the Puerto Rican nightjar. If her path had been uncertain, at least the end result had never been in doubt. Until now. Field studies would be difficult at best, straight research claustrophobic and unappealing, and dissections and laboratory work next to impossible, since it was becoming hard to hold a knife. She didn't want to leave school; she didn't see how she could stay. She needed to be alone someplace where she could sort out her thoughts.

The morning after her confrontation with Miss Pym, she'd packed some clothes and paid the boy across the hall five dollars to carry her suitcase downstairs and throw it into the back of her '68 Mustang. Her father had given her the coupe not long before he and her mother died on the Connecticut Turnpike coming back from a performance of *Promises, Promises* in the city. Ironic, considering how often her mother had used those very words in response to her father's assurances that he'd never miss another family dinner, or school performance, or fund-raiser again.

Her mother had sat at her vanity, brushing her décolletage with powder, happily dabbing Shalimar behind her ears, while Alice's father, tickets in hand, paced back and forth in the hall, jingling the change in his pocket and consulting his watch. Her mother hummed 'I'll Never Fall in Love Again' while she finished dressing; her father winked at Alice and pulled up her mother's zipper as he joined her in the chorus. Alice knew the notes to the song by heart; her pulse raced and her stomach pitched at the first few notes. She could never hear that song without imagining the two of them huddled next to each other in the front seat, her father singing against her mother's hair as she rested against his shoulder. Did they even see the truck? Had there been a moment of panic? A chance for them to think of her for even the briefest second?

Miss Pym had consulted a file while she'd chastised Alice in the airless office. *An emotional two years for you. The progression of your condition*—an apologetic clearing of her throat—*I mean, your disease, losing your parents. So many adjustments to make.*

Losing your parents. Who said things like that? As if they were hiding from her and all she needed to do was turn over a few pillows or open a closet door. They weren't lost. She knew exactly where they were. With her index finger she'd traced the stern granite of their headstones, side by side, just as they'd ended, sitting side by side in a car seat that still held the dirty impressions from the bottoms of her sneakers on its blue vinyl back.

Natalie hadn't wasted a breath before erasing them, not one article at a time, but with an emphatic swoop. Home for the summer at the end of her junior year, Alice had opened the door to her parents' bedroom closet and found it completely empty: the clothes, the shoes, the felted hats with their stiff bits of feathers, the tin box stuffed with mementos of their courtship, the rolls of wrapping paper and old Christmas tags with a tracery of ink barely visible, all gone. Their bedsheets were gone from the linen closet, their ice skates and tennis rackets absent from the attic. Their ashtrays, the coasters with their initials intertwined. All of it donated, Natalie had said, to the Salvation Army, because really, why would you want to be constantly reminded of what was over? Even the smell of them had vanished, replaced with the off pine odor of a cleaning product that now made Alice nauseous. The only thing she'd managed to salvage was the reed from her father's bassoon, still in the old Mercurochrome bottle in the medicine cabinet.

Her childhood home became a prison when she wasn't at school. Therese, who adored Natalie but had always frightened Alice, cleaned the house constantly when Alice was home on break, wiping the faint cloud of breath from a mirror, the ashy pattern of a footprint from the hall floor. Alice could not understand the woman's slavish devotion, or how she stayed busy in a household decreased in number by three, but Natalie insisted on keeping her, telling Alice, 'You can't understand how difficult it is to manage the house on my own. You aren't here, remember? I am.'

The ghosts of her parents wandered the halls, searching for earthly attachments. Alice heard them at night, their muffled voices falling into her ears as she twisted against her sheets. *'Darling, have you seen my apron? I just hung it here in the kitchen and it's gone.'* Or her father, morosely searching for his favorite tie, a gold and navy blue foulard with a tiny stain just above the point, saying, *'Your mother never liked that tie. She's secreted it away somewhere, hasn't she, Alice?'*

It had been eight years since she'd been to the cabin. Myrna Reston, keeping a low profile since a scandal involving her husband's investment group became known, had passed the job of managing the cabin rental to her oldest son, George, Jr. George had been a minion in his father's firm, lacking the ambition to do much more than fall into the guaranteed embrace of the family business. Alice remembered him vaguely as a pock-faced teenager who'd tried to shove a garden hose down the front of her swimsuit when she was still in grade school. Fortunately, he remembered her only as Natalie's little sister, and when she called to ask about the cabin, he'd sounded happy enough to hear from her and happier still at the thought of obtaining some rent in the off-season.

'You can have it for a song, doll,' he'd offered. 'It will be cold in the mornings, but I'll have our man lay in some wood for you for a few fires. There won't be much happening in town this time of year. Most places have already closed for the season. But you can still get groceries at Martin's and likely anything else you'd need.'

Alice had assured him she wasn't interested in shopping, only wanted a few days away from school, where there were too many distractions.

'Didn't classes just start?'

'Individual study this term. I just need a quiet place to do some research.'

'Hmm. How's Natalie, by the way?'

George had been as infatuated with Natalie as anyone else, but a stunning combination of arrogance and stupidity had made him noticeably more persistent. He'd always been quick to do her bidding, gifting her with expensive trinkets she hadn't known she wanted, providing her with the answers to high school exams, nullifying potential rivals with vicious rumors. Natalie had kept him on a long lead, reeling him in with a casual compliment, a fluttering of lashes whenever she needed something. When she was younger, Alice had thought him simply a troublemaker, but as she grew older she'd realized a streak of cruelty tainted his antics, making it difficult to shrug them off as typical eruptions of teenage temperament.

'Natalie's fine, thank you. As a matter of fact, I think she mentioned you just the other day, George. I'll be happy to tell her you asked about her. And I'll take you up on that offer of wood, if you don't mind.' The lie had slipped from her tongue without a thought.

'I'll have our man leave the key under the mat. Just let me know what day you want to come up and he'll have the place ready for you.'

'Tomorrow,' she'd said. 'If it's possible, I want to come tomorrow.'

'That's not much notice.'

Alice had held her breath.

'Let me call him. I guess we can make that work. I'll have to tack on something extra, though.'

She worried that the cabin would have become a miniaturized version of the way she remembered it, but nothing had changed except for the absence of voices. The house had always been full of other people and of other people's things, and now the sound of her suitcase dropped on the wood floor echoed through the empty rooms. *It's peaceful,* she reminded herself. *That's what you wanted.* But it was also lonely.

George Reston's man, Evan, had indeed laid up a stack of wood near the fireplace and opened the windows for airing. The rooms had a vague odor of mildew, except for the bedroom she and Natalie had shared for so many years, with its heavy beams crossing the ceiling and the knotty pine walls. The air in that room was dry and smelled of cedar. She remembered the two of them jumping up and down on the thin mattresses, clutching each other and squealing with delight when their father scratched at the window screens after dark, pretending to be a bear; staining their fingernails with juice from the raspberries they found in the woods; Natalie sitting cross-legged on the gravel by the side of the road, studiously working to free the cuff of Alice's jeans that had gotten caught in the bike gears, while Alice tried to balance the bike and stay upright. She pushed the checked curtain aside and looked out across the lake. Where had that sister gone? The sun was low in the sky, barely a half circle of it still visible on the horizon, and the water was the dull gray of pencil lead. Dead calm.

She collapsed onto one of the twin beds, pulling the chenille spread over her shoulders. The room grew colder and she considered getting up to close the windows, but didn't have the energy to do both that and climb back into bed. Instead she pushed deeper under the covers and listened to night make its way into the cabin: the muffled echo of birdcalls, the clicking of bats, the hesitant nocturnal rustling of small animals. She woke once, to find the bedroom filled with milky light, the moon, broadcasting loud across the sky. Everything she saw was sketched in shadow, as if it existed in another realm. She listened hard, then harder, waiting to hear the sound of her parents stirring in the next room. That was how she fell back into sleep, straining to hear something that wasn't there until her ears ached with the effort.

In her dreams that night she stretched, arms and legs waving like sea grass, her bones as flexible as bands, her spine arching and curving like a bowstring. Green water surrounded her, and her own buoyancy came as a surprise—grace restored, movement effortless. Stretching became swimming. Swimming became running through the water, until the viscosity of it increased and the push of it against her body was more than she could manage.

Coming out of sleep she smelled chimney smoke and the heavy tang of resin, and blinked, anxious to dispel the remnants of her dreams. Morning sun cut through the bedroom window, and with it came the familiar stiffness of limbs and joints, body parts that had long since betrayed her. The most necessary aspects of her skeletal structure had turned from useful bone into a series of nicks and catches, grinding against each other and melding into immobile pieces, petrified versions of the knots her father had taught her to tie when she was a child.

They were standing on the pier, Alice and Natalie and their father, twenty-some stone steps down from the cottage. The Restons' flat-bottom skiff bobbed back and forth, occasionally wedging against the piers until the water pulled it free with a groan. Natalie, just thirteen then, was already more intent on watching her reflection ripple back and forth in the water than on any sort of lesson, and Alice seized the opportunity to commandeer her father's attention.

'It's important both of you develop some basic nautical skills,' her father said, apparently oblivious to the fact that neither of his daughters had an interest in launching out across a stretch of dark water. The toe of one of his new deck shoes marked a page in a book of knots, and Alice recalled the crisp black-and-white illustrations, a frayed piece of rope magically turning in upon itself in one diagram after another until it become an intricate web of twists and circles that looked impossible to decipher.

Her father held a length of rope loosely between his hands. 'The end of the line you work with is called the 'bitter end.' The main length of line is the 'standing part.' Before the end of the summer, both of you are going to know how to tie a reef knot, a clove hitch, a bowline, a cleat hitch, and a becket bend.' Her father squeezed her shoulder. 'We'll have you weaving a monkey fist before you know it, Alice. A quarter for each of you for every knot you learn.'

All afternoon she sat on the dock, the planks warm against her skin, the smell of the lake filling her nose, working the rope over and under, under and around, around and through. After several hours, she had transformed the piece of rope into a series of misshapen knots. Natalie skipped rocks and lay on the deck, her sleeves rolled up to her shoulders, her jeans folded neatly up past her knees. She glanced at Alice occasionally through eyes slitted against the sun.

'Don't you ever get tired of doing what you're supposed to do?' There was no hint of sarcasm in the question, only a trace of confusion, as though Natalie was searching for something that eluded her.

'I guess one of us should probably try to.' Alice got up and sat beside her sister, picking up Natalie's piece of rope, biting her lower lip as she started her careful construction of knots again.

Natalie smiled at her before rolling over onto her stomach. 'Make mine look good, okay?'

What Alice remembered most from that year was not biking into town with her father or reading her mother's elegant script on the postcards addressed to relatives. It was not sitting between the two of them in the evening, watching her father's hand touch her mother's hair or the field of stars that sprouted across the dark sky. What she remembered most was the feel of smooth rope in her hands, the indentation of warm coins pressed against her palms, and Natalie's wink when their father counted out two equal shares of quarters.

Her body rebelled from the previous day's drive, but she'd been expecting as much. Her flares were almost always followed by a day requiring rest, and then it was usually possible to drift back to a state of status quo. She drew a bath and as the water lapped at her skin, she remembered the way her body had felt in her dream, fluid and lithe. Spiders criss-crossed the ceiling, skittering back and forth to escape the steam. She pulled her hair up in a loose knot, dressed, took a blanket from the basket next to the fireplace, and headed down to the lake. The sun glinted off the water's surface, blinding her with bright sparks. The skiff was in its same spot, tiny wavelets pushing up against its dented sides. Alice spread out the blanket, climbed into the boat, and lay down in the empty hull. The water rocked her, and the sun warmed her skin until she felt like melted sugar, liquefied to a soft gold.

She wasn't aware the boat had come loose from its moorings until she sensed the absence of land, until she lost the familiar smell of warming wood—the planks of the dock, the bark of trees painted with sunlight, the resinous, warped shingles of the cabin—and felt instead the languid pull of water surrounding her. She sat up, panicking when she saw how far she had drifted from the shore. But the lake was calm, the oars were securely in their locks. She pulled herself onto the boat's seat and let her hair down, feeling the breeze sift through it until it was dry. She might be able to row herself back with the help of an afternoon gust; if not, she could flag down a passing boat and ask for help. But it was late in the season and the lake was quiet. There were no other boats to be seen.

Alice ran her hands along the nicked wood of the oars. It was easier to think out here on the water, to contemplate a different course for her life. On land, her limitations announced themselves in a loud voice. But here, far from shore, the determined buoyancy of the ancient skiff and the steady rhythm of small waves worked their way under her skin. The wind picked up and billowed her shirt out in front of her like a spinnaker. Wisps of clouds knit themselves into a pale skein, whirling and unraveling over her head as they turned from dark to light to dark again. A light chop slapped the side of the boat. She could see a storm building at the sky's edge and watched with interest more than alarm until the curtain of rain appeared in the distance near the point and began its slow undulation toward her.

Lightning shattered the sky, and by the boom of thunder that followed she could estimate how far off the storm was. She levered the oars into the water, alarmed by their weight. Pulling on one to turn the boat back in the direction of the cabin, she winced at the pain that rocked across her shoulder and down her back. It took all her strength and the oars barely skimmed the water's surface. Unless she was able to gain more traction, she'd never make any headway. She set the oars back in the boat and pulled the blanket from the floor, draping it around her shoulders and attempting a rudimentary knot, all her chilled fingers could manage. She scanned the floor of the boat, looking for something she could use for cover or as a flag. There was only a plastic milk jug, its top sliced off to create a makeshift bailer. When she looked up again, a stinging rain began pelting her face. Shielding her eyes, she stared across the water, back toward the cabin. She thought she heard the distant sputter of an engine, but whatever the noise, it was stolen by the wind. She put the oars back in the water and pulled as hard as she could, gasping with the effort. Five ineffectual strokes were all she could manage before dropping her head to her chest. The shore was as far away as it had been. But there was something moving toward her, growing larger and louder, a motorboat cutting a deep V through the water as it headed in her direction. Maybe the Restons' custodian, Evan, had noticed the boat was missing. Or maybe it was George. Then she recognized something familiar in the posture of the figure steering the boat, and she knew it was him.

It seemed unlikely if not impossible. She'd followed his career without intending to, had read the reviews of his shows, noted the accolades and his success over the past years. There would be no reason for him to be here now. His parents, too, were gone, though not dead. She'd come across an article in *Architectural Digest* while thumbing through stacks of old magazines in the sterile waiting room of her rheumatologist. There was a grand stone house in France at the end of an allée, shaded by rows of olives. They lived most of the time in Europe these days, disappointed in 'the sad degradation of American culture.' The picture surprised her: two unlined, stoic faces with a dog perched artfully between them on a dark blue settee, the three of them equally coiffed and placid. So unlike the face she remembered when she thought of him, which she hadn't done for a long time. There'd been more important things to contend with, and she'd pushed her memories of him, accompanied by her feelings of disappointment and shame, to a dark place at the back of her mind.

She could smell the boat exhaust, even through the torrents of rain. He cut the engine and let the motorboat sidle up next to the skiff, reaching out to grab at one of the oars and pull himself closer.

'Take the rope,' he barked at her, but she didn't answer. Her joints felt fused into one ineffectual scrap of bone, and she couldn't move.

'Take it, Alice, damn it. What's wrong with you? You're going to drown out here.' He grabbed one of the oars and pushed the skiff back until he was close enough to the prow to thread a piece of nylon rope through the bow eye. He let out a long length of it and tied both ends of the rope together tightly around the middle seat in the motorboat.

'Hang on,' he yelled over his shoulder.

She rested her hands on the edges of the skiff, her fingers too numb and cold to grab hold of anything. The boat surged beneath her as it was pulled across the water, thumping across the motorboat's wake. Thomas had one hand on the tiller and looked back over his shoulder every few seconds, as if he thought she might decide to take a sudden swim. Unlikely, unless he went a good deal faster than he was going now and she tumbled out. She was more concerned with how she was going to get out of the boat and back up the steps to the cabin without his watching her every step. Her physical weakness was the thing she was most ashamed of, the thing she tried to hide whenever possible.

Her cheeks stung from the sharp rain nettling her skin. Why had she come back here? She saw the hazy outline of the Bayber house through the waving trees. She'd come because this was where her past was happily captive, woven into the woods, sparking off the surface of the lake. Her younger self still hid in the forest, deciphering the songs of birds, naming the stars in the night sky, half-listening for the reassuring call of her name by her parents, who laughed more and drank more and reminisced on the dock while dangling their pale legs in the cold, dark water. This was where she'd pushed her way through the thin paper skin of adolescence to feel the lovely stirrings of attraction, the polarized tugs of desire and insecurity.

Then there was all that followed: the realization she'd been foolish and naïve; Thomas's true character revealed, as well as Natalie's. This was where everything started, and where everything started to end. A few short months from then, the world would crack open in Dallas. Riding with her father in the front seat of the car that November, she would watch, alarmed, as he turned up the radio volume and shook his head in disbelief, pulling over to the side of the road along with all of the other cars, burying his head in his arms. Looking out the window, she saw a pantomime of emotions playing out in each car: tears, shock, fear. It was the first time she'd seen her father cry, the first time she understood there would be things in life he could not protect her from. That memory had its own tremor, the same as the one she'd felt months before when Thomas Bayber first walked onto their dock: the certain knowledge the world had shifted and nothing would ever be the same.

Thomas pulled back on the throttle as they neared the shore, killed the engine, and jumped from the boat to the dock. He tied up the motorboat, then grabbed the rope and coaxed the skiff in, putting his foot out to keep it from bumping the dock. Water ran off every inch of him, streaming down the sharp angle of his nose, bleeding off the ends of his hair where it was plastered against his neck. All she could do was sit and wait for him to leave. Finally he straightened up and held out a hand.

'If you're waiting for a formal invitation, this is all you're going to get.'

'Leave me alone.'

'Leave you alone? Have you lost your mind? It's practically a tempest, and you honestly think I'm going to let you sit here?' The wind tore the words from his mouth. 'Get up. You'll catch your death and I'm not having that on my hands.'

She glared at him. 'Don't you think I would get up if I could?'

That stopped him. She cringed at his casual observation of her stiff limbs, her oddly positioned hands, resting like pincers on the sides of the boat. But after a brief and frank appraisal, his eyes stayed on her a moment longer and there was another look, of the sort she wasn't used to seeing.

He wiped his hand across his face. 'Well, you might have thought of that before you decided to get in the damn boat. Can you at least scoot over to the side, so I don't send us both into the drink trying to get you out?'

That much she could manage. She bit her lip as he hoisted her out of the skiff, feeling like something rusted and long frozen.

'I can do the rest myself.'

'Don't be stupid. I can't very well leave you here, and while I doubt I could get any wetter than I already am, let's try something more expedient, shall we?' He swung her up in his arms, and she closed her eyes, her humiliation complete. He made his way up the dock slowly and paused at the base of the stone steps. Her ear bounced against his chest as he took the steps, and she could hear his ragged breathing.

'You're still smoking.'

'This doesn't seem like an appropriate time for a lecture.'

'You're wheezing.'

'You're heavier than you look. And I'm old, remember?'

He regretted using that word, she could tell, by the way he suddenly shifted her in his arms. But it was too late. Of course she remembered. She remembered everything. She shivered as the rain drove into her hair.

'Alice.'

'Don't talk. Please, don't talk.'

'You're determined to make this awkward, I see.' But he didn't say anything more, only continued the trek toward his house.

The path was uneven and spongy, half-obscured by decomposing leaves and branches of evergreens the storm was bringing down. She could feel the ground sucking at his every footfall, as if he was trudging through a bog. Ahead of them, light came from the main room of the Baybers' summer house, faint and watery behind the running wash streaking the window glass. At the back door he set her down gently, his arms shaking with the effort of placing her *just so.* He pushed the door open, and she came in behind him, weakened by the rush of warm air that enveloped her.

'I suppose now you're going to scold me for leaving the house with the fire stoked.'

'No. It feels too good to be warm,' she said, lingering in the hallway, her teeth rattling against each other. 'I'll only stay a minute to dry out, then I'll go back.'

'Alice.'

It was all he said, but it was enough. Crying was the stupidest thing to do, but in that moment she wondered how she'd managed not to for so long. The years of depending on other people were stacked up behind her and seemed incalculable ahead. Her one job had always been to maintain a certain good nature, a stoicism about her RA. But right now she just wanted someone to have the power to fix her. To fix everything.

'Why do I seem to have this effect on women? They're around me and they cry.' He offered her a handkerchief from his pocket, but it was as wet as the rest of him and when she grabbed it water trickled down the slant of her arm.

He was staring at her. When she finally looked up, he closed his eyes and shook his head. 'I was very sorry to hear about your parents,' he said. 'Myrna Reston, of course.' He went into one of the bedrooms and came back carrying some clothes.

'No buttons,' he offered. 'Do you need help?'

'I can't . . .'

'We're both soaked to the skin. The rain isn't going to let up anytime soon, and I can't imagine it's good for you to sit around in wet clothes. Please.'

She stood up, unhappy to separate herself from the steady, low flame of the fire, the comforting blue and orange of it toasting her skin back to life.

'There's a guest bedroom where you can change,' he said, gesturing toward a room at the far end of the hall.

She took the clothes from him and made her way down a dark hallway. The guest bedroom, if that's what it was, was three times the size of her dorm room at school. A high queen bed was centered against the far wall between two windows with faded coffee-colored curtains that skimmed the floor. An armoire took up most of the space on the opposite side of the room, its bonnet curled and fretted with scrollwork. A stale sweet odor of perfume clung to the bed linens, the suggestion of tuberose or gardenia.

There was a loosely wired, gold filigree cage on the bedside table next to the lamp and inside of it, a porcelain bird resting on a branch, the whole thing no more than five and a half inches from tip to base. Entranced, Alice lifted the bottomless cage and cautiously picked up the figurine, relieved the fire had restored some movement to her fingers. The bird was *Passerina caerulea*, a blue grosbeak, in his breeding plumage. The figure had been worked in intricate detail, and she ran the tip of her index finger along its back, admiring the craftsmanship. The head, mantle, and chest were all a deep cobalt blue with the brightest color appearing on the bird's rump and the crown; the wing and tail feathers were a dark gray. The wings were marked with two chestnut wing bars, and black masking extended from in front of the bird's eyes toward the stout, silvery gray bill. The grosbeak was perched on a branch of witch hazel, and even the leaves of the shrub, oval with wavy margins, had been accurately painted: a dark green above and a paler green beneath.

Alice turned the figure over, but there was no mark to identify the maker. Hanging on the wall above the bedside table was a watercolor of the same bird, in the same setting. Scribbled near the bottom of the painting in cursive that was barely decipherable were the sentences 'For Letitia Bayber, our friend. One model to another.' And the signature 'D. Doughty.'

Was this Thomas's mother's room? Alice had seen only the one picture of her, in the magazine article, and it was hard to reconcile the expressionless woman sitting with her husband and dog as the friend of someone who could make anything as wonderful as this bird. She looked around the room again and realized how out of place the figure was, the only delicate thing in a room full of dark mahogany furniture and subdued colors, all of it overscale and foreboding. Alice set the bird back on the table and replaced the cage, almost sorry that something so beautiful was consigned to a room where it was rarely seen.

The curtains at the windows were open, tied back with cords ending in woolly, frayed tassels. The house was surrounded by woods on all sides. When Alice looked out the windows into the flat black of trees and night, the only thing she saw was her own watery reflection in the glass. She struggled out of her clothes, leaving them in a damp pile on the floor. The things he'd brought her were his, she could tell by the way they hung on her. The soft T-shirt dropped well past her hips, its faded blue interrupted by a Rorschach splotch of ink across her stomach. The pajama pants were easy to pull on. She tugged the drawstrings at the waist, tying a loose, sloppy bow, then gathered up her own soggy things and went back out to the main room.

He had changed into dry clothes as well and nodded when he saw her. 'They look better on you than they do on me. Can you drink?'

She'd missed her regimen of medications, the kaleidoscope of pills she swallowed several times a day. 'Do you have brandy?' she asked, tired and reckless, longing for a degree of oblivion.

He raised an eyebrow but didn't answer, only poured something amber from a decanter into a glass and held it out to her, taking her clothes when she took the glass. She held it with both hands and took a cautious sip, feeling the warm liquid light a slow flame down her throat and stamp itself into the wall of her chest. She marveled at the liquor's impact, the sharp smell of it burning her eyes, the agreeable fuzziness left in its wake. He disappeared somewhere as she lowered herself into a high-backed chair close to the fireplace and shifted back and forth, searching for the position that was the least uncomfortable.

This room was the same as she remembered. It could have been yesterday she left her footprints on the chalky floor while trailing after him, and squirmed on the love seat while he frowned and sketched. It gave her the odd feeling of being in a museum, a museum whose curator was lax in his duties, she thought, noting the fine film of dust covering everything: a stack of books, the face of a clock, the tapers in their heavy brass candlesticks.

Thomas came back into the room and poked at the fire before sitting in the chair across from her. His feet were bare, pale, with high arches, the little toe on his left foot crooked, evidently broken at some point. There was an uncomfortable intimacy seeing him barefoot, and she felt every shift her body made beneath the fabric of his thin shirt. Eight years since they'd last seen each other. How little the difference in their ages mattered now.

'There's a porcelain figure in the other room.'

He poked again at the embers. 'I hadn't remembered that's where I'd put it.'

'Is it yours? It doesn't look like the sort of thing you'd have.'

'Because you know me so well?' He smiled at her. 'It can be yours if you like. Take it.'

'Why do I get the feeling it isn't yours to give?'

'Perceptive as ever, I see. I guess you're right. Technically, it's not mine to give away. I stole it.'

'I don't believe you.'

'You should. I took it from my mother. It was something she cherished, a gift, from a very dear friend of hers, and quite valuable, I imagine. Have you ever heard of Dorothy Doughty?'

Alice shook her head.

'She died ten years ago or so. She and her sister, Freda, were neighbors of my mother's in Sissinghurst. I think Freda used to watch after my mother sometimes, when she was a child. The sisters were both sculptors; they had their own kiln at the house. Dorothy was an ornithologist and a naturalist, as you can probably tell. She liked to do models of the birds she saw in their backyard garden. She and Freda ended up joining the Royal Worcester company as freelance modelers. Freda's models were of small children, but

Dorothy's were all of birds and quite lovely. The one in the bedroom was a preproduction prototype. She gave it to my mother the year I was born.'

'Why did you take it?'

He shrugged. 'I wanted to hurt her.'

'You did it deliberately to be cruel?'

'Does that surprise you?' He stood up and walked over to the bar, pouring himself another generous glass of brandy. He tipped the decanter in her direction, but her glass was still full and she shook her head.

'I wanted her to feel loss. The absence of something she treasured. Clearly, that wasn't going to be her son. I believe she was quite distraught over it. I was surprised to see she could muster that much emotion.'

He didn't sound angry, only matter-of-fact and distant, sipping his drink and staring into the fire. A chill skipped across Alice's skin, this one having nothing to do with the rain or her exhaustion. She rolled the glass back and forth between her hands, watching the liquid spike and draw against the sides, and took another drink. 'It sounds as though you didn't have a happy childhood.'

'Plenty of people in that club. I wouldn't let it bother you.' He looked at her evenly while she fought the urge to fidget. 'Do you miss your parents?'

'I miss them every day.'

He nodded, as if that was what he'd expected her to say. 'Yes. Of course you would. I've been estranged from mine for nearly eight years now. I don't feel anything when I think of them. Does that make me a bad person, do you think?'

'Not that.'

A thin smile. 'Ah. Now we're getting somewhere. The other, you mean then. That makes me a bad person.'

Did he think they could avoid falling back into that awful history, when he was here in the same room with her, standing so close she could have reached out and touched the hand that held his glass? The spreading warmth from the brandy lit her insides and coalesced into something weighty at her center, pulling her farther down into the chair's cushion. She took a deep breath. 'You think it makes you a good one?'

He pulled logs from a wicker basket and threw them on the fire, sending a spray of sparks racing up the flue. 'I took a nap after you left that afternoon, Alice. When I came back into this room, I knew you'd seen the drawing. It wasn't just that the sketches were in the wrong order—I'm not sure I would have remembered exactly how I'd arranged them, aside from the obvious intent not to leave that particular sketch on top. I saw your footprints in the chalk dust. And a thumbprint in the corner of that sketch. You didn't know you'd left that behind, did you?'

He stood in front of her and took her wrist. She flinched and tried to pull away, but he didn't notice or didn't care, only brought her hand closer to him, circling the pad of her thumb with a finger as if trying to erase something from it before he let go.

She held her hand against her chest, feeling the heat of her joints bleed through the shirt. 'It doesn't matter.'

'Don't be ridiculous. Of course it matters.'

'Maybe to you. Not to me.'

He finished his drink and set the glass down on a table with a dull thud. 'You're a bad liar, Alice. Thank God for that.'

'No. I'm only tired. I came here to be alone for a while; I didn't come here for you. I didn't come here to see you or to hear your voice, and I don't want to have to remember any of that. It makes me sick.'

If she were as bad a liar as he said, he'd have seen through her immediately. She felt alone all the time now; she didn't need to come to the cabin for that. Being with him was a balm, if only because he'd known her parents for those few weeks. She could ask if he remembered her mother being afraid of Neela, or if her father's grip was strong when he first shook his hand. She could ask him what he saw when he looked at the four of them on the dock that afternoon. Did he remember her father's toast at dinner the evening he'd finished his sketch? She could see glasses raised in the air, something rosy swaying inside of them, could hear the delicate clink, clink of the crystal, but the words paired with that particular memory had vanished. Everything else in her life seemed broken; she didn't want her connection to him, however vague or fractured it was, to be another thing counted as lost.

His face fell with her words. She was surprised to see she'd hurt him. The Thomas of her memory was callous and indifferent, existing to remind her of the meaning of betrayal.

'So,' he said, 'Alice has grown up after all. And in spite of her affliction, quite capable with a knife.'

She turned away, not wanting to look at him.

'Was she in your room while I was there that day?' She hadn't meant to ask, but now the words were out, she realized it was what haunted her most, the idea of her sister listening to their every exchange, burying her face in a soft pillow to keep from laughing. Maybe it was a vestige of Natalie's perfume she'd smelled in the guest room, Natalie's potent presence able to withstand even the ebb and flow of eight years.

'If that's what you think then you wouldn't believe anything I'd tell you.' His face was red, from the fire, from the drink. 'It's amazing. Years have passed and yet I still feel compelled to defend myself. Maybe because your high opinion was one of the few things that mattered to me.'

'The opinion of a fourteen-year-old girl? That seems unlikely. When I think of how my parents trusted you . . .'

'Your parents were far from saints, Alice. It would be generous to say they were ordinary people who made some very serious mistakes. Don't make them out to be perfect. That's too thin a wire for anyone to be able to keep their balance. And as for Natalie . . .'

She rose unsteadily from her chair, fueled by alcohol and fury. 'Don't say her name. I don't want to hear it.' Alice threw herself against him with all the force she had, arms flailing, hands useless, pounding against his chest anyway. Every hit sent shock waves spiraling across her body, a hammer to her bones.

He stood perfectly still and made no effort to defend himself. The rage left as quickly as it came and she sank to the floor at his feet, her useless ankles buckling under her weight, her forehead resting against his knees. She was breathing so hard she thought she might choke, and between gasping sobs, she said, 'I'm afraid. I'm afraid of everything. All the time.'

He touched her head, patting her awkwardly. She remembered how he was with Neela, the way he'd held the dog in his arm and rubbed the top of her head with his knuckles until her eyes closed and her tail thumped slow and heavy against his chest. But now his hand was stroking her hair, his fingers weaving themselves into her curls, his thumb barely skimming the side of her face.

He sat down on the floor next to her. 'There's ample evidence to the contrary.'

It struck her as hilarious. He was the only person she knew who actually said things like that—*ample evidence to the contrary*. 'Can't you talk like a normal person?'

'I only meant that if you're really afraid of everything, you hide it well. You haven't let this disease . . .'

'RA. You have to say it out loud. Rheumatoid arthritis.'

'And you're still interrupting, I see. You haven't let RA stop you. You haven't let what happened to your parents stop you. You're finishing your education, you're . . .'

'Quitting. I left school. That's why I came here. Everything is getting too hard. I can't do it anymore.'

'Can't do it? Or can't do it perfectly?'

'It's the same thing.'

'Not for most people.'

She let her head fall against his shoulder and leaned into the smell of him: damp wool and dust, smoke and the heady fragrance of grapes turned to must. His hand moved to her foot, his thumb tracing the curve of her instep, a spot where her skin still felt like silk. She wondered whether anyone else had touched her there, other than with a clinical hand, turning her ankle this way and that, asking her to describe her pain.

She closed her eyes and when she opened them, looked up at the ceiling. She'd had this view before, remembering the afternoon she'd seen the sketch of Natalie. She pulled her foot away.

'Alice.'

'No.'

'It wasn't what you think.'

'Don't insult me. I never thought of you as being predict-able, Thomas, so don't say what anyone else would—that nothing happened.'

'You think I slept with her? A teenage girl?'

She swallowed hard. 'Yes. I think your ego would allow you to do almost anything and find a way to justify it.'

He turned away from her, but his hand remained on her

shoulder, the tips of his fingers exerting a gentle pressure there.

'Natalie was what? Seventeen? That would have been illegal, Alice. To say nothing of amoral.'

'I saw the sketch. No one's imagination is that good.' She thrust her chin out stubbornly and shook his hand from her shoulder. 'Or that accurate.'

'She posed for me, yes.'

'In the nude.'

'Naked as a jaybird.'

'You think this is funny?'

'Not at all. I was just hoping you might appreciate the avian reference. Evidently not. But I have to admit, it makes me wonder how well you know your sister.'

'What's that supposed to mean?'

'No one could accuse Natalie of being inhibited. I never asked her to take her clothes off. She came over one afternoon and asked if I would do a sketch of her. She told me she wanted to give it to her boyfriend. I agreed and went to get my sketch pad and pencils out of the back room. When I returned, your dear sister was standing there with her dress around her ankles. *Sans vêtements*. She wasn't happy when I told her I wouldn't sleep with her.'

'You're trying to tell me that she asked you?'

He looked pained. 'Yes, Alice. She asked me. Natalie was angry, about a lot of things. She was very disturbed. I think she wanted to sleep with me to make a point.'

'I don't understand.'

'Don't you?' He looked at her closely as if trying to decide something, then shook his head and closed his eyes. 'Then it's not my place to tell you. Anyway, who knows? Maybe Natalie suspected I'd say no and was testing her powers. Or maybe she just wanted something she couldn't have.'

'Natalie? That's hard to believe.'

'Haven't you ever wanted something you couldn't have?'

'What do you think?' She held up her hands, afraid to imagine how she must look to him. The monstrous angles of her fingers, her knotty, swollen joints. Like she'd been constructed from a box of spare parts. In her head was a 'want' list of things she would never say out loud, never acknowledge to anyone else for fear they might think she felt sorry for herself. *I want to be able to hold a dissecting knife again. I want to walk in the woods alone. I want people to stop asking how I'm feeling, how I'm coping, how I'm doing. I want to forget the name of every doctor and nurse I've ever had, and the names of their spouses and their children. I want to buy clothes that fasten with buttons, and shoes with narrow toe boxes. I want everyone to stop telling me to lower my expectations.*

'I shouldn't have asked you that.'

'No, you shouldn't have. You don't know anything about me, or my life. You don't know what it's like to worry you'll start to despise the people who help you, the ones you should love, because they're healthy and you're not, because they're kind and you're this angry, frustrated . . . thing. When you know you're not going to get better'—she paused, the unspoken words *only worse* hanging in the air between them—'you become halfway invisible. People stop noticing you. No one likes to have to consider the specifics of illness too carefully.

'I've found I still serve a purpose. I remind people to pray, to calculate the odds, to thank the fates, the gods, good karma, whatever it was that made this happen to me and not them. I'm in the worst sort of club. The one no one else wants to be in.'

He looked at her, aghast. 'Alice.'

'Just leave me alone. Please.'

'I can't.' He stood up and held out his hand. When she didn't move, he reached down to pull her toward him. He picked her up and carried her over to the love seat, then sat next to her, drawing small circles on her upper arm with the tip of his finger, barely touching her skin. Everything inside of her felt weighted down and heavy, as though someone had tipped her head open and filled her to the brim with stones.

'What's the worst thing?'

'Don't ask me that.'

'You said I didn't know you. I want to. I want you to tell me the one thing that's worse than all the rest, something you've never told anyone else.'

'Why?'

'Because I'm asking, Alice. I'm trying, and I usually don't try. I want to know.'

Sleep pulled at her edges. Her lips moved against the skin of his neck.

'I worry there's nothing left of the person I was supposed to be, beyond the pain. Sometimes I can't separate myself from it. I think about how when I'm gone, then the pain will be gone, too. We'll have finally canceled each other out. Maybe it will be like I was never here at all.'

Then, because she couldn't stay there any longer without wanting him to touch her, she pulled away from him, stood up slowly, and said good night.

She came out of the guest room in the morning wearing a large denim shirt she'd found in the closet and managed to pull over her head, and the same loose pants. He was sitting in one of the chairs by the fireplace, where a pile of powdery ash remained from the night before. An easel with a medium-size blank canvas was set up in front of the chair.

'You're a sloth,' he said. 'I never would have guessed that about you. I've been waiting for hours for you to stir. But you sleep on, oblivious to the smell of coffee and the sound of cooking.'

'That was cooking? I thought we were being bombed.' She lingered in the doorway, lured by the familiar ease of his teasing. Seeing him again had brought something distant back to her: a love of conversation, the joy of easy banter. But it felt strange to be in his house at so early an hour. The room, a warm refuge last night, was weighted with the formality of morning, and she hesitated, unsure whether she should stay or go.

'Come here.'

She walked over to him, and he pulled her down gently into his lap. There was a scarf resting under his right wrist, draped over the arm of the chair.

'I may be unable to do some things, but I am still capable of standing, you know.'

'Pills,' he said, ignoring her and pointing to a collection of bottles on the end table. 'I brought all of them. And there's French toast if you need to take them with food.'

She wasn't sure whether to be more disturbed by the thought of him rummaging through her things or by the fact she'd evidently slept through his comings and goings. 'Weren't you worried Evan might object?'

'Evan and I are old friends. He takes care of most of the houses along the road here during the off-season. Besides, I didn't want to give you an excuse to leave. Now, which of these do you take in the morning?' She sorted through the bottles, and he handed her a glass of water, shaking his head at the mosaic of pills nestled in her palm. She gulped them down self-consciously.

'Put your arm on top of mine.'

When she did, he pressed his knee lightly against their arms, pinning them in place, and with his left hand, loosely tied the ends of the scarf around her wrist, joining it to his own.

'What are you doing?'

'Experimenting. Watch.'

With his left hand he placed a paintbrush between their fingers. Then he moved his right hand toward the palette, grabbing up a deep navy with a neat back-and-forth motion. He brought their hands toward the canvas and stopped.

'Now, you're going to steer.'

'I can't.'

'Of course you can. Don't overthink it, just close your eyes. What would you paint, if you could paint anything?' He stopped and laughed. 'A stupid question. Birds, of course. *Oiseau. Uccello. Vogel.* All right, imagine a flock in flight. Don't think of what you're seeing. Think of what it feels like when they surprise you, when they take your breath away. Think of what you're feeling, here.' He placed his left hand at the base of her throat for a moment, then wrapped his arm around her waist. 'That's what you want to draw.'

His mouth, so close to her ear. She envisioned a field of blackbirds rising up in a dark curtain against the sky, their calls swelling into a chorus that obliterated even the sound of her own heartbeat. Her hand moved back and forth in a steady rhythm, floating on his, weightless.

'There. Open your eyes.'

She peered through one eye first before opening both, astonished by what she saw on the canvas: a watery sky interrupted by brushstrokes that suggested birds in flight. 'We drew this?'

'You did.'

She was delighted to have created something, however rudimentary, as opposed to only examining something or documenting it. 'Let's do more. I want to paint your house. The way I saw it yesterday from the lake, in the rain.'

'I'm glad to see you're tempering your ambitions. We can paint anything you like, of course. It's just I'd hate for you to spend all of your energy on one endeavor.'

He untied the scarf from their wrists, and it floated to the floor. He whispered her name over and over until it sounded exotic, like it belonged to a stranger. She was the stranger, she realized, behaving in a way completely foreign to her, abandoning her usual efforts to conceal herself, to fade into the background. She pressed into him, feeling his ribs against her back. His breathing was fast; his fingers worked at the raised seam on the cuff of her sleeve. She turned toward him, resting her head against his neck. He'd already showered; his face was fresh and smelled of shaving cream, his breath with the dull echo of coffee and rum. She kissed the line of his jaw, wanting to touch him first. The color of his skin shifted just there, like a cleft in a dune. She slipped her hand inside his shirt, hiding it, and tilted her head back. Her neck was one part of her that was still fluid, still in its original condition. His thumb found a beating pulse point there and pressed against it, and she felt herself unraveling.

'Tell me what you're working on now.'

'Nothing with birds. I don't think you'd like it.' His hands skimmed her body with the lightest touch, deciphering the history written on her skin: the ghost stories of childhood scars, flesh that never saw the sun, creases etched from movements of habit. He'd filled the bed with so many pillows it resembled a fort; she was surrounded by down and foam, her joints resting on faded silk rectangles of lavender and buckwheat.

'How do you decide?'

'What to paint?' He shifted, pushing away the sheet and circling her waist with his arms, drawing her closer, burying his nose in the cloud of her hair. She could smell his sweat on her body, and on his upper arm, the lingering scent of the shampoo he'd used to wash her hair in the shower, sandalwood and citrus.

'I don't usually talk about it. It's not that I'm superstitious; art isn't a religion to me. But it's difficult to put into words.'

She kept still, pressing herself toward invisibility, as if, forgetting she was there, he might confess something.

He raised himself up on one elbow. 'I suppose I look for what isn't seen and try to put that on the canvas. Not the negative space, more the essence of a thing, of a place.'

'What if you were painting me?'

Thomas ran his thumb along her lower lip. 'If I didn't know better, I'd think you were fishing for a compliment.' He stretched, a seamless movement that pulled his body a fraction away from hers. 'There are some things so beautiful I would never attempt to paint them.' He climbed out of bed and disappeared down the hall. 'Don't go anywhere,' he called back to her. 'I have something for you.'

There was nowhere she wanted to go. With every leaving she waited for the sound of his steps retracing, coming back to her. 'I kept this for you,' he said, climbing back into bed, running his fingers down her side, across her breasts. Her skin rose and prickled. She was cold and hot at the same time; parts of her frozen, parts like magma. The book he tossed on the blanket was Mary Oliver's *No Voyage and Other Poems*. 'You probably owe the library quite a bit of money by now.'

Two days. Three. He had killed her desire for both food and sleep. She only wanted to be awake, in this bed, talking, or not talking. It didn't matter.

'Turn the light off.'

He did, but with the room darker, he seemed to grow lighter. His skin gleamed, pale and cold, like luminous marble.

'I'd prefer to see you,' he said.

'Then pretend you're painting me and close your eyes.'

Dressed in his bathrobe, she peeled the covers away from him. The sun was out for the first time in days and saturated the room with light. She pressed the tip of her tongue to the crest of his hip, tasting the salt of his skin. It was easier to ignore her pain when she focused on something immediate, something she wanted. He squirmed and grunted, only half-awake. She ran her finger down the center of his back, nudging each vertebra—cervical, thoracic, lumbar, sacral— admiring the perfection of his spine, then traced her finger over a pearly ring of scar tissue tattooed on his left buttock.

'What happened to you?'

'Hmm.'

She poked his shoulder. 'What happened?'

'Where?'

'Here.' She poked him again, circling the scar.

His voice was unintelligible, thick with sleep. He answered into the pillow. 'Neela. Vicious little cur bit me.'

A memory swam toward her, slow but deliberate, cutting clean through every obstacle she threw in its path. Natalie's words, yet they were coming from his mouth. *Vicious little cur.* She tried not to remember the rest, but her sister's words engulfed her, pulling her down. *That didn't stop her from taking a bite out of Thomas. I've seen the scar.*

She turned the lock on the door of the guest room. She closed the curtains and tore off his robe, hating the feel of it against her skin, welcoming the sharp stab of pain brought by quick movement. Her own clothes were stiff with muck and still smelled like the lake, but she struggled into them, then sat on the bed with her hands over her ears, blocking out the sounds of him pounding on the door, calling her name, then, later, cursing her. She heard him leave and come back and leave and come back. She heard his perfect back slide down the wall in the hallway. She heard the bottle and the glass, and the sound of his voice gone slack with liquor. She heard his breath and his regret, heard his apologies. Heard him sleep.

She looked around the room once before leaving, memorizing details. The dark curtains, the rug in front of the armoire stained with mud, the pillows piled high on the bed, stiff and formal, as if she'd never slept there that first night of the storm. The wire cage on the bedside table. She lifted the cage and ran a finger across the back of the grosbeak again, the deep, endless blue of it. What was it he'd said? *I wanted her to feel loss*. Alice set the cage back on the table and slid the bird into her pocket.

SEVEN
NOVEMBER 2007

Had he really expected to walk through the door of the summer house and find the two panels hanging on the wall, a large empty space between them? Why not a red *X* marking the spot for good measure? The man who let them in, Evan, kept his eyes on them continuously. Finch didn't even see him blink. He *requested* they both stay in the same room and stood guard at the door, as if he expected they might abscond with—what? The ratty sofa covered with a sheet? The cracked lampshades, yellowed, with enough webbing to hammock a small mammal? He checked the floor for spiders. The Oriental carpet had a larger bald spot than his own head. So much gone to waste, it made his stomach turn. There was no understanding Thomas. He could have sold the house and had enough money to live on for a while or, far less likely but infinitely more practical, paid off some of his debts. Instead it stood empty, concealed by the trees.

The lakeshore was fringed with ice, the surface a flat mirror that stretched to the horizon. Everywhere he looked, Finch saw nothing but white. The trunks of trees had been blasted with snow, their limbs shrouded in clouds of it. The piers of the dock, the stairs, the roofs of the neighboring cabins, all blanketed in the same. The perfect winter scene, he supposed, but to Finch, it felt claustrophobic.

'The owner is a friend of mine,' he said to Evan, the watchdog with a crew cut who stood ramrod straight, his back pressed against the door, his arms crossed and resting on the convex suggestion of a gut.

'Close friend?' Evan asked.

'Very,' Finch replied.

'Then you know he's dead.'

Finch's breath caught in his throat for a moment until he realized the man was referring to the elder Bayber. 'I see the misunderstanding. Not the parents. I'm a friend of Thomas Bayber. Their son.'

'He's not the owner. Never has been.'

'But if Mr. and Mrs. Bayber are deceased, surely their property would pass to their son?'

'Not my business. I imagine there's lawyers enough to sort it all out. Or not. I just watch the house is all. Keep the kids from ransacking it, make sure nothing goes missing.'

The last was said with slow emphasis, making Finch think he should have forged a postdated note from Bayber Senior, granting him permission to poke around in absentia.

'Finch. You've got to see this!' Stephen's voice rang out from the end of a long hallway where he'd wandered off on his own, despite Evan's admonishment that they stay together.

Finch looked at Evan, wondering if he could take him in a fight. The man couldn't be much younger than he was. Evan cracked his knuckles before shrugging. 'End of the hall,' he said. 'Probably the room on your right. I'll need to check your pockets before you leave, though.'

'Charming,' Finch mumbled under his breath. The gloom of the place was wearing on him, and he trudged down the hall thinking this had been a mistake, agreeing to join forces with Stephen on what would most certainly turn out to be a fool's quest. He was confident within the confines of his profession, but this was straining the boundaries. What did he know about tracking down missing art? And what if the whole thing was some dark joke on Thomas's part? No. He'd had an opportunity to look in on Thomas before they left. While the stroke had left him unable to provide any additional details or offer any explanation, there was hope and expectation in his eyes. It wasn't a joke.

Finch stood in the doorway of a large bedroom, peering in. 'What is it I'm supposed to be looking at?'

Stephen glanced over his shoulder. 'What's the matter with you?'

'You don't find it the slightest bit insulting that our friend in the other room presumes we're here to carry out some sort of heist?'

'You aren't picking a fight, are you? Good Lord, did you see how the man's built? His arms are twice the size of your neck, Finch. I mean he's old and all, but still.' Stephen was juggling the tools of his trade, his digital camera and magnifying glass, while examining a watercolor on the wall. 'Notice anything?'

'How can I see anything when you're standing right in front of whatever it is I'm supposed to be looking at?'

Stephen moved to the side, and the first thing Finch saw was a gold filigree cage on the bedside table. 'This was deserving of such an enthusiastic summoning? Thanks to you, we're going to have to go through a thorough pat down.'

'It's the cage in the painting.'

'Yes, I can see that, although I'm not sure what significance you're ascribing to it. The grandfather clock in the main room is in the painting. So is the love seat. And I'm guessing the moldering atlases on the coffee table are the ones in the painting, as well.'

Stephen didn't say anything, only raised his index finger and tapped the wall. Finch moved in closer to look at the watercolor Stephen had gestured toward, and though it hardly merited a quickening of the pulse, he was still pleased to find himself excited by the unexpected. 'Dorothy Doughty? What is it? A study for one of her models?' He took the magnifying glass from Stephen and worked his way meticulously across the painting from top to bottom, right to left, as if deciphering an ancient Chinese manuscript.

'Look at the text above the signature.'

'Letitia. That was Thomas's mother. But I don't recall this bird—do you know what it is?—ever being released by Royal Worcester. There were thirty-six pairs of American birds and three individual models done. Then nineteen British birds . . .'

'Twenty-one, actually.'

Finch took a breath, imagining his hands circling Stephen's slim throat. Old, he'd said? *Old enough to know better*, Claire chided him. He swallowed hard before coughing politely. 'Yes. Twenty-one British, but those weren't put into production until after Doughty's death in 1962.' He stared at Stephen over the top of his glasses, feeling the muscles between his shoulder blades contract. 'I imagine you have them memorized?'

'Redstarts on gorse in 'thirty-five. Goldfinches and thistle in 'thirty-six. Bluebirds and apple blossom, also in 'thirty-six, then Virginia cardinals and orange . . .'

'My point being, this isn't one of her later pieces. Thomas's mother grew up in England, in Cornwall. The Doughty sisters lived in Cornwall until after the war. It's more likely they would have known each other then, when Dorothy was doing the series of American birds.'

'Maybe you're right about that. So the cage is in both paintings, this watercolor and the central panel of our triptych. But what's more interesting is what's not here.'

'I'm not following you.'

'The inscription, Finch. It says, 'One model to another,' doesn't it? And the bird painted in the watercolor is inside of a cage. This cage.'

'You're wondering where the bird is? How do you know the gift wasn't just the watercolor?'

'Look at the table, Finch. Right here. You'll need my magnifying glass.' He handed it to Finch while rocking back and forth on the balls of his feet. Finch held the glass close to the table and noticed several fine scratches. Stephen had already pulled a plastic bag and cotton swab from his case, and when Finch straightened up, the younger man swooped toward the table, quickly moving the swab across the surface.

'If the bird in the watercolor was a prototype and never went into production, then we can assume it wouldn't have been on a plinth, likely only resting on its base. I can test this residue to determine its chemical blueprint and compare it with similar output from the company's factory around that time. If it matches, we can be fairly sure that Dorothy gave Mrs. Bayber a bird in addition to the painting.'

'Stephen, I don't mean to be a killjoy, but let's assume you're right, and there was a Doughty bird here at one time. What does that have to do with finding the other panels? Anything could have happened to it. Letitia could have taken it to France, Thomas might have it; maybe it was sold or donated to a museum. All we would know was that it was here at one time. Besides, there must be at least two decades of grime on everything in this room. Would you be testing residue? Or dust?' He watched Stephen's spirits shrivel a bit.

'You can't know for sure, Finch. Even if it doesn't have anything to do with the paintings, it would still be a find of some interest. It could be important.'

'Well, you have the key words down. It would only be important and interesting if you could find it.'

Stephen stubbed the toe of his shoe against the rug, and Finch could easily see him as a child, on the outskirts of every group, struggling to find something he possessed that would let him into the circle. A spark of guilt tripped through Finch's internal wiring. 'I suppose the best idea would be to test it and see what you come up with.'

Stephen brightened. 'Well, if you think I should.'

'I imagine Cranston will want us to explore every avenue. Is there anything else here we should be looking for? I was hoping there might be papers, maybe something with an address, but the desk's been cleaned out. Whoever shut the place up did a thorough job.'

'I'll just take a few quick shots of the main room,' Stephen said, a third of his face disappearing behind his camera. 'Unless you want me to try to collect fingerprints?'

'Can you do that?'

'Well, technically no. I suppose this means we'll have to get back in the car.'

The thought of jettisoning the gloomy house and leaving the eerie, snow-muffled landscape behind put Finch in a better mood. 'Providing we're able to get past security with our dignity intact, I know a nice place in Syracuse where we can have dinner. They used to serve a lovely roast pork with spiced apples. Hot food—that should perk you up. We'll get a good night's sleep and start for the Kesslers' first thing in the morning.'

As far as Stephen could tell, weather conditions had no impact on the way Finch drove: too fast, with too little attention paid to the rearview mirror and too much emphasis placed on passing cars observing the speed limit. He clutched the armrest when the wheels caught black ice and sent the rear of the car fishtailing.

'You need to remember, Stephen, when skidding, take your foot off the gas, avoid the brake, and steer in the direction you want to go.'

'I want to go home. What direction is that?'

'Good! A sense of humor helps the driver remain calm in adverse driving conditions.'

'I would have thought not driving in adverse driving conditions would help the driver remain calm.'

Finch seemed to be suffering from the delusion that Stephen planned to take up driving at some point in the future, when in fact, each minute spent in the car reinforced his affection for the public transportation system. When Finch finally pulled into the hotel parking lot, Stephen scrambled out of the car. His knees buckled. Fear, frost, a failure of his fibula; none of these negated the blessed fact he was standing on solid ground.

Over dinner, it took them all of five minutes to review what they'd found. Why would Bayber have wanted them to start at the cabin if there was nothing there? Stephen hadn't expected it to be easy—or had he?—but he had hoped there might be a smattering of clues along the way. Before they'd left for the cabin, he'd spent hours searching the Internet for some indication of where the sisters might be, but had come up with surprisingly little information. Natalie and Alice Kessler. Parents deceased in 1969, no living relatives. Two young women, ages twenty-six and twenty-three, and in 1972 they'd vanished from Stonehope Way in

Woodridge, Connecticut. Two *attractive* young women, which made it all more likely they'd have been noticed by someone.

'We can't go back empty-handed,' he said to Finch. The waiter had tried removing the breadbasket from the table while there was still a heel left, prompting Stephen to wrestle the basket away from him, while noting the consequences that removing food prematurely would have on his compensation. He gnawed on the crust while doodling across his napkin.

'You realize that's not paper,' Finch said. Stephen stuffed the napkin in his pocket, and Finch shook his head. 'Stephen, let me ask you something. What is it you expect to find?'

'The other two panels, of course. Don't you?'

'Not really, no.' Finch leaned back in his chair and signaled the waiter for the bill. He took a sip of coffee while holding up a finger toward Stephen, then patted his upper lip with his napkin. 'I know Thomas. He wants something.'

'He wants us to find the other pieces of the painting.'

'Why?'

Finch's question rattled Stephen. He far preferred to focus on the task at hand, finding the two triptych panels, as opposed to trying to intuit Bayber's motivation. 'I suppose because they're a part of his legacy. Imagine the worst-case scenario, Finch. We find the Kessler sisters and they don't want to sell the paintings.' This really *was* the worst thing Stephen could think of, since it put him on the fast track back to his office, appraising doll collections and relics from the Civil War. 'At the very least, they become authenticated works in his oeuvre. Maybe that's what's critical to him now. To have everything he's created in his lifetime accounted for.'

'You estimate he painted the pieces when, thirty-some years ago?'

'The original panel, yes. The overpainting, some years after that.'

'Why wait until now to try to find the other panels?'

'Really, Finch,' Stephen said, rearranging the salt and pepper shakers. 'I'm not sure that's our concern.'

'I just don't want you to get your hopes up, Stephen.'

Finch's tone of resignation sent him into a panic. 'I don't believe you completely grasp the seriousness of my situation, Professor. You heard what Bayber said. He will only sell the work in its entirety. If we can't find the panels, what incentive will Cranston possibly have to keep me on?'

'Your skill? Your knowledge?'

Stephen shook his head.

'You're counting on this one thing to change quite a lot for you.'

Stephen realized Finch had a great deal in common with his father: never wanting for approval or lacking in accomplishments; a bevy of friends and family; jokes that drew laughter; stories his students clamored to hear time and again, finding them more charming with each retelling. Had Finch ever watched people look uneasily at one another in his presence, or felt the tone of his voice rise unexpectedly until all heads in a room swiveled in his direction? Had he ever made a logical assessment of a situation only to hear people describe him as heartless? How could he possibly explain to Finch that this was the opportunity of a lifetime? Find the missing panels and he might once again be anointed with the gravitational pull of success; people would be drawn to him, whether they liked him or not.

'In terms of a career path, Finch, I am presently working in the basement. Dropped any lower and I become fodder for Jules Verne.'

Woodridge was a small town at the northern tip of Fairfield County in Connecticut. The Kessler house stood at the end of a long, curving lane bordered by sycamore and hackberry trees, the patchy, mottled bark of the former looking like a contagion the latter had narrowly escaped. It wasn't until he and Finch were halfway down the lane that Stephen saw the house, a yellow, three-story colonial revival that at one point must have sat like a cheerful ball of sun against the backdrop of evergreens. Now the house had faded to the color of Dijon mustard; the front porch sagged in the middle; the yard was littered with wheeled contraptions appropriate for a variety of ages: a Volvo station wagon, an old Mercedes up on blocks, two motorbikes, bicycles, and a tricycle with muddy streamers hanging from the handgrips. Dogs barked at the rear of the property when they got out of the car.

Finch appeared unhappy but determined and mounted the front steps with the enthusiasm of a precinct captain. An index card thumbtacked beneath the doorbell stated, 'Broken. Please knock loudly.' Finch's head dropped to his chest, and he waved Stephen forward. Stephen took off his gloves and thumped on the front door with his fist, watching chips of paint drift down onto the bristled welcome mat caked in mud.

The man who eventually came to the door had lank brown hair hanging to his shoulders, a plaid wool shirt, and glasses with the thickest black rims Stephen had ever seen. Finch offered a brief explanation, but the man seemed unconcerned about having strangers in his home and swept his bangs away from his forehead before shaking Finch's hand and letting them in.

'Winslow Edell,' he said. He turned to the dark staircase and yelled, 'Esme!' His voice echoed up the stairwell, a musical lilt sticking to the end of it. In spite of the collection of vehicles outside, there was not a sound in the house save for the dogs out back that had begun baying in tandem.

'She'll be down before long. Why don't we wait in the living room?' They followed him down a hall into a large room and waited while Winslow pushed newspapers off every piece of furniture and onto the floor. Stephen couldn't figure out why the room was so bright until he realized there were no curtains, no drapes, no shutters or blinds. The light streaming into the room was reflected from the snow outside.

'You're friends of the Kesslers, then?'

Finch cleared his throat. For once Stephen had no desire to interject, still absorbed by the overall state of clutter surrounding him. 'We are trying to locate Natalie and Alice for a good friend of the family.'

Winslow frowned. 'I doubt we can help you. We only met Natalie Kessler the one time, and that was thirty-five years ago, when we first looked at the place in 'seventy-two.'

'And you bought the house right away?'

'Oh, no. We're just renting. The Kesslers still own the house.' A woman in frayed jeans with a long chestnut braid entered the room and sat down on the arm of Winslow's chair. 'We fell in love with the house the minute we saw it. I was pregnant with our first then, and Natalie—Miss Kessler—was in a hurry to leave. I heard there was a younger sister, but I think she was ill, or maybe away, when we moved in. We never saw her. I'm Esme, by the way.' She got up and walked over to Finch, giving him a peck on the cheek, then did the same with Stephen. 'Can you believe it, Winslow? That we've been here for that long?'

'Through six kids and eleven grandkids. Lots of history here.'

The house seemed an odd combination of taste and dishevelment. Stuffing poked out of the arms of chairs with nicely carved legs; the coffee table was gouged but sturdy. A piano stood in the corner, buried beneath magazines.

'You play the piano, Mrs. Edell?' Stephen asked.

'Mrs. Edell?' Esme twittered. 'I thought my mother-in-law might have slipped into the room for a minute. Please, just call me Esme. We prefer informality. It's how we raised our children, having them use our first names. We wanted them to know that we considered them our equals.'

Winslow nodded. 'From the very beginning. People in their own right. Just smaller.'

So this was where the counterculture had come to die. Stephen avoided glancing at Finch, sure of his expression. 'Do you mind if I look at it?'

'Not at all.' She moved stacks of magazines off the top of the piano, and Stephen was stunned to see the instrument was a rare macassar ebony Mason & Hamlin.

'We never play it,' she said. 'We're not a musical sort of family. But it was here, so we thought, why not give it a whirl?' She punched D sharp repeatedly, as if encouraging the key to stay down. Finch's shoulders shot up toward his ears. 'The kids never took to it, though.'

'It was here?'

'Oh, it's not ours. It belongs to the Kesslers. Everything in the house does. We rented the place furnished.'

Finch appeared as confused as Stephen felt. 'Forgive me, Mr. and Mrs. Edell,' Finch began, pointedly using their surname, 'but you've been renting the house for thirty-five years? And in all that time, never had any contact with Alice or Natalie Kessler?'

'Well.' Her voice lowered to a conspiratorial whisper. 'We can hardly believe it ourselves. We never took the place with the intention of staying this long. The rent was steep for us for the first few years, but Winslow's parents left him a little money so we could make it work. The rent increases since we started living here have been very modest. Winslow's a bit of a handyman, so he keeps the place up.'

'Yes, I can see,' Finch said, pointedly looking at the raw edge of a windowsill.

'We just send our checks off every month to the property management company.' Esme stood in back of the chair where her husband was sitting and wrapped her arms around his neck. 'I suppose it will have to end, sooner or later. But we're prepared, aren't we, honey? We've been talking about getting a mobile home and just hitting the road for a few years.'

'I don't suppose you get any mail for the Kesslers?' Finch asked.

'Not anymore. There were the usual things for the first year or so we lived here. Catalogs, some magazines, lots of letters from people who must not have known they'd left. Packages. We were just supposed to send anything that came to the management company, so that's what we did. We haven't had any mail come for the Kesslers in at least, oh, twenty-five years, I'd guess.'

'The name and address of the management company, could you give them to us?'

Winslow popped out of his chair and walked over to a desk, pulling open a bottom drawer stuffed with files. 'It's in Hartford. Steele and Greene Property Management. Here's the address.'

'Anyone in particular that you deal with?' Stephen asked, making cramped notes in the pad he'd taken from his pocket.

'Deal with? No. We don't bother them and they don't bother us. Like Esme said, we keep the place up and send our checks in on the last day of the month. We're as reliable as the U.S. Postal Service. It's a sweet arrangement.' For the first time since letting them into the house, Winslow looked alarmed. 'You wouldn't be trying to get them to sell this place, would you?'

Finch gave nothing away, sitting perfectly straight in his chair. 'I can assure you we are only trying to find Alice and Natalie Kessler to pass a message on to them. It has nothing whatsoever to do with the property. Mrs. Edell, you said you only met Natalie the one time. Did she happen to mention anything about where they were going, or why they were leaving in such a hurry?'

Esme considered, but shook her head. 'Not that I recall. It was after Hurricane Agnes. She talked about the basement flooding, but Winslow never found any real damage to the foundation. Their parents had died about three years earlier. We thought maybe they just wanted a fresh start.'

'Didn't it strike you as odd, that they would leave all of their furniture behind?'

'It was providence,' Winslow said, smiling broadly at Stephen. 'Why question good fortune, I say. A man from Steele and Greene came after we signed the papers. Walked through and took an inventory of everything—all the furniture, the kitchen equipment, the artwork. We signed off on it. It's all still here, every piece of it.'

After the word *artwork*, everything was muted by the drumming of Stephen's heart in his throat. The missing panels were here. Finch, too, appeared dumbstruck that the problem should be so easily solved. 'The artwork you're speaking of, could we see it?'

Esme motioned for them to follow her. 'It's not really our taste, you understand. So we moved it all to the back hall. It's only us coming in and out that way.'

The back hall was dim, but even before entering it Stephen could see the shallow profiles of frames lining the two walls. He walked past several pieces with only a perfunctory assessment—lithographs mostly, some signed posters, and a few photographs. Then two thirds of the way down the hall, he stopped short and took a step back.

He'd been so focused on what they were looking for that he'd walked right past it. The Edells did not have either of the missing triptych panels; nothing hanging in the hallway was the right size. But what Natalie and Alice had left behind was a color pencil sketch, signed by Bayber and dated August 1963.

Stephen stood in front of the sketch, oblivious to the chatter of the Edells. This was one of Bayber's early pieces; he would have been only twenty-eight at the time. The artist's talent and skill were already apparent, though his style had yet to be defined. Even so, Bayber had conveyed the world of this family in a simple sketch, telegraphing their emotions in his choice of color, the weight and length of his strokes, the pressure applied.

The Kessler family sat together on a love seat, the same love seat depicted in the main panel of the triptych. Seeing the four of them together, Stephen could pick the pieces of the parents that had migrated to the children. Alice was perched on the left arm, looking younger than she did in the oil, though her personality was very much in evidence. Using only the position of her head and the arch of her brow, Bayber portrayed her as an intelligent and inquisitive young girl. The parents sat close together, closer than was necessary given the generous size of the love seat; Bayber had drawn them with the suggestion that they were leaning slightly into each other, but did so unconsciously, as if each was so used to the other's presence it would have been awkward for them to sit farther apart.

Natalie sat on the right arm of the love seat, next to her mother. As opposed to the others, the colors Bayber used to draw her were cool, the strokes short and sharp, her edges more angular. There was the impression of an insurmountable distance between the older daughter and the rest of the family. He'd exposed some fissure, an estrangement so apparent it was difficult to look at the sketch without feeling a degree of discomfort for the four of them. Stephen could understand why it had been left behind.

'Even then,' Finch whispered to him. 'You can see his abilities.'

The background lacked a richness of detail, but Stephen recognized several things from the cabin: books stacked on a low table in front of the sofa, a large clock in the background, the wide stone mantel of the fireplace. He pulled out his camera and took several pictures of the sketch.

'What do we do with it?'

Finch seemed surprised. He said quietly, 'You have your notes. You have your photos. That's all we can do. It's not ours, Stephen, just because we've found it. And it doesn't belong to Bayber either. He gave it to them, as a gift. It, like everything else, would appear to belong to the Kessler sisters. Wherever they are.'

Esme's attitude changed when Stephen started taking pictures. Her nose tilted up, as if she'd caught the scent of something akin to bad news. Stephen pointed at the Bayber and gave her a wide smile. 'My mother won't believe it. She has one just like this.'

That, he was pleased to note, even impressed Finch.

They took leave of the Edells, who saw them off with enthusiastic waves from the front porch as they wound their way through the maze of junk in the yard. Esme continued waving as they drove off, and Stephen was forced to respond in kind, counting the seconds until they rounded the curve and were safely out of sight. It was only then that he sat back in the seat, shell-shocked.

'How can they not realize what they have? What if something happens to it? What if they decide to sell it?'

'Stephen, it's been there for thirty-five years. I don't think we need to worry about it going anywhere in the immediate future. And isn't it of some satisfaction to you, knowing of its existence? Think of it—in good likelihood, there are only a handful of people in the world who know about that Bayber sketch: Natalie and Alice, Thomas, the person who took inventory of the house's contents, the Edells. And you and me.'

'You had no idea?'

'Evidently, there's quite a bit I don't know when it comes to Thomas.'

'I still feel it was irresponsible to leave it there.'

'As opposed to doing something responsible like stealing it, for example? Stephen, you'll just have to have faith it will be there. Add the sketch to our list of reasons,' Finch said.

'List of reasons?'

'To find Natalie and Alice as quickly as possible.'

EIGHT
AUGUST 1972

How Natalie found the house was anyone's guess. She might
have closed her eyes and laid the tip of her index finger on
the map, on Orion, a small town clinging to the western
edge of Tennessee on the Gulf Coastal Plain. It was past
midnight when they drove up, long before the landscape
took on the flat gray of near morning, and the dark was
plush and heavy. The house anchored the middle of a block
of similar houses, old Victorians with crumbling porches and
pillars, and the tidy silhouettes of boxwood hedges. They
stumbled as they headed toward the broad porch steps, the
front walk cracked and erupting at its seams as though plates
of continents converged there. The stairs creaked under their
feet, sagging with the weight of suitcases, and while Natalie
fumbled for the keys Alice stood stock-still, feeling as odd
as a cat burglar; she'd fallen asleep in one life and now woke
to find herself breaking into another.

We can afford it was the explanation Natalie offered, along
with *the weather will be better for you*. She ignored Alice's
hysterics, her pleas to stay in the home where they'd grown

up, where her parents still moved at night from room to room, their breath a cold draft; the house where, Alice prayed, her daughter may have opened her eyes for the briefest of moments, to take everything in before closing them again. Natalie had pried Alice's hands from the door-frame. *We can't stay here.* She'd locked the car doors as she pulled out of the driveway at a speed that sent gravel arcing up in a spray from the back tires. For twenty hours Natalie had driven as though the devil was on their rear bumper, her face set and determined, fueled by coffee and wide-open windows; Alice had sat like a zombie for most of the trip, drifting in and out of oblivion and half-wishing the car would crash, thinking only that then, she could be with her daughter.

By light of day, the look of the house hadn't improved. Tendrils of green were knit into the grubby lattice beneath the porch, firmly locking the house to its damp bed of mud. The shutters gaped at their hinges, and strips of paint peeled from the wood siding like streamers. The house had been sold furnished, with furniture that was mismatched and scabby: bites of wood missing from chair legs, permanent depressions in the sofa cushions, indefinable stains. A pungent humidity cloaked everything, making it hard for Alice to breathe. *It's the medicine*, Natalie said. *It's making you groggy.* But Alice knew better. It wasn't the gold salts or the penicillamine, which had become necessary again almost immediately once she was no longer pregnant. The baby had cast a spell over her body, fending off her familiar symptoms with a protective charm. What arrived in the aftermath surpassed the worst her arthritis had previously offered up: the physical jabs and volleys it threw, her intimate relation-ship with exhaustion, the detours her illness took when new drugs set up roadblocks. This pain was different, even from the grief that still hugged her in its arms after her parents' death. This pain was fresh and searing and made a home for itself in her very core.

She had neither the strength nor the endurance to climb the long flight of stairs leading to the second story, so the main floor of the house became hers. She occupied only two rooms, and did not occupy them so much as move between them—the high-ceilinged living room, with its expansive windows which ran from the front to the back of the house, and the small bedroom on the opposite side that at one time must have been a study, but was now as spartan as a monk's cell, with only the wrought-iron frame of a double bed pushed up against the wall. At night, Alice rolled onto one hip and moved as close to the wall as she could, resting the flat of her palm against it, waiting to hear the house breathe and speak in its creaky voice.

After several weeks she detected a pattern in the hall carpet, the path her footprints left as she dragged herself from her bedroom to the chair in the corner of the living room and back again. Saisee, the housekeeper Natalie found shortly after they arrived, placed an ottoman in front of the wing chair and a throw across the back. Alice passed the days wrapped in a blanket, staring out the back windows, their swollen, mildewed frames barely able to hold the panes in place. The old glass distorted the trumpet creeper and morning honeysuckle, turning the garden into something watery and tropical. The few birds she recognized, thrashers and yellowthroats and towhees, moved sluggishly, as if anesthetized by the heat.

She lost her appetite, her sense of time, the ability to sleep. Saisee coaxed her with breakfasts made for an invalid: delicate rice puddings, milk toast and softly coddled eggs, cornmeal mush. But the food had no smell and tasted of lead. The hours closed ranks against any change in routine, and the days fell in line, one after another. The heat swelled and retreated, then swelled again through the long months of August and September. Daylight pasted itself to the sky, refusing to fade. Such unbearably bright rooms, the white paint glinting like ice and burning her eyes. Even when she squeezed them shut, the light burrowed in beneath her lids.

At night the insects called to each other. She lay awake listening to their chirps and saws, their singing impossible to tune out. After long hours, the bed stopped being a bed and instead turned into a deep well, its sides slick with moss, impossible to climb. She woke from shallow fits of half sleep, shivering, damp with sweat, the sheets twisted in knots beneath her. The dreams left behind an echo of water which she heard all day, the quiet, certain slush of it chasing away the oppressive heat, soothing her fiery joints, calling to her as it rose past her ankles and knees, washed the sweat from beneath her breasts, lapped at her shoulders, chilled her lips, then filled her ears. She drifted between rooms, caught in an undertow. No *Kaboutermannekes* appeared to guide her.

Was it day or night? Friday or Tuesday? Had she taken her pain medication? Best to take more, in case she hadn't. Natalie shook her by the shoulders, the flash of pain throttling her back into the world.

'For God's sake, Alice. Get dressed. Walk around the yard. Do something useful with yourself.'

She stood up, wishing she could shake Natalie back, shake her hard enough to loosen her teeth. 'You're a monster.'

Natalie's face remained impassive. She plumped the pillows on the sofa where no one ever sat and turned away from Alice. 'If you haven't got any more spirit than this, it's just as well. You wouldn't have had the stomach to be anyone's mother.'

That cruelty sparked something bitter and caused it to rise in Alice's throat, refusing to be swallowed. 'And you wouldn't have been selfless enough.'

It was the worst she could imagine. Her sister's face showed a flash of anger, but it was gone just as quickly. Natalie stared at her, with a tight, frozen smile. Alice couldn't help but shiver.

'Do you hate me, Alice?' Natalie asked, almost eager. 'You probably should. But I must say I'm surprised. I didn't think you had it in you.'

Alice sank back in the chair, her spine settling into the familiar curve there. Could she hate her own sister? Wouldn't that make her every bit the monster she accused Natalie of being? She remembered Thomas's attempted warning and the way she'd cut him off, refusing to hear anything negative about her family. It was one thing to number their faults in her own head, quite another to listen to an outsider recite them.

She shook her head. 'I don't hate you.'

Natalie shrugged before moving to the clouded mirror at the end of the living room, poking loose strands of hair back into her chignon and straightening her skirt.

'I've got an interview. I'm not sure when I'll be back.'

'An interview?'

'For a job. Someone has to work to keep you in those little bottles of pills you run through so quickly.'

'But there's the money from the house.'

Natalie outlined her lips in pink and pressed them together, watching herself in the mirror. 'That's gone.'

'Gone?' Alice's mouth went dry. 'How can it be gone? We haven't bought anything.' She'd envisioned whatever they'd made from the quick sale of their house coupled with the small protective trust their parents had left, as her only assurance she wouldn't end up on the street. 'Are you saying we don't have any money?'

Natalie's patience had expired. 'We have enough money for groceries and the house payments. For a while. The lawyer and I worked everything out.' She tucked a curl behind her ear and smoothed it into place.

Alice remembered the probate lawyer they'd met with after their parents' death. And she remembered his response to Natalie, how the smell of her perfume drove the blood up his neck and into his drawn cheeks; the number of times he'd blinked—four—when Natalie rested her hand, palm up, on his desk.

'But where . . .'

Natalie cut her off. 'There may have been a scholarship, Alice, but that doesn't mean your playtime at a private college didn't cost us anything. Not that there's much to show for it. And all of those doctors' visits? I don't mean the rheumatologist and the physical therapist and the blood work and the drugs. I'm talking about the obstetrician. You might have stopped to consider that.' She pulled a compact from her purse and patted away the shine on her nose. 'I didn't see the father stepping forward to pay.' She paused and examined Alice in the mirror, her face taking on the studied casualness of a cat.

Alice sat perfectly still, holding her breath, feeling muscle tremble against bone, unable to remember whether she'd called out for him in her delirium, whether she'd inadvertently said or done something to give them away, wondering if Natalie might somehow know about Thomas.

Her sister pulled the pins out of her hair and shook her head. 'I think down is better. I don't know when I'll be back. Not that it matters. You'll be sleeping. You know, Alice, you really should get some air.'

The idea of being penniless shocked her into action. She and Natalie were both adults now and both unemployed. There was no medical insurance. Alice started cheating on her medications, taking half of what had been prescribed, counting on physical pain to shift her focus from the dead spot in her soul to the job of surviving. She forced herself to stretch her fingers and toes several times a day, and practiced walking the perimeter of her bedroom instead of napping, thinking all the while of what Thomas had told her of Edith Piaf. And then she walked the room some more, trying to think of anything but Thomas.

Work was the greater problem. There would be little use here for a biology major, less for an ornithologist. Natalie, on the other hand, would have no trouble finding a job, if a job was what she wanted. As predicted, within a week Natalie was working at the bank. Within two she was dating the married bank manager. And while any income provided a boost to their dwindling funds, Alice was now aware how uncertain her situation was.

Orion was a place with little impetus for change, little tolerance for disruption. That was how she and Natalie were viewed, as disruptions. Saisee informed her of this, not unkindly, while they sat in the kitchen one afternoon, Saisee snapping beans for dinner, Alice clumsily folding napkins. Phinneaus put it differently the first time they met, when he came knocking on their door from across the street, bearing a plate of something uneven and deflated in the center, covered in a heavy blanket of frosting. *This town, it's like a slow, deep river cut well into its banks. Take something biblical to make it change course.*

'That's Mr. Lapine,' Saisee said, drawing out his name—'Lay-pee-en'—until it sounded more like a medical condition than a surname. The woman peered through the starched lace curtains Natalie had chosen, then moved to where Alice sat propped in her chair in the corner of the living room and leaned over to whisper to her behind the wall of her hand, standing so close that Alice could smell the curtains' same starch on Saisee's apron. 'He's your neighbor from across the way. Lives in that house all by himself. Nice enough young man, but people are none too sure about where all his kin come from, and seems he's in no hurry to tell.'

'Looks like I'm the official welcoming committee,' he said, taking off a boonie hat in camouflage print to reveal shaggy blond hair streaked darker in spots from sweat. His shirt stuck to his skin, damp along the front placket. 'I understand you ladies are from up North. How are you finding Orion so far? I hope our temperatures aren't too disagreeable.'

'Small, Mr. Lapine. My sister and I are finding it small. But charming, of course,' Natalie replied.

'I'll only answer to Phinneaus, please.'

Natalie favored him with a lukewarm smile, but her rapid appraisal made it clear she thought him a misfit more suited to her sister. She excused herself with a half nod, begging a previous appointment.

'Phinneaus, then. I'm afraid I'm on my way out. But Alice will be delighted to entertain you. She thrives on attention. Always got the lion's share of it from our parents. I believe it might have spoiled her. She's having a hard time adjusting to all this'—she swirled her hand in the air, as if spooling cotton candy—'quiet.'

Alice gasped, but Phinneaus's only response to Natalie was a penetrating gaze before he shrugged and turned his focus to Alice. He looked at her face, ignoring the parts of her hidden beneath the lint-colored throw, the tender perimeters of her body that Saisee had thoughtfully concealed. He was either kind or savvy enough not to offer his hand by way of introduction, which made Alice suspect he had been forewarned, that the entire town knew of her predicament already, after only a few short weeks. Natalie had likely used her as the tool, prying open the stern casing of neighbors and those who might prove useful to her. A lovely stranger in town, not as reserved as she should be. A northerner with a trace of superiority, unbecoming in one her age with no apparent reason other than looks to assume herself superior to any of them. But then there was the sister—a whiff of scandal, a horrid affliction. With what Natalie had to endure, saddled at her age with such responsibility, her beauty certain to be wasted, could they not make allowances? Alice understood she was useful to Natalie in this way, gifting her with a humility she did not actually possess.

'I'm sorry. I don't know why she would have said that.'

'Neither do I,' Phinneaus replied. 'But then, I'm an only child. Us only children, we haven't mastered the knack of sibling rivalry for some reason.'

Alice was too embarrassed even to grin. The conversation seemed destined to end there, Natalie having set her up all too well for failure.

'It's an interesting name,' he said, moving closer to her. The knees of his pants were stained a faint red from the clay soil Natalie said filled all of the yards in the neighborhood. His face, too, carried a thin layer of the same red dust everywhere except for two owlish circles surrounding his eyes. Spectacles. She could imagine him wearing them. How serious he must look with his soft, downturned eyes.

'Alice? What's interesting about it?'

His laugh surprised her—warm and round, as if the air inside of him was the same temperature as the air outside. 'No,' he said. '*Phinneaus*. That's usually the first thing people say to me. *Interesting name.* I thought I'd beat you to the punch.'

How long had it been since she'd engaged anyone in conversation? She struggled for something to say, wondering if she'd lost that art along with any ease of motion. Silence spread over the space between them, and he shifted from one foot to the other, holding the sorry cake slightly out in front of him.

'Saisee, could you please take that from Mr., er, from Phinneaus and bring him some tea?'

'Lazy daisy,' he said, handing the plate to Saisee. 'My mama claimed it was the perfect 'welcome' cake because if you didn't know the person well, at least there wasn't much about it to offend. Unless of course you didn't like pecans, and she always said if a person didn't like pecans, then they weren't worth getting to know anyway.' He stopped talking long enough to accept the glass of tea Saisee offered and took a long drink, wiping his mouth with the back of his hand.

'You aren't joining me?' he asked Alice.

The other glass Saisee had brought sat untouched on the table beside the chair. 'I'm not thirsty just now, thank you.'

'I see.' His eyes flicked over her hidden body, and she saw a hesitation, the suggestion of recognition. 'I've come at an inconvenient time. I won't impose myself on your hospitality any longer. I just didn't want another day to go by without making myself known to you and your sister.'

'Thank you for the cake.' She tried to keep her tone neutral, not wanting to sound as dismissive as Natalie, but wishing he would leave. She shifted her limbs beneath the throw, distinctly aware of how close he was standing. For the first time since moving into the house she had a fleeting thought of vanity, wondering how she appeared to a stranger.

'My pleasure. I imagine I'll see you and your sister in town sometime.'

I imagine. Not *I hope.* 'We'll return your plate right away,' she said, her voice more curt than she intended.

He stared her down until she flinched. 'No need. Plenty more where that came from. Saisee, thank you for the tea. I can see myself out.' He nodded at the housekeeper, and Alice kept her eyes on the floor until she heard the front door close.

Saisee headed to the kitchen, muttering under her breath, but Alice caught her words clearly enough: *uppity, rude, unfriendly. Have my hands full with these two.*

***

She could see him in the late mornings if she pushed the edge of the curtain aside, always waiting until Natalie left for work and Saisee was occupied elsewhere. It started as something to pass the time, a diversion to keep grief at bay when it tried to swallow her whole, but grew into a ritual. She was conditioned to be an observer. It was a talent she'd nurtured and honed, one she still possessed since it required patience and stillness as opposed to movement. There was comfort in viewing even a fragment of him, like a compass point to help set her bearings. On those days she didn't see him she felt unmoored and spent the hours nodding through a muddy fog of memories and nightmarish dreams.

In late fall, his movements were methodical as he dropped warty knots of bulbs into deep holes, neat mounds of dirt on all sides, white arcs of bonemeal staining the lawn. In the winter she could see him hunched over a snub-nosed car in his driveway, the steam of his breath the only sign of life coming from under the hood. Spring came. The leaves of the bulbs he'd planted pushed up through the mulch like verdant spears, and he cut his hair and kept it short, so tight to his skull that she could see the shape of his head. An umbrella took up permanent residence on the front porch, evidently never quite dry enough to close. Then summer, when the heat was a battering ram against the house. His image wavered before her like a mirage, yet she could still make out the contours of his bare upper body, his arms tan and muscular, something inked on his right arm just below the shoulder. A heart? The name of the mother who had schooled him in the suitability of lazy daisy cake? She was too far away to tell.

With autumn came the reckoning. She'd turned lax in her observations, inventing a life for him gleaned from stolen moments of surveillance, and from the sound of his car leaving some evenings, most often Fridays and Saturdays, which she interpreted to mean he had a social life. There would be a girlfriend, of course—Alice pieced her wardrobe together from fashion magazines Natalie left lying around— someone freckled and petite who favored halter tops and platform shoes and lip gloss bearing the scent of ripe fruit. Or perhaps she'd be older, with a hard edge, lacquered hair, and a regular stool at a bar on the edge of town.

In late October, the air through the screen door smelled of dried grass and earth forked over. Phinneaus was raking leaves into a ragged pile in his front yard when he suddenly stopped moving and looked directly to where she stood watching him from the side of the living room window. She froze, but it was for nothing. She'd been discovered. Even after she let the edge of the curtain drop back into place and was safely hidden again, she turned red with shame. Her interest would be rightly translated as loneliness, evidenced by her pitiful behavior.

She didn't need to wonder for long whether he would let it pass. The doorbell rang the following afternoon, and before she could plead with Saisee not to answer, he was standing in front of her in the living room, and she was, as she'd been the first time she'd seen him, sitting in her chair in the corner of the room, a blanket hastily thrown over her lap.

'Do you suspect me of something, Miss Alice?'

'I . . . no. Of course not.'

'Because I must say, I hadn't pegged you for much of a sleuth.'

There was kindness in the word he chose. 'That's a generous way of putting it, Mr. Lapine. I'm not sure I'm deserving of such generosity.'

'Phinneaus.'

'Phinneaus. I owe you an apology. I'm ashamed of myself.'

'You should be. There must be better ways for you to spend your time.' He looked at her straight on, his eyes sharp and appraising, as if he'd already decided something about her. 'Perhaps we should just admit to having a mutual curiosity about each other.'

'You were curious about me?'

He nodded. 'Most people here are. Do you find that unexpected?'

She'd been determined to take what she had coming, but her hackles rose at his tone. 'I suppose you wanted to see if the rumors were true.'

'That I did.'

Her chin tilted up as she said, 'I'm sure they are. Every one of them.'

'Well, not every one. I can see for myself you're not cross-eyed. You don't appear to be the result of a mixed marriage. And you haven't said much yet, but I don't believe you suffer from Tourette's. Although you could still surprise me there.'

She couldn't help herself. The absurdity of it burst forth from her in a laugh just short of a cackle. 'That's what they're saying about me?' She pushed the blanket off and let it puddle on the floor around her ankles, resting her hands in her lap, where they would be visible to him.

'I see,' he said, more softly, something other than pity in his voice. 'Arthritis?'

'Yes. I can't offer anything more exotic. That's the full extent of it, I'm afraid.'

He motioned to the chair on the other side of the table. 'May I?'

She nodded. He sat down and methodically rolled up the right leg of his pants. His calf was pale as a fish, but muscular in that same way. He winced as he got closer to the knee, and Alice steadied her mouth as the last turn of fabric revealed a jagged wound like uneven joinery—two thick-edged pieces of skin that didn't quite meet, but shared a crater of dull red and purple scar tissue with a flat sheen. The scar continued, snaking above his knee and out of view.

'Vietnam.' She stated it as fact.

'Shrapnel. I was lucky compared to most. On the ground for four hours before the medics came, and the infection was pretty bad, but they still managed to save my leg.' He viewed his limb impersonally, thumping a spot just below his knee like he was knocking on a door. 'Not much feeling in it with the nerve damage and all. But the doc told me he'd kept his part of the bargain. 'I kept it attached to you, Lapine. How well it works is up to a higher power.' I told him I wasn't particularly religious. He said it might be a good time to reconsider.'

'Did you?'

Phinneaus rolled his pant leg back down. 'In a way. I decided God wasn't going to be willing to save me unless I was willing to save myself first.'

She sat perfectly still, studying her hands in her lap. 'And how does one do that?'

'One day at a time.' He nodded when Saisee came into the room and asked if he wanted some tea, then settled back in the chair and waited until she left again before continuing. 'Maybe you could do me a favor.'

Her interest was piqued. What sort of favor could she possibly do for him? It had been more than a year since he'd met Natalie in this same room, so the usual request she received from men—*introduce me to your sister*—could be eliminated. 'We still haven't returned your cake plate. I guess I owe you something. But only if you call me Alice.'

'All right. Alice. Orion's the same as any small town. Gossip is currency. Seeing as how we're neighbors, and we've expressed a mutual curiosity in each other, I was thinking you might tell me something about yourself.' He raised an eyebrow and gazed at her intently.

If he expected her to shrink from the challenge, he'd be disappointed. 'So is this payback?' she asked. 'Or are you just saying you'd prefer to get the news straight from the horse's mouth? Fair enough. What don't you know, aside from the fact I'm not cross-eyed?'

'I can think of a few things. What's your middle name, for example?'

That made her smile. A ridiculous question, but at least unexpected.

'Katherine.'

'Alice Katherine Kessler. Were you named after your mother?'

'My grandmother. Katherine was my mother's middle name.'

'Hmm. Well, that might get me a beer at Smitty's, but not much else. Do you have a favorite tree? A secret crush? A flower you're partial to?'

A flare of suspicion made her sit up straighter in her chair. What he'd asked was perfectly innocent. But it was like the child's game of Pelmanism, turning over cards one at a time to find the match. The answer to one question revealed nothing at all. But pair it with the answer to another, and she'd provided him a clue. That was something she had no interest in doing. Let people think what they liked. She wasn't about to offer up her past as after-dinner conversation.

'The flowers in the yard are pretty enough. I don't have a favorite.'

'Maybe you would, if you got out more.'

'Now who's doing the spying?'

'I wouldn't rate our offenses as being quite the same. We're neighbors, after all. I live across the street. You've been here for more than a year and yet I never see you in town. Your sister, yes. But not you.'

Of course he would have seen Natalie. Natalie had taken whatever steps were necessary to ingratiate herself with the people of Orion, aside from inviting them across the threshold. Alice had even noticed her sister watching Phinneaus on occasion, though there was nothing covert about her observations and nothing concealed in her smile when she looked at him. It made Alice want to warn him.

'Unless you've nothing better to do than stare at this house all day, I don't know how you can be so sure of my comings and goings. Or lack thereof. Did you stop to think I might go out while you're at work?'

'No, ma'am. I did not. Of course I work out of my home, which,' he said pointedly, 'I imagine you know. Maybe you even have it written down in a notebook somewhere—*my* comings and goings. But I acknowledge it could be a possibility.'

'And what is it you do, Phinneaus, when you're not concerning yourself with my presumed lack of egress?'

'Your *lack of egress*?' He grinned, and she knew he'd seen through her feeble attempt to change the subject. 'I believe we were speaking of you, Alice, but I'm glad to tell you anything you want to know. Although I warn you in advance, my story won't even get you a beer. I fix things for people. Help with their taxes, come April. Jack of a few trades, master of one.'

'What would that be?'

'It will sound like a boast, but it's just the truth. I guess God gave me a gift for understanding how things work, how they're put together. Give me something broken and I'll figure out what makes it run. It doesn't matter what the parts are: gears or wires, circuits or levers or an engine. I'm happiest when I have something in front of me to puzzle out.'

His honesty disarmed her. She could tell it was true by the way his eyes flashed and his fingers twitched when he talked about making things work. His body tightened with a kind of intensity she recognized. He knew how to be still and focus on one thing.

'You and I have some things in common. You might not believe it from my inexcusably forward behavior, but I'm a private sort of person myself. I settled here after the Army. Most folks in town have been here all their lives, and their parents and grandparents before them. This isn't the sort of place people come to; it's the sort of place people grow out of. That's what makes you and me curiosities. People want to know why we came.'

She had to admit, there were things about him she wanted to know: why had he come here; where had he lived before; did he have family? He wasn't much older than she was, and the wound to his leg would have brought him some measure of scrutiny, the sort of wary observation she was used to. They had those things in common. Plus they were both here, in this place. In spite of her reservations, she wondered what it would be like to have a friend. Someone to confide in. Though she and Natalie barely conversed, her sister's absence during the day only added to the emptiness of the house. And as much as she was growing to like Saisee, the woman was wise enough to know who paid the bills, and was scrupulous in getting her work done, leaving her little time to talk. Alice had started to wonder if loneliness would be her undoing, despite the raft of other possibilities.

'That's an interesting theory,' she said. 'But you're right, I doubt it's worth much on the market. What about a deep, dark secret?'

'I showed you my scar.'

'We sound like children.' She laughed, the sound of happiness alien to her own hearing. He joined in. 'But a scar,' she said. 'I've got plenty of my own. That's not enough.'

'What do you want to know?'

'You have a tattoo.'

She watched his mouth tighten as though he'd suddenly tasted lemon.

'That's none of your business.'

The sudden reprimand caught her off guard. She wished she could take it back, ask him something else instead. His laughter had opened something inside her, and she realized how badly she wanted to talk to someone, even if the only thing they discussed was the weather. 'Maybe I do have something to show you. Will you wait here for a minute?'

His expression didn't change, but he nodded. 'If you want.'

She got up from the chair and started the trek to her bedroom, the act of trusting as foreign to her as running. When she came back into the living room, she stood in front of him. 'Hold out your hands. Palms up.'

'And close my eyes? I know the drill.'

She watched the blue of it disappear into the well of his hands and took a step back. It was too late to change her mind now. He couldn't know what it meant to her, but he handled it as though he did, cradling it like something with a beating heart, a piece of sky captured inside his tightly pressed fingers.

'This is a grosbeak.'

'Yes.' She was delighted. 'You're familiar with them?'

'I am, ma'am.'

Iyammam.

'I haven't seen any here,' she said.

'No, and you won't. They stick closer to the woods on the outskirts of town. Lots of cowbirds and warblers, too.' He examined the bird carefully. 'I've never gotten close enough to one to notice the way the wing feathers are stacked. And these little tips of gray on the chest. Have you seen many of them?'

'No.' She turned her head to the window. 'Only this.' A stain of memory spilled into her: a locked bedroom door, the sound of knocking.

'But you know your birds?'

'Yes. I know them all.'

He rubbed one hand across his chin. 'Maybe there's something you could help me with. There's a scout troop in town, pretty much a ragtag operation, but I'm trying to help the boys get some of their badges. Camping, fishing, rifle shooting. There's a badge for bird study.'

'Oh, no. I'd rather not . . .'

'Just hear me out, Alice. I suppose it seems like a small thing, but it means a lot to them to earn a badge. It won't be easy for some. They have to be able to label fifteen different parts of a bird. They have to identify twenty species, and keep a field notebook. And of those twenty, they have to identify five by their song or call alone. You did say you knew your birds.'

So much she'd learned only to store it all away. What good did the knowledge do, cloistered in a dark corner of her brain? Facts swooped like swallows, darting across her mind; there was a rush of pride in things still remembered. Singing was limited to the perching birds, the order Passeriformes. Nearly half the birds in the world didn't sing, but they still used sound to communicate—calls as opposed to song. Most birds had between five and fifteen distinct calls in their repertoire: alarm and territorial defense calls, distress calls from juveniles to bring an adult to the rescue, flight calls to keep the flock coordinated, even separate calls for commencing and ending flight. Nest calls. Feeding calls. Pleasure calls. Some chicks used calls to communicate with their mothers while they were still in the egg. The thought of it made her heart hurt.

'I won't push you. Give it some thought. It would mean a lot to the boys' families.'

So he was giving her a lever of her own. Help the children and the parents will have to accept you. He passed the figurine back, still warm from being in his hands.

'Whoever made that took a lot of care, you can tell. Something handed down to you?'

'No.' Anticipating a certain pleasure in shocking him, she said, 'I stole it. And to think you want me to teach Boy Scouts.'

'Well, there is a badge for crime prevention.' He looked at her intently, but she kept her face still. Despite his potential as a friend, she'd shown him enough of herself for the time being.

'Alice Katherine Kessler,' he said, shaking his head. 'It's too bad I can't tell anybody. Information like that would definitely be worth something.'

NINE
NOVEMBER 2007

'Is this a pity invitation?' The idea that Lydia might consider him someone requiring sympathy was deflating, but her response to his question was a bright laugh, a burst of joy pushing through Stephen's phone line, and exploding in his dim living room like a flare. At least he could make her laugh. That was no small accomplishment. And at this hour of the morning, too. Nine o'clock and her voice was as limber as though she'd been up for hours. She was probably a whistler. Perpetually cheerful.

'No, Stephen. This is not a pity invitation. You and my father have been working such long hours on your project, whatever it is, I thought it might be nice for the two of you to do something more social, especially with the holiday coming. Say this Saturday? At seven?'

'Your husband will be there?' What was the man's name? He recalled an effusive handshake and overly warm palms. Warm, that was it. Something about temperature or the Protestant Reformation. Which was it? Hmmm, definitely temperature. Fahrenheit. Celsius. Rankine. Kelvin. That was it—Kelvin, with a null point of absolute zero. An appropriate description. Zero. Why were women drawn to men with such white teeth?

'Since I'm inviting you to dinner at our home, yes. Kevin will be there.'

'Oh.'

He counted the seconds of the pause that followed, getting to the far edge of four before she asked whether 'oh' meant he would join them.

'Yes. It means yes I will. I don't eat spinach, though. In case you were considering it.'

'I'll keep that in mind. You know, I can see why you and my father get along, Stephen. You have a great deal in common.'

Did they? He contemplated the possibility after hanging up the phone. He liked Finch, and he supposed Finch deserved some of the credit for Lydia, whom he had become infatuated with the first time he met her at Finch's flat, so they did have that in common. She'd come bearing food, a warm and spicy curry, telling Finch she'd read turmeric helped reduce inflammation and treat digestive problems. Finch had rolled his eyes, but Stephen was smitten, the impediment of a husband notwithstanding. He contented himself with worshiping her from afar, at least until she came to her senses and lost her less-than-significant other.

As to their *project* as she'd referred to it, he wondered why Finch hadn't told her what they were working on. Of course he'd changed the subject himself when his mother had asked the same question over Thanksgiving dinner the week prior. *And what are you working on these days, Stephen?* He'd started to tell her, but then stopped, recognizing that, whatever it was he and Finch were up to, there was an element of the clandestine about it he quite enjoyed. If he told her he'd met

Thomas Bayber, she would either clamor to know the details, in which case he would become exasperated with her frequent interjections, or she would be completely uninterested, in which case he would be insulted. In addition to which, any discussion of painting would make them both think of his father, and the holiday meals they shared were awkward enough without him sitting at one end of the table watching his mother's concerted efforts not to cry.

Saturday, the first of December, was five days away, which meant there was a good deal of time needing to be occupied before seeing Lydia. A hostess gift would be important. Soaps, maybe. Women liked little soaps; they seemed to act as some measure of a woman's achievement in the art of gracious entertaining. There was an assortment of intricately wrapped and beribboned soaps in a bell-shaped jar in the guest bath whenever he visited his mother. He wondered what became of them after a single use—were they discarded? Rewrapped? It seemed wasteful to him, but of greater concern was the thought that such a gift would give Lydia the impression he found her to be either less than hygienic or deficient in entertaining skills. Maybe a bottle of perfume? But there was *the Kelvin* to contend with, and Stephen imagined a gift of scent wouldn't be looked on favorably.

Stephen had agreed, albeit reluctantly, with Finch's suggestion they divide in hopes of conquering, or at least in hopes of unearthing something that would prove useful. Finch committed to spend the week reviewing the file of personal correspondence Mrs. Blankenship had collected for him, admitting to Stephen that his initial evaluation of such things had likely verged on perfunctory. Stephen was to focus his attention on the main panel of the triptych. They planned to meet on Sunday to share their respective findings.

In an attempt to put a date to the painting, Stephen spent the first part of the week poring over details of Bayber's previous works, committing them to memory, looking for aberrations, noting anything that seemed unusual or out of character: a difference in the way Bayber used negative space, places where his brushwork seemed crabbed and intentional, the introduction of a new color into his usual palette. By Thursday morning, he was itching to leave the confines of the library and get back to the lab.

Realizing the potential windfall for Murchison & Dunne, to say nothing of the prestige that would accompany bringing a Bayber to market, Cranston had coughed up a princely sum to allow Stephen access to a private, state-of-the-art forensic lab with the sort of equipment that made his pulse race every time he passed his security badge in front of the sensor pad: hyperspectral imagers to analyze historic documents; multi-spectral digital imaging cameras to inspect works of art; a gas chromatography machine to identify oils, resins, and waxes; even a new X-ray machine with lovely, long grenz rays.

Stephen showed his identification again at the second security checkpoint and paused for an iris scan, required to access the room where the painting was kept. It was mildly unsettling that an image of his own personal iris was being housed somewhere for all eternity, but the beauty inherent in the science of biometric authentication thrilled him.

He laid his notebook on the lab table in an empty study room and ran through the list of tests needing to be done. Cranston had been definite about the importance of estab-lishing documentation for the piece that would stand up to extreme scrutiny, so Stephen started at the beginning, with the signature.

The lab had a comprehensive collection of signature and monogram dictionaries. Stephen had photographed Bayber's signature on the triptych panel earlier in the week and now removed the photo from a manila envelope, examining it with a magnifying glass and comparing it to earlier records of the artist's signature. He projected scans of the signatures from the painting and from the dictionary onto the wall at an expanded scale, and inspected them side by side. At that size, the dips and curves of letters became roads cutting through a muted landscape. By studying an artist's signature over time, he could detect changes to the central nervous system and diagnose conditions such as Parkinson's, obsessive-compulsive disorder, schizophrenia. He could even make a reasonable judgment in regard to long-term substance abuse. But Bayber's last documented work had been painted when he was still relatively young, age fifty-two, and his signature gave no indication of any serious degradation of his physical or mental condition.

Stephen took exhaustive notes, thankful no one was interested in examining *his* handwriting. He went into another room to make arrangements for the X-ray tests with one of the technicians, who possessed the skills required to run the equipment but seemed to lack interest in the specifics of what he was scanning. Stephen and Cranston were concerned any leak regarding the existence of the painting would be disastrous. While Bayber had signed papers giving Murchison & Dunne the right to sell the work, the agreement was contingent on Stephen and Finch finding and retrieving the other two panels. In Stephen's experience, agreements were ephemeral things, be they between business partners or lovers; a cadre of expensive lawyers could muddy any waters quickly enough, and if word spread that there were two Baybers floating around, Stephen didn't have nearly so much confidence that he and Finch would be the ones to find them, minus divine intervention.

Which seemed to come a few hours later. After poring over the other test results and taking several more pages of notes, Stephen was summoned by the technician to review the X-ray results. 'I think you're going to want to see this' was what he said.

Stephen looked at the images on the monitor. His heart fluttered in his chest. 'This can't be right.'

'It's right,' the man said.

'Maybe there's something on the lens.'

'On both sides of the painting? I don't think so. Look, you're good at what you do. I'm good at what I do. It's there, I'm telling you.'

'Shoot it again, with more kilovoltage. I want to bring up both of these areas.' Stephen pointed to the right and left sides of the screen. 'And with a shorter exposure time. We need to go deeper here, and we need to get more detail on the left side.'

'We.' The technician snorted under his breath.

Finch had assumed the role of Bayber's gatekeeper, and Stephen was sure he wouldn't approve of any unannounced visits, which seemed an excellent reason not to tell him. After all, it was a Thursday afternoon, he hadn't called ahead, and there was no guarantee Mrs. Blankenship would let him past the front door. Bayber's unexpected trip to the hospital the morning after he'd first shown them the painting had resulted in a week's worth of tests and second opinions from a variety of specialists, but since Cranston's expectations had been elevated, Bayber's lack of finances, as well as the absence of any sort of medical insurance, were rendered immaterial. Once the doctors agreed whatever recuperating there was to be done could be managed at home as well as in the hospital, Cranston had spared no expense, bringing in a hospital bed, a wheelchair, and a private nurse to help Mrs. Blankenship, as well as a host of laborers to address the leaks and overall draftiness of Bayber's flat. The first and last of those generosities were the only ones that made sense to Stephen, since Bayber had yet to speak, let alone move from his bed, and Mrs. Blankenship seemed peeved by an additional female presence.

She buzzed him up without asking what he wanted and answered the door after the first knock.

'The two of them are driving me to the brink,' she said and pointed a finger toward the bedroom. 'Him looking at me like I'm supposed to be a mind reader and that other one . . .' She paused and bit down on her lower lip. 'She may be a nurse, but I don't think that gives her the right to try to reorganize the linen cupboard.'

'It does seem presumptuous,' Stephen said.

'Yes, that's the word for it.' Mrs. Blankenship sighed, clearly disappointed that her efforts in the arranging of linens might be considered subpar. 'You might as well go in. I'm sure he'll be glad to see someone's face other than mine, although you won't be having much of a conversation with either of them.'

Stephen nodded and made his way down a dark hall that led to the bedrooms, astonished by the lack of natural light in the apartment of a painter. The heavy curtains in the main room still hung closed, and most of the lights were off. Not that Bayber necessarily did any painting here, but how could the man see anything?

It was a surprise then to enter the airy master bedroom and find himself blinking against the afternoon sun. One of the large windows was cracked open, and the curtains in this room had been pulled back all the way. There was a woman sitting in a small chair in the corner, reading a gossip magazine. Her clothes gave her away as the nurse, even if Mrs. Blankenship hadn't already made it obvious: a dull maroon top with a pattern that looked as if it had been chosen to hide patient mishaps—the regurgitated remains of partially chewed pills, drools of cherry-colored medications, spills of pudding—paired with white polyester pants and the ubiquitous white shoes. The arrangement of her fingers suggested the keenly felt absence of a longed-for cigarette.

Bayber, paler now than when Stephen had seen him in the hospital, was propped up in bed on an enormous pile of pillows; he looked like something skeletal, half-emerged from a cocoon. The nurse watched as he pulled a folding chair next to the bed but said nothing to him. He took Bayber's hand, but the man's eyes remained closed.

'Mr. Bayber, it's Stephen Jameson. I've come to ask you a question.'

Bayber's eyes jerked open, and he moved imperceptibly toward Stephen, his lips parting to show an even row of teeth, a blue cast to their faint translucence. Stephen watched Bayber swallow and heard the gentle hiss of breath being drawn in. But the only sounds that escaped from the man were formless clicks of trapped air, coming from deep in his throat. He did not blink. Stephen shifted uncomfortably in his chair, a familiar sensation rising in his stomach. Guilt. This was what he had missed with his father, all these last unpleasant bits: the diminishment, the infirmity, the slow fading; he had left all that to his mother. And though he doubted he would have been much consolation to either of them, he was still astonished she did not despise him for his absence.

This reduced version of Bayber had not the strength to lift a finger to his mouth or instruct the nurse to banish him.

It hardly seemed possible such a short time ago Stephen had stood next to this man and looked him square in the eye, desperately trying to control his stuttering tongue, his shaking hands, while making impertinent suggestions. But now he knew things, at any rate suspected them, and wanted to voice his suspicions aloud. And there was nothing Bayber could do to stop him.

'Mr. Cranston has allowed me a great deal of latitude in researching the painting in order to authenticate the work. A number of forensic examinations and scientific tests needed to be done to provide the eventual buyer with the necessary documentation and to establish an irrefutable case.'

He paused, unsure how best to continue, hoping for a response of some sort. His palms turned damp, and he wondered if Bayber was perhaps becoming impatient or disgusted, but since the artist was unable to convey either, it was impossible to tell. Stephen sat back in his chair and looked over his shoulder at the nurse, who appeared engrossed in her reading material.

'I began with the signature. As you can imagine, it was a match. But forensic analysis goes beyond simply detecting patterns, Mr. Bayber. It is more than comparing the smoothness of strokes connecting letters, noting where the artist picked up the brush, or when he put it down.'

Stephen felt the same sense of excitement he had in the lab, dwarfed by its high white walls, examining the giant brushstrokes illuminated on the sterile surface. As he spoke he felt himself slipping out of the room, away from the light streaming in through the window, away from the cool, papery skin of Bayber's hand, away from the sound of magazine pages being turned with the sticky pad of a thumb. He heard the quiet of the lab pulsing around him and stood in front of Bayber's enormous signature, studying the curving map of letters that crisscrossed the wall like intersecting paths of a maze.

'I can detect certain qualities in a signature, you see. Pride, boredom, humility. Arrogance. I can differentiate between signatures painted quickly, and those put to canvas with a painstaking exactitude, as if the artist hesitated to leave the work behind.' Did he imagine it, or were Bayber's eyes narrowing? The man's hand in his remained perfectly still, but Stephen thought he felt a surge of pulse.

'There's no question the signature on the triptych panel is yours. The degree of pressure applied, the point the brush was lifted from the canvas, the descender on the *y*—all virtually identical to signatures of record. But one thing wasn't the same. There was a good deal more paint on the brush, leading me to believe you signed this work slowly, maybe even lingered over it. You were reluctant to be done.'

He dropped Bayber's hand and stood up to stretch, walking to the end of the bed. Bayber's eyes followed him, the raspy breaths growing quicker.

'The first time I saw the panel, I noticed substantial over-painting in two areas. It's possible you were reusing an old canvas. That wouldn't be unusual. But it did pique my curiosity, so I conducted some tests: UV, visible, infrared images of the painting. Helpful, though not enough to provide us with the whole picture, if you'll forgive the pun. But X-ray, that's another story. The lab has a computed radiography system so scans can be displayed on a high-resolution monitor. You shoot onto reusable phosphor imaging plates. There's no more need for film, which was informative but tedious in terms of process.'

At the word *tedious* Bayber's eyes closed and Stephen stopped talking. How was it no one else seemed to appreciate the beauty and genius inherent in such equipment? The mere mention of the word *thermoluminescence* had the same effect as a sleeping pill on most anyone, but for Stephen, science was magic and majesty. It was science that allowed authenticators to peek beneath the surface of a painting to see its skeletal beginnings as a sketch, science that revealed the age of paintings on oak panels by counting the growth rings of trees back to 5000 B.C., science that determined whether the blue cloak of the Virgin in an illuminated manuscript was painted with ultramarine from precious lapis lazuli or colored by the more affordable azurite.

'Your fatigue is noted, Mr. Bayber. To the point, then. This is what an X-ray tells me. It tells me if there are small tears in the canvas that have been repaired. It tells me if there are holes in the support panel or losses in the ground layers. It lets me see cut-down edges and transfers. But perhaps most important, it tells me what was there before. It tells me what you painted over. Alice's hand wasn't resting on the birdcage in your initial painting, was it?'

Now he had Bayber's attention. The artist's breathing quickened and his mouth moved, the dry lips struggling to form some word. His face had gone from bone white to livid, and his hand twitched at his side.

'Her arm was stretched out toward the edge of the canvas, at least to what is now the edge of the canvas, and she was holding someone else's hand. The other person's fingers are clearly visible in the previous layer. That was interesting. Who was she linked to? Then I noticed something else. In the painting, Alice is wearing a ring on her left index finger— a thin band with a heart in the center. Much of her hand is covered by yours, but that detail is clearly visible. I took a few more scans, decreasing the exposure time to get the clearest possible image. The musculature and the size of the fingers indicate the hand of the person in the underlying composition is that of a woman. Oddly enough, this woman is wearing a similar ring—a thin band with a heart in the center. But she's wearing it on the little finger, not the index finger. Her joints appear slightly swollen; the angles of the fingers off by a few degrees, as though her hand was somehow disfigured. I enlarged those two sections, the hand of the woman in the hidden painting and Alice's hand in the surface painting, and compared them side to side. The shapes of the nails, the comparative lengths of the fingers in relation to each other, the closeness of the bones to the skin. Allowing for some minor changes attributable to age or perhaps illness, the hands are virtually the same.'

Stephen went back to the chair beside the bed and sat down again, taking a glass of water with a straw from the bedside table and steering it toward Bayber's mouth. He watched as Bayber strained to drink; then, apparently exhausted, the man's head fell back into the deep nest of pillows.

'You've been praised for your rendering of minute details.' Stephen paused, thinking about the first time he'd seen one of Bayber's paintings. 'It's like looking at a puzzle, isn't it? The longer and closer you look, the more you see. And once something is seen, it cannot be unseen. The viewer is never able to take in the piece as he did the first time; the initial impression is gone and can't be recalled.'

The room was quiet. When Stephen listened for the sound he was not hearing, he realized the absence was of pages being turned. The nurse was listening. He leaned in closer to Bayber and whispered the rest of it in his ear.

'The details told me everything. You gave Alice a sliver of a scar on her index finger, barely visible. It's like a single strand of spiderweb running from the bottom of her nail to the top of the first knuckle joint. It took me a while to notice

it, but now I know that it's there, it's all I see, the first thing
my eye goes to when I look at the painting, as if it might
have vanished, or I'm afraid I might have imagined it.'
Stephen was sweating. When had the room become so
warm? There was a drop running down between the furrow
in his brows, and he felt his shirt pasted to his back. He held
his breath, willing Bayber to find his voice, to tell him what
it was he really wanted from them.

'That same scar is on the hand Alice is holding in the
hidden painting. Which means it's Alice, or some older
version of Alice, in the missing left panel, isn't it? I haven't
had as much time to analyze the other half of the painting,
but since that side has been overpainted as well, it stands
to reason some older version of Natalie is in the missing
right panel.'

It was saying the word *missing* out loud that started a
chain reaction in his brain. The answer to it all, the thought
he needed to catch, skipped and sprinted ahead of him at
such a clip he had to grit his teeth in order to focus and
keep up, igniting a dull throbbing in his jaw. A few false
turns, a detour around flickering synapses, but then the
thought was there, trapped in a dark dead end. When he
grasped it, everything became illuminated, obvious—exactly
what it was Bayber was looking for. The light in the room
lanced at his eyes, and Stephen felt the full force of a migraine
charging toward him like a rolling ball of furnace air and
lightning. He squeezed his eyes shut against it, but it was
too late.

'You don't care so much about the other panels of the
painting,' he whispered to Bayber, clutching the sides of his
own head to keep his brains from spilling out. 'It's the sisters,
isn't it? You want us to find Alice and Natalie. You've wanted
us to find them all along.'

Stephen scarcely remembered the ride back to his apartment, unsure of how he'd ever managed to hail a cab. He drew the blinds shut and fell onto the bed, shivering and nauseous. His upper arm ached, and he touched it gingerly just below the shoulder, anticipating the bruise that would bloom—first inky, then pea green, then an alarming jaundiced sulfur— where Bayber's nurse had grabbed him and tossed him out of the bedroom. The woman had transformed into a monster the minute her charge was provoked, possessing the enthusiasm and strength of a professional wrestler.

Stephen rubbed his wrist, trying to erase the feel of Bayber's grip. Bayber had erupted at the mention of the girls' names. Whatever remained of his vigor was channeled into his fingers, which wrapped around Stephen's wrist with a stubborn tenacity, firmly locking onto him. Spittle flew from the edge of his mouth as he hissed the same sound over and over—*sssssuh, sssssuh*—and pawed at the open air between them with his other hand. Stephen, terrified that he'd pushed Bayber past the brink, thought he might be having a second stroke. But if anything, Bayber grew stronger not weaker, and his eyes fixed on Stephen with a single purpose as he struggled to express himself, whether to confirm or to deny what had been suggested, Stephen did not know.

He rolled onto his stomach and pulled the pillow over his head. In the dark, women floated past: Chloe, Alice, Natalie, and Lydia, all interested in ministering to his aching head, their delicate hands fluttering about his face, caressing his cheek, smoothing his hair. They came together in the person of Mrs. Blankenship, not quite as interested in his well-being, grimacing and shaking her head in disappointment. Mrs. Blankenship in turn became the nurse, who gave him a shove so severe he hit his head and saw stars blinkering about until he realized he'd fallen onto his bedroom floor, the pulsing flickers no more than the neon wink of the bar sign across the street. He pulled the blanket down from the bed and tossed it over the half of his body he could easily reach, staying there for the night, one ear pressed against the cold wood floor.

Around midmorning the next day, when he could finally open his eyes without squinting, he pulled himself back onto the mattress. His head was a soupy mess of leftover aches and twinges, punctuated by the occasional sharp stab behind his left eye. He propped himself up on a pile of pillows recognizing the irony, he was Bayber's doppelgänger in such a position, and sat frozen, breathing as shallowly as he could in deference to the still-lurking migraine. After a period of perfect stillness, the static in his brain gave way to a more tolerable white noise. His thoughts slowly flocked back to him and resettled, nesting out of order.

Without turning his head, he reached over and pulled a pencil and sketch pad from the top drawer of the bedside table. There was something soothing in the rhythmic place-ment of graphite lines, and before he knew it he had sketched a cartoonish version of the painting that haunted him, the Kessler sisters sitting on the sofa with a wolfish Bayber insinuated between them. He flipped to a new page and this time drew only the hands and forearms he had seen in the hidden layer of the painting, those belonging to Alice and to the woman he imagined was the other Alice, the older Alice, their digits companionably intertwined. Then he did the same for Natalie.

From the angles of their forearms, it was easy enough to imagine how the older Alice and Natalie might be positioned in their respective panels. He was sure enough of their pres-ence, certain he'd gotten that much right, but it was the only part he could envision: a vertical slice of an Alice and another of a Natalie, the visible musculature in their arms suggesting they were pulling their younger selves toward the future. But he had no idea if Bayber had overpainted sections of the missing panels as well, and if he had, why? Had the triptych, when finished, disappointed him? Stephen thought of the man lying in bed, the stunning ferocity of his grip. Disappointment in the work seemed an unlikely reason.

Stephen sat up, looking at the walls of his bedroom, covered with reproductions of Bayber's cataloged works and with the photographs he'd taken of the painting, close-ups and distance shots. Looking at all of it in such close proximity, he could easily see that nothing else Bayber had done was as captivating as *Kessler Sisters*. When he lay back on the bed again, myriad figures swam around him, but he had eyes only for the girls on the sofa and for Bayber, the trio surrounding him from all angles until he was inside the painting with them, the breeze that rifled the curtains pricked his flesh, the toasted green of summer at its zenith filled his nose. What of it was real?

He got out of bed and picked up the backpack he'd tossed in the corner, looking for his camera. He reviewed the shots he'd taken of the sketch at the Edells', pleased to see he'd remembered most of the details correctly. The color pencil sketch was easily placed at the beginning of Bayber's career and was consistent with the date, 1963, before his style had completely developed. There they were, the uncomfortable Kesslers sitting on that same sofa, the husband and wife in the center, Alice with her wild mane of blond hair, next to her father on the left; Natalie on the right, her eyes cast down. The background was rough, but Stephen recognized things he and Finch had seen at the cabin: the grandfather clock, the stacks of atlases, the rugs.

Then there was the cage. Three appearances: in the Doughty study, in the oil, and in all of its decrepit physical glory, sitting on the bedside table at the cabin. Stephen looked at the photos pasted on the walls in front of him, on the ceiling above him. Only in the panel of the triptych was the door to the cage slightly ajar, as if something precious had flown away.

He stumbled into the kitchen and made a bowl of instant oatmeal, drowning the dusty particles of oats with milk on the edge of turning before spooning the watery porridge into his mouth with a ladle, the only clean utensil he could find. What was he overlooking? He turned to a clean page in the sketch pad and scribbled notes in his usual shorthand. Where had the Kessler sisters gone, and why had they left in such a hurry? After thirty-five years, why had the house never been sold? And the bird. Although Finch had convinced him this last was of little consequence as far as finding the paintings, Stephen's instincts hummed the moment he'd seen the empty cage. *Everything means something to someone*, his father had often told him, hoping to entice Stephen to discover what an artist was trying to convey. So, the bird. He outlined the letters heavily in ink.

His unappealing breakfast dispensed with, he set the bowl and ladle in the sink to join the week's worth of dishes gathered there and went back to the bedroom to retrieve his laptop. He sat down at the kitchen table and swept his arm across the face of it, sending every bit of paper and crumb to the floor.

He focused on a speck on the opposite wall, determined to approach the problem from a different angle. It all revolved around the girls. Everything went back to them. He pulled up the searches he'd saved shortly after Cranston tasked them with finding the paintings. He'd checked the Social

Security Death Index several weeks ago, and found neither of their names, which meant he wasn't tracking a pair of ghosts. And the living left trails, dropped little bread crumbs of data unintentionally. He just needed to find the trailhead.

His search on Natalie Kessler had turned up little more than the most basic information. Graduated from Walker Academy, an all-girls prep school, in 1965, then from a small local liberal arts college four years later. There was no need to search the names in small print at the base of her class photo. Among the staggered rows of square-shouldered, serious-looking young women, her face stood out: a penetrating gaze, a frozen prettiness.

He added the black-and-white photo to the other images of her he carried in his head and realized he was becoming accustomed to her beauty, her unapproachability keeping him safely at arm's length everywhere but in his dreams. That was where Natalie and Chloe became interchangeable. It would be Chloe he was in bed with; Chloe's long, pale body stretched out next to his, the bends and folds of her as sinuous as a river cutting its course through soft earth. But at some point her skin turned to gold; her hair lightened to wheat and grew longer, curling up at the ends; her fingers dug sharply into his shoulder, fusing herself to him. And realizing suddenly she was the wrong one, he'd be ashamed of what he'd done to her, this woman he'd never met; the way he'd pressed her down, laced her hair through his fist. He would wake in a sweat, willing the women out of his head, out of his limbs, the lingering scent of them away from his nose, their taste from his mouth.

He accessed Murchison & Dunne's Intelius account, then dug around more deeply on the Web. Nothing for either of them after 1972. But searching for images proved more fruitful, if only by one. What popped up on his screen was an old newspaper photo of a group of young people clustered together, raising glasses in the air. The caption read, 'New Fairfield County College Grads Celebrate the Fourth' and the photo was dated July 5, 1969. There was Natalie, front and center, hands folded in her lap while everyone surrounding her was a pixilated blur of black and white. And standing behind her, her shoulders disappearing into his hands, a hulking young man. Stephen zoomed in on the caption to check the names. George Reston, Jr.

George Reston, Jr. had no qualms about leaving a trail. By carefully turning the dial—a different query here, some fortunate logic there—Stephen opened a vault of information, a digital portrait of George Junior almost embarrassing in its comprehensiveness: his father's brief imprisonment for securities fraud, articles in the society pages regarding his parents' donations in support of several arts organizations, property ownership records, including a summer house on Seneca Lake. Stephen checked the address and stunned, leaned forward in his chair, the planks of his arms stretched out on the gritty tabletop. Surely, it couldn't be that simple. The most basic of ties and he'd been blind to it. Friendship. Why had he not considered the house next door to Bayber's? The house rented, every August, by the Kesslers. The house owned by the Restons. That Finch had overlooked the connection as well only disheartened Stephen more. Perhaps this was what Lydia had so easily detected, their commonality: an obtuseness in regard to friendship.

Once he'd found the map, the trail unfolded before him. The Edells mailed their monthly rent checks to Steele and Greene. When he cross-referenced Steele and Greene with George Reston, Stephen found several entries. A brief newspaper article from 1972 detailed Constellation Investments' launch of a newly formed subsidiary, Steele and Greene, a property management company. George Reston, Jr., age twenty-eight, had been named president and CEO.

There was a grainy, black-and-white head shot of George Junior looking annoyed and bored, his chubby, bland face sporting a topper of closely cropped curls. He had the same face as the nameless hundreds Stephen passed on the streets of the Financial District daily; the same starched collars, the healthy sheen of wealth coloring their cheeks, a purposeful stride, out to mind the business of the world. *At least have the humility to smile, you prig,* Stephen thought, a quick tang of envy coating his tongue. But it dissolved when he clicked on a page listing Constellation Investments' management team and found that in 1972, a George Reston, *Senior,* had served on the board of directors, having previously held the position of president of the investment company. Wouldn't Stephen's own father have done the same for him? Hadn't he tried?

There was no website for Steele and Greene, no telephone number. When he looked up the address Winslow Edell had provided, Stephen found it was for a postal service center in Hartford. If Steele and Greene had any physical presence, it was well-hidden. A quick check of a few real estate websites confirmed the Kessler property was zoned only for single-family residential. As far as Stephen had been able to tell, there wasn't much acreage associated with the property; it seemed unlikely the land could be subdivided and sold for development. So why would a property management company bother with the headaches involved in renting out a single-family home in a small Connecticut town, in the middle of nowhere? He went back to the picture of the Fourth of July celebration. George's firm grip on Natalie's shoulders looked as if he was trying to pin her into that chair, into that particular moment. *What one wouldn't do in the name of friendship,* Stephen thought. *Or in the name of love.*

Short of staking out the mail center in Hartford, he'd reached the end of his investigative skills. If the house still belonged to the Kesslers, and he could find no property records to indicate otherwise, then either the rent the Edells were paying was lining George Junior's pockets or he was passing it on to Natalie. By following the money, Stephen might be able to find her. And if he could find her, quite possibly, he could find the other two panels of the triptych.

It was enough for him to have solved the puzzle. Let Finch and the others discern what the work meant. Stephen wanted only for his reputation to be restored, for there to be another painting and then another and another, each waiting for him in unattributed limbo. Wasn't that all he cared about, the discovering and the naming? The satisfaction in being right? He was accustomed to living in a state of agitation when tracking the provenance of a piece. He was not accustomed to being haunted by one, weighed down by the gravity of its story, imagining beginnings and endings for people existing in more than two dimensions.

He shook his head, refocusing on the task at hand. Mining a warren of dead ends and false starts in an effort to follow a trail of money was not his specialty. But after staring at his laptop screen for a few minutes more, he realized there was someone who might help him. Simon Hapsend, the person whose office he had inherited at Murchison & Dunne, could likely find the answers in his sleep.

Stephen had received an e-mail message not long after Simon left the firm, typically cryptic, reading only, 'In case of emergency. Memorize and delete. SH' followed by ten digits. In the two and a half years that followed there had never been occasion to use it, until now. The area code had been easy enough to remember—347—and Stephen had assigned each of the remaining seven digits to one of the letters of Simon's last name. He picked up the phone and dialed. When he heard the beep at the end of the message, a computer-generated recording requesting he leave his name at the tone, he stumbled, blurting out, 'Simon, you said in case of emergency. Well, this is an emergency. I need someone with your particular skills, your talents, shall we say, to help me locate a missing person. I need you to follow a money trail. Probably nothing illegal, although you would know better than I. Contact me as soon as possible, please. Oh, it's Stephen. From Murchison & Dunne.' He left his contact numbers and e-mail address, and hung up the phone. He would see Finch at dinner the next night, and there was no point in calling him until he knew whether or not there was anything of value to share. So he picked up his pencil, made a list of the clothes he owned that might be appropriate for the following evening's dinner, and waited for Simon Hapsend to call him back.

TEN

'What'd she look like, Miss Alice?'

A hundred times, by her count, she'd asked Frankie not
to call her that. Miss Kessler or Alice, either would have
been preferable to the title that sent a quick shiver down
her back, the unattractive hiss of it combined with her name.
It made her feel every one of her fifty-eight years. But
Phinneaus had raised his nephew with southern manners,
and try as she might, she could not dissuade him.

'You're supposed to be studying. And that's an extremely
impolite question to ask. What would your mother say?'

Frankie had the good sense to look mortified, at least
momentarily, although Alice's mortification probably
surpassed his when she realized how thoughtless it was
to bring up the boy's mother. Fortunately, Frankie seemed
more concerned that a report of his ill manners would find its
way back to his uncle. 'You won't tell, will you, Miss Alice?
I never knew a dead person before. I didn't mean nothin'
by it.'

She looked at the boy, his mouth pursed, waiting for some
word from her, and she widened her eyes. 'Miss Natalie

looked the same as she always did.' She paused for effect. 'Only stiffer.'

She felt awful the moment she said it, macabre and unhinged. What was wrong with her? But Frankie whistled. That was just the sort of detail he'd longed for, gruesome enough to satisfy his cohorts and generic enough to allow for embellishment.

'And it's *anything*. Not *nothing*.'

His face crumpled with the effort of sorting out her corrections. He had the vigorous curiosity of an eight-year-old boy; an expression like *one foot in the grave* opened the door to a whole universe of sinister imaginings. Frankie had heard Saisee use the expression some weeks ago about an aunt who was lingering. It was clear the idea had unnerved him by the way he clung to his uncle's side until they'd passed the long block of the cemetery on the walk home from school.

'That's what the fence is for, isn't it, Phinneaus?'

'This fence?' he'd asked, grabbing hold of one of the speared iron posts.

'To keep people's feet out. So they don't get grabbed.'

Phinneaus told all of this to Alice later, the two of them collapsing into laughter. She'd felt a flood of affection for Phinneaus, thankful for the space he'd carved out for her once Frankie had come into his life, taking pains to keep their friendship intact. Frankie wasn't hers, she'd never thought that. There was a mother, Phinneaus's sister, who might someday decide to claim him again. But until then a part of the boy felt tethered to her, and for that she was grateful.

'You realize this means he thinks we're old,' Phinneaus said. 'Maybe not a foot in the grave, but he's worried there's a toe or two there. No wonder he keeps pullin' me to the other side of the street.'

'Are we old?' Time had flown away from her, minutes like birds, gone in a flash of wing. How odd it was, all those years spent feeling old while she'd been young. And now that she couldn't be considered young anymore, not by anyone's standards, she didn't feel old. Instead, she felt like she'd finally caught up with herself and was exactly the age she was supposed to be.

Frankie bent his head over his schoolwork with an audible sigh of discontent. Alice smiled—being a monitor was one of her better skills—and looked around the room. When had the house turned from strange to familiar? Those things that used to annoy her: the slope of the hardwood floor from front to back, the web of cracks etched into an upper window, the musty smell of turnips clinging to the walls, drifting up from a long-abandoned root cellar; those things had inter-laced themselves so firmly into her consciousness, they became hers. Even the house itself was hardier than she'd initially given it credit for. Thirty-five years she had lived here, much of it spent reassuring herself she did not belong. Thirty-five years of living a half-life, like something radioac-tive, encased in concrete and buried away.

If she had lived only part of a life, then Natalie had taken the rest. Her sister had grown older, but railed against the process with an arsenal of creams and potions, with under-garments that realigned her soft flesh, with hair dyes and tooth whiteners and contact lenses. She kept her hair long when other women cut theirs short, smoothing it with mayonnaise. She wore her skirts well above the knee, exposing a creamy expanse of thigh, when fashion magazines trumpeted the return of the maxi skirt. When others opted for punch, Natalie asked for a second gin and tonic, and enjoyed more than one Ramos gin fizz with her friends, or with those who gave the appearance of being friendly in order to partake of the latest gossip. *At least she's drinkin' ladies' drinks*, Saisee said, as if that redeemed Natalie, but only barely.

She walked three miles every day with the goal of staying the same size she'd been in high school; past Ruby's salon, past the hardware store, past the bank and the market. Past the post office, where she stopped to pick up mail not delivered to the house—never to the house—because certainly she deserved to have some privacy in regard to her own affairs. (A statement Saisee interpreted as a personal slight.) Past the diner, where she waved to the men perched on stools in front of the window, the same men who looked up in unison from their *New Herald*s and continued smiling long after she went by before returning to squint at the lines of fine print. Past the cemetery with its fence and scraggly hedge of forsythia and box, and American flags the size of postcards, screwed into the hard ground next to the plainest of markers.

All that walking. Then, two weeks ago, she'd simply dropped while walking from one side of the living room to the other, as if the carpet had gained some severe gravity, pulling her to the floor in a rush. The vase full of blazing star and bellflower and great blue lobelia, cut from the wild edges of their back garden, had slipped through her fingers like it was oiled. It landed with a dull thud on the Oriental, painting a stain of water on the wool, which Alice swore she could still see an outline of. Alice had found her legs more capable of quick motion than she would have imagined possible. On the floor next to Natalie, alarmed by the expression of disbelief on her sister's face, she'd held Natalie's hand, forgetting for once to envy the strength of it as Natalie's fingers locked around hers, encircling her wrist like the talons of a fierce bird.

'Sorry,' Natalie had said, her breath catching in her throat.

Alice bent down, her ear close to Natalie's mouth. 'It's all right,' she said.

'No. I'm sorry.'

***

'Did her fingers curl up?'

'Like mine, you mean?' Alice held out a hand, giving it a blunt appraisal.

'Nah. You can still move your fingers, can't cha?'

'On a good day, yes.'

'My cousin told me when folks pass, if they don't want to go, their fingers curl up like they're trying to hold on to their lives with all their earthly strength. Like they're clawing to stay where they are.'

'Your cousin's imagination is more vivid than yours, Frankie, which I find almost impossible to believe.'

Alice had pulled Natalie's hand away from her wrist to feel for a pulse and finding none, held on to her sister's hand again. *Not yet,* she'd whispered. *Don't go yet.* But then Natalie's fingers, the same fingers Alice had known all her life—long and slender, the nails cut straight across, not too short or too long, the polish growing a little dull—had relaxed. The funeral director's assistant had hounded her for two days until she finally gave in and picked a bottle of nail color, a dreadful, calamine lotion shade called Pinkee Doodle Dandy.

'Miss Natalie would have wanted her nails to look their best,' he'd grumbled.

'You pick something, Albert. I grant you dispensation.'

'Wouldn't be right. She wasn't my kin. Family does for family.'

'Albert, I've picked out the dress and the shoes, the necklace and earrings you told me she'd need. Can't you please stop bothering me about something so unimportant?'

'Wouldn't have been unimportant to her,' he'd said.

In that, he was right. It would have mattered to Natalie, and he knew that about her. The whole town would have known it. Orion, Natalie's mysterious choice after fleeing Connecticut, was exactly the sort of place where the most critical concern following the loss of a loved one would be the determination of appropriate attire. Natalie had landed them in a town that valued good gossip as much as it did propriety, a place that embraced the long-suffering older sister like a lost lamb in spite of her *northernness*, and kept Alice at arm's length, uncertain as to whether she was more deserving of suspicion or of solicitude. All except for Frankie and Phinneaus.

With Albert's insistence that she 'pick out something pretty for Miss Natalie,' Saisee had dumped the collection of nail polishes into Alice's lap, the diminutive, half-empty bottles with their slick black tops, the sort of thing Alice had never worn when she might have, and couldn't open now had she wanted to. They were as foreign to her as currency from a tropical island: sunny corals and gummy-looking pepper-mints, eraser pinks and taffeta ivories, raucous fuchsias that made her think of exotic birds she had never seen but could imagine in all of their screaming plumage. The idea of doing anything to draw attention to her hands, to her fingers, could not have been more unfamiliar to her. The thought of it loosed a dark laugh from her that turned into a melancholy cry.

Pick out something pretty. Pretty. The word stuck in her throat, the odd syllables trapped in the wrong mouth. That was a word she had eliminated from her vocabulary a long time ago. The words she could claim for herself had steelier tones: *whip smart, pigheaded, distant, determined.*

Before, there had always been Natalie to war against, always Natalie to bring out her sharpest teeth; to force her into battle over the smallest slice of life to which she could still lay claim. Her determination to hold her own against her sister was the strong motivation that allowed her to get through each day. Now that Natalie was gone, Alice felt something else moving in to take her place: the anxious embrace of defeat, always waiting its turn.

'Phinneaus says we should eat dinner with you tonight,' Frankie told her, the croaky rasp of his voice bringing her back.

'I didn't realize inviting yourself over for dinner was mannerly.'

'Phinneaus says you could use the company. That you shouldn't be alone right now, Miss Alice.' His eyes widened. 'Are you scared?'

'Scared? What would I have to be scared of?'

Frankie lowered his voice, and though she knew it wouldn't be worth the pain, she bent her head closer to hear his answer.

'Haunts.'

'Haunts? You mean ghosts? Frankie, what in the world are you talking about?'

His eyes were fixed on her feet. 'Miss Natalie.'

Would Natalie take any pleasure in haunting her now? The only reason for haunting would be if there was anything left unsaid between them. *Haunting, taunting*. The words somersaulted back and forth across her brain, the opposite ends of a baton. No, she decided. There were ghosts enough to fill up the rooms of this house, all of them. There wasn't space for another.

'You tell Phinneaus if it's all right with Saisee, then yes, I think it would be nice to have the two of you join me for dinner.'

'Saisee doesn't have to cook. We're gonna bring the food to you.'

'Unless your uncle's suddenly become a master chef, I'm not sure that's anything to look forward to. But as for the company, well, I don't see how I can refuse an offer like that, do you, Saisee?'

The housekeeper sniffed and smoothed down the pleats of her skirt. 'I'm not sure how I feel 'bout someone else cookin' in my kitchen. There's nothin' wrong with my hands.'

'You're invited, too, Saisee,' Frankie piped up. 'I forgot to say.'

'Just because Miss Natalie's gone, no reason for everything round here to fall to pieces. I still got work to do.'

But for how long? Alice wondered. Yesterday hadn't been a day to think about money, neither was today. But soon. Soon she would have to ask Phinneaus, who eschewed the convenience of a calculator, to sit down with his sharpened pencil and review her finances with her. She would watch him print on ledger paper, the numbers meticulously scratched in one column, then transformed by a horrible alchemy, only to appear much larger in another. The resulting sum was a crystal ball, hinting at her future— where she would have to go, what she would have to leave behind, when she would need to start doing without. She envisioned her available funds dwindling like her own fragile architecture until there was nothing left after all the subtractions: the cost of her medicines, the doctors' visits, Saisee's salary, the property taxes and the water bill and the electric bill and the food. Death leaned over her shoulder, breathing Natalie's breath, making Alice feel reckless. *I could leave it all,* she thought. *I could stop trying to be better, stop trying to outwit my disease, stop being tired. I could just stop.*

But there was Frankie, sitting at her feet, looking up anxiously.

'This grand feast of ours,' she said, stroking his head. 'What will we be having?'

'I can't tell a thing. I swore.'

'Well, in that case, I won't tempt you to break your word.'

He scrambled to his feet, all awkward limbs and clumsy edges, and lucky, freckled-boy health. 'I got to tell Phinneaus.' He looked back at her before pushing the screen door open. 'I could say we're havin' somethin' cold. That's just a hint, not a whole tell.' He winked at her, clearly pleased with himself, and the door slammed behind him, his feet clumping down the porch steps and echoing across the walk as the noise of him pushed out into the world.

'Saisee, you should join us.'

'I'm gonna pack up some of her things, Miss Alice. No use leaving them out now. Don't want nothin' callin' her back here.'

Alice shook her head. 'Not you, too? I know for a fact you don't believe that. Natalie's gone and she's not coming back, not as flesh or haunt. You hear me?'

'Not a thing wrong with my hearing.' Saisee balanced a basket of linens on her hip and sashayed out of the room. But like Frankie, she stopped in the doorway to give Alice a parting word. 'I know she was your sister. I know it's a sin to speak ill of the dead. But I'm glad she's gone. You can send me away for saying so, but I mean it clear to my bones. I'm glad she's gone. Always criticizing, always holdin' you down. Trying to keep you afraid. Your sister never wanted nothin' more than hurt for you.' Saisee turned and walked into the kitchen.

'Don't say anything against her, Saisee.' Alice's scold was no more than a whisper and the housekeeper was already out of earshot, but Alice felt compelled to defend her sister anyway, even if it was only to the still air in the room.

It would have been less painful had Saisee used Natalie's name, providing Alice with the smallest amount of emotional distance. *Sister* was the person of her childhood. *Natalie* was the other, the one who'd taken that sister's place so many years ago. Alice waited, hoping to feel indignation or anger rise up in her on Natalie's behalf, but there was nothing other than the sad knowledge that Saisee was right. Alice heard Natalie's familiar voice over the years, delivering venom laced in her adopted drawl: *I saw Phinneaus at the dance last night. I didn't know he was seeing a redhead. You wouldn't believe the way that girl moved. I'd say indecent, but people couldn't stop applauding. Phinneaus will be needing a wife to help him now that he's got that boy. Someone energetic enough to run after a three-year-old, don't you think? Do you really need a new dress when you never go anywhere? I'm not sure we could afford it anyway, not with the cost of all of your prescriptions.*

There had been small fissures in their strained relationship, occasions when something just beyond civility was called for, birthdays and holidays, meals shared in the presence of others. But then there were other things, unexplained. A night years ago when she'd been unable to sleep. The thought of what she'd lost suddenly stormed her defenses without reason. It had not been a particular date, or time of year; no trigger she could put her finger on. Maybe it was the quiet that invited the thing in, that called it down upon her. The shock of loss rolled over her as if it was brand-new. She doubled over, crying, the force of her sobs rattling the bed against the wall. She couldn't stop. The sudden touch of Natalie's hand on her shoulder was so foreign, the anguish in her voice so real when she said, 'Alice.' Alice threw her arms around her, listening to Natalie's

cracked voice start, then stop. Then try to start again.
'Alice, I need to . . .'

'Don't say anything. Just stay with me.'

'Shhhh. I know.'

'You don't know. You can't understand. Just stay. Please.'
She'd fallen asleep like that, half sitting up, her arms wrapped
around Natalie.

The next morning, when Alice stumbled into the kitchen
for coffee, Natalie was leaning against the refrigerator, a glass
of juice in her hand.

'Natalie, thank you for—'

Natalie interrupted, holding up her hand in response.
'I don't know, remember?'

The sister Alice longed for had vanished overnight; Natalie
had carefully folded her back up and secreted her away in
some unknown place. But those rare instances had given
Alice hope; they had led her to believe her sister was there,
buried beneath something she did not have the strength to
move.

Thanksgiving came and went with minimal fanfare, and the
night of reckoning descended shortly thereafter. Phinneaus
arrived carrying his tools: the sharpened pencils, legal pads,
the calculator she'd bought for him as a present before she
knew him well, which he always carried but never used.
After dinner, Saisee and Frankie stayed in the kitchen to
clean up and to practice his vocabulary words. Alice and
Phinneaus retreated to the dining room. She lapped the
dining room table with her stuttering walk and pushed aside
the curtain, peering out the window into the dark.

'I miss winter.'

'We have winter, Alice. Some snow most years. You know
that. You're stalling.'

It was a gift, having someone who knew her so well. 'I know. But it's true. Sometimes I miss northeast winters. Still. After all this time.' The promise of quiet, the blanket of solitude stretched out over everything and everyone at once, expected, but still surprising when it came, the sky shaking off its feathery coat. How the rest of the world slowed, for a month or two, to her own hesitant pace; everyone taking care, moving with greater caution, pushing forward into a battering wind that pushed back. How much closer she felt to normal then.

'Something on your mind?'

She wasn't good at hiding anything from him, but this, especially, seemed so visible. Not just to him, but to anyone who looked at her.

'You love your sister, don't you, Phinneaus?'

He twirled the pencil between his fingers before drawing tic-tac-toe squares on a blank piece of paper. 'I think what you mean to ask is, do I love my sister *still*, even though she stole from my folks and broke their hearts and abandoned her child to her broken-down older brother without thinking twice about it. Even though she's reckless and irresponsible and a criminal and a junkie. Even though I don't think she'll change. I believe that's what you mean to ask me.'

'Well, do you?'

'Hell, nobody's perfect.' Phinneaus grinned at her, and marked an *x* through the middle square, sliding the paper across the table toward her. She didn't respond, and he tried again.

'Yes, Alice. I still love her. I know that doesn't make it any easier for you.'

'But how can you?'

He wasn't someone who found it necessary to explain his opinions or his actions, and most of the time she was content to fill in her own interpretation. But not now. She'd hoped for a different answer, one that would allow her to justify her own feelings. 'How can you?' she asked again.

He sat back in his chair and let the pencil roll across the table. 'I spent a lot of time hating people, Alice, during the war, and after. It was a useful emotion—let me do things I'd have never thought I could bring myself to do. I hated governments and politics. I hated the food and the weather and the noise. I hated the men I was fighting against, and half the time I hated the men I was fighting next to just as much. Every time I used the word, every time I thought it, it deadened me a little more.'

She remembered. He'd gotten to Orion two years ahead of her, but had been almost as dead to the world as she'd been upon arriving here. It was five years before he told her about the tattoo on his upper arm, a bow bisected by a flaming arrow, and that had happened only after he'd stumbled across their front yard late one night when Natalie was gone on one of her biannual vacations, drunk and talking to himself, cursing when he fell into the boxwood hedge along the front walk. She'd shooed him around to the back of the house, started a pot of coffee, and let him talk, gradually piecing together a story from his few coherent sentences. It was why he'd come to Orion, he said. His best buddy in his unit had been a local boy, always talking about his idyllic childhood. He'd died holding on to Phinneaus while they both waited for the medics to come, the same medics who later saved Phinneaus's leg. The friend had a little brother, one of the itchy, grimy boys in the first scout troop Phinneaus helped. But no one knew he and the man had served together, and he meant to keep it that way. *I promised him I'd do what I could,* Phinneaus had told her that night, *but no one's gonna make me tell his momma about his last hours on this earth. Bow and arrow. Orion. The hunter.* Those were his last words before his eyes closed and he fell asleep on the kitchen floor. He was gone before Saisee arrived the next morning and avoided Alice for a good two weeks after. The look he flashed her the next time she saw him was all the warning she needed, and she'd never said a thing about it to another soul.

'When I found out about Sheila dumping Frankie, I thought it would push me over the edge, the way she'd left him. I wanted to hate her. But the moment I saw him—he was, what, three years old?—there wasn't any hate in him, no matter he'd been passed around from one relative to the next ever since he was born. He didn't hate his momma. I don't know why, but he never has. And if he didn't, then how could I?'

Phinneaus had changed when Frankie came into his life five years ago. Up until then, he and Alice had been equally reticent, content to inhabit the fringe of Orion's small society. She was the one who tutored the town's children, awarding a feather for a right answer. She was the one who peered from the window at Halloween, watching Saisee dole out candy, occasionally nodding to the watchful parents on the sidewalk. She was the one who ambled around the block in the early morning or just after dusk, preferring to limit her exposure to adults to the gray hours of the day, be the living ghost they acknowledged but didn't speak of outside of polite inquiry, in deference to her sister. And Phinneaus was . . . Phinneaus. Plainspoken and private, he had little need of conversation or attachments with adults, but was a champion of the town's children. There'd been little about him to dislike, so people let him alone, as he clearly wished. But with the arrival of Frankie, he turned into a de facto parent. He fretted and bragged, laughed and scolded, taught and learned in equal parts. He joined the PTA, coached Pee Wee football, threw birthday parties for Frankie with water balloons and garter snakes and do-it-yourself ice cream sundaes that made the boy the envy of his friends. He left Alice behind in some small way, yet she was happy for him. Now he had Frankie to care for, she didn't need to worry his sense of nobility would make him feel somehow responsible for her.

'Any particular reason you were asking about my sister?'

'I'm wondering if I hated Natalie.'

He drew another *x*, in the top middle square, then put the pencil down and slid his hand over hers. 'I imagine you did.'

'I thought maybe, after she died, I could change it into something else. Maybe just feel sorry for her. But I can't.'

'Give it time. You might end up surprising yourself.'

Frankie had fallen asleep on the couch, his body all long limbs and angles, the curve of his belly spilling out from where his shirt rode up above his waist, his face slack with the ease of slumber. Phinneaus set out stacks of papers in neat piles, having agreed with Alice there was nothing to be gained by delaying any assessment of her *obligations,* as he referred to them.

'It sounds better than *debts.*'

'It's meant to.'

She thumbed through the largest piles. The one closest to toppling over was the pile with all of her 'explanation of benefits' paperwork; the others were invoices from doctors' offices and insurance companies.

'What's in here?' she asked, peering into a large cardboard box filmed with dust.

'Don't know. Saisee brought it down from your sister's room. Said she found it in the closet.' He paused, and she sensed he was looking for the right words. 'It might seem too soon, after only a couple of weeks, but it will have to get done at some point. It's a spare room now, and you might need it.'

She smiled at him. 'What would I need it for? You think the view's better from the second story?'

Phinneaus cleared his throat. 'You might need it for a boarder.'

He looked up to see if she was going to object, and even though the thought of having a stranger in the house, in her house, made her uneasy, she kept her tone light, realizing her options were limited.

'So now you and Saisee are conspiring against me?'

'I could take you upstairs if you want to do it yourself, but Saisee thought it'd be easier if she brought things down. You know, do a little bit at a time. She started cleaning up in Natalie's bedroom so you could see what you wanted to hold on to. What you wanted to sell.'

'What I might want to burn?'

'You're taking this better than I expected.'

'I don't have much choice but to be practical, do I?'

If she could choose, would she have designed a life without Natalie in it? To tell Phinneaus they had never been close would negate their whole childhood, a time when they took turns licking the backs of S & H Green Stamps and pasting them into the stamp book; when Natalie pulled Alice's head toward hers and worked their long hair into one joint braid, saying, *Now we'll go everywhere together.* Those occasions when she pushed Alice's tormentors to the sidewalk with hard shoves, her face a picture of controlled fury; when she took the blame for Alice's small failures: the stolen gum, the broken vase, the school yard spat, going head to head with their father, matching the punishments he doled out with her own willful indifference. Why had that changed? What had she done?

At some point in their adolescence a magnetic force developed between them, running barely below the surface. Polar emotions of anger and love, of loyalty and jealousy, were volleyed back and forth. Natalie knew better than anyone how to hurt her. Alice had assumed her arthritis was to blame, with its twin shackles of money and attention—the attention the disease required from her parents when they'd still been alive; the money that bound Natalie to her after they'd died. Her sister's way of being in the world, of pulling people close only to cut them loose with a calculated cruelty, unraveled whatever ties the two of them had once had. They had lived their older lives like strangers from different shipwrecks, washed up on the same island, without the benefit of a common language. But now Natalie was gone, it was not only absence Alice felt but an incompleteness; like with a phantom limb, she was tormented by something no longer there. Frankie was half-right to talk about haunts. The older sister who had been her protector, her defender, was the one still haunting Alice's memory, the one who refused to relinquish her grasp on Alice's heart.

Phinneaus hunched over his legal pad, moving *obligations* from one side of the table to the other while she rummaged through boxes from Natalie's room. She was shaken to see her sister's broad, familiar script on the first piece of paper she pulled out, some sort of legal document from a property management company, Steele and Greene.

'What's this, do you suppose?'

He held it up under the light, his lips moving as he read the document, then he scowled and read it again.

'Alice, didn't you say you and Natalie sold the house in Connecticut?'

Without warning she was propelled back thirty-five years, at a speed that left her struggling to breathe. She could hear pellets of hail exploding on the roof and smell the sulfurous remains of lightning strikes. The wind roared around her like an animal, shrieking and moaning and clawing to get in. She felt a deep, striking pain low in her back that almost doubled her over.

'We did sell it. Right after the hurricane. Natalie said there was structural damage to the foundation from the flooding and that we couldn't afford to do the renovation work. We listed it for sale 'as is.' The real estate agent found a buyer right away. A young couple.' *With a baby*, she thought, but did not say the words out loud.

'This looks like an agreement between the Kessler Trust and Steele and Greene, a property management company. They're acting as rental agents for a property owned by the trust. A residential property at 700 Stonehope Way in Woodridge, Connecticut.'

'That can't be right. That's our old address. The house we sold. Maybe the real estate agent worked for Steele and Greene?'

'You don't remember signing anything?'

'No, of course not. I wouldn't have signed away our house. I never wanted to leave it in the first place.'

Phinneaus rummaged through the box, pulling out more papers. 'There's a signed lease agreement here. Alice, your old house, it wasn't sold. It's a rental property. Natalie must have been receiving rent checks from the management company.'

'But she said we had to leave. And there's never been any money . . .'

Memories she'd tried to tamp down came back in jagged, broken pieces. The bluish-green wallpaper in the foyer that felt like silk when she trailed her fingertips along it, pretending it was the surface of a lake; the sound of the doorbell, one note mysteriously missing from its chime; the creak beneath the third step leading to the second floor; her grandmother's piano, left to her mother on the condition she play it once a day; the furnace-like heat and low ceilings of the attic, the heavy air colored with the scent of mothballs and yellowing paper and the cry of a small bird piercing the dark, brilliant and fierce, close to her ear, then fading.

'Alice, I'm not sure about any of this. Let me look through these other papers first.'

That time immediately following the storm was all darkness and confusion to her, punctuated with shame that she'd been so weak, that she'd let herself drift away from the pain so easily, that she'd wholeheartedly embraced the drugs and the stupor that followed, wanting nothing more than to be dead to the world.

'I don't understand. She wanted us out of that house. Why?'

'I'll just have another look . . . make sure I've got this straight. Why don't you bring us some tea?'

She walked to the kitchen to fill the kettle, swatting at memories as they rose up around her, uncertain of where she was. Which hallway? Which kitchen? By the time she came back with the tea, Phinneaus had emptied the box. He'd moved all the other paperwork onto the floor; the table was covered with papers from the box that had been in Natalie's closet. There were checkbook registers and deposit slips, ledgers with dates on the covers, newspaper clippings, a bundle of letters, some postcards, a book.

'Maybe we should forget about all this for tonight. Tackle it in the morning. What do you say?' There was just enough concern in his voice to be noticeable, not enough to be intrusive.

She shook her head. 'You go on, Phinneaus, and get Frankie to bed. I'm fine, really. But I don't think I can sleep.'

He reached for a checkbook register from the pile nearest him and tore a clean sheet of paper from a legal pad. 'Sleep's overrated. Besides, bed, sofa, I don't think it makes much difference when you're his age.' He started turning through the pages of the register, periodically writing down numbers.

She loved the sound of his voice, only there was never enough of it. The sweet drawl of his words floated toward her on a river of honey. If she was braver she would have pulled him to her, taken his words into her mouth, swallowing them down like a balm for everything wrong in the world. Instead she picked up the book, a softcover copy of *Franny and Zooey*, and thumbed through it. She stopped to read the notes in the margins, Natalie's fat, loopy cursive barely contained in the narrow white space: *Franny's book—does Salinger mean for green to symbolize innocence?* and *Where is the spiritual conflict between F. and Z.?*, then stopped when the book opened to a page where a postcard and two glassine envelopes containing negatives had been stuffed close to the spine.

The postcard was of a painting: a red sports car driving in front of an American flag, with the word 'Corvette' printed in large black letters across a white border. The image was ghosted with webs of white where it had been bent and creased. There was no postage attached to the back, just a date, *March 22*, and a few sentences written in chunky, boyish letters: *We can go away—maybe California? I've always wanted to surf. (Kidding, babe.) Give me a couple of days. Tell me where to meet you.* There was no signature, and Alice turned the postcard over and back again. Who had Natalie intended to meet?

She took the glassine envelopes from the book and pulled out a strip of negatives from the first, holding it to the light. A flat history in tones of burnt orange. There were only four exposures on the strip, and even though there was no date, after looking at the first image Alice could guess when the pictures must have been taken: in 1963, early in the summer, before they'd made their yearly trip to the lake.

Natalie was wearing a shift with a deep square neckline and braided straps tied at the shoulders, a dress that had been a present for her seventeenth birthday, in October. Alice remembered how Natalie had preened when she put it on, the royal blue making her skin glow like it had been dusted with nacre. Their mother had waited until the dress showed up on the out-of-season sale rack before buying it, and Natalie complained she'd have to wait at least eight months before it would be warm enough again for her to wear it. But here she was, the summer after that birthday, her blond hair pulled forward to curl over her shoulders, her hands resting defiantly on her hips, the look on her face undecipherable.

The setting was unfamiliar: a pond surrounded by tall clumps of grass and half-submerged rocks, a split rail fence behind, a leafy backdrop of shade trees. Natalie had been gone the first three weeks in July that summer, sent off to visit friends of their parents who were showing her around Smith, tempting her with a taste of college life. Maybe the sudden push to ensure Natalie went to college meant her parents had found the postcard? Alice vaguely recalled how tense things had been just before Natalie left—the score of slammed doors, the raised voices accompanying every meal. She also remembered, with a stitch of guilt, how relieved she'd been once Natalie left and the house settled back into its steady, quiet routine.

The photos must have been taken at the house of her parents' friends, Alice decided, her eyes moving from one frame to the next. But it was the last frame that caught her attention, and as the negative strip fell to her lap she put her hands up to her mouth, a sickness swirling in her gut.

Natalie, turned sideways in that same dress, was circling her belly with her hands, one above, the other below, pulling the fabric of her dress taut over the small dome of her belly. And even in that two-dimensional world of several lifetimes ago, Alice suddenly understood exactly when it was that Natalie had changed, and why.

'Alice?'

Phinneaus had left his chair and was standing behind her. His hands rested lightly on her shoulders.

'I didn't know,' she said.

'What didn't you know?'

She handed him the strip of negatives and the postcard. He put on his glasses and looked at the images without saying anything, then read the postcard and set it down on the table. His hands went back to her shoulders, and she could feel the cool steadiness of them through the thin fabric of her shirt.

'She had the baby?'

'No.' Alice shook her head, her own sadness swimming back to her, reaching for her with needy, grasping fingers. 'She was only gone for three weeks. I thought she was visiting friends. That's what they told me.'

'Your parents?'

'Yes.'

She'd never understood why Natalie had consigned her to the ranks of the enemy that summer. The change in her sister had been sharp, definite; it was as though something had discovered the plane of weakness in their family and cleaved them in two, splitting Natalie off from the rest of them. But now Alice realized it wasn't some*thing* that had chipped her sister away. It was the beginning of some*one*. She looked at the date on the postcard again. Late March. Natalie must have been about four and a half months pregnant. Her horror deepened as she recalled the tentative flutters that had teased her own belly; the increasing sensation of breathlessness whenever she'd climbed the stairs.

The knowledge that her parents could have forced her sister to do such a thing unraveled her bond with them, a connection she'd always thought unassailable. In little more than a moment, they'd taken on the masks of monsters; their expressions of care and worry replaced by something stern and immobile. She felt herself drifting through the darkness of space, away from them and toward the cold place where Natalie must be, wanting only to apologize, to comfort and console, to take back words she'd uttered, unknowing, that would have trumped, time and again, any step toward reconciliation. There had been no one for Natalie to confide in, no one to take her side. And then Alice remembered Thomas's words of caution, his veiled remarks about her parents: *They were far from saints, Alice. They made some very serious mistakes.* Of all people, Natalie had chosen to confide in him. To her shame and regret, the familiar ache of jealousy deadened her bones. Thomas had been her confessor as well, and it was painfully obvious just how insignificant and childish her secrets had been when weighed against Natalie's.

'Alice.' Phinneaus had taken the negatives from the other glassine envelope and was holding a strip up to the light. There was a hushed, strangled sound to his voice. 'Maybe I shouldn't be looking at these.'

'Is it Natalie?'

'No.' He handed her the negatives. 'It's you.'

How she wished she could go to the girl in those images now, take her hand and push aside the mass of wild blond curls, whisper in her ear, *Run. It's not too late.* But people never believed that what was going to happen to them would actually happen. When she was fourteen, she had not believed her body would start a war with itself. And later, she had not believed she could fiercely battle the creeping progress of her disease, yet continue to lose. Someone telling you about the future did not prepare you for it. Nothing prepared you for it.

The Alice frozen in time, living within the confines of those few small squares of film, felt better than she had in years. The baby had fought her disease, the hormonal rush of pregnancy had cascaded through her, and for the first time she'd felt both love and respect for her body, marveling that it could simultaneously tear down and create, yet not destroy her in the process. Instead of her treacherous medications, she'd swallowed large, innocuous vitamins and gorged on milk, on icy green grapes she pulled from the freezer, on saltine crackers slathered with butter, and sometimes just on butter itself, licked from the tips of her fingers.

She'd spent hours roaming the woods near their house, avoiding Natalie for as much of the day as she could, coming in only when the air turned chill, with remnants of the forest woven into her hair, sticking to her coat, cemented to her boots. Natalie had never asked about the specifics of her pregnancy, something that made Alice both uneasy and grateful. Instead, there was an odd combination of calculating appraisals and casual indifference, as though there was some other logical explanation for clothes that no longer fit and the waddling gait she'd developed. She'd wallowed in bottomless sleep, falling into the canyon of it the moment she crawled between the sheets and waking to find her hands resting on the hard knot of her belly.

That was the Alice who had started several letters to him, but stopped writing each one after the first paragraph, before she put to paper words that would have made a difference. She'd torn the letters into tiny pieces and carried them into the bathroom in the pocket of her robe, flushing them down the toilet, thinking it would be better to wait one more day before telling him, then another, and another. And as the days, then weeks, passed, she'd begun thinking of the baby as only hers, and whenever she wavered, she'd reminded herself of the lie he had told, the sort of life he likely led, and how ill-suited to parenthood someone with his temperament would be.

In the negative she held between her fingers, she stood in the backyard of the house where she'd grown up, on an early summer day with birds cartwheeling across the sky. Her body was turned sideways, her hair curling over one shoulder, her hands circling the broad expanse of her belly— one above, one below—in a pose almost identical to that of her sister nine years earlier, completely unaware anyone was taking her picture.

'Oh, Natalie,' she whispered, wondering where the photograph was that went with the negative. 'What did you do?'

ELEVEN

How glad Finch was for the excuse of the holidays. Back in the cozy warmth of his own familiar rooms, the city glowing with temporary good cheer, peace on earth, kindness to one's fellow human beings. Dinners with Lydia and her husband became something to look forward to, in part because the menu changed to reflect the generosity of the season, and for these few shining weeks, he could partake of food he enjoyed: potpies with their napped, buttery crusts; roasts with interesting chutneys—quince! Why didn't he eat quince more often? It was delightful! Potatoes that were whipped and swirled, peaked and marshmallowed. It was even possible to finagle Kevin, his son-in-law, into slipping him the occasional tipple of eggnog when Lydia's back was turned.

His daughter's Federal-style row house was festooned with greenery, evergreens dripping from the chandeliers and spiraling around the banister. There was mistletoe, with its ghostly spray of pale berries, suspended from a fixture in the front hall. After a glass of port, he had but to close his eyes and Claire was waiting for him to slip his arm around her waist and waltz her slowly across the room until they stopped directly beneath it. The ivory curve of her neck beckoned, and her delighted trill danced in his ears. *Denny,* she would say in a slightly breathless whisper, her mouth pressed against the shoulder of his jacket. *Time to go home now, don't you think?* And when he looked down at her face she would smile at him and wink. Ah, there was nothing subtle about that woman when she wanted something, and his happiest memories were of those times she had wanted him.

Thanksgiving, just the week before, had been worse than he could have imagined. He and Lydia had muddled through the anniversary of Claire's death together, even though their grief and grieving weren't the same. Lydia was silent when he offered up memories of her mother, seeming content just to spend time with him, while he was comforted by saying Claire's name out loud, squeezing her into sentences and paragraphs and rambling stories where she took center stage. Thanksgiving itself had been a maudlin affair; the holiday table groaning under the weight of too many dishes. He and Lydia pushed food around their plates, not interested in eating, leaving Kevin to supply the small talk that served as a bridge between their mourning. After the meal, he'd walked into the kitchen to find Lydia standing in front of the open refrigerator like a waitress, plates of food slicked over with plastic wrap balanced up and down her arms, but no place to squeeze them in.

That night the two of them had promised each other that they wouldn't spend Christmas or New Year's in the same way.

'She would hate this,' he'd said.

'Yes,' Lydia had replied. 'She would be very angry with us.'

'Likely throw things. Breakables. I'm not willing to risk

it. Are you?' She'd shaken her head, laughing and throwing herself into his arms. And so they moved forward from there.

Finch felt his spirits lift as the season bloomed. He knew this, too, was because of Claire, not so much because she'd loved the holiday but because she'd loved what it did to him: turned him giddy with happiness and overwhelming gratitude. *Count your blessings*, he'd say to himself year after year, and he had: Claire, Lydia, a satisfaction with his life's work, the ability to acknowledge it for what it had been. That was more than enough. He was a sentimental fool, to be sure, but this was the time of year he welcomed it. Finch, he told himself, you could use a little *peace on earth*.

He was beginning to think the whole thing with Thomas was a mistake, just a sad, sordid chapter from his past he was determined to resurrect. In spite of finding Thomas's study of the Kessler family in the Edells' back hall, he and Stephen were no closer to finding the other two pieces of the triptych than they'd been when they started. He'd finally convinced Stephen that it might be wise to spend some time apart, focusing on their respective strengths in an effort to turn up some new information. Frankly, Finch was looking forward to spending a few weeks *not* thinking about any of it. He hummed a carol while he rolled up his sleeves and patted the outside of a roasting chicken with salt and pepper.

'Claire,' he said aloud, between verses, 'I plan to prepare a green vegetable for myself this evening, in keeping with the spirit of the season.' Even the ring of the phone couldn't shake him from his reverie, and he was delighted to see Lydia's number on the display.

'Darling daughter. Apple of my eye. You'll be happy to know that I bought broccoli today when I was at the store and may even go so far as to cut up some of the dastardly green crowns to have with my dinner.'

'Dad? Are you feeling all right?'

'Right as rain. Snow if we're lucky. Now, to what do I owe the pleasure of this conversation?'

'I was calling to invite you to join us for dinner on Saturday. If you're free.'

'Love to! Can't think of anything I'd rather do. Can I bring something?'

'That was Stephen's exact response. You two have been spending so much time together, I believe you're starting to think alike.'

Finch felt his mood dipping precariously. 'Jameson? What does he have to do with this?' Surely she hadn't . . .

'I invited him to join us, too.'

She had. He could barely contain a groan. 'Lydia, listen here. I'm old enough to arrange my own playdates. If I wanted to eat dinner with Stephen, I'd call him up and say, 'Stephen let's have dinner.' And I don't recall having done that.'

'Dad, it's the holidays. He's alone. You said yourself that you thought he'd benefit from having a little more social interaction. Consider it a charitable act.'

There had been charity enough as far as he was concerned. For too many hours in the close confines of a poorly venti-lated car he had been forced to listen to Stephen's discourses on *wavelet decomposition* and the wondrous methods now being used to convert a painting to a digital image in order to analyze it mathematically and statistically.

'And the purpose of all of this analyzing . . .' he'd said.

Stephen's eyes had glowed with delight at being asked to elaborate. 'To allow us to chart techniques particular to a specific artist, and to the artist's use of certain mediums. Giving us another tool that can be used to identify forgeries or works not done in their entirety by the artist to whom the work is attributed. Think of it. At some point in the not too distant future, science will allow us to ascertain authenticity to an absolute degree.'

'How lovely,' Finch said. 'And in the midst of all this *decomposing*, does anyone stop to consider the painting? The subject matter? The emotion the artist was trying to translate?'

'Please.' Stephen had waved his hand dismissively. 'When was the last time you went to an exhibition? Do you know what's happening there?'

'When was the last time *you* did?'

'I asked first.'

'Ridiculous,' Finch had said. 'This argument is ludicrous.'

'I don't believe *ludicrous* is the word you want. My argument is far from senseless and is in no way absurd or farcical.'

'You are giving me a headache.'

'If you had simply answered my question . . . people go to museums to see an exhibition someone has told them they *have* to see. The implication being that unless they see this particular exhibition, and have the appropriate reaction to the work, they have no real appreciation for art. So they stumble around a crowded space, wearing headphones and squinting at captions in tiny print. This is nothing more than a model designed to exploit herd mentality. People are told what to think about a painting, what they should see in it. They're denied the opportunity to stand back and contemplate perspective or technique without the benefit of someone else's overly large head getting in the way. Then they collapse onto banquettes that are too hard and have accommodated far too many people with who knows what standards of hygiene. Honestly, Finch. I hardly think emotion plays a role in the experience at all.'

It made him want to hit something or, more accurately, someone. The thought of such thinly veiled belligerence serving as dinner conversation in the sanctity of his daughter's home was more than Finch could bear. And he was in no mood to act as Stephen's keeper for the night.

'Lydia, perhaps it would be better if we changed the parameters of the invitation. Maybe we could meet Stephen at a restaurant, instead?' He regretted ever introducing the two of them, though since Stephen had been at his apartment when Lydia stopped by with Kevin, he'd had little choice. The flash in Stephen's eyes when he took Lydia's hand had made Finch immediately suspicious. Smitten. Just like that. Stephen's face had melted into bovine simplicity as his eyes watched Lydia's every move. It was unconscionable.

'You said he's not very good in public places.'

'Did I? I don't recall. I may have been exaggerating.'

'Dad, it will be fine. You'll see.'

How could it possibly be fine? He'd lost all interest in dinner. It wasn't until the smell of singed chicken skin filled the house that he remembered his meal at all. The remains of the bird, dry and crusted, were relegated to the sink, the broccoli returned to its plastic bag in the refrigerator. Finch retreated to his study, taking solace in a chocolate Santa he had surreptitiously removed from a dish next to the teller's window at the bank. He became more angry with Stephen as the evening wore on. *Why must he usurp my family?*

But the moment the thought entered his head, there was Claire, chiding him for his stingy behavior.

He is in need of a friend, Denny. As are you.

'I have friends.'

You don't. Not to put too fine a point on it, my dear, but we had friends. You have acquaintances. It isn't the same thing.

'I only want you. You and Lydia. I don't need anyone else.'

You have me. And you will always have Lydia. But you know as well as I do that that's not the same thing either. Her image frayed before him, then evaporated. A flickering bulb, dimmed.

He poked the logs in the fireplace, poured himself a glass of burgundy, and fiddled with the digital music player that had been a gift from his daughter, thinking *Five Variants of Dives and Lazarus* a suitable companion for his evening's work. His desk was a disaster zone, a week's worth of mail hidden beneath stacks of files which Mrs. Blankenship had dropped off for him, years of Thomas's mail and clippings, which Stephen had suggested Finch search through in hopes of finding something pertinent. With a new appreciation for Mrs. Blankenship, Finch tried to think of the task as something other than secretarial, but his mood worsened as he leafed through the odd collection of papers, many of them a tallow yellow and crumbling round the edges.

There were announcements of shows from years ago, faded newspaper pictures with gallery owners and patrons circled around Thomas, who often seemed to be contemplating something in the far-off distance with an expression of bemusement. There were the expected offers of teaching positions, invitations to speak, and pleas from young artists offering to size canvases, sharpen pencils, haul slop, anything to be able to share the same rarefied air with someone who possessed, as one supplicant put it, 'a supreme knowledge of that which is universal within us all.'

Tripe. Finch rubbed his forehead, hoping to alleviate the tightness spreading between his brows. Such adulation was exhausting to read about. But to experience it, day after day? No wonder Thomas had become reclusive. Weaned as he was on constant attention and praise, groomed to engender superlatives, it was understandable that at some point admiration had ceased to mean anything to him, that he'd reached the point where all he wanted was to be alone. When one was the recipient of a great gift, was one forced to live in service to that gift, unable to do anything else?

But the more Thomas withdrew, the greater a subject of fascination he became. Where did he live? How did he live? What inspired him? If he was discovered frozen in a block of ice on the peak of Kangchenjunga, there would be those who'd opt to cut open his brain to determine what accounted for his talent. The clingers and the hangers-on, the wannabes and the has-beens, and those-who-never-would-be; no one in their right mind would ask for such a life, if they understood the consequences of it.

Finch continued thumbing through the stack, trying to establish some order. Bills that had never been opened. Bank statements, unused check registers, reviews that had been forwarded by Thomas's various representatives over the years. Letters, most marked 'personal' (underlined), all addressed in an obviously female hand, although few had been opened. Finch flipped through them, distracted, until one caught his eye. In the upper left hand corner of a card-size envelope was printed, '700 Stonehope Way, Woodridge, Connecticut.' The house he and Stephen had just visited. The Kessler house.

The envelope wasn't sealed, although it was hard for Finch to know whether the glue had failed with age or the envelope had been opened. The postmark was difficult to make out, but it looked like the letter had been mailed on either the eleventh or seventeenth of June 1972. He worked a snug card out from the envelope and set it on the desk. It was from a museum gift shop, the type of card produced to accompany traveling exhibitions. The picture on the front was one of Thomas's earlier works, an oil painting of three women standing in a dark hallway dragging branches of ash behind them, their hair rising up from their heads in snake-like coils, shooting toward a ceiling lit by one bare bulb. When he opened the card, a photograph fell out. 'Thomas,' he whispered, feeling the air knocked out of him in a single punch.

The picture was of a young and very pregnant Alice Kessler, standing in the backyard of her home on Stonehope Way, cradling her belly. And written in flowing, liquid script on the back of the photograph were the words *I know what you did. N.*

Finch pushed his chair back from the desk and walked over to the fireplace, carrying the photo with him. He sat down on the leather ottoman, holding the edges of the photograph with both hands. There was a sick panic in his stomach, and he wished he could reverse the last minute, pushing the picture back into the card, the card back into the envelope, the envelope back into the stack, flipping past it without ever taking notice of the address.

What had Thomas said to him? *No more than I have envied you the companionship of a daughter.* Finch felt the weight of overwhelming sadness press down on him, thinking of Lydia, unable to consider the absence of her, a hole in his life never to be filled. He looked at the postmark on the envelope again—June 1972—and tried to recall that year, whether he had noticed anything different, anything unusual in Thomas's behavior. As soon as he started thinking along this line, he abandoned it. In the first place, it was more than thirty-five years ago. He had reached the age where it was a struggle to remember in what room he'd left his shoes, his password for the computer, the names of his graduate students, even the pretty girl with the red hair and the low-cut blouse, the one who leaned in dangerously close to him in a cloud of woodsy scent whenever she visited his office.

Beyond questioning the accuracy of his memory, there was an implication in looking back so far that his life has been intimately intertwined with Thomas's; that they'd shared confidences, sought each other's opinions, revealed their deepest hopes and fears, even in the veiled masculine language of their generation. This was untrue. Finch had accepted it when climbing the long flights of stairs to Thomas's apartment just over a month ago. They did not have a friendship in the true sense of the word. Their relationship was symbiotic at best, based on mutual need.

And what Thomas needed now was for Finch and Stephen to find his child.

How old was he when he'd found out—thirty-seven? Had he not been ready to have a child in his life even then, after the years of women and parties; of indulgence coupled with self-imposed isolation, dropping away from the world when it proved too much for him, resurfacing to be lionized once again. And now, when he was frail and impaired, this was when he chose to be a father? Finch felt Claire's hand on his shoulder and leaned into her, almost losing his balance. *Why do you assume he didn't want the child, Denny? You're that sure of his heart?*

'I can't stand to hear you defend him. Not now. Why don't you defend me?'

I suppose because you've done nothing to require it, you foolish gizzard.

That private endearment funneled into his ear and was more than Finch could bear. His longing for her physical presence eclipsed everything else; he was desperate to hold her, to have her sitting next to him and touch the side of her cheek, to bury his head in her chest and take in the spicy smell of carnation soap that lingered on her skin. The ethereal substitute sent to him in her stead had no more weight than a breeze, a dash of smoke. He pulled away.

She turned up her nose, insulted. *Suit yourself, then.* Within moments the air next to him turned cold and heavy, and he shivered even though he was sitting next to the fire. It didn't matter. Her words had accomplished what she'd intended, as always.

Why had he assumed Thomas didn't want the baby? Admittedly, Finch knew nothing of the situation beyond the photograph he held in his hands. He had not been privy to any conversations or decisions, did not know the outcome. His conclusion was based entirely on the flaws and faults he'd ascribed to Thomas over the years. Or had it been instead the result of his own insecurity, his need to be the better man in at least this one respect—as a father?

The noises of the room came to him separately: the soaring and diving strings running over the harp of the Vaughan Williams, the hiss of flame from the slightly damp wood he'd set on the grate, the traffic from the street. Finch looked around and saw his life in all of its pieces: his books, the papers strewn across his desk, the still photos on the wall, the globe in the corner fixed to its one perspective, no longer set spinning on its axis now that Lydia had grown up and claimed a place of her own. The room was small and dreary, everything in it insignificant. He had never felt so much loneliness.

He pulled a copy of his catalogue raisonné on Bayber from the bookshelf, flipping through pages until he found what he'd written of Thomas's work that year.

In 1972, Bayber's work underwent another metamorphosis, yet refused to be defined by or adhere to any specific style. Elements of

abstract expressionism, modernism, surrealism, and neo-expres-
sionism combine with figurative art to create works which remain
wholly original and highly complex, both delighting and terrifying
at a subconscious level. There is nothing fragile here, nothing dream-
like. No protections are offered, not for the artist himself and not
for those viewing his work. All is called forth in a raw state, human
values finessed on the canvas, softened and sharpened, separated
and made aggregate. While there are certain motifs in these works—
often a suggestion of water, the figure of a bird—and various elements
are repeated, aside from an introverted complexity, the context in
which they appear is never the same from one piece to the next.
What ties these works together is the suggestion of loss, of disap-
pearance, and of longing (see figs. 87–95).

The figure of a bird. He had forgotten his own writing. Finch
took the book back to his desk and pulled a magnifying glass
from the top drawer to study the color plates. Thomas had
completed six paintings in 1972, four of them after July. In
each of those four, Finch managed to find what he had seen
long ago, the figure of a bird. Was it Alice, flown away from
him? Or was it meant to be the child?

He looked at each of the paintings prior and could find
nothing. But every painting Thomas had done after July of
'72, regardless of the style or subject matter, contained the
suggestion, if not the image of a bird. They were often
included as hidden objects, rarely in a central role, and in
a few instances Finch wondered if he was seeing something
that wasn't really there, only because he wanted to. It
reminded him of reading *Where's Waldo?* to Lydia when she
was eight, his daughter perched on the arm of his chair like
a bird herself, scouring the page to find Waldo before he
did. Once either of them found Waldo, he was the first thing
they noticed when they read the book again, his place in

the crowd indelibly imprinted on their memory. Finch found himself looking at Thomas's paintings the same way now, searching only for the bird and having found it, unable to see the meaning of anything else.

His envy fell away as it often did when he thought of his family, especially since it seemed increasingly likely Thomas's plea would be a last request. If Finch brought his best efforts to the task of finding Natalie and Alice, he could close the book on this chapter of his life with a clean conscience. He flipped through the rest of the personal correspondence quickly, looking for anything that might provide him with direction. There was nothing. Then, close to the bottom of a stack of bills, he found another envelope of the same size, written in the same hand. There was no return address, but the card had been postmarked in Manhattan, on June 25, 1974. The flap of the envelope had been previously opened, and inside he found another card, this a reproduction of one of Thomas's more recent works, ironically one of the 'bird pictures,' as Finch had quickly come to think of them. The painting was of a man fishing on a grassy shore, his decapitated head resting on the ground beside him, sitting next to a giant kingfisher with a pole between its wings. Inside the card was a color snapshot of Natalie Kessler, holding a dark-haired toddler in her arms.

The child was a girl. There was nothing written on the back, and the photo wasn't dated. Natalie was standing in front of a tall window, but the background was indistinct and Finch couldn't make out any suggestion of landscape to tell him where the picture might have been taken. He turned his magnifying glass to Natalie, noting the slight fullness of her face, her long hair, straight and parted in the center, and her clothing—a fringed skirt that looked to be suede and a Mexican peasant blouse. Only the style of clothing had changed; Natalie at twenty-eight did not look much different than she had at seventeen. She had posed in a way to show off her figure, the curves of which had only slightly softened with age. She was still unnervingly attractive, but her expression was cold and distant, even with a child in her arms. Or did she look that way because the child she held belonged to Thomas?

Finch could see the resemblance to Thomas in the little girl. They shared few physical traits other than Thomas's long nose and eyelashes, but her expression was definitely his: firm, stubborn, intelligent. Loose, dark curls framed a face that was angular, with a high forehead and cheekbones, and a dash of freckles sprinkled across her nose. Her mouth was the same Cupid's bow as her mother's, though the little girl's lips were pursed in frustration. The eyes were pale, with those heartbreakingly long lashes, and she looked directly at whoever was taking the picture. The child knew her own mind. One hand pushed against Natalie's chest while the other stretched out toward the camera, as if beseeching the photographer to take her away.

Why was Natalie holding the child instead of Alice? Perhaps Alice didn't know the picture was being taken; perhaps it had been her intention to keep the child a secret from Thomas all along, and it was only Natalie who thought he should know of her existence. But that supposition didn't mesh with Finch's mental image of Natalie: her possessive grip on Thomas's shoulder in the main panel of the triptych, her hard look. He doubted those were details painted from imagination. She seemed more the type Thomas favored: women who were strikingly attractive and aloof, and used to being the center of attention in their own right, already accustomed to the thrum of crowds and the flash of cameras that followed Thomas wherever he went.

Alice, on the other hand, seemed a wholly different kind of creature. The Alice in the photograph was pretty in her own sort of way, with her lean frame and long limbs and the mass of wild blond hair, her eyes as pale as glacial ice. But he suspected the greater attraction would have been in the inquisitive tilt of her head, the keenness in her eyes, the refreshing lack of awareness she seemed to have of her own physical presence.

Alice would have been twenty-three when she had the baby. The Kessler girls had been on their own, with little money to speak of. How could she have raised the child? What would she have done for a living? In his initial Internet searches, Stephen had uncovered a school record indicating Alice left the university shortly after starting her graduate degree work in ecology and evolutionary biology in 1972. He hadn't found a reason for her abrupt departure, but Finch imagined even in the early seventies, the private Roman Catholic university she was attending would not have continued providing a scholarship to an unwed mother, no matter how intelligent she may have been.

Still, at twenty-three Alice would have been young and strong. She had a college degree; she would have been able to find work more easily than many. Not an easy life, but the world was full of single mothers who had found ways to manage. That was the head of the coin. The tail was a mirror image of the way Thomas lived now—dingy, damp rooms filled with squalor, the choice between spending available dollars on groceries or on heat. Still, in spite of the fact he had never met her, Finch thought of Alice as being responsible and resourceful. As long as the child was healthy, and with a bit of luck and support from her older sister, no doubt things had turned out all right for everyone involved, with the exception of Thomas.

Finch jotted a few notes—questions, primarily—on the pad he kept in his jacket pocket and tucked both of the photographs back inside their envelopes for safekeeping, envisioning Stephen's reaction when he saw them. The look he imagined on Stephen's face gave him an enormous sense of satisfaction. *Maybe an old dog brings something to the mix after all.* The prospect of having dinner with Stephen suddenly became much more appealing.

By the time Saturday arrived, Finch had worked himself into a state. Despite firmly insisting to Stephen that anything they discovered regarding the paintings was not to be made a topic of dinner conversation, he found himself dialing the younger man's number before he left for Lydia's. Merely alerting Stephen to the existence of the photos, he reasoned, was hardly the same as showing him the pictures between courses, passing them back and forth under cover of Lydia's tablecloth. But there was no answer, just the same odd message on his machine: 'It's me. Stephen. Speak *after* the tone'—the emphasis on *after*, Stephen had explained, because he found it annoying when people said '*at* the tone,' which implied the person leaving the message should try to estimate when the beep was going to occur and start talking at the same moment. Finch hung up without leaving a message.

Holiday music drifted onto the stoop from behind Lydia's door, but when she opened it to invite him in, her face was pale and drawn.

'What's wrong?' Finch asked, but she only shook her head and put him off, staring nervously into the dining room. He heard the high sound of laughter, a giddy, tinkling bell of a noise, and low conversation. 'Is Stephen here already? Am I late? Good grief, has he brought someone with him?'

'No,' she said, not meeting his eyes. 'It's nothing. Let me take your scarf.'

'Lydia?'

'Go on in. I won't be a minute.'

Finch walked into the living room to find his son-in-law handing a glass of wine to a stranger, a woman whose clothes were all a variation of the same tone, beige, and whose platinum hair was swept up in a stiff swirl around her face.

'Dad!' Kevin exclaimed. Finch thought his enthusiasm was tinged with a touch of nervousness. 'I'd like you to meet a colleague of mine from the office. This is Meredith Ripley. She heads up CSR at Brompton Pharmaceuticals.'

'CSR?'

The woman extended her hand. 'So many acronyms these days. I can rarely decipher what anything stands for anymore. Corporate social responsibility. I work for the Brompton Foundation, overseeing some of their charitable initiatives.'

'How nice. That must be very . . . satisfying work.' Finch was completely at sea. What was the woman doing here? And where was Lydia?

'Oh, it is.'

An awkward silence followed, during which he swore he could hear every heartbeat, swallow, and thud of pulse coming from those in the room.

'I was thinking, Dad, it would be good for you and Meredith to meet. Lydia and I are such poor company when you talk about art, and Meredith has been looking to expand the work Brompton does in their Arts for the Schools Program. I thought you could give her some ideas.'

Finch glanced at the woman again, this time estimating her age—certainly older than Kevin, but decidedly younger than himself—the absence of a ring on her hand, her own slight look of unease. *Lydia and I are such poor company*. How dense he'd become. No wonder Lydia appeared distressed. She was likely imagining his reaction.

He arched an eyebrow at Kevin and cleared his throat. 'I'd be delighted,' he said. 'I know a graduate student who has been looking for an outside project. This sounds like a perfect fit.'

There. Satisfactorily dispensed with. No need to mention all the free time he'd have if he was forced to take a sabbatical. Meredith Ripley pulled back from him slightly, her smile tightening, and he felt a trace of guilt until he recognized that after a moment's hesitation she, too, seemed somewhat relieved. Kevin adjourned to the kitchen, offering a transparent excuse, leaving Finch alone with the woman.

'Kevin didn't mention he'd invited me, did he?' She wasn't going to beat around the bush.

He admired that and was sorry if he'd made her uncomfortable. 'It makes no difference. I'm always pleased to meet someone who works with my son-in-law.' It was late to be gallant, but at least no one could fault his manners.

'I have a theory about married people, Professor Finch, having been one myself for quite a time. By nature, they abhor a vacuum. I'm sure your son-in-law meant well. Don't be too hard on him.' Her smile was warmer now, genuine, and she sounded wistful when she mentioned having been married.

'I guess I'm not used to thinking of myself as single yet,' he said.

'A little over a year since you lost your wife?'

Finch wondered what other bits of his dossier Kevin had thought it appropriate to offer up. 'I still feel very married. I imagine I always will.'

'My husband died three years ago. I keep anticipating it

will get easier. There are days I only think of him a few times, usually when I'm doing the strangest things. Taking out the trash, sniffing the milk to see if it's gone bad. Why then, do you suppose? Then there's the other kind of day, when I don't want to get out of bed. I'm sorry, I must be making you uncomfortable. It's just nice to talk with someone who doesn't offer up the standard condolences. *Time is a great healer. You were lucky to have the years together you did.* But here I'm presuming you understand and we don't even know each other.'

'It's all right. I've been on the receiving end of a few of those myself. Were you married long?'

Her eyes were bright, and Finch cursed himself for asking.

'Thirty years. Right out of college. He was a symphony pianist. He proposed to me in the orchestra pit of an empty theater.'

Finch didn't say anything, only nodded. Her husband had been a romantic. He himself had asked Claire to marry him while standing in front of her favorite painting at the Met, Harry Willson Watrous's *The Passing of Summer*. It said a great deal about her, he'd always thought, that she was drawn to a work so quiet on the surface, yet suffused with longing. *Tell me why you like it*, he'd asked, and Claire had replied without hesitation, as if she'd often wondered the same thing, *There's something wonderfully melancholy about it—the cherries in the cocktail glass, the dragonflies hovering in the air. Such a lovely girl, yet she's so lonely. It reminds me there are times to be sad, but you should never search for them, or find them too often.* He fell in love with her exactly then, the whole of him opening in a way he hadn't known was possible.

Meredith Ripley was running her index finger around the rim of her wineglass. She looked close to miserable, and Finch wondered if this would be his fate as well: holidays the polar opposite of what they had once been, days so weighted with solitude he'd lie in bed, unable to move.

'If there was an occasion when talking about your husband over coffee with a friend would help,' he said, 'I would do my utmost not to resort to meaningless drivel.'

'You're kind. I'm guessing you'd say that even if you didn't mean it.'

'I can safely assure you, you're wrong. Never has anyone accused me of being too kind.'

He cornered Lydia in the kitchen, where she'd been hiding, but before he could say anything, she rushed at him, enveloping him in a hug. 'It wasn't my idea.'

'I'm relieved to hear it. If I'm spending too much time here . . .'

'Of course not. Kevin just thought, after our horrible Thanksgiving, both of us seemed so lost without her. I never should have agreed.'

'Lydia, your mother was the love of my life. Not everyone gets to have that. I did. Yes, I miss her, but I'm happier being alone and missing her than pretending not to miss her while being with someone else. Does that ridiculous statement make sense?'

'Yes.'

'Good. Then will you try to dissuade Kevin from further matchmaking attempts on my behalf?'

She nodded, though Finch thought she still looked anxious and upset. Stephen was late, and he hoped she wasn't worrying about him. They pecked at hors d'oeuvres and Finch consumed too many glasses of wine while the four of them waited, the effort of small talk and feigned interest wearing him down. When Meredith began shredding her cocktail napkin, Kevin convinced Lydia they should go ahead and start dinner. What the devil was keeping Stephen? Candlelight turned the surface of the dining room table into a long stretch of dark water. And even though they were in the same room with him, Finch felt an almost insurmountable distance between himself and those he loved.

When the doorbell finally rang, at eight o'clock, Finch groused in his chops, calling to Lydia as she got up from the table, 'If his piece of roast is dry as sawdust, it's his own fault.' But then he heard his daughter's gasp and worried exclamations, and she raced past them into the kitchen, returning with a bag of frozen vegetables just as Stephen entered the room.

'What in the world . . .' Finch started, but stopped when he saw the state of Stephen's face, his lip split, his eyelid drooping, the skin around his socket and cheekbone purpled as a plum.

'I've brought little soaps,' Stephen said, sinking into a chair.

'Good Lord, are you all right? Have you been mugged? I'll call the police.'

Lydia pressed the cold peas against his cheek, and Stephen smiled at Finch while squinting, as if he found the sudden attention pleasing, worth whatever pummeling he'd taken.

'No need,' he said. 'Just a misunderstanding between myself and a previous employee of Murchison. We hold different views of what constitutes an emergency. Did you know some people don't take kindly to one being too detailed over the phone in regard to their specific talents, especially when that call may be being recorded?'

'Are you delirious? You've hit your head, haven't you?'

'Finch,' Stephen said, leaning back in the chair and sighing contentedly as Lydia ministered to his eye, Kevin and Meredith circling in the background. 'I know I'm not supposed to say anything now. But after dinner remind me to tell you—we have to go to Tennessee.'

Finch drove Stephen home after dinner and insisted on walking him to the door of his apartment, concerned about the possibility of concussion. The application of frozen peas had only partially slowed the swelling of Stephen's face, and his enthusiastic response to the discovery of the pictures came out in lisped half sentences. In spite of Stephen's own findings, for once Finch found the majority of praise being sent in his direction.

'You wa genis, Finsh,' Stephen slurred as he slumped into a chair. While Lydia had opted for the equivalent of a cold compress, Kevin had administered several doses of brandy, and it was readily apparent which measure was having the greater impact. Finch covered Stephen with a blanket he'd retrieved from the bedroom floor, and slipped a sofa pillow behind his head. Stephen blinked at the photo he held in his hand, the picture of Natalie and the child. His eyelids fluttered. 'Angwy,' he said, pointing at Natalie.

The accuracy of the word startled him, and Finch remembered what had made him ill the first time he saw the painting: his certainty that Thomas had slept with Natalie, despite her age, and that it had meant something far different to her than it had to him. It was evident in her eyes, in the set of her mouth, in her posture and the position of her fingers on Thomas's shoulder. *Mine*.

Yet it was Alice who was the mother of Thomas's child. Finch eased the photo from Stephen's hand. He looked at it again, at Natalie's cold face, her controlled expression, and wondered if she had somehow found a way to punish them both.

TWELVE

Alice woke up on the couch that had last accommodated Frankie, bent and stiff as a rusted piece of wire. A weak winter sun illuminated the room. For hours last night she'd stared at the papers spread across the table, searching for some explanation that would let her weave this new information into the fabric of her past. Finally she'd given up, making a nest of her arms and burying her head there, too tired to care about the paper clips leaving indentations on her cheek. She gave in to the undertow of memory, letting it drag her down into a dark and dreamless oblivion.

Phinneaus's olive-colored jacket covered the upper half of her body, and she burrowed into it, wanting only to hide awhile longer, her nose against the corduroy collar, smelling the bay of his shaving cream.

He was sitting in a chair on the other side of the room, watching her.

'What time is it?'

'You lost the morning, I'm afraid. It's coming up on one o'clock.'

'Have you been here all night?' Without waiting for an

answer she said, 'You didn't need to stay, Phinneaus. I'm all right.'

'I know you are.'

'Is there coffee?'

'Hardly the breakfast or lunch of champions, but yes, coffee and pills, comin' right up. Maybe some eggs?'

Eggs. She grimaced as her stomach flipped. The apprehension she'd experienced last night had returned as soon as she opened her eyes, and her gut felt full of it. The thought of food was not appealing.

'Humor me,' he said, in response to the face she made. He got out of the chair and walked over to the sofa, his halting gait so familiar she felt it in her own bones. He pushed the hair away from her face with a quick swipe of his thumb before heading to the kitchen, calling for Saisee.

She'd fallen in love with the choreography of his upper body, what remained of a soldier's grace: the ease with which he claimed a buddy, draping an arm across Frankie's shoulder; the effortless swivel of his neck when he heard something behind him; the fluid bend of his elbow. She marveled at the dance of his fingers when he shuffled a deck of cards or pulled the silk from an ear of corn. The speed with which he shouldered his pheasant gun, in one swift, unbroken movement. *Phinneaus be nimble, Phinneaus be quick.*

She reached for the back of the sofa and pulled herself up into a sitting position, groaning as she slipped her arms into the sleeves of his jacket. How long did it take to become a gracious person? One who could accept help and give thanks without being resentful of it? She thought of Frankie, struggling through his schoolwork, wrestling with the onset of early adolescence, trying to come to terms with the fact his mother was in prison and had never shown the slightest interest in hearing from him, or finding out anything about him.

'Thank you, Miss Alice, for trying. Phinneaus says I'm a work in progress,' he'd said the other day, earnest and patient, even though she'd been short with him after reviewing the same story problem for the fifth time—trains coming at each other from opposite directions, one carrying oranges, the other carrying pineapples, an ambrosial disaster in the making. *Maybe that's what I am, too,* she thought. *A work in progress.*

Phinneaus came back into the room carrying a tray and set it on the coffee table. He poured coffee into her mug, one of a set of six bone china pieces with a chintz pattern he'd found at the flea market. He'd wrapped the handle of each of them with a piece of inner tube to act as a sort of cushion. Seeing the cup always lifted her spirits, the combination of materials so idiosyncratic, a veneer of sophistication coupled with the reality of limitation. He fixed her coffee the way she liked it: one healthy pinch of sugar and so much milk he often shook his head before handing it to her, snorting, *why bother?* Over the years they'd learned each other's habits slowly, carefully, with moves as cautious as hunters', taking care to camouflage their concern. She knew he preferred to sit with his right leg to the fireplace. Ever the scrounger, he would scan the For Sale column in the local paper before any other section. He was respectful with the prey he shot, his fingers lingering admiringly on the feathers of a turkey or a nutria pelt. And he was an intent and neutral listener; she was never quite sure what he was thinking until he spoke.

'I take you for granted,' she said.

'You do at that.'

It alarmed her, hearing him agree so easily. 'But I don't mean to.'

'Alice, if this is because of Natalie . . .' He stopped, and she watched him consider the right words to use. 'I'm not going anywhere. I mean, Frankie and I, we're still here.'

She took measure of that. *Frankie and I*. He had allowed them both the safety net of a third party, even if that third party was an eight-year-old boy.

'You're the last one standing, Phinneaus. You've known me longer than anyone else now, except for Saisee, and you know me better than she does.'

'Not quite longer than anyone else.'

Thomas. The moment she'd seen the negative she'd felt him beside her, an old ghost, a shadow stuck to her skin. She couldn't shake him off. She heard his dry laugh ring in her head, felt his breath on the small of her back. She shivered, and it was the trace of his fingers as they trailed over her mouth, his words whispered against the skin at the base of her neck, the taste of brandy resurrected in her throat, her eyes burning from the strength of it. Phinneaus had handed her the strip of negatives and not asked a single question, and in turn, she hadn't volunteered a single answer. Had she imagined the quickly hidden look of disappointment that washed over his face? No. It was a look she'd never seen from him before, and one she'd now have to try to forget.

Thomas was a lifetime ago. She'd kept her memories of him and the cabin separate from everything that came after, and convinced herself it was a kindness that he never knew, that she'd never been able to bring herself to seek him out and tell him. What had become of him, she didn't know. It was Phinneaus who'd thrown her the rope and pulled her out of grief; Phinneaus who'd coaxed her into another life, one guarded step at a time; Phinneaus who'd made her feel her contributions, however small she counted them, were of value. And it was Phinneaus who sat across from her now, staring down at the carpet, the rise and fall of his shoulders so slight she knew he was half-holding his breath, waiting for her to tell him.

'I don't know him, Phinneaus. Not anymore. Not since we came here.'

'It's not my business.'

He said it too quickly, too casually, and if he meant for it to hurt her, it did. She rolled the mug back and forth in her hands, letting the heat slowly thaw them out until she could bend her fingers a little. *I can't do it,* she thought. *I don't want to have to go back and remember all of it, not even for you.* He shifted in the chair, and as if he had disappeared, Alice suddenly saw what it would be like without him, his absence a greater weight than Natalie's and her parents' combined. The panic that gripped her was unbearable, and she wanted to tell him it *was* his business, his more than anyone else's.

'I haven't thanked you yet.'

'I'm happy to pour you a cup of coffee anytime, Alice.'

He wasn't going to make it easy for her. Well, fine. She could be just as stubborn. 'I meant for staying with me last night.'

He shrugged. 'Finding out about the house and Natalie, having to go through her things. It seemed like a lot to take in all at once. I thought it might be better if you weren't alone.' He rubbed his hands back and forth over his knees, something he did, she'd learned, when weighing his options. 'She hasn't been gone long, Alice. Maybe none of this has sunk in for you yet, I don't know. But I'm worried about what will happen when it does.'

The feelings of tenderness she'd felt for him only a moment ago were replaced by anger. 'I don't seem sad enough, is that what you mean? Would you feel better if I dressed in black? Is it ghoulish I'm not flailing on the floor or tearing my clothes? That I don't need a sedative or a tonic? That's what people around here think, isn't it?'

The veins stood out on his neck, and he clenched his jaw, clearly annoyed with her. He stood up and paced back and forth across the living room. 'I don't know which part of that question makes me want to throttle you more. The fact that when you can't deal with your own feelings, it's easier for you to put them off on someone else—or in this case, on an entire town—or that after thirty-five years you're still determined to make yourself an outsider, living on your own little island. Give us some credit, Alice. We may not meet your standards of refinement *around here,* as you so delicately put it, but I imagine we know well enough that people grieve in their own ways. If you'd for once stop worrying about what everyone else thinks and let yourself get close to someone, you might be surprised to find folks understand. You're not the only person in this world who got handed a life different than the one they expected.'

'Is that what you think? I'm feeling sorry for myself? You know that's not true.' They'd never really been angry with each other, and now the feeling was so palpable she could see it flaming between them, a rising red-hot wall. She stuck her chin out. 'I am close to people. I'm close to Saisee. I'm close to Frankie.' She looked through the window at the cheerless yard, the outside world frozen and still, even the birds perched on branches motionless, as if carved from ice. *What would I do without you, Phinneaus?*

'I'm close to you.'

'Are you?' He turned away from her and said quietly, 'Damn you, Alice. When are you going to stop pretending we have all the time in the world?'

It was an honest question. She longed to go backward, to start the day over from the moment she'd opened her eyes. But now they'd said things that made that impossible. She cradled the mug against her chest. He didn't say anything more, but moved over to the couch and sat next to her. She could feel the heat coming off of him, the wash of it stretching toward her, and without intending to, she rested her head on his shoulder, feeling the welcome scratch of his shirt against her cheek, something sharp and real. Would he stay if he knew she was capable of hatred? That sometimes she felt so full of resentment, there wasn't room for anything else? Would he ever want to talk to her again, or would he take Frankie and go, leaving her more alone than she'd been when she first came here?

'Hold your hand up.' He gently took her hand in his and held it in front of them. 'Like this. Bend your wrist and point your fingers and your thumb upward. Now hold it this way for five seconds. Does it hurt?'

She shook her head, wincing, but kept her hand up.

'Now who's lying? That's good enough. We'll do it again later.'

When she looked at him, he only said, 'You haven't been keeping up with your exercises. You know you have to do these every day if you can.'

'I like having the occasional day without being reminded of everything I can't do. Besides, physical therapists don't grow on trees.'

'You've had several of those *occasional days* in a row now, seems to me.'

They were talking around each other, clinging to the safe territory so familiar to both of them: her illness, the lack of finances that forced them to make do. But he hadn't let go of her hand, and in return, Alice sensed something more was required: an admission or confession showing she trusted him, even with her worst self.

'I'm afraid what you'll think of me.'

He whispered into her hair. 'You already know what I think of you.' His voice so tender it made her ache. 'I saw well enough how she treated you, and I should have stopped it. She kept you worried about money, scared about your disease. I watched her pick the words to beat you down same as I picked up a weapon to fight with. But I don't think she knew who she'd be without you.'

'Natalie and I battled with each other for most of our lives, Phinneaus. It's just the way things ended up between us. But it wasn't the ways things started.'

He nodded. 'Go on.'

He was asking her to shed her skin, to display the darkest part of herself. Years of misshapenness had conditioned her to people's eroding manners. The staring no longer bothered her; she only stared back. Let them see the dropped longitudinal arch of her feet and the metatarsal drift of her toes. Let them gawk at the deformities of her hands, the swan neck of her fingers, the dinner fork of her wrists, such whimsical descriptions for her state of disrepair. All that was tolerable when she could pretend a pristine interior, unblemished by the dark spot of a nasty thought, a malignant wish.

She looked down at her hands, the tips of his fingers loosely threaded through hers. 'It's so tempting to make everything Natalie's fault now. But she didn't force me to stay. After a while, it was just easier to be afraid. I got comfortable letting other people do everything for me, and then at some point, I stopped trying to figure out how to do things for myself. How could you—how could anyone—want to be with someone like that? But Natalie stayed. Natalie was always here.'

'The devil you know?'

'I kept hoping there was something keeping us together, that underneath it all, we still knew we could count on each other. That we loved each other. I don't think I believe that's true anymore. Maybe all these years just boiled everything down to jealousy and hate.'

'There's no law says you're required to love your kin, Alice.'

'All I know is, we turned into each other's best excuse for not doing the things we were afraid of. Maybe you're right; maybe it just hasn't hit me yet. I only know everything feels off balance without her.'

She whispered the rest of her words into the front of his shirt, trying to diffuse their meaning. 'The odds were never in my favor to be the last one. It's horrible to realize there's no one left who knew you at the beginning; no one to see how you've turned out, good or bad.' She sensed Natalie's presence withdraw from the room, as if her sister were collecting the small dust of herself left behind. 'I'm sorry for her, Phinneaus. I'm sorry she never had what she wanted. Maybe if she had, she'd have been a different person. Maybe I'd have been a different person then, too.'

She felt such ugliness, not physical for once, but a black hole swallowing her from the inside. 'Something happened at the lake that summer, after Natalie came back. I blamed her for it, at least in part. She was always the one people paid attention to, the one everybody wanted. When I found out what she'd done, it was easy enough to hate her. But it doesn't carry the same weight, does it, thinking you hate someone when you're a child? You can't understand until you're older what people are really capable of.'

'So now she's blameless?'

Alice shook her head. 'No. But at some point I realized I wouldn't want to trade places with her, not even if it meant having her looks, her good health. No one took her seriously. Natalie was so pretty—what else did she need to do? All that attention conditioned her to a certain sort of life. She was never going to eat her lunch out of a paper bag, or take a bus, or share a walk-up with four other girls. And the terms of the trust our parents set up were very specific. There wasn't much money, but what was there was designated for my medical care, with Natalie as trustee. It must have been their way of ensuring she wouldn't be burdened, but only because they assumed she'd marry, and have means of her own. So we were stuck together, the two of us. I always felt like half of my life was hers, but I wonder if she didn't feel that half my disease was hers, too; so much in her life had to be worked around me, around what I could and couldn't do.'

Alice sat up and wiped a hand across her face. 'Then I made it worse. I had something Natalie never could. Even if only for a minute. She couldn't forgive me for that.'

'What do you mean?' His fingers traced careful circles on the back of her neck, under the weight of her hair. A door opened, and she slipped backward, her history racing past.

'I was home for Christmas break my sophomore year. Natalie was engaged to someone—I don't remember who; I'm not sure I ever met him—then suddenly she wasn't. No one would tell me what happened. I remember being in the kitchen with my mother and seeing her standing at the sink, washing the same dish over and over, staring into the water. Eventually she said it was a misunderstanding, two people who hadn't known what they wanted. Better forgotten.

'I heard the two of them talking later, in Natalie's bedroom. I'd left one of my medications downstairs, and when I came back up, I heard Natalie saying she never should have told him, that she knew no one would want her once they found out. She said it was my mother's fault. Hers and my father's. She sounded so desperate; it was painful just to hear her voice. My mother left the bedroom, crying. She saw me standing there but waved me away.

'The next morning I was packing to go back. My mother came into my room and sat down on the bed next to my suitcase. She started folding my clothes, the way she did when I was little. She didn't say anything for a long time. Then she picked up one of my blouses and held it against her mouth, shaking. She wouldn't let me touch her. Once she stopped crying, she told me Natalie had gotten an infection years earlier and would never be able to have children of her own. She was talking so softly I could barely hear her. Then she folded the blouse again and smoothed out the wrinkles with the back of her hand. 'I'm good at this part, aren't I?' she asked. She laid the blouse in the suitcase, and left. We never talked about it again. She was dead before another year went by.'

Alice sat up and took a sip of her coffee, gone cold and bitter, and forced herself to swallow. 'Natalie must have gotten the infection after she had the abortion. I can understand it now, why she felt the way she did. It wasn't only because of my RA.'

'You mean, because you got pregnant?' He was still holding on to her hand. She closed her eyes and turned away from him, giving him the chance to let her go.

'Yes.'

'And the other picture? The one of you?'

It was like being a wounded bird in a box: trapped, everything dark. She couldn't see. All she could hear was the sound of her own heart beating its way out of her chest, so desperate to be away. Yet someone's hands held her carefully, gently, not wanting to do more damage. She could barely feel him holding her, began to wonder if it was her imagination and she was alone; but then he started to murmur, so quietly, and she knew he was still there. Alice took a deep breath and closed her eyes.

'There was a storm.'

They were in the attic, the three of them, trying not to listen to the wind tearing the house away. It wanted to get in. Like something rabid, it was shrieking and moaning, throwing things at them: bricks, trees, whatever it could find. She could hear the squeal of nails being pulled from wood and the steady slosh of water against the foundation of the house, as if they'd already lost their moorings and been set adrift.

All morning the forecasters had reported on the tortured path of Agnes; first a hurricane, then merely a depression, and finally, unexpectedly, back to tropical storm when it combined with a nontropical low, exploding over Pennsylvania. It sent the Genesee, the Canisteo, and the Chemung over their banks; swelled the Chesapeake and the Susquehanna; threatened to overtop the Conowingo Dam; swept away train tracks, then houses, then people. But it was never supposed to make it so far north.

Natalie threatened Therese, who had been ready to abandon her longtime charges and head for higher ground. Between the two of them, they'd managed to haul Alice up the stairs once they realized water was coming into the basement. Alice lay on a thin quilt, propped between two pillows, sensing the movement of humid air as Natalie paced in the dark, the electricity long gone. She tried to focus on the ragged sound of her breathing, her own panting preferable to the unrelenting bellow of the storm.

'You have to call the doctor.'

Natalie's hair was pulled back in a sweaty knot, and even

in the milky beam of the flashlight, Alice could see red flowering in her face. She wiped a hand across her forehead, then crouched down next to Alice, pulling a blanket up over her midsection. 'And how am I supposed to do that, Alice? It's a hurricane. Listen to me.' She fought off Alice's grasping hands. 'No, listen to me. The phone lines are down. No one's coming. It's just us.'

Her back was going to break into pieces, she was sure of it. Everything inside of her was on the verge of exploding, and all she could think was *Yes, let it. Let me blow apart into a million bits, as long as the baby is all right.*

'Natalie, promise.' She willed all the strength she had into her hand and grabbed her sister's arm with a death grip, squeezing it through the surprise of another contraction. 'Don't let anything happen to my baby. Promise.'

'Stop talking. Therese knows what to do. She's done this before, haven't you, Therese?' Therese nodded, but her eyes were static with fear. Alice could see Natalie's pale fingers fanned across Therese's upper arm, the three of them linked together. *We're like a barrel of monkeys,* she thought, sliding into delirium.

'Promise. *Kaboutermannekes.*'

'Alice.' Natalie grabbed her by the shoulders and shook her hard. 'Stop talking gibberish or I swear I'm going to throw something. I can't think.'

'Don't let our souls be lost. Promise.'

'You need to sit up. Bite down on this and let go of my arm.'

Natalie was behind her then, holding her up, and there was a damp towel that tasted of something medicinal, the alcohol burn of it running down the back of her throat. She felt Therese's hands slide under the blanket and over her belly.

'Don't push until Therese says to, Alice. Do you hear me?'
She nodded and bit down hard on the towel.

'*Tijeras,*' Therese said. *Scissors.*

Alice fought to get away from them then, from everything, clawing at anything within her reach.

Natalie pulled her arm back and slapped her across the face, screaming, 'Damn it, Alice! It's for later. For the cord. You've got to calm down. You're going to hurt the baby if you keep this up. Understand?'

Then there was a pain so sharp it had its own teeth, its own breath, and in its wake, a monstrous cracking noise in her head that sped down the length of her spine like a bullet, setting each of her nerves on fire as it passed. Her body glowed like a hot coal, orange to white, then started shaking, trying to loose itself from her center. Some other force was in charge of her now, a force that made her bend and buckle, and welled up in her throat, pushing out of her with a howl to match the storm. *The house is coming down,* she thought. *The house is falling down around us.* And even though she was sure her eyes were open, no matter where she looked, she could see only black.

'I had a girl.'

She was caught in a splice of time. Phinneaus rocked her with the steady rhythm of a metronome, his arms a safe haven from the spell of the attic that reached to pull her back. The storm had passed, the wind reduced to whispers. She couldn't understand what was being said; the words were too fuzzy and indistinct to interpret, but someone there needed her. She heard the sharp cry of a bird, then nothing.

'A girl. Tell me what you called her.'

'I wanted to call her Sophia.'

'Sophia Kessler. I like the sound of it. You would have

been a good mother, Alice. I'm sure of it.' He stroked her hair, and she felt the swirling specks of memory congeal and settle back into their usual place, a safe distance away, their outline hazed by the accumulation of years.

'When I woke up I was in a hospital.' She remembered the room, so white it seemed to reverberate. 'There was an older woman in the bed next to mine, with her leg in a cast. She cried in her sleep. I understood what it meant. I wasn't in the maternity ward.' She'd asked for the baby, and the nurse, young and inexperienced, had looked away for a moment to compose her face before turning back again, smiling as she tucked in the sheets. *Someone will be in to talk to you.*

'After that, I only wanted sleep. I chased after it, prayed for it. The doctors were very accommodating with their drugs.'

She pulled her hands away from him and stuffed them into the pockets of his jacket. It was too much—this touching, the telling. A low sun glazed the window. At some point it had become late afternoon.

'Natalie explained everything later, once I was home. She was sitting in a chair next to the bed. She kept her hands on the arms of the chair. She didn't touch me. She told me when Therese delivered the baby, it was stillborn. I said I'd seen her. I'd held her in my hands. She was moving. Natalie just kept shaking her head.'

You're just remembering it the way you want to, Alice.

But I heard her. I heard Sophia crying in the attic.

Only because you wanted to.

'Natalie had taken care of everything by then. She drove me to the cemetery the next day, showed me the grave under an oak. There was a bench nearby. I wanted to sit there, but it was raining so hard we couldn't get out of the car. She told me she'd chosen something for the headstone, part of a verse from Psalm eighty-four—'Yea, the sparrow hath found an house.' I never got to see it; the headstone was still being engraved.'

"And the swallow a nest for herself.' That was one of my mother's favorite psalms,' he said.

'I thought it was kind of her, to try to pick something meaningful for me. I was grateful for that. When we got back to the house, she gave me all of my medicine and watched while I took it. As I was falling asleep, she told me she'd sold the house. That we'd be leaving in two days.'

Phinneaus stood up and walked over to the corner window, looking out at the yard. Alice watched as he rested his open palm against the glass, the breathing aura of fog that flared around it. His silhouette was a pillar holding up the entire room.

'What about the father. Did he know?'

She'd been waiting for him to ask. She kept her head down and didn't say anything. Then she got up from the sofa and walked to the window to stand next to him. She put a hand on his shoulder and gave a little tug until he faced her, then shook her head. 'No. He never knew anything about it.' She paused and let go of him. 'Do you hate me?'

He looked away from her but shook his head. 'No. But if it was me, I'd have wanted to know.'

'He wasn't you.' It wasn't the pardon she'd hoped for, but it was what she deserved. 'I don't know what he would have thought, but I should have given him the chance to tell me.'

'I'm not judging you, Alice. I imagine you had your reasons.'

'I'm not the person I was then.'

'None of us is.' He folded her up in his arms, and she

leaned into him, overcome with tiredness, barely able to stand on her own feet. *I could stay just here,* she thought, *never moving again and I'd be happy.*

'What about the other woman? You said her name was Therese?'

She rested her head against the crook of his neck. 'I never saw her after the night of the storm. Natalie let her go. She said she didn't think I'd want to see her again. Not after what happened.'

'What was Therese's last name?'

'Something with a *G*. Garza, I think.'

'She'd been with you a long time?'

'Ever since I got sick when I was young. She came in twice a week to help with the housework after I was diagnosed. It was too much for my mother to handle, between all of my doctors' appointments, and her social commitments. Why are you asking?'

'No reason, really.' He bent his head and whispered in her ear, 'You're tired. It's been a long afternoon and I need to check on Frankie. The boy's getting too sly for his own good. Who knows what he's been up to today.'

'That boy is a sweet and lovely child, which you well know.' She pressed her lips to the back of his hand and laughed at the look of shock that spread across his face, the tinge of delight. 'Phinneaus Lapine, I believe you are blushing.'

'You're making me forget there's anything outside of this room.'

'What was it you said to me earlier? That you were still here? I'm not going anywhere, either.'

He looked at her, his face marked with caution. 'I hope that's true.'

It was strange to sleep without the wish of being someone else. Like the hoary frost of winter that iced the evergreens, her skin cloaked her bones differently, fitting her well. That was the gift he'd given her. Her pillow was sweet with lavender, the sheets cool. Instead of pinning her hair up, she fell back onto the bed and let it float around her, a wild mess of tangle and curl. There was an unaccustomed comfort in being only herself.

In the morning she came into the bright kitchen, ravenous, and surprised Saisee by asking for green tea and a second biscuit.

'Do I know you?' Saisee asked, peering over the rim of her glasses. She laid out a column of morning pills for Alice to swallow and put the kettle on the stove, a crock of honey on the kitchen table. 'Mr. Phinneaus said if it's all right by you, he'd be over later.'

'When did he call? I didn't hear the phone.'

'Did I say he called? I did not. He showed up early this morning, not long after I got here, and went straight on into the dining room, workin' on all those papers of yours. Whole dining room table's covered with 'em. I don't know where we're gonna have supper.' She beat a wooden spoon against the side of her thigh and arched her eyebrows.

Alice went into the dining room. Saisee was right. The table was blanketed with neat stacks of papers, arranged edge to edge, each stack topped off with an index card bearing a brief description of its contents. *Bills. Bank statements. Lease agreement. Receipts. Steele and Greene.* She circled the table, wondering how he'd managed to do all of this in the space of a few hours. A marvel of orderliness. At the center of the table, the hub to his many spokes, he'd set his yellow legal pad. There were two questions written across the top of the page in Phinneaus's precise script: 'T. Garza?'

and 'ASK?' A chill ran up the center of her back. She returned to the kitchen to finish her breakfast, but she'd lost interest in eating the second biscuit and couldn't keep from glancing at the table in the other room. The tune she'd been humming in her head dissolved and seeped away.

'Saisee, did you bring everything down from upstairs?'

'Her clothes are still up there. All those perfume bottles. No room for 'em anywhere else. I only brought down what papers I could find, like Mr. Phinneaus said to. You lookin' for something in particular?'

Did she expect there to be something addressed to her? A letter of apology, an acknowledgment that however their relationship had evolved, the blame was theirs to share? That wouldn't have been like Natalie, who'd remained resolute in her detachment. 'I guess not,' Alice said.

There was a rap on the door, and Phinneaus swept into the room, stomping his boots on the mat under Saisee's watchful eye.

'Good morning.' He came over to Alice and kissed her lightly on the cheek. His lips were cool as paper and carried a hint of the outdoor chill. 'You slept well?'

Daylight drew the apparent change in their relationship with a deft stroke. Saisee cleared her throat and went upstairs, but not before favoring Alice with a knowing smile that reddened her face. Manners aside, the lack of space between them made it clear something had shifted since the previous day. She leaned back in her chair, not yet used to such immediate closeness. 'I slept very well, thank you.'

He seemed not to notice, clearly distracted by his own thoughts. 'Good. You're done eating?' He gestured toward the half-moon of biscuit left on her plate and the tepid remains of her tea. 'I need you to look at something.'

He hustled her from the kitchen, pulled a chair out from the dining room table, and nudged it toward her. She sat down and folded her arms in front of her chest, wishing she'd stayed in bed longer.

Phinneaus began his usual pacing. 'Alice, yesterday you said you thought the name of the housekeeper who worked for your family was Therese Garza, didn't you? And that Natalie let her go after the storm?'

She nodded. 'Phinneaus, what is it?'

'I feel like I'm snooping into something that's none of my business, but you did ask for my help in looking over your expenses.'

'I know I did. And I appreciate it. I don't suppose you've discovered millions of dollars stashed somewhere, have you?'

He ignored her attempt at levity. 'The night before last, I told you it looked like the property in Connecticut had never been sold, that your house was being rented through a property management company, Steele and Greene. When I went through Natalie's bank statements, I found out she was receiving deposits into her checking account once a month.'

'Maybe those were from her job.'

'I don't think so. There were other deposits made every two weeks. Natalie wasn't a salaried employee; her checks varied a little from one pay period to the next depending on the month and the number of days she worked. These deposits were made by a bank in New York, and they were always for the same amount. But that's not what's interesting.'

'No?' She felt a prick of annoyance at the word *interesting* and sat up straighter in the chair. All of this was fine for him. He had the suspicion of something undetonated and was in his element, cautiously digging away the soil to unearth it, while schooling her in his plan of attack, undaunted by any bones he might run across. But those bones belonged to her family, not his. And if Natalie had found a way to make some extra money, what difference did it make now?

Phinneaus took his reading glasses out of his shirt pocket and frowned at the stack of ledgers piled on the table, tapping his pencil against them. 'For the past thirty-five years, from September of 'seventy-two through this past September, Natalie wrote a check once a month to Steele and Greene, always in the same amount.'

He paused and turned to her. She was alarmed to see his look had changed from excitement to one of both pity and concern, as though he was trying to gauge how what he was going to say would affect her.

'There's a notation in these ledgers next to every one of the checks dated from September of 1972 through June of 1990—eighteen years. Always the same notation: 'ASK—T. Garza.' Therese Garza. But starting in July of 1990 and through this September, the notation changed to just 'ASK.' Why would Natalie be sending checks to Therese Garza every month for eighteen years? And why would she be sending them through the company that's renting out your house?'

'It has to be a mistake.'

'For thirty-five years?' Phinneaus sat down next to her and pushed the stack of ledgers toward her. 'I don't think so.'

His tone had modulated, his voice the rational and measured one he used when trying to explain life's ponderous questions to Frankie: why evil occasionally seemed to win out over good; how things tended to equal out in the end; why you couldn't make people change even when it was for their own good, they had to want to change themselves. She realized Phinneaus was trying, in the only way he knew how, to tell her something very bad, something neither of them was going to be able to fix. Her breath came faster, and she felt it moving up high in her lungs. She wanted to hold it there, to stop what came next.

'Alice, do you hear me?'

What she heard was a pounding ocean in her ears, a field of static obscuring all logical thought. *Breathe,* she thought. *Just breathe.*

'Maybe Natalie felt guilty for letting her go.'

Phinneaus held out his hand, and when she didn't move he covered both of hers with his. 'I think it must have been for something else.'

'What else? And 'Ask Therese'? Ask Therese what?' She shook him off and stood up, relieved her legs still functioned even if her lungs were letting her down. She felt the urge to knock all of his carefully arranged papers off the table. 'Neither of us may have thought very highly of her, Phinneaus, but it sounds like you're suggesting Natalie was involved in something criminal. That's not possible. There has to be a simple explanation for this.'

'There is. It's just I don't think you're going to want to hear it.'

'Try me.' She couldn't look at him. She'd already made up her mind whatever he said wasn't going to be true.

'All right.' He pulled the legal tablet from the center of the table and turned over the first page. Out of the corner of her eye she saw he'd drawn an elaborate diagram—paragraphs and arrows, question marks and suppositions. He'd already worked the whole thing out in his head.

'I don't think Natalie told you the truth. Not about why you had to leave Connecticut, not about what happened that night in the attic. Not even about the grave she took you to see that day it was raining. I think something else happened. And I think Therese and Natalie were the only two people who knew anything about it.'

Her nose was flooded with the scent of something sickly sweet, and she choked on it, gasping for air. She was drowning, drowning on land, and Phinneaus was just standing there, watching her go down. The simplest thing in the world would be to tell him to stop right now. She could think the word, but could not get her lips to form it.

He pulled her back down onto the chair. 'I know this is hurting you. And I'm sorry to be the one doing it.'

'Then don't.'

'Alice, you need to hear the rest of this. Natalie kept meticulous records. I'm guessing she needed documentation for the insurance company regarding all your medications, blood work, X-rays, your visits to your rheumatologist. Which makes sense, considering the terms of the trust would have required her to document any expenses before receiving disbursements. But there's absolutely nothing documented regarding your pregnancy. You saw a doctor, didn't you?'

'Of course I saw a doctor.'

'But there aren't records of any visits to an obstetrician. There's no record of a hospital stay; no receipts for pain prescriptions, antibiotics. There's nothing.' His voice dropped, and he looked away from her. 'There's no certificate of still-birth, and there's no record of any payment to a cemetery.'

'You mean it's as if I was never pregnant.'

'Yes. At least, I think that's how Natalie wanted it to look.' He shuffled through another stack of papers and brought out an envelope, hesitating before he handed it to her. 'I'm guessing her bitterness caused her to do something even she couldn't imagine, Alice. And then after the fact, she just couldn't find a way to undo what she'd done. I found this with her papers.'

It was a business envelope, a standard number 10 in ivory with 'Steele and Greene Property Management' printed on the back flap in dark ink and directly below, a return address in Hartford. It was heavy when she took it from him; a cotton bond, woven, with a watermark. The weight of fine stationery. Her mother had always had good stationery: response cards, envelopes in two sizes, creamy standard sheets with her initials, raised and linked at the top. She'd opened all of her mail with a sterling letter opener, as if each piece of correspondence deserved its own small ceremony. Alice turned the envelope over and saw who it was addressed to: *Agnete S. Kessler*. ASK. Agnete. Natalie had named her after the storm.

The envelope dropped from her hand and lay faceup on the carpet at her feet. An address in Santa Fe, New Mexico. The words 'Return to Sender' followed by three exclamation points, written emphatically in black and underlined three times. *Someone should pick that up*, she thought. But she couldn't move.

It was too much to comprehend, not that she could understand it any better in another ten minutes, or ten days, or even a year. It was inconceivable that her sister—with whom she shared blood, DNA, history—might be the architect of her suffering, her slow unraveling. And yet Alice could conceive of it, now, when faced with a room full of evidence. Her mouth opened, and she turned to Phinneaus, but her voice had already floated away from her, beyond this room and toward the west, calling out for a grown woman who might be her daughter.

So she was someone's mother, but she was not. And hadn't been for thirty-five years. Mother. But evidently not the sort who would know, instinctively, her own daughter was alive. She felt a horrifying kinship with Frankie's mother in jail, knowing him yet uninterested in the circumstances of her son's life, his small triumphs, his ongoing battles. Were they that different? How was it possible she'd accepted everything Natalie told her, every detail, every lie? She'd allowed grief to make her slow and stupid.

Phinneaus picked up the envelope from the floor. 'Alice, we don't know anything for sure.'

'You wouldn't have told me any of this if you weren't sure. You believe she's alive, don't you? And that Natalie was hiding her from me all this time.'

'For as long as I've known you, Natalie's gone away twice a year, for about two weeks at a time. From what I remember, she left right before Thanksgiving the first year you were living here, and then went away again in the spring. Same thing every year after that.'

'But those were vacations. She went to New York to visit friends. New Orleans for Mardi Gras. California for . . .' Her voice trailed off.

'Four weeks of vacation every year? On what she was making at the bank?' Phinneaus shook his head. 'And what friends would she be visiting, Alice? She was in New York, but I think she must have been seeing someone at Steele and Greene when she was there. I couldn't find much in her papers about the company, but there was one signature from the firm on a lease document.' He looked at his notes. 'Have you ever heard of a George Reston, Jr.?'

It was like a building coming down, this collapse. The last hope she harbored that Phinneaus might be wrong, that there could be some other explanation, shattered and turned to dust. She pictured Natalie's face as her sister lay on the carpet, clutching her hand, her look of surprise and regret. Alice had always considered herself the smart one, but as it turned out, she'd been the one most easily fooled. She'd underestimated George's capacity for cruelty and how desperately he wanted to win Natalie's affection.

What had they cost Natalie, she wondered, favors of such magnitude? She could only guess. All she really wanted now was for Phinneaus to help her find George Reston. To hunt him down and then leave her alone with him in a locked room. She had nothing more to lose.

Phinneaus was still talking, but it was little more than a buzz in her ear.

'I checked Natalie's credit card statements. There are airline charges for tickets to New York, and then a day or two later, another flight to Albuquerque. I found charges from a car rental company, too, but no hotel charges. She must have stayed with them.'

'Them?'

He cleared his throat. 'Therese and Agnete.'

She struggled to pay attention. 'Why would Natalie leave a trail for someone to follow? Wouldn't she pay cash for everything if she didn't want anyone to know where she was going?'

'Have you been upstairs in this house since the two of you moved in? Who was there to go through her things? Saisee? Maybe she felt sure you'd never see any of this. Or maybe Natalie wanted to be found out. I don't know.'

Alice gestured toward the envelope, still in Phinneaus's hand. 'This letter, is there anything after that?'

'Not that I've been able to find. But Natalie did have tickets. They were for October twentieth.'

'The last letter was returned.'

'Yes.' He handed her the envelope.

'The postmark is from two months ago. She could be anywhere by now.'

Phinneaus was circling the table again, gathering things

up. 'I suppose she could. But it seems like the best place to start.'

'To start?'

'Looking for her. So you can find her and tell her the truth. There's no knowing what Natalie might have told her. She's got to understand you didn't . . .' He stopped when he noticed Alice shaking her head.

She'd been afraid she would disappoint him at some point; he thought too much of her. She just hadn't anticipated these would be the circumstances of that disappointment. She'd thought it might be with the offer of her body, when that came, although they'd both reached an age where perfection would be more intimidating than alluring. This was who he was, an organizer, a resolver of problems. Nothing was more satisfying to him than the offer of solutions. But this wasn't anything he could fix for her. He was assuming they wanted the same things, dreamt the same dreams. And now he would realize he didn't know her at all.

'I need some time to think, Phinneaus. I appreciate everything you've done, but I want to be alone for a while.'

'You're afraid.'

Of course I am. Stop asking me to do things I can't do. She pulled her sweater tighter around her. 'I need some time.'

'Alice, Natalie's gone. The only person you're at war with now is yourself. Let me help you.'

She shook her head and stumbled away from him, retreating to her bedroom. She locked the door behind her, an action completely unnecessary and meant more to keep her in than him out. But the house, old and poorly insulated, continually gave itself away. She knew he would hear the turn of the bolt and be offended, and she stood waiting with her forehead pressed against the doorframe, perfectly still.

It was only another minute before she heard the kitchen door slam.

Saisee had already cleaned her room. The bed, so comfortable last night, looked orderly and sterile, the pillows stacked against each other, the sheets pulled tight and tucked into crisp corners beneath the blanket. She sat down on the edge of it and pulled her hair back, knotting it loosely at her neck. There was no way to make him understand.

How many times had she sat on this bed and smoothed her imaginary daughter's hair, or dragged a thumb across the furrow between her brows? How many years had she sung a silent 'Happy Birthday,' imagined what school clothes to set out for the first day, written down a child's Christmas list? When the students she tutored gathered in the dining room for their lessons, clustered together with their chittering voices, their fidgeting, their anxious glances at each other's notes, hadn't she counted her daughter's head among theirs? All of it pretend. She was a pretend parent, even in her attentions to the children she taught. She had them for an hour or two, then released them and like homing pigeons they flew back to their nests, any thought of her forgotten until the next time they walked into her house.

Phinneaus was right, of course. She was a coward. If her daughter had known her from the start, things might be different. It wouldn't seem strange to have a mother who moved at a turtle's pace on a good day, and didn't walk at all on a bad one. She'd think of her mother's swollen joints no differently than the bloated plastic snap-and-lock beads she would have pushed together and pulled apart as a toddler. All that time spent resting in bed would have included fairy tales and poetry, crossword puzzles and Chinese checkers. The child's arms would be strong, her fingers limber.

But that hadn't happened. There seemed to be no upside

in throwing herself into a stranger's life now, rather, a woman's life. At thirty-five, her daughter was an adult. Alice's imagination carried her only to the point of Agnete as an adolescent; she didn't try to picture the woman her daughter had become, fearful of seeing the legacy of her own genes passed on. Natalie was dead, but she had won.

There was the whole day left in front of her. She couldn't sleep. Walking the perimeter of the hooked rug again seemed equally useless. She left the refuge of her bedroom and took her coat from the back hall, pulled on mittens, and wrapped a scarf across the bottom of her face. The air outside was crisp with the scoured scent of winter. She looked down as she walked, watching for cracks in the sidewalk, for the treacherous spiny fruits of sweet gum, for patches of ice. While most people learned their neighborhood by the houses they passed, the people they waved to, Alice had learned hers by looking up and down. She could tell where she was by an abandoned nest in a tree, by the odd pits in the sidewalk cement, by the shabby brick border that contained Mrs. Deacon's roses, and the trowel stuck halfway in the ground near the edge of the church driveway, marking something unnamed.

At some point during the years the town had stopped being a way station and turned into her home. It claimed her in spite of her efforts to remain isolated, her attempts to keep herself away from judgment, speculation, and pity, the thought of the last especially repugnant. But Saisee, Frankie, and Phinneaus dismantled her defenses. They threw down casual crumbs for her to follow, luring her out of hiding and into the world. They brought in tantalizing threads of gossip and took out with them evidence of her commonness, the small seeds they planted to establish her not as ghost but as flesh and blood—*Alice caught Frankie's cold; Alice*

*loved the recipe for Mrs. Whittaker's corn bread; Alice said she
thought the PTA should have a fund-raiser to get new books for
the school library.* She had done nothing to deserve them.
And Phinneaus? Already her hand missed the thin, worn
flannel of his shirt, her face the scratch of his day-old beard.

She circled the block twice, letting everything inside of
her tick down until her feet were too heavy to lift and the
air too heavy to breathe. When she came back in the house,
Saisee had lunch waiting: hot tea, beef and vegetable stew,
and a plate of crackers with a relish dish of pimento cheese.
The housekeeper stood with her back to the sink, her arms
folded in front of her, her eyebrows raised as if waiting for
an excuse.

Alice looked at her friend. 'You know, don't you?'

'I don't know what you're talkin' 'bout.'

'The pimento cheese gave you away. The only time you
make it for me is when you're trying to coerce me into doing
something I don't want to.'

Saisee sniffed. 'Not my fault these walls are so thin.'

Alice pushed the food aside and laid her head on the
table.

'You gonna eat that perfectly good lunch I made?'

'Not hungry.'

Saisee slapped her hand against her side, and Alice jumped.
'Don't go makin' me any madder at you than I already am.
Listen to me now. It's not for you to decide how somebody
else is gonna feel about you. Whether they gonna want you
or not. That girl deserves . . .'

'She's not a girl anymore, Saisee.'

'You know what I mean. This person deserves to know
what happened.'

'Why? Because it absolves me? And what about her?
Natalie went to see her twice a year, Saisee, ever since she

was a baby. Agnete must have loved her. I doubt she even knows Natalie's gone. How can I tear their relationship down, if it's just to force a place for myself in her life? Would I be any less cruel than Natalie?'

'You never once tore down Miss Natalie when she was alive. I don't suppose you have to do it now. Truth will out. Always does.' Saisee sat down next to her. 'You tellin' me you don't want to see your own girl?'

See. That was the word that tripped the switch and started the machinations. She wouldn't actually have to say anything to Agnete. If there was some way to find her, wouldn't it do just to see her face, to stand close enough to feel the echo of her walk, to memorize the tilt of her head, the curve of her fingers? It was equal parts subterfuge and deceit—the sort of thing Natalie would have done. But the idea had already taken on a life of its own and was running rampant in her brain, stoking a small, steady flame at her core. *I could see my daughter.*

THIRTEEN

The sky was purple when she looked out the window of the train, somewhere in the middle of Kansas, a state wider than she would have imagined. Phinneaus had driven her south the hour to Newbern to catch the 58 City of New Orleans and waited with her, both of them shifting back and forth on a hard bench in the depot, until she boarded the train shortly after midnight. They were talked out, having spent much of the previous week arguing, first about her insistence on going alone and second, about her chosen means of transportation. All of the squabbling and wheedling had left them done in, and she worried about him driving back so late, as tired as he was, but he was still too angry with her to act sensibly, and she didn't have the strength to fight another battle. Once she found her seat in the coach car and the attendant put her bags up, she slept through most of the eight and half hours to Chicago. Then there was a six-hour wait at Union Station before boarding the Southwest Chief to Lamy, fifteen miles south of Santa Fe. She slept through that, too, unconcerned with what she looked like, or whether anyone would try to take her bags or knock her over the head. It was so long since she'd been reckless she scarcely recognized the feeling. It felt oddly liberating to test her physical limits after such a long time.

'This is ridiculous,' Phinneaus had said. 'You should be flying. I don't know why you won't let me get you a ticket. You could be there in four hours instead of forty.'

'Maybe I don't want to be there in four hours.'

'No, you'd rather jostle your aching joints around for a couple of days. That makes perfect sense. Alice, you can't do this.'

She'd wished for the ability to hit something, hard, without her body suffering the repercussions, understanding the *something* would be him. 'Don't. That's what Natalie would have said, had I ever given her reason to. You can't do everything for me, Phinneaus.'

He'd looked shell-shocked, and she was almost sorry she'd said it. Comparing him to her sister was inexcusable, but in this case it was true.

'Except for the hour's drive to the physical therapist's office, I haven't really traveled anywhere since college. I can't deal with getting on a plane in one state, and just a few hours later, getting off five states away. I need more time to figure this out in my head before I get there.' She'd felt guilty saying it, knowing the implication was that she planned to meet Agnete and talk to her. In reality, finding her was the only challenge she'd actually considered.

At the station in Newbern, he'd grabbed her arm, making a last-ditch effort to get her to change her mind. His skin was pale and the hollows under his eyes a faint purple. 'Alice, I've pushed you into this. Even the doctor said it probably wasn't a good idea for you to go alone. Of all the things to be stubborn about, please don't choose this.'

'Probably.' She was giving a lot of weight to that one word. 'Phinneaus, you have to let me do this my way. I'll call you when I get to the hotel in Santa Fe. I promise I'll be fine.' *And if I'm not, at least you won't have to see it.*

An odd time to become an optimist, she realized, swaying back and forth in the Sightseer Lounge. She'd planned to sleep her way across the plains, but her internal clock had other ideas, so she stared out the long window, seeing nothing in the dark but her own reflection. She'd never been good at sleeping when she was supposed to, not since she'd been a little girl. Always up before the sun, lying in bed and listening to the house come slowly back to life, its predawn creaks and groans so different from those when it settled into itself at night. Did Agnete have the same habit? Not something she was likely find out, only watching her from a distance.

On the surface, the plan was simple enough. Barring any complications, she'd be in Lamy in the early afternoon and after a brief shuttle ride, arrive at her hotel in Santa Fe. She'd rest for a few hours, have an early dinner, get a good night's sleep, and then, in the morning, take a cab to the address on the returned envelope in hopes of finding out where Agnete had gone. That was the extent of it. She'd been aware from the beginning there were several inherent flaws in the plan, and Phinneaus was probably aware of it, too, one reason he'd been dead set against her traveling on her own. Inquiring after her daughter's whereabouts was in itself problematic. Who would she ask? Neighbors? She pictured herself going door-to-door, asking if anyone knew Agnete Kessler and would they mind telling her, a complete stranger, where Agnete had gone. There was no guarantee Agnete would have told anyone, and even if someone knew, what would compel them to pass that information on to her? The one thing working in her favor was her apparent frailty. *At least no one's going to mistake me for a stalker.*

But inspiration came when she realized the odds favored any neighbor of Agnete's knowing Natalie as well. All those years of visits would have counted for something. In spite of everything Natalie had stolen away, she'd given Alice an unplanned gift in her passing: not only knowledge of Agnete's existence but a reason to contact her. The envelope served as proof of her connection and allowed her to maintain the anonymity she desired. She could be anyone—a family friend, a close relative—coming to deliver the news in person, knowing how close Natalie had been to her niece. She was shocked by how quickly she'd sacrificed her principles and was willing to shade the truth, if not discard it all together, first to Phinneaus and Saisee, then to strangers; possibly to a daughter she'd never met. *I owe that to you, Natalie. I should have paid closer attention. Imagine what else I might have learned.*

Her thoughts wavered and shifted in the glass in front of her. *Imagine what else I should have known.* With a jolt, her own culpability came into sharp focus. Natalie and Thomas. Natalie's inability to have a child; Alice's inability to care for one on her own. Had she honestly expected her sister would help her raise her child without knowing who the father was; that there would be no repercussions?

Alice's sole attempt at manipulation—telling George Reston, Jr. that Natalie had mentioned him—had been the start of her undoing. George would have eagerly filled in any blanks once Natalie started asking questions: what reason did George possibly have for speaking with Alice? Why had she called him? And when was she at the cabin? With a shudder, Alice realized her sister must have known Thomas was the father of her child from the start; she had met Alice's burgeoning perimeter, her dense, selfish joy, with a tortured silence. All this hell Alice had blithely called down upon herself, for once choosing to be completely unaware, not only of her surroundings, but of everything that had been written on Natalie's face.

The few travelers hoping to spend time in the observation car took one look at her and kept moving, their eyes fixed on the door at the opposite end of the car. Her inability to atone for her past actions was transmitted in hollow cries, in waves of tremors. No one stopped to ask whether she was all right or if she needed help. It must have been clear, even to strangers, that no simple comfort was going to provide redemption.

Alice was worn down to nothing, raw and empty, by the time night gave up its turn to dawn. The Southwest Chief had crossed into Colorado just as the sun was coming up. The high prairie caught fire with the advancing light; dusty ranchlands took the place of dusty farm fields, clots of cattle stood together as the train sped past. The scrappy blocks fronting the rail line could have belonged to any town: strip shopping centers and gas stations, a stucco maze of storage units, an auto yard, the boarded-up skeleton of a pancake house, all relegated to the monochromatic landscape paralleling both sides of the tracks. But between La Junta and Trinidad, the scenery changed. She noticed the ragged outlines of mountains in the distance, the scraped tabletops of mesas. After the low-speed climb up Raton Pass, she entered a different world. The train headed toward Glorieta, then spilled down into Apache Canyon, the closeness of the canyon walls taking her by surprise; she sat back in her seat. The train was moving too fast to see much beyond the pines stepping up rock walls, but she knew from memory the bird species that would be endemic. She could picture the colored plates in her textbooks—the greater roadrunner, with its shaggy pompadour crest; the yellow eyes of burrowing owls; the shiny, jet-black plumage of the phainopepla, which gobbled up hundreds of mistletoe berries a day.

She'd missed the Festival of the Cranes by only a few weeks. How tempting, to find herself just hours from Bosque del Apache and the Rio Grande. She imagined lying on her stomach, binoculars trained on the sandhill cranes and snow geese in their winter quarters, watching in wonder the mass morning liftoffs and evening fly-ins. It was an old desire, but even now, though she knew the impossibility of it, it persisted; the world as one giant aviary she ached to see, all of its feathered inhabitants in their natural environment, a thousand times better to hear their cries dampened by verdant jungle foliage or echoed across the wells of canyons than to listen to abbreviated bits of captured songs emanating from a machine. It was infinitely easier to consider all of this than to think of her daughter, the engine pulling her closer to Agnete with every S-curve of track.

In Lamy, the attendant took her bags down and helped her off the train, pointing her in the direction of the shuttle stop. Once the train departed, Lamy looked like a ghost town, and even though the air was fresh and the sky a pale washed blue, she was relieved to see the shuttle pull up shortly after. She was the only passenger, and the young woman driving the van was friendly, anxious to find out Alice's plans, to recommend restaurants, and to suggest which galleries she might want to visit.

'Are you interested in Native American art? Contemporary Hispanic? Photography? American modern?' She rattled off a few more options, but Alice lost track of the conversation, watching the land roll away from the van's shaded windows, the arroyos, the ghostly skeletons of aspen among the pine, the Sangre de Cristos. The girl was wearing a western-style shirt in a floral print, and her plump braid of blue-black hair bounced as the shuttle jounced. Bounce. Jounce. Alice's joints rebelled, but the girl's voice was resolutely upbeat, hypnotic in its cheerfulness. For the first time since she'd left, Alice thought of Thomas and how odd it was Agnete had ended up here of all places, in a town with as many art galleries as restaurants. Her hands were shaking. How had she thought she could do this?

'I'm just here for a short stay. I'll probably try to see a little bit of everything.'

'That's a good plan if it's your first time here. You probably want to take it easy for the rest of the day anyway, to let your body adjust to the altitude. It can give you a killer headache, if you're not used to it. By the way'—the girl fished a business card out of the ashtray and handed it over her shoulder—'I do massage if you're interested. Shiatsu, Thai, hot stone. Craniosacral therapy. The works.'

'I'll keep it mind,' Alice said, discreetly slipping the business card into the crack of the seat cushion.

Her hotel room smelled of piñon. The adobe walls were dun-colored, the furnishings in somber tones: a brick-red sofa with cocoa-colored pillows, a Navajo-patterned throw, and two chocolate leather chairs, all a welcome respite from the bright outdoor light. There were several pieces of Indian art on the walls and a carved bear fetish in an arched niche near the door. After the bellman left, having told her where the ice machine was and how to turn on the gas for the beehive fireplace in the corner, she crawled into the large bed, not bothering to undress, and pulled a rough blanket up over her shoulders. There was a strange atmosphere, something she couldn't put her finger on until she scanned the room again and realized what was missing: the presence of another person. She was alone.

She hadn't been alone since the day they'd come to Tennessee. There had always been Natalie or Saisee to start with, and then later Phinneaus and often Frankie. The majority of her life had been spent in the company of care-takers. No matter how self-sufficient she wished to be, she had, to a great extent, been dependent on the kindness of others. *Could you help me lift this? Could you just open that? Would you mind holding the door, taking my coat, carrying my books?* Being completely alone felt as strange to her as visiting the North Pole. The shimmering silence was cold and clarifying, absent the dialogue of assistance she was accustomed to.

What is the worst that could happen? She cataloged her body parts, acknowledging the tenderness of this, the flame of that. It was, for once, a dispassionate appraisal. *I could die.* That seemed melodramatic; a remote possibility since she was ensconced in a comfortable hotel room with a telephone a mere arm's length away. But it was a relief to think the thought without the usual burden of guilt that accompanied it. At home, it would have seemed sinful to contemplate such a thing, no matter how disloyal her body, when there were people fluttering around, sacrificing their time; their ministrations part of a daily ritual undertaken for her benefit. But in this atmosphere of mysticism and enchantment, to consider she might choose at some point to let go of the tether binding her to earth was not so alarming.

The music coming from the CD player on the bedside table was an ethereal combination of pipe, didgeridoo, chanting, and percussion that sounded like shakers and rattles. All of it lulling her into dreams of flight. As she slipped into sleep, she thought she heard the repeated high howl of a wolf or coyote outside her window and couldn't tell if she was in Tennessee, dreaming of New Mexico, or in

New Mexico, dreaming of Tennessee. The bed was the only place that didn't seem foreign, and she clutched a small corner of the sheet in her hand, rooting herself to it.

She woke up, disoriented, in a dark room. She couldn't remember where she was at first, fumbling to find her glass of water, her familiar clock; her feet had already swung over the side of the bed, searching for her slippers. It was only after she bumped her shinbone against the table that she remembered and stuck out her hand, feeling for the lamp. Nine o'clock. And she hadn't called Phinneaus. She punched his number into the phone, thankful there was only an hour time difference between them. His voice when he answered was stilted, the distance between them expanding as she talked.

'I fell asleep.'

'I called. Did you have your phone turned off?'

'I must have.'

'And the Do Not Disturb sign on the door? I couldn't get anyone to put me through to your room.'

She couldn't remember hanging anything on the door, in fact, could remember little about her arrival other than that she was here now, and in the dim light of the bedroom lamp, the room seemed strange and immense, odd shadows flickering on the walls, music wafting up from the courtyard below.

'How's your room?'

'It's what you'd expect, I guess.' Then she remembered the care he'd taken in booking it for her—not next to the elevator but not too much of a walk; on a low floor, but not the ground floor; a corner room if possible, with a fireplace; a view onto the courtyard or the square, but not the parking lot. She quickly amended her statement. 'It's lovely. I just haven't had a chance to get used to anything yet. It's odd for me, being alone. No Natalie, no Saisee. No you.' She paused, waiting for him to say something and when he didn't, added, 'It feels different than I expected it would, Phinneaus. I feel different.'

'Not sure if you mean that to be a good thing or a bad thing.'

'I mean I wish you were here. Not because I need something. Just because I wish you were here.' It was ridiculous even to try. She'd never been good at explaining her feelings, too used to keeping things to herself. This was more painful than the adolescent crushes exposed at recess.

'Where are you?' he asked.

'Sitting on the edge of a very large bed.'

'Don't bother flirting with me when I'm too far away to do anything about it. Is there a door leading out to a deck?'

'Yes, I think so.'

'Throw a blanket on and go outside. Tell me what you see.'

She climbed out of bed and walked across the room to the French doors. The afternoon had been so warm the cold air took her by surprise, but it cleared her head and she felt immediately awake, and transported. 'Phinneaus. It's beautiful here.'

'Tell me.'

The deck wrapped around the building. The trees in the empty courtyard were studded with white lights, and there were fire pits with licks of blue flame curling up from under their copper caps, surrounded by Adirondack chairs. A single guitarist stood next to the fire pit on the far side of the courtyard, strumming softly and singing something in Spanish, stopping occasionally to rub his hands together, his voice a bell in the dark. The air was scented with resin, and when she turned the corner and walked to the other end of the deck, it was dark, stars dotting the sky overhead.

'I see Ursa Minor,' she said, her breath a puff of fog.

She heard a door slam on his end of the line, followed by a booming crash. 'Uh-huh. I see Ursa Minor, too. We can't be all that far apart then.'

'Phinneaus Lapine'—she laughed—'it's raining there. I'm not a fool, I can hear the thunder. Tell me the truth. You can't see anything at all, can you?'

'To be perfectly honest, no,' he said. 'But I imagine the stars are still where they were the last time I looked.'

His voice was everything she equated with home. She knew he would try to understand, even if she made a decision other than the one he would have made. 'I don't know what's going to happen. Maybe no one will know where she's gone and I won't be able to find her.'

'But you'll have tried.'

'You think that will make a difference?'

He hesitated before answering, then said, 'Yes. But the more important thing is that you think it will, too.'

If she was standing on the edge of a cliff, her decision to take a step backward would have seemed perfectly logical. But he wanted her to throw herself off into a free fall, and enjoy the view on the way down.

'Alice? You still there?'

'Hmm. Still here.'

'Don't stay away too long.'

'I miss you,' she said quickly, then hung up before he could answer and huddled down in one of the chairs on the deck, looking out into the dark.

She stayed in bed, dead to the world, waking to the sound of a vacuum cleaner in the hallway. She knew she'd overslept even before looking at the clock. Already late morning. She'd planned to walk around the square early, map in hand, to get her bearings before the streets were filled with clumps of tourists, objects to be negotiated around and avoided. She got out of bed and hobbled over to the window, regretting she hadn't thought to put on socks before her outdoor conversation with Phinneaus. She bit her lip as she pulled the curtain aside.

The courtyard was a flurry of activity, grounds people clipping bushes and planting trimmed pines in large terra-cotta planters before stringing them with lights and ropes of small red chiles. Christmas. She'd almost forgotten the holidays and realized she should pick up something for Phinneaus, Frankie, and Saisee while she was here. She ordered room service and ran a bath, dumping the contents of a package of bath salts into the deep tub and inhaling the scent of cedar and sage while swirling her hands back and forth in the warm water. The trip had taken its toll, and she barely had the energy to dress. Walking around town would be out of the question.

On to Plan B. If she couldn't walk, she could at least plot. She wrapped herself in the ample hotel robe and settled down in front of the fireplace with a map she'd taken from the top drawer of the desk and one of Phinneaus's legal pads. She knew she was delaying the inevitable—trying to locate Agnete's address—but decided to make a list of things to buy first, looking for shops close to the hotel and purpose-fully ignoring her uncertain finances. She dunked a sopaipilla in her coffee and brushed powdered sugar from her lips, the plate of chile-flecked fried polenta, chorizo, and eggs already finished. It might not have been a vacation, but it felt like one. She was on her own, eating strange foods, planning to spend money she wasn't sure she had, and no one was paying the slightest bit of attention to her. She had fallen down the rabbit hole.

It was easiest to come up with ideas for Saisee, whose pride in her cooking shone in everything she concocted, tossing in a pinch of this and a smidgen of that. Alice had even watched her hold crushed spices in the palm of her hand and blow them gently over the pot. *My momma taught me that. Best way to get flavor to every part of the pot.* For her there would be white posole and blue cornmeal, a collection of chile powders, and *piloncillo,* the little cones of unrefined Mexican sugar Alice imagined she might use to make caramelized custard. Frankie wasn't difficult either. She'd passed a glass case in the lobby gift shop and spied a handsome horned toad fetish on the second shelf. Phinneaus would cluck at her, but she wanted Frankie to have something not handed down, something exotic and unexpected he could instill with powerful childhood magic. That would take care of him, along with some train paraphernalia she'd already purchased at Union Station, since his sole experience of rail travel to date was confined to the treacherous mystery of the story problem.

That left Phinneaus, and the thing she wanted to give him wasn't easily wrapped. If she could cast a spell, she'd offer him this new, slightly careless version of herself, but that person might easily vanish before she boarded the train again. She'd already chosen one thing for him. It was wrapped and hidden under her bed at home, her old textbook with the beautifully colored plates, *Birds of the Northeast.* He would know it meant something to her, that she was giving him a bit of her own history, a piece of the person she was before he knew her. And she thought he would find the book every bit as fascinating as she did—the different bird species depicted in their natural environments, claws curling across a slender branch or feet obscured in a tangle of brush, heads cocked, considering a plump cluster of berries, or eyeing grubs inching unaware across the delicate grasses along the bottom of the page. The meticulous drawings of individual feathers: the pennaceous and plumulaceous barbs of the vane, the after-feathers, the intricate patterns of stippling, dotting, and dashing that were as telling to her as a fingerprint. The illustrations of nests with their perfect eggs, some mottled, some speckled, some plain and small as her fingernail.

But since he was the one who had encouraged her to come, it seemed only fitting she bring him something back. There was an article highlighting local artisans in one of the magazines on the desk, and a picture of a cutting board made from alligator juniper. The wood had a tight, beautiful grain, its color running from pink to rose. It may not have been a romantic gift, but besides his honesty, his sensibility was one of the things she most admired; she knew he would appreciate the fine craftsmanship.

Having finished the list, she set it aside and picked up the map again. Her stomach turned queasy at the sudden thought of Agnete, of standing in front of the house where her daughter had lived all the time Alice had been in Tennessee. The address from the returned envelope was on the east side of town, a street called Calle Santa Isabel. She found it on the map, a short stub of a street, the exact width and length of several others. But Alice wanted more than the pale charcoal line on the map. She wanted a life's history.

The enormity of all she'd missed rolled over her. Had her daughter been happy living on Calle Santa Isabel? The name sounded cheerful enough, but names could be misleading. Had there been trees for her to climb, neighborhood children to play with? Had she decorated her front door with the red pepper Christmas lights Alice saw everywhere? Did she walk to school or take a bus? And had she come home clutching ragged pieces of construction paper in her fist, covered in thick trails of crayon meant to be turkeys and pumpkins and umbrellas? Cutout paper snowflakes? If Alice stood on that street, in front of that house, would she be standing in the dust that had powdered around her daughter's feet?

Staying in the room thinking was making her nervous. She could probably manage a short walk around the block, just to become familiar with her surroundings. She swallowed a handful of pills and pulled on her clothes, thankful Saisee had packed things easy to get into and out of. The light outside was brilliant, the sky the same crystal blue as the day before. It was warm, and even though there were people out, the sidewalks weren't crowded. She passed a small café, lingering by the open door to take in the smell of cinnamon and coffee, then made her way down the rest of the block, stopping to look in the window of one gallery or another.

When she turned the corner, she saw a gallery on her left with a bench outside and sat down to rest, positioning herself sideways so she could look in through the window. Inside, a tall man—he must have had to stoop to walk in and out the front door—was gesturing emphatically to a young couple studying a landscape on the far wall. His dark hair was pulled back in a ponytail, and he was wearing a black jacket and a large turquoise ring, which looked to be in jeopardy of sliding off. Alice could tell by the way the young woman smiled and nodded she was losing enthusiasm; her nods become fewer, her sideways glances at her partner more frequent. Perhaps they had only wandered in and were staying to be polite. It was a process Alice had never understood, the buying of art, especially while on vacation. Would a particular piece suddenly attract you? Would you be drawn to an image or a palette? The situation seemed rife with the opportunity for buyer's remorse. The couple exited the shop and walked briskly away, arm in arm, as if urging each other out of the gallery owner's clutches. The man in the gallery, meanwhile, looked out at Alice and smiled, shrugging his shoulders. A moment later he was standing in the doorway, only slightly hunched over, she noticed, holding two cups of coffee.

'Another beautiful day in paradise,' he said, handing one of the cups to her. It was Styrofoam and easy enough to hold, the warmth spreading through her thin mittens. She smelled the same hint of cinnamon and something spicier she'd caught in the doorway of the café.

'I'm sorry about your sale,' she said.

'There'll be another. There always is.' He looked at her and cocked one eyebrow. 'I don't suppose . . .'

'Oh, no. It would be wasted on me.'

'You mean to tell me you don't like art? I don't believe it. Everybody likes art. It's just a matter of finding the piece that speaks to you.'

Up close, she could see his face was etched with fine lines. She imagined he'd spent most of his life here, living in the thin air and the warm sun, the desert carving its way into his skin until his face resembled that of a dried apple doll from a craft fair. 'You're probably right. I might be a fan of Audubon, I suppose.'

'Ah, birds. I can tell a lot about a person by the type of art they're drawn to. You say Audubon, and I think of someone with a meticulous eye for detail. But that's an easy assumption, isn't it? Not the sort of thing that impresses someone like you much.'

'Like me?'

'Uh-huh. Skeptic.' He studied her intently, and she was surprised to find herself unaffected, buffered from his scrutiny by her coat and her mittens, her ugly shoes and her padded socks, her warm cup of coffee and her anonymity.

He rubbed his chin with his knuckle. 'I would say a person who hangs Audubon on her walls is a person who believes in God, but not necessarily religion. A person who believes in free will, but also in the existence of a natural pecking order, pardon the pun, in all societies. Aware of it, and accepts it. I would say such a person has the capacity to be awed by nature and horrified by it, in equal amounts. A scientist's brain, but an artist's soul. How am I doing?'

Alice smiled. 'Remarkable.'

'You're not impressed. I see I'll have to up my game.'

He looked at her face, her eyes, and she looked back at him blandly, keeping her sharp corners hidden. She had little practice talking to strangers but embraced the thought that she could play the role of anyone she chose, trying on imagined identities to see what fit: businesswoman here for a meeting, opera impresario, wealthy collector, lover en route to a secret assignation.

'Hmm,' he said, narrowing his eyes while he watched her. 'It's not so much an admiration for the artist as it is for the subject matter, correct? What is it about birds? People envy them the ability of flight, of course, but it must be more. Maybe not just their ability to fly, but to fly away *from*, is that it? To leave trouble behind, be free from boundaries, from expectations.' He smiled. 'I admit to envying them that.'

Was that where it came from? She'd loved birds long before her physical limitations kept her grounded. She'd found a birding diary of her grandmother's in a trunk in the attic when she was Frankie's age, and when she asked her father about it, he dug through boxes on a shelf high above her head, handing down a small pair of binoculars and some field guides.

She'd seen her first prothonotary warbler when she was nine, sitting alone on a tupelo stump in the forest, swatting at mosquitoes targeting the pale skin behind her ears. She glanced up from the book she was reading only to be startled by an unexpected flash of yellow. Holding her breath, she fished for the journal she kept in her pocket, focusing on the spot in the willow where he might be. A breeze stirred the branches, and she saw the brilliant yellow head and underparts standing out like petals of a sunflower against the backdrop of leaves; the undertail, a stark white. His beak was long, pointed and black; his shoulders a mossy green, a blend of the citron yellow of his head and the flat slate of his feathers. He had a black dot of an eye, a bead of jet set in a field of sun. Never had there been anything so perfect. When she blinked he disappeared, the only evidence of his presence a gentle sway of the branch. It was a sort of magic, unveiled to her. He had been hers, even if only for a few seconds.

With a stub of pencil—*always a pencil*, her grandmother had written. *You can write with a pencil even in the rain*—she noted the date and time, the place and the weather. She made a rough sketch, using shorthand for her notes about the bird's coloring, then raced back to the house, raspberry canes and brambles speckling bloody trails across her legs. In the field guide in the top drawer of her desk, she found him again: prothonotary warbler, *prothonotary* for the clerks in the Roman Catholic Church who wore robes of a bright yellow. It made absolute sense to her that something so beautiful would be associated with God.

After that she spent countless days tromping through the

woods, toting the drab knapsack filled with packages of partially crushed saltines, the bottles of juice, the bruised apples and half-melted candy bars, her miniature binoculars slung across one shoulder. She taught herself how to be patient, how to master the boredom that often accompanied careful observation. She taught herself how to look for what didn't want to be seen.

She set her empty coffee cup on the arm of the bench. 'Maybe you're right.'

He smiled, looking pleased with himself, and nodded. 'I told you. There's one piece of art for everyone.'

What possessed her to ask? Maybe it was because she was thinking about Agnete and she couldn't think about her daughter now without thinking about him, too. 'What do you know about Thomas Bayber?'

'Bayber? I know if I owned anything of his, I wouldn't have to work. Not here or anywhere else. My pockets aren't that deep, and besides, there's nothing more to be had. His paintings are all in museums, except for a few pieces in private collections. New York or Miami, I'd guess. Maybe Japan.' He seemed puzzled she'd asked. 'I didn't peg you for a serious collector. And here you led me to believe you'd never had much interest in art.'

'Not serious so much as curious. I know the name is all. Not much about the artist. He's talented, then?'

'An understatement. He was.'

A dull wave shifted across her, and she closed her eyes, making her fingers into fists inside her mittens, waiting for the familiar stab of a sharper pain to take this one away. She'd never considered the possibility. The Thomas she knew was frozen in his midthirties, cocksure and indefatigable. He would have been in his early seventies now.

'When?'

'When what? Oh, no, I don't believe he's deceased. But he stopped painting twenty years ago. Dropped completely out of sight. Rather mysterious, considering he was fairly prolific up to that point. But I see! That's why you asked about him, because of the birds! You were just testing me, then? Not that I object. You wouldn't want to work with a dealer who wasn't experienced and knowledgeable. You know your art.'

It was her turn to be puzzled. 'I'm not sure I understand.'

'Wait here. I'll be right back.' He dashed inside the gallery, and when she looked through the window she could see him shuffling through a pile of large books, turning over papers, fumbling for something under a desk. When he came back outside he had a large volume tucked under his arm, *The Art of Thomas Bayber* by Dennis Finch. He sat down next to her and rested the book on the bench, flipping through pages until he got to the middle, a section of colored plates. He read a paragraph of text to her.

'*In 1972, Bayber's work underwent another metamorphosis, yet refused to be defined by or adhere to any specific style . . . There is nothing fragile here, nothing dreamlike. No protections are offered, not for the artist himself and not for those viewing his work. All is called forth in a raw state, human values finessed on the canvas, softened and sharpened, separated and made aggregate. While there are certain motifs in these works—often a suggestion of water, the figure of a bird—and various elements are repeated, aside from an introverted complexity, the context in which they appear is never the same from one piece to the next. What ties these works together is the suggestion of loss, of disappearance, and of longing (see figures 87 to 95).*'

'Nineteen seventy-two. He stopped painting fifteen years

after that. But look at this plate. Can you see the bird, there in the corner? They're not always easy to find. It's that patch of blue.'

She didn't have to hear the year repeated again to guess the reason for Thomas's metamorphosis. And she didn't have to look at the picture of the painting to be able to identify the bird. *What have I done, Thomas? What have I done?*

'Blue grosbeak,' she said.

'I don't know my birds as well as you do, so I'll take your word for it. He was incredibly talented. It's a shame he stopped painting.'

There was more than enough shame to go around. Alice rose to her feet with effort, swaying unsteadily. 'Thank you for the coffee. I'm sorry to take up so much of your time.'

'On the contrary, I should be thanking you. I hadn't thought about Bayber for quite a while. It's a great pleasure to look at his work again, even if it's only in the pages of a book.' He stood up and tipped his head toward her. 'I hope you enjoy the rest of your day. Maybe we'll see each other again if you're in town for a while.'

'Maybe so.'

Her only thought was to get back to the hotel room. She maneuvered past the tourists pausing by shops and the couples strolling hand in hand; steered clear of café tables set on the sidewalk and the large sculptures near the fronts of souvenir stores. The hotel elevator was slower going up than it had been going down; the door to her room took longer to unlock, the small red light above the handle stubbornly refusing to turn green. Once inside, with the dead bolt turned behind her, she walked over to the wooden luggage rack holding her suitcase and ran her hand underneath the clothes she hadn't unpacked, patting her way along the bottom until she found the heavy, thick sock. Tugging it out, she reached inside of it and worked her hand down toward the foot until she felt cool porcelain beneath her fingers. She pulled out the figurine of the blue grosbeak and sank to the floor.

He hadn't aged. He sat on the edge of one of the leather chairs in her room and whispered her name. 'Alice.' Then, 'Are you awake?'

She was sure she had been and squeezed her eyes shut, not wanting to see him, only to find they were already closed.

'Alice.' His voice was more urgent now, more demanding. 'I didn't know.'

'You hid her from me.'

'No, I would never have done that. I didn't know she was alive, Thomas. I've missed as much of her life as you have.'

He was standing over the bed, staring down at her. He reached out a hand, and she shrank away from him, but he only touched her cheek, and she felt the warmth from his fingers move across her face like a tide. His hands were as long and slender as she remembered, their paleness a beacon in the dark room.

'You didn't trust me enough to tell me?'

'You wouldn't have wanted to be a father.'

He sat on the bed next to her, and she moved over so he could lie down. He cradled her face between the palms of his hands. 'Did you know me so well?'

She shook her head. It was something she could never fix, and that was what made her cry, a deep sob she choked on. With one decision she'd altered the lives of three people, cracking them into jagged, separate pieces. Had she wanted to hurt him so much? 'I should have told you.'

He wrapped an arm around her waist and pulled her close to his body. She rested her hands against the solid wall of his chest, feeling the breath go in and out of him, the certain pulse of his heart. Her every inhale ferried some remembered smell: the clean linen of his shirt, linseed oil and turpentine, the dry must of tobacco, the powdery cast of graphite.

'Would we have been a family, do you think?'

'We might have tried.' He stroked her hair, and she tucked her head under his chin, her body automatically curling into him, a habit imprinted in the memory of her skin, her muscles, her bones.

'Natalie told you.'

His eyes were closed, and he lay so still she wondered if he really was dead, come back to her as a vision. 'She made sure I found out.'

'Did you look for me?'

'I looked for both of you. But you'd already flown away.'

She woke up on the floor, the early glow of morning seeping in through the windows. Her fingers of her left hand were frozen tight around the bird, and she thought how fitting a punishment it would be if they were to stay like that, clutching at the freedom she'd longed to capture, unable to set it free, watching it die in her grasp. She pried her fingers apart with her right hand and set the bird on the dresser, then fell into bed. She had no idea what time it was and didn't care enough to turn her head to see the blinking digits of the clock. All she could think was that she had never known such tiredness; that it was possible she was too tired to be alive. But sleep wouldn't come, no matter where she searched for it: in the comforting, smooth tones of Phinneaus's voice; in the clover smell she could find at the top of Frankie's head; in the warm cup of tea Saisee poured out for her, sliding down her throat like a dull ember. It was not beneath the down blanket, or the starched sheets, or even in the feathery pillow that collapsed under the weight of her head. There was only guilt, and the repeating voice, over and over. *Agnete.*

She was forced to lie there for the sake of her body. She'd asked too much of it and now it was letting her know, in no uncertain terms. It was torture, trying to turn off her thoughts. She watched the sun slowly paint the walls with day, concentrating on the slow creep of it across the room. The lead weight of her limbs pinned her against the mattress; she didn't have the energy to so much as turn over. And when she realized there was no more running from it, she ran toward it, her arms open. She ran toward Agnete and sucked her into her arms, a tornado of pent-up love and remorse. She sat down with the child in her lap and took her birding notebook out of her pocket and started at the beginning, showing her daughter every sketch, describing every bird, the curious cock of its head, the fluff of its down, the secret things woven into the fabric of its nest. She went through each page, leaving out no detail, watching her daughter's fingers outline her drawings, watching her daughter's head nod when she was ready for the page to be turned.

When the room turned bright enough to hurt her eyes, she tested her body, flexing first one foot, then the other, slowly moving each in turn up the mattress until her knees were bent, then sliding them back down. She drew circles on the backs of her wrists and moved her fingers as though she were halfheartedly playing the piano, tapping at invisible keys, just to test her flexibility. Tentatively rolling onto her side, she anticipated a warning flash of protest, but the pain was tolerable. She lifted the phone receiver and called for breakfast: dry toast, green tea, and one egg, scrambled. Then she sat up and reached for the robe at the end of the bed, the same spot where Thomas had sat, and held it against her face, anxious for a clue of him. But she smelled only the cedar and sage bath salts from the day before.

The breakfast was tasteless; the clothes she slipped on her body weighed nothing. When she stepped outside the air was sharp, the stair rails etched in a mosaic of frost, as if someone in authority had decided if Thursday was autumn, then Friday should be winter. The bellman called a taxi, and she gave the driver the address.

'Nice day today,' he said.

'Yes,' she answered, and watched the shops and low, flat-roofed houses tumble by, a blur of adobe. She turned her body toward the window to dissuade him from additional conversation. The short blocks were lined with cars, and the driver's turns were quick, first in one direction, then another, until she felt lost in a maze of brown walls and tall grasses. Finally he pulled half into a gravel drive and stopped.

'This is it. Eleven Calle Santa Isabel.'

They'd gotten here more quickly than she'd expected. The house was a small adobe, neat in appearance, with a low wall in the front bordered by clumps of coppery big bluestem and plume grass. Paper bags lined the top of the wall, and a wreath of cedar hung on the front door.

'Do you know what the bags are for?'

The cabbie turned and squinted at her as if she were the thickest tourist he'd ever encountered. 'Farolitos. There's sand in the bottom of each paper bag and a candle. In my great-grandfather's time, they lit bonfires on the corners to light the way to Christmas Mass. Maybe too many places caught fire, eh? Now we use paper bags.'

'Can you wait for me, please?' She handed him twenty dollars and stepped out of the cab. 'I won't be long.'

She stood next to the car with one hand resting on its side, thinking if she could just stay in this one place, she'd be safe. The speech she'd practiced on the way over—*I'm looking for the woman who used to live here. I'm a friend of her aunt's. There's been a death in the family and we're trying to locate her*—sounded suddenly wrong. She was in an unfamiliar land, lost, missing the words to communicate.

The driver tapped the horn and rolled down the passenger-side window far enough to yell out, 'Lady! You all right?'

She nodded and kept her eyes on the front door, on the wreath, thinking it was only the first time that would be hard; once she'd done it, she could ask a hundred strangers at a hundred different houses if she had to. Her feet carried her across the slabs of the stone walk and through the wide opening in the wall, into a courtyard garden planted with desert holly and sumac, bearberry and winterfat. She stopped.

The garden was full of sculptures, modern stainless-steel pieces in varying sizes, but all of them sharing the liquid quality of movement. They might have been abstract figures or merely forms, she wasn't sure. Sunlight bounced back and forth between them. She ran her fingers across the curve of the one nearest the walk. The metal, cool and slick, was smooth beneath her hand, the solid heft of it clear even from the slightest touch.

The front door was a deep orange, the familiar color of bittersweet. Before she knew it her hand was on the door, the small echo of her rapping drifting straight back to her heart. She listened for the sound of footsteps and half-hoped for the heavy soles of a man's shoes, thinking a man might be less suspicious. But she didn't hear footsteps. She didn't hear anything, save for the taxi's engine idling. She knocked again and waited, but there was nothing.

She started back down the walk. A movement caught the corner of her eye, and when she turned, she saw a young woman stepping around the side of the house, dressed in khakis and a denim shirt, wearing bright red gardening clogs. She was carrying a rope of cedar garland over one shoulder. Alice could smell the spicy scent of it from where she stood, a few feet away.

'I heard someone at the door, but I was working in the backyard and didn't want to go through the house, it's so muddy back there. Can I help you?' Her smile changed to a look of alarm as Alice began weaving on her feet, drifting down suddenly, toward the path.

He was standing in front of her. That was the arch of his brow, his long nose, his high forehead. As the woman rushed forward, Alice saw she moved like Thomas: quick, purposeful, sure of her step. Thank God, there were his beautiful, straight fingers grabbing her arm. But she saw herself mirrored in the pale eyes and freckled skin, in the intensity of the gaze, the tangled curls of hair that bounced around the shoulders, though the inky black of it was from him.

'Let's get you to a chair.'

But she didn't want to sit. She didn't want to move from this spot; didn't want the hand firmly holding her arm to move an inch up or down. Or away.

'Agnete Sophia Kessler.' Her own rite to speak the name, not as a question, but as a baptism.

'Yes. Do we know each other?' There—her father's tone of suspicion.

Yes, Alice wanted to say. *I know you the way I know my own heart, the way I feel my own pulse. I know what your laugh will be, how you wave good-bye, the crescent of thumbnail you worry between your teeth. I have known you from the second you entered this world, and if I were to leave it now, I would know you still, were I to dust or ash.*

'I came to tell you . . .'

Agnete waited, her face composed and patient. *Such a false premise,* thought Alice. *Such a complicated story.* So much explanation was going to be required. She could think of no other place to start.

'I'm your mother.'

FOURTEEN
DECEMBER 2007

Finch was green. He didn't really believe his own excuses for not flying, but repeating them often enough had evidently affected his psyche, and to his humiliation, outside the terminal he'd succumbed to a full-on panic attack, desperately trying to reinsert himself into a cab that was already departing. He and Stephen were pulled from the security line for extra screening, no doubt thanks to Stephen's black eye, which had turned a menacing aubergine. And Stephen's insistence on holding his boarding pass in front of his mouth while whispering instructions clearly audible to anyone within a ten-foot radius did nothing to endear them to the TSA.

'Try not to look suspicious.'

'I don't look suspicious.'

'You're practically panting. It makes you look guilty of something.'

Finch hissed at him through clenched teeth. 'That's because I can't breathe.'

'Can we get some oxygen here?' Stephen asked loudly,

waving in the direction of the security desk despite the jabs Finch inflicted to his rib cage.

'You're going to get us arrested!' Other passengers had the sense to move away, leaving the two of them as an island in the security line, easily identifiable, easily tagged.

Stephen looked wounded. 'I'm only trying to help you overcome what has clearly turned into a phobia.'

'Don't help me.'

The two-hour flight to Memphis was delayed an hour and forty-two minutes. The wait practically undid him. He sat in one of the molded plastic chairs with his eyes closed, palms sweating. Claire might have helped him, but he refused to summon her. He'd devised his own set of rules for penance, chief among these being where he was allowed to talk to her. Airports, airplanes, waiting in line for Chinese takeout or to pick up prescriptions, these were not on the list. He would not use a conversation with her as an antidote for boredom or to soothe his feelings of incapacitation. He tried to limit their exchanges to those places she had loved: their ancient kitchen table with the one wobbly leg, Shakespeare Garden in Central Park, the Holiday Train Show in the Haupt Conservatory, their bedroom. Especially their bedroom. It wouldn't be fair to break the rules and bring her here of all places, just because he was experiencing a small breakdown, especially since it was his fault she'd been alone at the airport in the first place.

'It wasn't this one, was it?'

Stephen's voice in his ear had the whine of a dental drill, the shiver-inducing screech of crumpled foil.

'This one what?' Finch opened one eye and saw an Indian woman in a red sari seated across from them agitatedly tapping her husband's shoulder while giving him a look that would have sent St. Francis straight to hell.

'This airport. I thought I asked you and you said it wasn't. You did say that, didn't you?'

'Please stop talking,' Finch said.

By the time boarding began, Stephen nearly had to carry him onto the plane. To make matters worse, Stephen insisted on the aisle seat, telling Finch it was part of his flying ritual. Once they were airborne, Stephen downed several glasses of Bloody Mary mix and moved all three of the airsickness bags to the pouch in front of the middle seat.

'They shouldn't provide them. It's the power of suggestion—you see the bag, you feel ill. If you even check to see there *is* a bag, you're already anticipating the worst.' He shifted closer to Finch and lowered his voice. 'It's critical to be early in the boarding process so you can move them before your seatmates arrive. For some reason it makes them uneasy. I don't understand it. It's not as though I'm taking theirs.' In response to his raised eyebrow, Stephen added, '*Repositioning* is not taking. Technically speaking.'

Finch was sure his heart must have been exiting his chest. His hands were still slick with sweat, and the lingering smell of jet fuel made his stomach lurch. At least all three airsickness bags were in front of him; he supposed he should be grateful for that. The woman in the window seat had pushed herself as far away from him as she could manage, legs tucked up, arms wrapped around her sides, her body a compressed sponge that would magically expand once they landed.

'Here.' Stephen shoved a small plastic box toward Finch before pulling a black eyeshade out of his carry-on and snapping it across his forehead.

'What's this?'

'I'm surprised you don't recognize them.' Stephen pushed his call button and waggled his empty glass at the flight attendant, who rolled her eyes. There must have been a description of Stephen somewhere in the training manuals of the travel and hospitality industries, denoting him as—what was the kindest way to put it?—*challenging*.

'And I'll take his peanuts,' he said to the flight attendant when she returned with his fourth glass of Bloody Mary mix. 'Odds would seem high he's going to vomit.'

The woman in the window seat pulled a blanket over her head. Finch put his head in his hands.

'Open it,' Stephen said, gesturing at the box in Finch's hand. 'Acupressure bands. You helped me when we drove to the cabin. I'm returning the favor. And don't think I'm giving you a used pair. I had to open the container to make sure there were directions, then the clerk insisted I purchase them. I would have preferred the gray to black. Black seems so militant for an acupressure band.'

Finch hated to admit it, but he was touched. Why hadn't he thought of this himself? He pulled the bands over his hands and positioned them just below his wrists. 'It was thoughtful, Stephen. Thank you.'

'I know. Please remember that when you get behind the wheel for the two-hour drive to wherever it is we're going.'

Finch started to tell him, but Stephen held up his index finger. 'I'll get it. Just give me a minute.' He squeezed his eyes shut and started mumbling. 'Thank you. Thanksgiving. Turkey. Wild turkey. Bourbon? No. Hunting wild turkey. Hunter . . .' He smiled and pulled his eyeshade down. 'Orion,' he said.

Finch shook his head. 'Amazing.'

While Stephen dozed, Finch worked on a plan of action. Thanks to Simon Hapsend, their search had been narrowed from fifty states to one. Guilt over Stephen's pummeling had prompted Simon to provide the information they'd been most in need of: Natalie Kessler was in Tennessee. Whether Alice was as well, there was no way of knowing. But Natalie had taken great pains not to be found, which made Finch doubtful about the welcome they'd receive.

He was confident getting straight to the money part of the discussion with Natalie would be their most expedient route to the missing panels. As to Thomas's daughter, that was another matter. She'd be a young woman now, only a few years older than Stephen, and he had no idea what the sisters might have told her regarding her father. Perhaps they'd made him out to be a monster or a disinterested party; maybe they'd vanished him into thin air. Regardless, that conversation was going to require delicacy. He dreaded the thought of inserting himself into family politics, especially when details surrounding the supposed transgressions of all parties were murky. But the daughter was no transgression. She was a living, breathing link to Thomas, and since Thomas couldn't speak for himself, what other alternative did Finch have?

He reached into the carry-on he'd stuffed under the seat and pulled out a map of Tennessee on which he'd highlighted their route, preferring the physicality of paper to a phantom voice with a British accent, repeating the word *recalculating* ad nauseam. Orion was a pinpoint; he had to put on his reading glasses to distinguish it from a mark left by his pencil. How they'd settled in such a place, even found it, escaped him.

The pilot announced their descent into Memphis, and Stephen stretched in his seat, sending peanut wrappers and the empty plastic glasses he'd assigned to the four corners of his tray table into the aisle. He ignored the Fasten Seat Belt sign and collected his things from the overhead bin, jamming them beneath the seat in front of him. The flight attendant glared, and Finch was sure he'd been relegated to her same low opinion, if only by his proximity to Stephen.

'You're like a tornado,' he said.

'Your face is a much better color than it was earlier. The bands must have done the trick.' Stephen looked pleased with himself. 'Have you figured out what we're going to do?'

'Not at all.'

***

They landed in a light drizzle, the airport in Memphis looking much the same as every other airport Finch had experienced. He wanted to be out of the terminal as quickly as possible and hurried to the car rental counter, queuing up with the other travel-weary passengers who had donned raincoats and held their computer printouts. Stephen looked the most road worn of the bunch, which was saying something, with his spotted rain poncho, his backpack slung over one shoulder, and his scuffed briefcase clutched in his hand.

Out of gratitude for Stephen's earlier thoughtfulness, and because he remembered Cranston was footing the bill, Finch upgraded them to a larger vehicle. They stood in the rain waiting for the shuttle to pull up, but once he stepped onto the bus, falling into yet another plastic seat, Finch felt enormous relief, as if he'd endured a great battle and managed to come out on the other side, all his parts intact and where they should be.

At the car rental lot, Stephen tossed his backpack and briefcase into the back of their designated vehicle, and settled into the passenger seat with minimal complaint, immediately adjusting the vents and temperature controls before fiddling with the radio.

'Lots of country music stations.'

'We're in Tennessee,' Finch said.

'It's not my favorite type of music.'

'Then perhaps you should consider turning it off.' They were getting a later start than he'd planned. They still needed to stop at the motel in Dyersburg, and Finch wanted to be in Orion well before dark, before the Kesslers sat down to their evening meal, before the small amount of energy he had in reserve was completely expended.

Instead of turning off the radio, Stephen hummed over it, stopping his percussion solo on the dashboard to ask, 'Do you wonder what she looks like now?'

Finch knew who he was referring to. Their conversations always circled around Natalie, as opposed to Alice. Natalie had been a beautiful girl, but manipulative and calculating. Finch thought it quite possible her personality had settled into her face as she'd grown older, drawing a shallow channel between her brows, scratching lines of disappointment around her mouth.

When he'd first found the photos among Thomas's papers, he'd thought the anger in Natalie's message, *I know what you did*, had been for Alice's sake, in her defense. But after studying both the main panel of the triptych and the drawing at the Edells', he no longer thought that was the case. On canvas at least, the sisters seemed to have no connection to each other, circling in separate orbits, whether around their parents or around Thomas.

Alice's role was less clear. For some reason Finch was willing to give her the benefit of the doubt. Maybe it was the photo of her while pregnant, the joy emanating from her so palpable he could swear there was a change in temperature whenever his finger touched her image. Or perhaps it was because, at least when she was younger, she'd seemed immune to Thomas's spell. Maybe it was the intelligence he noted in those pale blue eyes. Whatever sharpness she had to her was in her intellect, not her personality. Regardless, his mood lifted when he thought of her.

'She'd be the type to have invested heavily in keeping herself up, don't you think?' Stephen said.

'We're here to find out about the paintings, and if the gods choose to smile upon us, maybe something about Thomas's daughter. Not to indulge your Mrs. Robinson fantasies.'

'Don't ask me to believe you haven't wondered what they look like now.' Stephen let the air push his arm back against the edge of the open window. 'Why would they come here, anyway? There's so much space. So much . . . nothing.'

'A number of people might find that appealing.'

'Would you? If you were young, and looked like they did?'

'No. I don't suppose I would.' Thinking about it made him uneasy. They were operating minus a well-crafted plan, with a vast number of unknowns, and he felt at a distinct disadvantage. He wanted the whole thing done with. He wanted to be home with his family for the holidays, and as satisfying as it might have been to deliver Thomas a family of his own, neatly tied up with a bow, the odds of that happening were infinitesimal. 'Dyersburg is another fifteen miles. Once we check in, I suggest we get cleaned up and then leave for Orion as quickly as possible.'

'You want to ensure we make a good first impression, is that it?'

'You never get a second chance,' Finch said. He fought the urge to point out the miscellaneous stains on Stephen's poncho. 'I believe we'll need all the help we can get.'

They pulled into the parking lot of the motel and got their

room keys from the front desk manager, an elderly woman whose hair was the shade of a Spanish onion. After nodding in affirmation of her stern warning not to smoke in the rooms, they dragged their luggage up an exterior flight of stairs and closed the doors to their adjoining rooms synchronously.

A hot shower erased the chill Finch had caught standing in the rain, and the change of clothes improved his mood, if not his overall health. But their brief time out of the car did not have the same restorative effect on Stephen. Without constant feeding, Finch realized Stephen was inclined to become surly and argumentative, neither of which would aid their cause. He pulled into a gas station and drummed his fingers against the wheel while Stephen dashed inside, coming out with his hands full of chip bags and candy bars.

'Do you have any idea how much sugar and sodium you've consumed in the past several hours? I mean, four cans of Bloody Mary mix? We should just get you your own salt lick.'

Stephen only waved his hand at this reproach and started tearing open wrappers.

By the time they reached Orion, the temperature had plummeted. Finch's nose was running and his eyes burned. Someone had hung a large evergreen wreath on the billboard at the edge of town, welcoming all travelers. 'Orion—old town! New attitude!' Stephen looked at him and smirked.

The main street could best be described as quaint, only three blocks long with nary a chain store in sight. The late afternoon sky was stuccoed with heavy clouds, and there were few people on the street. A woman raised her head as the car passed, then quickly tucked her chin back against her chest, any curiosity regarding an unfamiliar vehicle not worth the curl of cold air that might slip down her neck.

'Mint?' Stephen asked, thrusting a tin under his nose.

'I'm fine. Thank you.' Finch drove past a cemetery and then slowed down, noting addresses. He pulled over in the middle of the next block, in front of an ancient-looking three-story Victorian. A narrow brick walk, lined with boxwood hedges, led to the front porch.

'Stephen, I think it would be better if you let me do the talking.'

'You're afraid I'll say the wrong thing, aren't you?'

'I'm concerned your combination of enthusiasm and directness might be misinterpreted.'

Stephen shrugged. 'Have it your way.'

Finch locked the car doors out of habit and trudged up the walk with Stephen trailing in his wake. He could hardly believe they were here. In spite of what he'd said to Stephen earlier, in the last few hours it had been difficult not to imagine Natalie and Alice, what they might look like now, their expressions when they heard the name Bayber. He had prepared himself for almost anything, but not for the young boy who answered the door after he knocked.

Finch adjusted his gaze downward and held out his hand in his most amiable fashion. 'Good afternoon, young man. I'm Professor Finch and this is Mr. Jameson. We've come to see your mother. Is she home?'

As if Finch needed reminding that they were no longer in New York, the boy flung the door open, looking not in the least suspicious, or skeptical someone was trying to sell him something, or scamming for cab fare.

'Nope. She's in jail. Are you a teacher?' The boy looked around Finch to where Stephen perched on a lower step. 'Whoa! What happened to your eye, mister? You been in a fight?'

Stephen smiled at Finch. 'Am I allowed to answer or do you still want to do the talking?'

Finch nodded weakly, unable to get beyond the *in jail* portion of the boy's response. Stephen stepped onto the porch and crouched down in front of the young man. 'I have indeed been in a fight. With a large and frightening man. As you can see, I wasn't the winner.'

The child held an index finger close to Stephen's eye. 'It's a good one. I got in a fight once. Uncle Phinneaus told me he'd get out his belt if I did it again.'

Finch regained his composure and started over. 'Is your uncle here? Maybe we could talk with him.'

'No, he's at home. We live across the street.' Finch turned to see a neat two-story folk Victorian painted gray with white posts and a covered wraparound porch.

'I see. So you live over there with your uncle. Do the Kesslers live in this house?'

'Yep.'

The relief he felt was immediate and sweet. 'Good. Maybe you can help us, then. The person we'd like to speak with is Natalie Kessler. Would you happen to know her?'

'Miss Natalie? Sure do. But you can't talk to her, either.' The boy leaned over to whisper loudly in Stephen's ear. 'She's dead.'

Finch leaned up against the doorframe. His body responded to this news from the top down: head swimming, breath fluttering, chest tight. Arms so heavy he wished he could ask Stephen to unscrew them from their sockets and set them aside. His knees wobbled. Tears welled up at the corners of his eyes. He was suddenly sorry for all of them, Alice and Natalie and Thomas; for all of the mistakes they'd made, and for all of his own.

'Frankie, get away from there. What do you think you're doing?' A woman's voice echoed up the hall, and Finch watched the boy, Frankie, shrink away from them until he was standing inside the door.

'These men want to talk to Miss Natalie, Saisee. But they can't, can they?'

'Get along with you. Go fetch your uncle.'

'All right, but this fella don't look good and the other one's been in a horrible fight.' The boy seemed more interested than scared and didn't look pleased by the prospect of being shooed away from whatever was going to happen next. The woman scowled at him, and he turned and jumped off the landing of the porch, skipping all three of the broad treads and landing on the walk, then running across the street.

'Can I help you?'

Here was suspicion. Finch recognized it in the woman's tightly folded arms, the raised eyebrow, the frown. But he no longer cared. He was utterly defeated. There would be no other undiscovered works by Thomas Bayber, and there would be no joyful family reunion.

'Natalie Kessler is dead?' he asked, his voice strained.

'Who wants to know?'

Stephen stepped up and put his hand on Finch's shoulder. 'I'm afraid it's a shock to both of us. We've been looking for her for the last two months.' He held out his hand. 'I'm Stephen Jameson and this is Professor Dennis Finch. Could we trouble you for a glass of water? Professor Finch was ill earlier, and I'm concerned he might be experiencing a relapse. Nothing contagious though, I'm reasonably sure.'

'Stay here.' She closed the front door, and Finch heard the click of the lock. *Ah*, he thought. *Maybe not so far from New York after all.* Stephen was patting him on the back as if he were trying to burp a baby, and Finch held up a hand and moved away from him, spent and discouraged.

'I realize you're trying to help, but I just . . .' He sat down on the edge of the porch, feeling the cold of the brick cut through his pants.

"Is your mother home?' Really, Finch, don't you think the boy is a little young to have a sixty-one-year-old mother?' Stephen snorted. 'Don't tell me you haven't been thinking about them. They're stuck in your head at a certain age, the same way they're stuck in mine. I have to say, you're taking this harder than I would have expected. You never considered the possibility?'

Finch looked at him in amazement. 'You did?'

'Well, statistically the odds are against it, but we know absolutely nothing of the woman's history. She might have been a smoker, may have had cancer. Maybe she suffered from heart disease or was simply bored to death.' He stopped. 'Sorry.'

'I promised him. It was an incredibly stupid thing to do, but I did it. Every day since I found out Thomas had a daughter, every single day, I think about Lydia and how I'd feel if I knew I had a child somewhere and couldn't find her.'

'I'm lucky. The only thing I'm disappointed about is the painting.' Stephen sat down on the brick porch, rubbing his hands back and forth across his thighs.

Finch glared at him, unsure whether he was being honest or trying to jolly him out of his depression. 'I can't believe you would be that callous.'

'I would if I were you. But really, Finch, you're very quick to give up. I find it disheartening.'

'You heard what they said. Natalie Kessler is dead.'

'Exactly. *Natalie* Kessler is dead. No one's said anything about Alice.'

'And what would your interest be in Alice Kessler, gentlemen, if I might ask?'

Finch and Stephen jumped to their feet. A tall, sandy-haired man stood near the corner of the house, leaning on a hunting rifle. He started walking toward them with an uneven gait, *a hitch in his get-along*, Finch's father would have said, swinging the gun at his side. At the same time the front door opened and the woman they'd spoken to earlier held out a glass of water.

'This is Mr. Phinneaus Lapine,' she said. 'If you have questions about Miss Natalie or Miss Alice, you best ask him.' She handed the glass to Finch, who stood frozen on the steps, never having been in such close proximity to a real gun. *This is where the finesse portion of the conversation becomes critical,* he thought, forcing himself to concentrate even though his head had turned muzzy.

'Yes,' he started, 'Mr. Lapine . . .'

Before he could continue, Stephen jumped off the front porch in much the same manner as Frankie had earlier, holding his hand out. 'Phinneaus? Now that's an interesting name. Is it biblical? Mythological?'

The man smiled at Stephen, but his hand stayed firmly on the gun. 'I believe it's after P. T. Barnum, but my mother had a peculiar way with the spelling of things. Never met a vowel she didn't like. And you?'

'Jameson. Stephen Jameson. Oh, and this is Professor Dennis Finch. Maybe you've heard of him? He wouldn't tell you himself—quite modest, as it turns out—but he's extremely well-respected in the art world. Writer, historian, lecturer, that sort of thing. I wouldn't be surprised if he'd appeared on public television at some point.' Stephen raised his eyebrows hopefully at Finch, who cringed, wishing he was elsewhere.

'Is that so? Forgive me for not seeing the connection, but what would any of that have to do with the Kesslers?'

'We've come for the paintings, of course,' Stephen said. 'Let's cut to the chase here. It's late. We're all cold and we can wrap this up in no time. The way I see it, odds are pretty fair you'd make an obscene amount of money, but if you prefer to focus on the bigger picture, great art can't be kept to oneself. Well, it can of course. Wealthy people do it all the time. But it's selfish, don't you think? Let me put it in perspective for you. It's your moral obligation to share it with the world.'

Finch put his hand to his head, now feeling truly ill, and sank back down on the porch. He was going to end up shot by a stranger with an unusual name, and from the looks of him, the man knew his way around a firearm.

'Better get him inside,' Phinneaus said.

Stephen stuck his hands under Finch's armpits and hoisted him to his feet. The woman, Saisee, held the door open and pointed to a sofa in the living room 'You'd better put him there. Who drinks cold water when they're sick? What he needs is some tea.'

He started to protest but found his legs uncooperative. Let Stephen steer him then. He'd managed to make matters about as bad as they could be. *I wash my hands of it*, thought Finch, tired of being the voice of reason. Let someone else take a turn being in charge. He leaned back on the comfortable pillows of the sofa, balking when Stephen tried to remove his shoes. He had no plans to expose his socks to strangers. Was he even wearing socks? He'd gotten so cold he couldn't feel much of anything below his knees and couldn't remember what he'd put on in the hotel room. All he knew was his head was pounding out a fierce rhythm and his teeth were chattering away, keeping time.

Saisee brought out the tea and poured him a cup, taking care to move it close enough to the edge of the table so he could reach it without sitting up all the way. As he lifted it to his mouth, a cloud of cinnamon, cloves, tea, and orange wafted up from the cup. He closed his eyes and inhaled deeply.

'Is this Russian tea? I haven't had it for years. My wife used to make it for me, when I was in danger of losing my voice. Too many lectures, I'd tell her. Too long-winded was what she'd tell me.'

Saisee nodded with a satisfied smile.

He took a large gulp. It was elixir, working its way down his throat, soothing his head, thawing his extremities. 'Thank you. I apologize. This is very . . .'

'Embarrassing,' Stephen interjected.

Finch's energy was limited and he chose not to waste it conveying his annoyance to Stephen. 'I suppose that's as good a word as any. Miss . . . I'm sorry, I don't know your last name.'

'Saisee's fine.'

'Saisee. Mr. Lapine. I appreciate your hospitality, especially seeing as how we've forced ourselves on you at a late hour with no warning, and I seem to be operating in a diminished capacity. I want to assure you we don't mean to intrude or cause any disruption. I assume Alice Kessler is not here?'

Phinneaus nodded.

'And I would imagine both of you are friends of the Kesslers?' Since Phinneaus's nephew seemed to have the run of the house, and Saisee had called Phinneaus in as reinforcement, Finch thought he must be, or have been, involved with one of the sisters. While the man wasn't willingly offering up information, Finch suspected from his guarded responses he knew more than he was going to share.

'Neither myself nor Mr. Jameson is personally acquainted with Natalie or Alice Kessler, nor are we friends of their

family. But we would have recognized them.' Finch patted
the pockets of his coat and removed from one a long envelope, handing it to Saisee, who in turn passed it to Phinneaus.
He opened it and pulled out the photographs that Stephen
had taken of the main triptych panel and the sketch at the
Edells'.

'I don't know whether either of you have ever heard of
the artist Thomas Bayber. My colleague Mr. Jameson generously exaggerates my accomplishments. It is, in fact, Mr.
Bayber whose work is well-known and respected. The sketch
you see in the photograph is one of his earliest works. It
hangs in the Kesslers' home in Connecticut, where both the
girls were born.'

Finch saw a flash of curiosity. 'Seven hundred Stonehope
Way?' Phinneaus asked. 'In Woodridge?' The man's tone
changed.

'You're familiar with the house?'

'I know Natalie and Alice grew up there.'

'Yes. And then disappeared from that same house rather
abruptly when they were both in their early twenties. No
one was able to find them.'

Phinneaus stared at the photograph of the triptych panel.
'Which implies someone was looking for them,' he said.

Finch nodded.

'This man,' Phinneaus said. It was not a question.

Finch's acquaintance was with Thomas, not the Kesslers,
so his protective instincts were somewhat tempered, and the
shock he'd felt the first time he saw the painting had dissipated over his many subsequent viewings of it. Nonetheless,
he could easily recall that initial reaction; his immediate
understanding that something had transpired between these
three people that should not have. Everyone who'd looked
at the painting was discomforted and uneasy, as if barbed

wire was the thing linking Thomas to Natalie and Alice, piercing the heart of each. Regardless of the physical distance between the sisters, there was the feeling that Natalie and Alice were barely cognizant of each other's presence, that each girl was alone with Thomas in the painting.

What was equally obvious to Finch now, seeing the pained expression on Phinneaus's face, was that this man was in love with one of the girls. A man might desire Natalie based on the painting, providing he didn't look too closely. Viewed from a distance, Natalie hypnotized and beguiled; she was a study in gold—her hair, her skin, her eyes, her youth, all of it swirled together and shimmering up from the canvas. But when one looked closer, what was beneath her expression became visible: a quiet, contained rage, a measure of ruthlessness, a determination to have her way. No, Finch decided, Phinneaus would be in love with Alice. In that moment, he felt as if something small and private had been stolen from him.

'Mr. Bayber's family had a summer house in upstate New York. The Kesslers vacationed there as well, staying at the home of a family friend. Thomas Bayber met them in the late summer of 1963 and composed the sketch of the family, most likely as a gift for them. The painting was done at a much later date.'

'And who is the man in the painting?' Phinneaus asked.

Finch swallowed, wishing there was a way not to have to answer the question. 'Thomas Bayber.'

Phinneaus closed his eyes for a moment, and his expression did not change, although Finch could tell by the way he clenched his hand into a hard knot he was exercising a great deal of control. 'The artist.'

'Yes.' He rushed on, hoping a barrage of facts would defuse the situation. 'Mr. Jameson is an authenticator. He believes this panel of the painting was done sometime in the early seventies, maybe ten years or so after the family sat for this sketch.'

'This panel?' Phinneaus turned to Stephen, who had assigned himself a corner chair and was folding and unfolding his napkin like a piece of origami. 'You mentioned coming here for the paintings. There are more like this?'

Stephen nodded. 'Two. The painting you see is the main panel in a triptych. We are looking for the adjoining panels, which would have hung on either side.'

'I know what a triptych is. This may be a small town, Mr. Jameson, but you'd be wise not to make assumptions about the people who live here without getting to know them, and I doubt you're interested in staying around long enough to do that. What makes you think the other panels are here?'

'Because Bayber said he sent them to her.'

Phinneaus stood up suddenly, nearly knocking over his chair. Whether he was angry or confused, Finch wasn't sure, but Stephen's tone, which Finch had long ago become accustomed to, wasn't helping the situation.

'Saisee, we've imposed upon you so much already, but I wonder if I might ask an additional favor?' Finch said.

The woman had been standing all the while, still and listening.

'Mr. Jameson suffers from low blood sugar and usually becomes intolerably rude just before he faints. Is it possible you could find something for him in the kitchen?'

She nodded, perhaps sensing it would be in everyone's interest to separate Stephen and Phinneaus before they came to blows, although if Stephen's eye was any indication, he'd again be on the receiving end.

'You come with me, Mr. Jameson. I was making cheddar grits and a pork roast for dinner. We have plenty, and I'd be happy to make you a plate. You ever had grits before?'

'I've had mush.'

Saisee laughed. 'Well, unless you had it dipped in flour and pan-fried in butter 'til it turned a real pretty golden brown, and then you doused it in honey, you didn't even have grits' poor cousin.'

Stephen followed her from the room like a puppy dog, and as soon as he was out of earshot, Finch sat up and put his feet firmly on the floor.

'Mr. Lapine, I've handled this badly. I came here to keep a promise to Thomas Bayber, a promise I shouldn't have made. I don't know Alice Kessler, and you don't know Thomas, but of the two of them, whatever faults they may have, I have little doubt Alice is the better human being. You question Thomas Bayber's character. I can't blame you for that. I had similar feelings the first time I saw the painting, and I've struggled at times to remind myself it is a painting, not a photograph. It's Thomas's vision, interpretation, and imagination you're looking at. He's far from perfect, but I cannot begrudge him his talent, and his talent is very great, indeed.'

'You gave him your word to do something. So he's a friend of yours?'

Finch smiled and shook his head. 'You're asking a complicated question. There have been times when I thought perhaps we were friends. I've come to the conclusion I'm not sure friendship is something he's capable of, at least not in the way you or I might define it. I've studied him, and his career, for more years than I care to count. Like many of the artists I've met, he can be difficult to understand, and even harder to get to know. Thomas is driven by inner demons, hasn't had a relationship that's lasted more than a year as far as I know, and is reckless with his health. His initial reaction to everything and everyone is suspicion, because he believes anyone who has an interest in meeting him wants something.'

'Forgive my saying so, but he doesn't sound like a good person.'

'No. I'm not portraying him in a very positive light, am I? The thing of it is, Mr. Lapine, I'm afraid the same could be said of any of us at some point in our lives. Would you agree?'

Phinneaus considered this, then said, 'That may be true. But it doesn't make me want to help him, and it doesn't explain why you would want to either. Is he paying you?'

'No. My sole reward would be in seeing another of his works come to light. But you don't know anything about the other two panels, do you?'

'I'm sorry. I don't. It's odd I never considered it before, but there hasn't been any art on these walls since the day Natalie and Alice moved in. Plenty of mirrors—that would have been Natalie's doing—but no artwork.'

'You didn't like her?'

'Natalie died a few months ago, so whether I liked her or not doesn't have much bearing on anything.' Phinneaus's look was honest but indifferent. Finch understood the man had his own code, which he would not violate.

'Mr. Lapine, there's something else I should tell you. Thomas had a stroke in late October, almost immediately after he asked Mr. Jameson and me to try to locate the missing panels of the painting. He's been unable to speak, his health is very poor. The doctors aren't optimistic about his recovery.' Finch took a deep breath. If Phinneaus knew what he was about to say, he wasn't giving anything away with his expression. But if Alice hadn't confided in him about her past, how much could he tell the man, guessing the impact it might have?

'As the person responsible for cataloging Bayber's works, I was given access to all his correspondence. There were years of it to sift through—articles, letters, requests for showings.' Finch cleared his throat. Where was the damn glass of water when he needed it?

'Natalie Kessler sent Thomas a photograph in the late spring or early summer of 1972. The return address she used was that of the house in Woodridge. Bayber was in Europe for several months that year, and didn't return to the States until late in the fall. When he had a chance to review his correspondence, he was very anxious to get in touch with the sisters, Alice in particular.'

'When did you find out the letter existed?'

'A few weeks ago.'

'If you only found out about the letter a few weeks ago, how can you know he was anxious to get in touch with Alice?'

Beads of sweat pearled on Finch's forehead. In his nervousness, he had clenched and unclenched his toes with a degree of ferocity that gave him raging foot cramp. When did the task fall to him, to speculate and hypothesize about what Alice and Natalie may or may not have done? Why couldn't he have remained pleasantly ignorant? None of this was his business after all. He was not cut out for a life of treachery and innuendo.

'I found several letters Thomas wrote to Alice and to Natalie, all of them returned, unopened. I believe there was another reason he wanted me to find the paintings, the primary reason. It has nothing to do with the work itself. However, his present condition has prevented me from confirming any of this, and I am a poor excuse for a detective.'

Finch's sympathy for the man standing in front of him,

challenging him, grew in direct proportion to his anger with Thomas for putting him in this position in the first place. 'Mr. Lapine, are you a parent?'

Phinneaus's face lost its color, but he did not seem surprised by the question. A flood of relief washed over Finch. *He knows. Thank God, he knows.*

'I am, you see. I have a daughter, Lydia, and I cannot imagine my life without her. You asked me earlier if Thomas Bayber was my friend. The truth is I have a great deal of sympathy for him in this one regard—as one parent to another.'

'I wish I could help you.'

The dismissal was not unkind, but it was clear. Phinneaus wasn't going to tell him anything. Whatever he knew, he would keep it to himself in order to protect Alice.

'Wherever Ms. Kessler is, when she returns, would you ask her to contact me?'

'Of course, although I have no idea when I might see her again.' Phinneaus took Finch's card and fingered the edge of it before sliding it into his shirt pocket. 'It's not that I don't sympathize, Professor. You said you didn't know Alice, just as I don't know this Bayber. You're right. But I can tell you this. Whatever you might think of Natalie Kessler, you'd be correct. And whatever you think of Alice, you'd be mistaken.'

'The older I get, Mr. Lapine, the more I realize it's sometimes preferable not knowing the answers to things. In fact, I often wish I'd never heard the question.' Finch stood up and pulled his coat around him, feeling steadier on his feet. He had done all he could. Before he knew it, he would be home again. 'I'll collect Mr. Jameson, and we'll leave you to your much-delayed dinner.'

But there was no need for him to collect Stephen, since

he was very nearly run over by him in his mad rush into the room.

'Finch, well enough to travel? We need to go. Now.' Stephen tugged on his coat sleeve like a three-year-old, pulling him toward the door. With a glance over his shoulder he said, 'Phinneaus, I meant no offense. I hope none was taken. Saisee, just to review, the ratio of liquid to grits is five to one, and salt the water first, correct?' He left Finch's side just long enough to dash over to the woman and peck her quickly on the cheek. 'My expectations in regards to grits were extremely low, but I believe you may be a culinary genius. I've never tasted anything so wonderful in my life.' She put her hand to her cheek while Phinneaus and Finch looked at the two of them in amazement.

'Have you lost your mind?' Finch asked when they were once again safely in the car.

'Finch, I hope you really are feeling better, because we're flying to Santa Fe.'

Much of the ride back to Dyersburg was spent in a circular argument, Stephen insisting they get to Santa Fe as quickly as possible and Finch equally insistent they abandon the enterprise altogether.

'You gave him your word. How can you possibly stop now?'

'And you tricked that woman. You don't feel guilty about that?'

'Not in the least. And how did I trick her? I only asked if she would write down her grits recipe for me so I could try to make it myself.'

'Do you even own a pan?'

The genteel niceties and false flattery, the obsequious politeness required to tease information from someone; it devoured an obscene amount of time, and Stephen had no patience for it. There was a far more straightforward approach to the problem. Go to the kitchen. The kitchen was always the hub of information. Finch had been brilliant to suggest it, actually. He should have thought of it himself. He'd been a little disappointed to learn Finch had really thought he was hungry, or in danger of being punched.

Regardless, it had turned out better than he'd expected. There was a calendar hanging on the wall next to an old-fashioned wall-mounted telephone in a horrid shade of mustard. He'd scanned the calendar while Saisee had her back to him, copying down the recipe, and found two notations that provided him with everything he needed. The first was from four days ago—'Amtrak NBN, 58—CONO, Union, 3—SWC.' The second notation was a phone number. He'd only had time to see the area code, prefix, and one other digit before Saisee turned back to the table, but that was enough.

There were 282 area codes assigned to locations in the United States and its territories. The entire state of New Mexico had used area code 505 since 1947, but just two months ago, those areas outside northwestern and central New Mexico—the majority of the state—had been assigned a new area code: 575. Santa Fe, Albuquerque, and Farmington were still 505. The prefix 982 was for the city of Santa Fe.

If he mentioned any of this, Finch would assume he'd memorized the entire list of 282 area codes. The truth was that Dylan Jameson had had dealings with several galleries in Santa Fe, and Stephen had memorized all of the numbers in his father's Rolodex over several long and tedious summer afternoons while he was a teenager. Alice Kessler was in Santa Fe, New Mexico, and had already been there a few days. Stephen had the feeling they didn't have much time.

'The point is, Stephen, we're causing damage. It's enough. I'm tired of trying to undo others' transgressions. I haven't the stomach for it. I want to go home and spend the holiday with my daughter and son-in-law and forget this entire business.'

'Finch, be reasonable. You say we've done everything we can, but that's not true. We won't have done everything until we find Alice and ask her about the paintings. We don't have to ask her anything else.'

Finch rolled his eyes. 'Oh, and you'd stop there. Do you have any idea what the population of Santa Fe is? No, don't answer. I'm sure you do and that will only depress me. You think she's going to be walking around Santa Fe waving a sign that reads, 'I'm Alice Kessler'?'

'I can find her.'

'I'd argue the point, but say you can. What makes you think she'd tell us anything about the painting or her daughter? You don't have children. You don't understand a parent will do anything necessary to protect a child. For whatever reason, she chose not to tell Thomas. Do you honestly think after all this time she's going to open up just because two strangers stroll into town, track her down like a felon, and start peppering her with questions?'

'Think of Bayber then, never getting a chance to know his own daughter. Is that fair?' Unfortunately the more agitated Stephen got, the more apparent his motivation became. Finch knew why he didn't want to stop looking until they found the paintings.

'Of course it's not fair, but it's beyond our control, Stephen. You think solving this is going to change your life. That would seem to be an unreasonable expectation, to say nothing of a wholly selfish one.'

'These aren't just any paintings and you know it.'

'So this is all about reclaiming your former glory? To hell with anyone who gets hurt along the way?'

'You've picked an odd time to develop a conscience, Finch. I'm only doing the job I've been asked to. Maybe that's why he wanted me in the first place. Because he knew you'd become too emotionally involved, let yourself get entangled in all these relationships or nonrelationships, whatever they are. Whereas I can focus solely on the task at hand. What's unreasonable about that?'

Finch wheeled into the motel parking lot with a spray of gravel. 'I don't know why Thomas wanted you. Maybe he felt sorry for you. Maybe he felt he owed something to Dylan. Whatever the reason, it doesn't matter. I'm done.'

'Then I'll find her on my own.' Stephen jumped out of the front seat, slamming the door behind him. Unfortunately, since Finch had upgraded their rental, the resulting gesture was not as dramatic as he'd hoped. He took the outside stairs to the second floor two at a time, unlocked the door to his room, and slipped in. He left the lights off, preferring the forgiving dark to the harsh reality of the motel room lamps, and leaned against the wall.

He hadn't expected that from Finch, the sucker punch, the suggestion Bayber felt sorry for him. It was disappointing to consider Bayber might have been aware of his dismal prospects, his clumsy tumble from grace. Stephen had opted not to reflect too intently on why he'd been chosen, imagining it was the result of a confusing web of connections—his father, Finch, Cranston—with the weight of his prior reputation sealing the deal. Self-pity he'd had in spades, but the pity of others was something he hadn't considered. The thought of it rooted in him like a weed.

He sat on the bed, opened his laptop and checked flights, then booked himself out of Memphis at noon the next day.

He called the front desk and asked for a taxi pickup at seven-thirty. At least he'd be spared the torture of another drive with Finch. He pulled up a list of hotels in Santa Fe. Only five had the prefix and initial digit he'd seen marked on the calendar. He turned on his cell phone, punching in the first number on the list, then stopped and turned the phone off. What if she wasn't at any of the hotels? What if she'd already checked out and was on her way back to Tennessee? She'd be chugging east on the return leg of the Southwest Chief while he was soaring overhead in the wrong direction.

And then there was the problem of what to say. He'd been counting on Finch to smooth the way with Alice. The two of them had Bayber in common, and what did he have? Nothing. Finch would have known how to start, how to ease into the conversation so that they might discover something before getting the door slammed in their faces. Although Stephen hated to admit it, while he'd found out where Alice was, Finch was the one who'd gotten them into the house.

Finch was right. He was constructing a future based on the successful outcome of this one venture. He *could* call each of the hotels now and ask for Alice Kessler, but if there was no guest by that name he'd be going back to New York empty-handed. Cranston would cut him loose. Stephen foresaw a move back to his mother's house, the terse snippets of conversation, the Help Wanted section she'd slide beneath his door, her suggestions evenly highlighted in yellow marker. He groaned and rolled onto his back, staring at the moonscape of the popcorn ceiling before falling asleep in his clothes.

FIFTEEN

The next morning Stephen dragged his suitcase down the steps behind him, not caring much who he woke. Where was the damn cab? He stamped his feet on the frost-tinged asphalt trying to warm them up. After a few minutes of waiting and pacing, he walked to the front office. The clerk was nowhere to be seen, but Finch was waiting for him, holding two cups of coffee.

'I canceled your cab. I hope you don't mind.'

Stephen couldn't recall ever being so glad to see someone and chuffed Finch on the arm, nearly upending both cups of coffee.

'You changed your mind?'

'It would appear so.'

'But . . .'

'I had a conversation with my spiritual adviser last night. She convinced me it was the right thing to do, and that I owed you an apology. She was right, as usual. My suggesting Bayber wanted you for the job because he pitied you was inexcusable, Stephen. In all the years I've been acquainted with him, I've never known Thomas to do something out of kindness or concern for another human being. I see no reason for him to start now. I think he asked for you because you are talented and determined and, as you reminded me last night, not easily swayed by emotions.'

'You do realize this means another flight?'

'At least it's not raining. I'll sock in a supply of pink pills when we get to the airport.'

'Finch, I've narrowed it down to five hotels.'

Finch nodded. 'You're steering this boat now, Stephen. I'm just along for the ride.'

'I don't know who your spiritual adviser is—I wouldn't think you'd go in for that sort of thing—but I love her.' Stephen threw his bags into the backseat of the rental car.

'Get in line,' Finch said, under his breath, and Stephen saw him look to the heavens and shake his head.

They had an hour-and-a-half layover in Houston. Finch spent the time trading e-mails with Lydia, and since Stephen didn't want to push his luck, he ignored the impulse to ask Finch if he might mention him favorably in one of his replies. On the flight to Albuquerque, he was so jumpy the flight attendant asked if he was ill. For the first time since they'd undertaken the endeavor, Stephen was less than one hundred percent sure they would succeed. If only he'd been able to communicate with Bayber. There were so many questions he wanted to ask him. Though it was illogical, Stephen still fostered the hope that finding the missing paintings would initiate Bayber's miraculous recovery. Seeing the old man gasping for breath had been a horrible experience, one he wasn't anxious to repeat. He longed to see all of them together in a room: Bayber, Finch, Cranston, his mother. They'd beam at him, and in unison speak one simple sentence: *Your father would have been proud.*

'I reserved a car for us while we were in Houston. The trip to Santa Fe is just over an hour,' Finch said as they landed. 'What are our plans?'

'I made hotel reservations for us downtown. One of the five hotels on the list. I thought we could have an early dinner, turn in, and get started first thing tomorrow.'

'You don't want to start tonight?'

Stephen didn't answer, only rubbed his hands together, trying to rid them of peanut skin flakes and the grains of salt lodged beneath his fingernails. 'What if you're right, Finch? She could have come and gone by now.'

'Well, it's doubtful she'll be holding a sign with our names and waiting for us in baggage claim.' Finch thumped him on the back. 'Stephen, let's take advantage of this one night, before we have any inkling of what the outcome may be. We'll spend a bit of Cranston's money on good wine, sleep in comfortable beds, have a ridiculously large breakfast tomorrow morning, and then we shall see what we shall see. Agreed?'

'Agreed.'

The cars Finch rented were getting larger with each trip, which Stephen took to be a bad sign. The professor was spending Cranston's money while it was there to be spent, and as he slid back and forth across the seat of the SUV with every curve, he was sure Finch was only humoring him.

Finch tapped the leather-wrapped steering wheel and smiled. 'It's like manning a boat. Four-wheel drive, heated seats, DVD entertainment system in the rear.'

'Should I be sitting back there?' Stephen asked.

'It'd be impossible to manage a hulk like this in the city. But out here we're practically alone on the highway.'

'Maybe we're just sitting up too high to see any of the other cars.'

Finch gave him a wary glance. 'This would not be a good car to be sick in.' He pressed a button, and Stephen's window opened a crack, flooding the interior with cold, sharp-scented air that tickled his nose.

'It's the elevation I'm not used to,' Stephen said. He'd practically had to vault himself into the front seat.

'You're right. The air is thinner.'

Stephen couldn't remember the last time he was surrounded by so much open space. The sun was a purpled orange disk, its lower third sliced off with scalpel-like precision by the table of a mesa, the rest of it backed by clouds in sherbet hues. The mountains rising above Santa Fe were dusky blue, interrupted by dark saw blades of pines crisscrossing the lower slopes. Elsewhere he saw dead beige: the mat of dun-colored grass running along the highway, the plains stretched out in front of them. It was late afternoon, and as dusk settled it fuzzed the outlines of things and flattened them out.

Santa Fe, by contrast, was a sparkling maze of low, blocky buildings and shadow-casting lights. A pale gold suffused the town. It glowed from ranks of paper bags outlining the tops of buildings and walls and the borders of drives; it twinkled from the branches of trees and the undersides of eaves; it blinked at him from tangled clumps tossed over hedges like nets flung across dark water. It was all magical and enchanting, and he entertained the notion that things might right themselves after all.

The restaurant, too, was warm and glowing, painted in candlelight. He and Finch ate and drank, settling into comfortable, sparring conversation. No mention was made of the painting, of the Kesslers, of the letters, or of the child. It was the kind of conversation Stephen would have loved to have shared with his father, but could not remember the two of them ever having had.

His phone buzzed in his pocket, and Finch scowled. It was a piece of technology the professor had no use for, bemoaning the slow death of written correspondence, the U.S. Postal Service, and the corded phone, all of which, he said, allowed for occasional, and necessary, interludes of blessed silence. Stephen checked the device under cover of the tablecloth.

'It's Lydia,' he said, and Finch's indignant look melted. 'She's texting me, asking why you don't have your phone on.'

'Is she all right? What's the matter?'

'Well, we can assume her thumbs are fine,' Stephen answered. 'As happy as I am to be the go-between, why don't you turn on your phone and ask her yourself?'

Finch stood up and dropped his napkin on the table. 'It's after eleven there, late for her to be calling. Can you sign the check, Stephen? I'll try calling her back from the phone in my room. The buttons are bigger.'

Stephen woke the next morning with the buzz of a headache circling the back side of his brain and swallowed aspirin with the water he found on the bedside table. Altitude, drink, and apprehension were not the makings of a productive day. He took a hot shower and scrubbed himself with the entire bottle of eucalyptus body wash he found in the bathroom. His head cleared, and smelling like a forest, he went downstairs to meet Finch in the restaurant.

Finch didn't look as though he'd slept at all, his face the color of skim milk, a hint of stubble bracing his chin.

'Lydia's not ill, is she?' Stephen asked, with some degree of trepidation.

'Not in so many words,' Finch said, looking preoccupied. 'She's pregnant.'

'Oh,' Stephen said. Well, that wasn't going to advance his cause. No doubt she'd be even fonder of *the Kelvin* in light of this development. 'Aren't you happy about it?'

Finch nodded, a ridiculous grin taking over the lower half of his face. He had the doting expression of a grandfather already. Stephen worried he was looking for someone to hug.

'Boy or girl?'

'I don't know. What I mean is, they don't want to know in advance.'

The man was practically giddy. Stephen had never heard so many consecutive contented sighs; he feared Finch might be hyperventilating. But the professor gave him a quick embrace, slapped him companionably on the back, then wrinkled his nose at the smell of eucalyptus still lingering on Stephen's skin. In the hotel's dining room, Finch ordered champagne, then interrupted Stephen's drinking of it with several toasts: first to Lydia, then to the grandchild, then to himself, employing the word *grandfather* as often as possible.

'Finch, this is all well and good, and I am happy for you, but we have important business to attend to. You haven't forgotten?'

'Of course not.' But his expression was one of muddled distraction. Stephen shook his head and forced himself to eat the toast crusts that remained on his plate.

After breakfast they walked to the lobby and sat next to each other in stiff leather chairs, the house phone on a table between them. 'I don't suppose there's any point in waiting,' he said.

'No. Best to get on with it.'

Stephen picked up the receiver. 'I'd like another guest's room, please. Could you connect me with Alice Kessler?' There was a pause while the desk clerk ran through the list.

'I'm sorry, sir. I don't show a guest by that name staying with us.'

Stephen put the receiver back and shook his head. 'Should I try the others?'

'What say we walk to them? After all, it's a lovely morning. Might give us the chance to look at a few galleries along the way. You did say the other hotels were on the square, or nearby, didn't you?'

Stephen had to give Finch credit for putting up a front. After all, it was no pressing concern of his anymore. He'd be going back to his cozy apartment, the lovely mushrooming Lydia, and after the holiday break, his classes. There was a family waiting for him in the truest sense of the word. Stephen thought of his mother's dusty artificial tree, its branches bent at odd angles, the painted metal showing through where needles had dropped like teeth, after years of being crammed into and pulled out from the same too-small box.

In less than an hour they had checked the remaining four hotels. No Alice Kessler at any of them, nothing further volunteered as to whether or not she had already come and gone. 'Against our policy to provide that sort of information' was the repeated refrain. Aside from going back to Orion and throwing himself on Phinneaus's mercy, Stephen was forced to admit they'd run out of options. He could feel the walls of his tiny office at Murchison & Dunne closing in and hear the screech of the elevator as it passed his floor and set the odds and ends on his desk rattling. Would Cranston keep him through the holidays or dispense with him immediately, putting his meager paycheck toward the expenses incurred funding this wild-goose chase? He stopped walking and leaned against a light pole, suddenly exhausted, his hand on his forehead.

'Stephen.'

'I'm all right. Just give me a minute, please.'

'Stephen.'

'For God's sake, Finch, you have to admit it's horrible.' He looked up to see Finch standing in front of a gallery, staring through the window at a piece of sculpture.

'Look at this,' Finch said, then ran inside.

Stephen walked to the window and put his hand to the glass, shielding his eyes from the sun. Finch was gesturing expansively to a young woman in a denim skirt and dangling earrings that brushed the tops of her shoulders. The sculpture was stainless steel, a sensuous form, like a cross between a cloud and a splotch. The edges were curved and exquisitely smooth, and the metal gleamed with reflected and refracted light, throwing prisms of color at the ceiling. The sign at the base read, 'Vertical Puddle #3—A. Kessler.'

A. Kessler. Alice. It hadn't occurred to him she might be an artist. Admittedly, he hadn't given much thought to how she'd earned a living after she dropped out of graduate school, though a career in ornithology seemed a far leap from sculpting. But if she was a sculptor, it made sense for her to be in Santa Fe. And if she was here, she could be found. He reached for the window ledge to steady himself. They had actually managed to track her down.

He headed into the gallery at the same time Finch was coming out, running square into him in the middle of the doorway.

'We've found Alice!' He was suddenly ravenous and breathless and happier than he could ever recall being. 'Did you get a number? Where is she staying?'

Finch had an odd look on his face, wistful and uncertain. 'It's not Alice we've found.'

'What do you mean? 'A. Kessler.' It says so right beneath the piece in the front window.'

'Agnete. A. Kessler is Agnete. Stephen, we may have found Thomas's daughter. Not Alice.'

'But Alice was here, in Santa Fe. I saw the note on the calendar. Maybe she was coming to visit her daughter. This is perfect.'

'Hardly the word I would use, but I suppose we'll find out soon enough. I left my card with the gallery owner. She's going to contact Agnete and try to set up a meeting.'

'But what did you say?'

'I lied.'

A lie had never come to him so quickly. He hadn't stopped to think—A. Kessler could only be Alice—and he'd charged in, asking about the sculpture in the window.

'A local artist. She does the most beautiful, unique pieces. Most of them are quite large; she did this one especially for me to showcase in the gallery. Agnete Kessler.' The woman pushed her hair behind her ears and smiled warmly, assessing his potential as a buyer.

'You said Agnete?'

'Yes. Would you like some information? I have a tear sheet here somewhere.'

He'd panicked, completely unprepared to stumble upon her so easily, now, when he thought the whole thing finally finished. *I want to talk to her about a commission.* A total fabrication, and once he'd said it, there was no way to circle around to his real reason for wanting to see her. The tear sheet was already creased; he'd folded it immediately and tucked it inside his coat pocket. He didn't want to see Agnete's face. Alice was the one they had to talk to first, not her daughter. There was nothing he could say to Agnete without betraying Alice, and he wasn't willing to do that to the young woman who stared at him intently from the painting, or the slightly older girl in the photograph, the one who'd looked so blissful.

'She might not contact us at all.'

'Finch, why wouldn't she? She's an artist, it's a commission; she's likely starving, most artists are. The thing is, I actually like her work, at least this piece. It is just like looking in a puddle. Or a fun-house mirror. Or both.'

'Fine. You offer to buy something and we can leave it at that.'

'You're joking.'

'I'm not so sure.'

'Finch, we have to find out if she knows anything about the painting. That's the whole reason we're here. If she happens to want to come back to New York with us and meet her father, so much the better. We're heroes on all fronts.'

'Heroes?' Finch shook his head, stunned Stephen could be so oblivious to the larger picture. 'Do you seriously suppose Alice will see it that way? Don't you think it's her decision when and what Agnete should be told about Thomas, if anything at all? You can't get that sort of news from total strangers.'

'Well, we haven't found Alice, have we? And aren't you supposed to be on Bayber's side in all of this? As her father, shouldn't he have a say in whether or not she knows?'

'It's not a question of taking sides.'

'Finch, I know you think I'm only concerned with myself, and that's mostly true. I'm honest enough to admit it. But I have to see those paintings. I lie awake at night thinking about Natalie and Alice, wondering if I've gotten it right. The only thing I know about with any certainty is the hands, nothing else. Not how old they are, or what they're wearing; not if there are other people with them, or if they're alone.

Look, whatever sordid mess the three of them made of their personal lives isn't my business; I'm sorry for them if that counts for anything. But for the first time in my life, I actually want to know the story, Finch. I want to know what Bayber was trying to say, not just what the other panels look like. It's the closest I've ever come to feeling like my father. How can you not want to know? How can you not do everything in your power to find out?'

Finch held up his hands, having heard enough. An overwhelming weight bore down on him; he could hear the dominoes falling, one against another, the solid click echoing in his ears. 'It's done. It doesn't matter whether or not I want to know. It's too late to stop it now.'

'So what do we do?'

'We wait for Agnete.'

She called midafternoon while they were sitting in the hotel lobby, Stephen gorging on the complimentary crackers, cheese, and sherry. Finch noted the landscape of scattered crumbs surrounding his napkin; the man ate mindlessly when nervous. He had set his cell phone on a small table between them, and when it rang they both fixed on it, watching it vibrate across the dark wood surface before Stephen grabbed it and thrust it toward Finch, trying to swallow a mouthful of cheese.

Her voice was not what he'd imagined, but how could he imagine it at all? He might have expected her to sound like Alice, but did Alice have a sound? An intelligent shyness that was halting and melodic? The voice of a songbird, bright and crisp against the morning air? Or Agnete might have claimed Thomas's suspicion and wariness, speaking briskly, with a cool detachment. All were assumptions likely fed by his own guilt. Instead, Agnete's tone was warm and confident. She would swing by the hotel and pick them up; they could see more of her completed work, as well as some of the pieces that were in progress, at her studio adjacent to the house, which was not far from the square.

'It's not a hard walk if you're inclined, but you've probably been walking around town all morning, and if you haven't been here long you can get turned around. I wouldn't want to lose you en route. You could end up at someone else's home, in someone else's studio, looking at their work instead.' She laughed.

Finch's laugh was more forced and uncomfortable. Shame gnawed at him, at his extremities, his gut. She was charming. He had the scruples of a flatworm. By the time he hung up, Stephen was a dog in heat, pacing around the sofa, hands in his pockets, then out, then in again.

'Well?' he asked.

'She'll pick us up in half an hour. We're going to her house, to her studio, to look at her work. I hope you were serious earlier about buying something.'

'Could I borrow some money?'

Finch scowled at him, determined to share some of his dark mood. 'No, but I wouldn't let that stop you.' They both went to their rooms to freshen up and met in the lobby with five minutes to spare. Stephen had his briefcase, and Finch grudgingly clutched a black leather portfolio into which he'd inserted pertinent pieces of information, as well as the same photos he'd shared with Phinneaus two days earlier. Now that he'd accepted his role, he wanted the whole thing to be over with as quickly as possible.

He checked his watch every fifteen seconds, hoping she'd changed her mind. She'd described herself in the briefest terms: curly dark hair, blue eyes, work boots—practical, she said, for tromping back and forth between the house and the studio. Several young women passed through the lobby who might have been Agnete, but not a one glanced in his direction, and he was again reminded that being old rendered him invisible, whether he wished to be so or not.

Then she was there. He recognized her immediately, and was loosed from his moorings by the shock of a female version of a Thomas he had never known: younger, happier, radiant with health. Agnete had the best of Thomas, his characteristics visible only in the way they strengthened what would have been Alice's soft features. Her eyes were the same startling pale blue as her mother's; the fair skin could have come from either of them. Her hair was as inky as it had been in the photograph he had of her as a child, black curls spilling electrically over her shoulders; her walk spritely, as if there were too much of her to be contained in one tall, slender person. Out of the corner of his eye, Finch saw heads swivel as people watched her cross the room.

She headed directly toward them with her hand outstretched, and he felt himself pulled into her orbit. He wondered if she might have the power to heal; if Thomas, upon seeing the happy, whole person he had helped to create, someone living and breathing, not of oil but of flesh, might be imbued with some of her liveliness, her strength. He turned to Stephen to find him staring at his feet, his face flushed, his hands hidden behind his back. Finch poked him sharply in the ribs and put his hand out, asking, even though there was no need, 'Agnete?'

'You must be Professor Finch. I'm delighted to meet you. And you are Mr. Jameson?'

Stephen nodded and tried to say something but was overtaken by a coughing fit. Agnete promptly thwacked him hard on the back. 'Better?' she asked.

'I'm fine, thank you. And I'm just Stephen. Finch and Mr. Cranston are the only ones who call me Jameson.'

'Mr. Cranston?'

Finch jabbed him again. 'It's very thoughtful of you to pick us up. I'm sure we could have managed on our own.'

'Not nearly so thoughtful as you may think. I'll have you captive, won't I?'

She offered him a small, secret smile, and he was caught off guard—her attractiveness reminded him of Natalie, but she seemed completely guileless and genuinely warm. Before he could ask anything else, she waved them toward the door and they clambered into an old Volvo wagon wearing a film of dust, Finch in the front seat and Stephen in the back. He wanted to keep as much distance between them as he could, not trusting Stephen to contain himself. The inside of the car was spotless, as if she'd been expecting she might need to offer a ride to two strangers. She was a fast but competent driver, taking the corners without touching the brakes, and Finch thought she might have been equally at home in the city, maneuvering in and out of traffic, zipping into rare parking spots, ignoring insults hurled her way by less fearless drivers.

'Here we are,' she said, after a quick ten minutes. They pulled up in front of a low wall softened by clumps of grasses and low-branching trees on either end, and sprays of arching, red-berried shrubs that bordered a wide opening just off center, where a stone path cut through. There was a scripted metal address mounted on one side of the wall that read 'Eleven Calle Santa Isabel.' The wall, similar to others they'd seen in town, was decorated for the holiday, with neat paper bags lining the top and swags of cedar garland draped along its length.

'I have a few smaller pieces in the front courtyard you can look at to get an idea. The larger pieces are in the back.'

They followed her down the walk, past the wall, and into the courtyard. Finch was transported. He looked to his left and heard the fountain before he saw it, partially obscured by pots of cactus and holly and the bare stems of things already done for the year. Stephen gasped and when Finch turned his head, he saw why. The other side of the courtyard was full of movement; shaped pieces of stainless steel throwing light in every direction. There was a piece that looked like a school of fish, and as he approached it, he saw their movement was actually a reflection of himself, bloated and shrunken, swimming across the shiny metal surface of each individual piece. Beneath a bower of leafless trees was a sculpture of birds, a tornadic flock whose mass of silver wings darkened then gleamed as the sun moved in and out from behind clouds. Everywhere he looked there was some bit of magic to catch his eye, something beautifully fluid and deceptively simple.

'They're incredible,' Stephen said, staring at a comma of metal that appeared to be solid and heavy but was balanced on a thin rod. He turned to Agnete, who was standing with her arms crossed, watching both of them. 'Where in the world did you learn to do this? Where did you study?'

Finch wondered the same thing, though he wouldn't have asked. Not yet. Her talent was obvious. She had her father's imagination, his gift for seeing not only what was there but the space taken up by what was not, and melding them into what could be. Her work had a fresh, playful quality that excited him. The fact he'd never heard of her, never even seen any of her pieces, reminded him how isolated he'd become, so many of his years focused on only one subject—Bayber—to the exclusion of anything else. He was saddened to think of the talent he'd missed. All the up-and-coming artists he hadn't seen.

She shrugged. 'Nowhere, really. I suppose I'm a product of my environment. Practically everyone here is an artist. You know what they say. Something about the air.'

'I'm very impressed,' Finch said. 'I mean that. It's not something I say often.'

'I believe you.' She smiled. 'You're a collector, then?'

Ah, here was where the difficulty started. 'There are certain artists I'm very interested in,' he said, stumbling over the words, trying to feel his way into an explanation and looking up at the cloud-streaked sky as though divine intervention might save him. 'Mostly paintings, though. Do you paint, Ms. Kessler?'

'Please, call me Agnete. Or Aggie, if you like. I used to paint, but I wasn't very good at it. I always wanted to know what was going on behind the canvas. Don't you wonder that, when you see a painting that intrigues you? What else must be happening that you don't know about?' She laughed. 'I guess two dimensions aren't enough for me.'

Stephen piped up. 'I feel that way, too. What else is going on? What don't we know?'

'Exactly,' she said, looking pleased to be understood. 'Why don't you come in and I'll pour us all some sherry before we go out back.'

A chill lingered at the base of Finch's spine as they walked to the front door, a flat, persimmony orange that seemed in keeping with Agnete's style, understated but unique. She ushered them into the house and took their coats, hanging them on a rack by the door.

'We're here,' she called out.

Finch stopped. He hadn't anticipated having to do this in front of anyone else; a spouse, a boyfriend. 'We're interrupting, and it's getting close to dinner. Please, let me call for a taxi and we can talk more another time.' He had the urge to flee, but Stephen was standing in front of the door, blocking his way, shaking his head.

'Not at all,' Agnete said. 'I told you once I had you here, you were a captive audience. And you wouldn't want to leave now, not before you've seen everything.'

She disappeared around a corner, and when Finch hesitated, Stephen gave him a shove. He walked down a short hall and turned the corner, then froze as Stephen, close on his heels, bumped into him and nearly knocked him off the top step of the two leading down into the living room.

The two women were sitting on the hearth of a fireplace in the corner of the living room. Stephen grabbed his upper arm and squeezed it so hard Finch felt his fingers go numb. Hanging above the fireplace was a painting, the right triptych panel, a young Natalie cradling a child in one arm, with the other arm reaching out to her side beyond the edge of the frame.

Stephen let out a puff of air, a small 'oh,' before sinking down with an ungainly thud on the step where he was standing. The woman sitting next to Agnete cocked her head and stared at Finch evenly, her hair spilling around her face, a cloud of faded gold dashed with silver; her eyes the same ice blue they'd been in her youth, but more intent and fierce than he'd imagined. He realized it was not Thomas who had given Agnete her look of determination, but her mother.

'You must be Dennis Finch,' Alice Kessler said. 'I understand you've been looking for me.'

SIXTEEN

Agnete had whispered in her ear, 'I'll ask them to stay for dinner, shall I?' The rush of her daughter's breath was like a flutter of wing displacing air, a sensation she wished she could capture in a jar. 'Yes,' she'd said without thinking. 'That would be nice.' So she was in Agnete's kitchen, clumsily steering a wooden spoon through a pot of thick chili, while Mr. Jameson was outdoors, no doubt assailing her daughter with questions she would not know the answers to, and Professor Finch sat at the kitchen table nursing the dregs of a glass of wine, observing her from beneath his brows as though she might be a fata morgana.

She had not expected to feel so trapped, or so relieved. Her body was at odds with itself: her back and shoulders rigid with tension, her muscles as languorous as sap. Let them be the ones to tell her daughter. In the two precious days she'd had with Agnete, Alice had searched for where to begin, had struggled to pull the right words from the air. *Thomas Bayber is your father*. She'd gotten that much out and quickly, too, feeling something unlock in her as she said it, giving him the gift of finally being known. Agnete hadn't pushed, but Alice knew explanations were going to be required. How could she say what she needed to? It seemed easier to let someone assign her a role—be it perpetrator or victim—and she would play it. She let the spoon drift in the pot and swirled the reddish liquid in her mug, an herbal tea Agnete had procured from someone local, claiming it had healing properties. It tasted like summer: marigolds and something else peppery and ripe.

She watched through the bay window as her daughter pulled Stephen Jameson around the backyard, showing him the rest of her work, their dark heads bobbing almost in unison in the dimming light. It was fine as long as she kept her in sight, but every time Agnete disappeared around the corner of the house or went into another room, Alice was seized with a panic that she'd been dreaming and would wake up in her bed in Tennessee, alone and unknowing.

'She's very talented, your daughter,' Finch said, tilting his glass toward the window. Agnete's hands danced through the air, pointing first to the sky and then to a piece of sculpture. Stephen appeared to be completely absorbed by them, setting their intricate parts in motion with the touch of a finger or a purposeful breath. Finch was relieved to have him out of the house for a while so he could talk to Alice alone.

'And she must have magical powers. Unless he's sleeping or eating, I haven't been able to keep him quiet. Agnete's worked a spell on him.' He drummed his fingers against the tabletop in a rapid staccato until he noticed Alice watching.

'A bad habit,' he said. 'Something I do when I'm ill at ease.'

'I'm making you uncomfortable?'

'You? Not at all. It's everything that comes next.' He shrugged his shoulders and shook his head, his glasses sliding farther down his nose. 'I don't know how to do this. I was so certain we'd never find you that I didn't give enough thought to what would happen if we did.'

'If it puts you at ease, we're in the same boat.' She brought the wine from the shelf and refilled his glass, then sat down across from him, using both hands to pour tea into her mug.

Considering her image over these past months, he'd presumed an intimacy between them, as if she'd returned his every inspection, wondering about him from the confines of her gilded frame, making assumptions of his life. He understood now he knew nothing of the living, breathing Alice sitting across from him, a woman who had never so much as imagined his existence. Phinneaus might have given him some clue about her illness, however cryptic, but he'd chosen not to say anything, his sole concern to protect her. Finch admitted to a grudging respect for the man, knowing he would have done the same for Claire.

'I'd like to join you,' she said, nodding toward his hands, 'in the tapping. I still get a great deal of pleasure seeing the mechanics of the body work as they were meant to. It isn't quite the same as phantom limb syndrome, but I can almost feel your movements, or a distant memory of them, in my own fingers. It's like being visited by a friendly ghost.'

'You talk as though you've had to contend with this for a while.'

'Since I was fourteen.'

He blanched. At fourteen, Lydia had been playing piano sonatas and racing up and down the block with her friends, her feet flying beneath her in a blur of speed. He tried to imagine a lost adolescence, a lifetime of physical pain. 'You've been living with this for most of your life?'

She nodded and gave him a wry smile. 'My most constant companion.'

'Then you were sick when you were pregnant.' He heard Phinneaus's words. *Whatever you might think of her, you'd be mistaken.* 'I'm sorry. That's none of my business.'

Alice laughed, and his face reddened when he realized she was laughing at him, though not unkindly. 'I imagine I've been your business for several months now, Professor. It's not unusual for women with RA to feel better while they're pregnant. Before that, and then again after, I was on the standard regimen: cortisone, gold injections, antimalarials, d-penicillamine, methotrexate. Some things worked for a while. Most didn't.'

She set her cup down on the table, rubbing her hands. 'There's an alphabet of reputed cures for my disease, only a few of which I've not checked off my list: *C* for crow's meat—mixing it with spirits is supposed to be an ancient Chinese cure. *E* for earthworms. You store them in a container in a dark place for a few weeks, then rub the rancid oil on the affected joints. And *W* for standing inside the thorax of a whale carcass. I looked, but I couldn't find one. I will confess to going barefoot in Christmas snow—that counted as my *X*—and to green-lipped mussels, gin—which I very much enjoyed, by the way—bee venom, nettles. All of those in times of desperation, because they'd worked for somebody, at some point, so I thought, why not?'

'But you stayed in school. Your degree from Wesleyan, your graduate studies . . .'

'At a religious university, on a scholarship. Which was revoked once they found out I was pregnant. And unmarried. Not exactly in keeping with their moral code. It wasn't as devastating as I thought. The life I'd planned for had started to seem increasingly unlikely.' She held up her hands. 'Ornithology. It's hard to imagine holding a live bird with these, isn't it? Tagging specimens? Doing dissections? Even my ability to take photographs or notes in the field would have been dependent on whether I was having a good or bad day.'

'You left school and went home to have the baby.'

'Yes, in the very early spring. I was deliriously happy. I felt good. Strong, even. I didn't give much thought to how I was going to manage, once the baby came. I had faith everything would fall into place.' Alice stood up slowly and walked to the stove, turning the fire down under the pot. 'I was wrong.'

It was unpleasant, this excavating of another person's life. Stephen might be able to view it dispassionately, as ancient history, but then he wasn't in the same room with her, seeing Alice glance out the window at her daughter like someone lost at sea who has just spotted land. Watching her flinch at every question as he dredged through her past. When her phone rang and she excused herself, he found he was happy for the interruption.

She came back into the kitchen a few minutes later. Her demeanor had changed; there was a tinge of color to her cheeks and her eyes sparkled. 'Phinneaus sends his regards.'

'I assume Phinneaus was the one who told you we were coming to Santa Fe?'

Her body seemed to unspool at the sound of his name; some rigidness went out of her. 'He guessed you might be. We're opposites in that respect. He has a sixth sense; he lets himself be guided by his intuition. I tend to react first, then think about what I should have done once it's too late. After Stephen pulled you away so quickly, Phinneaus went into the kitchen and sat in the chair where Stephen had been sitting. He saw the notes Saisee had jotted on the calendar.'

'So you had the opportunity to alter your plans, but you didn't?'

'I decided to leave it to chance, whether you'd find us or not. I was almost hoping you would.'

'I don't understand. Why?'

Alice looked out the window. 'Because I'm a coward.'

'From what little I know of you, Alice, I would have to disagree.'

'Then call it the long-awaited judgment.'

She turned toward the picture in the living room, Natalie holding Agnete as though she were her own child, her arm curled protectively around the girl's body. Finch recognized something in Natalie's face, the same unambiguous expression of ownership he'd seen in the main panel of the triptych, where Natalie's hand gripped Thomas's shoulder.

'You haven't seen the other panel?'

'No,' she said. 'I knew nothing about the triptych. I only saw this painting a few days ago. He captured her very well, wouldn't you say?'

'Agnete? Or Natalie?'

'Both of them. It's the only image I have of Agnete as a child, other than the one I carried in my head. Now that I've met her, my imagined Agnete is gone. I can't seem to bring her back.' She turned away from the painting as if it was physically painful to see. 'What were you planning to tell my daughter when you found her?' Alice asked.

He'd rehearsed a speech in his head numerous times since seeing Agnete's work in the gallery. But it was primarily speculation, with a hefty measure of conjecture and supposition. 'Only about Thomas. I would have been guessing at anything more. There were times I felt his right to know trumped everything else, your feelings, and hers. He put me in an untenable position, Alice, I just didn't realize it when I agreed to help him. By the time I found out there was a child involved, he was already ill. He couldn't speak, couldn't write. I wasn't sure how much he understood. It seemed too late at that point to assign parameters to our agreement.' He paused, uncertain of how to continue. 'What does she know about Natalie?'

'Just that her aunt died quite suddenly in September. I told her Natalie was planning a visit in October; that I'd seen her airline ticket. Agnete was very upset. The last time Natalie visited, they'd argued about money. She'd been telling Natalie for years she didn't need any financial support, but Natalie wouldn't listen. Agnete finally gave up and started putting the checks Natalie sent into a savings account. She was planning to use the money for Natalie later on, in case she needed it when she got older.' Alice lowered her voice and looked toward the door. 'I could tell she felt she was betraying her aunt by confiding in me, but Agnete thought the money was meant to make her feel in some way obligated. When the last check came, she simply returned it. That was the letter Phinneaus found when we went through Natalie's things. It was marked, 'Return to Sender.' We both assumed it meant she'd moved. Luckily, we were wrong.'

Alice shook her head. 'Beyond that . . . let's say we're cautious with each other. I find my daughter to be amazingly kind and patient. I can't imagine where she gets those qualities.' She smiled at him, but her eyes were wet. 'I know she has questions. And there are so many things I want to ask her. But there isn't any outline for this discussion, and I desperately need one.' She reached out and touched the sleeve of his sweater. 'You said you have a daughter?'

'Lydia. She's twenty-eight.'

'Then you already know what I am just coming to understand. That a parent will do anything to protect their child.'

Finch let his eyes close for a brief moment and thought of his daughter. She came to him as a child, running to meet him at the door after work, her arms wrapped around his waist, her stocking feet resting lightly on the tops of his shoes as he walked her backward into the living room. 'Yes,' he said. 'I would do anything necessary to protect her.'

'And if telling her the truth about Natalie, about what Natalie did to me, to the both of us, would only cause her more pain? What then?'

He thought carefully before answering. 'Agnete is your child, but she is not *a* child. She's an adult. I think you have to trust she'll come to her own conclusions regarding what you tell her, and make her own judgments of those involved.'

Finch set his portfolio on the table and opened it, taking out the cards Natalie had mailed to Thomas. He handed them to Alice one at a time. She examined them briefly, holding them by the edges as if they were hot. Then she set them down and buried her head in her hands.

'Alice, I think your sister must have been a very disturbed young woman.'

'He knew she was alive. He knew, and I didn't.'

It was what Finch had suspected, but it seemed too cruel to contemplate. He would not have thought Natalie, or almost anyone, capable of such a thing had he not seen the expression on Thomas's face when the four men first looked at the triptych panel two months ago.

'Would Thomas have made a good father, do you think?'

Finch thought of the dark, smoke-filled rooms, the empty liquor bottles, the squalor. How hard had Thomas tried to find the two of them? He and Stephen had stumbled their way to the treasure, albeit with a good deal of luck, in a few months.

'Perhaps he'd be a different man than he is now.' It was a roundabout way of answering the question. In spite of everything, he still felt some loyalty to Thomas. Who else was there to defend him?

'That seems like an awful burden to put on a child, the responsibility of bringing out the best in a parent.' She wiped her face. 'Parent, child, daughter. I have a new vocabulary, words I'm not used to using, at least not in regard to myself.'

'Does it really make a difference, finding out he knew about her from the beginning?'

'Each of us only knew what Natalie wanted us to. But I had a chance to tell him at the first, and I didn't take it. I can blame her for almost all of it, but not for that. Had I not thought Agnete was . . .'

Alice clearly had trouble thinking of her daughter as being anything other than vibrant and alive. 'I'd like to think I would have told him after she was born, that I could have swallowed my anger and given him the opportunity to know her. To become a different person, as you suggest. I'm not sure I know how to make peace with that.' She ran her fingertip over a spot on the table, trying to erase it. 'It's the second thing I've stolen from him.'

'The second?'

She turned in her chair and reached into the pocket of the sweater resting across the back of it. 'I wonder if you would give him this when you see him.'

She held her closed hands out in front of her. He saw the knuckles, swollen and red; the wayward position of her fingers, the fatigue of years carved into the skin. He held out his hands, and though he'd thought there was nothing left to surprise him, he had not expected what she put there.

'I was so angry when I left the cabin that day. He'd done something I didn't think I could forgive. I wanted to hurt him in return, but the truth was I didn't know how.' She ran a crooked finger across the back of the bird in Finch's hands. 'This belonged to his mother. In spite of how she and his father rejected him, he kept it. I thought it might mean something to him, so I took it. Even when I thought I'd never speak to him again, I'd always intended to return it.'

'You could give it back to him yourself.'

She shook her head. 'No. I meant it when I said I was a coward.'

The Doughty figurine was warm in his hands. He examined it, the careful details of its coloring, its anatomy. 'I don't believe Thomas ever had much experience with rejection, Alice. Adulation, adoration, yes. But aside from you, and his parents, I can't think of anyone else who ever chose to leave him. He doesn't give people that opportunity, you see. You walking out must have been a unique experience, one he preferred not to repeat. If you wonder why he didn't try harder to find you and Agnete, maybe it's because he believed you didn't want to be found. At least, not by him.' He reached into his briefcase and pulled out the packet of letters, all of them addressed to her, all of them marked, in Natalie's hand, 'Return to Sender.'

She was still, looking at the envelopes but making no move to touch them. 'Natalie succeeded, didn't she?'

'She didn't stop him from thinking about you. You're in every piece of work he did, from the time he found out about the baby until he stopped painting. Am I wrong to tell you?'

'You mean the birds.' She stared at her hands and smiled. 'I didn't know about that until I came here. If I hadn't stopped to rest outside a gallery, I don't know if I ever would have.' She reached across the table and rested her hand lightly on his. 'I don't think those images were meant for me, Professor. I saw him in a dream the night before I found Agnete. I think he meant them for her.'

'Alice, I'd like to help your daughter, if you think she'll

let me. I still have some contacts in New York, a few gallery owners I know, and it appears I may have some time on my hands. Her work is very special.' He waited for a sign of approval, uncertain as to whether he'd made the offer to please her, or because he felt a spark of a kinetic energy when he viewed Agnete's work, something that hadn't happened in years. Regardless, his offer was sincere.

'She has his talent.'

'She has her own talent.'

He hesitated, then asked, the last thing he intended to do on Bayber's behalf. 'Have you forgiven him?'

Stephen and Agnete were still outside, bumping against each other, racing toward the back door. He thought how young they were, the blush of red high in their cheeks, their long limbs, their dark hair.

'We've made our peace,' Alice said.

They pushed through the kitchen door together, jostling each other in a race to the house, then fell into the two remaining chairs around the table, laughing, shaking their hands to break the chill.

'Alice,' Stephen started, reaching across the table for the bowl of crackers. 'Is it all right if I call you Alice?' He went on without waiting for an answer. 'I wonder if I could get a picture of you and Agnete standing beneath the painting. I don't mean for you to think I'm presuming anything, but I did promise my employer I would keep him up-to-date. Regardless of the outcome, I'd like him to know we've found one of the missing panels.'

Stephen saw a look pass between Alice and Finch before she answered.

'The painting isn't mine, Mr. Jameson. But, if it's all right with Agnete, it's fine with me.'

'After dinner,' Agnete said, her tone, Stephen noted, a caution to him. *If you expect anything from me, don't push her.*

Agnete's responses to his questions in the backyard had been clipped when he strayed from the topic of art in general or her sculptures in particular. Finally, he stopped following her around and perched on the cold edge of a wrought-iron love seat in the courtyard, waiting until she realized she'd lost her audience and wandered back to him.

'Are you tired? Or just tired of hearing me talk?' she'd asked.

'I'm trying to understand how this must be for you. First your mother, who you've never met, shows up at your door with news your aunt has died. A few days later, two strangers claim to want to see your work, which is very impressive by the way, which I wouldn't say if I didn't mean. My good opinion of it would have meant something a few years ago. Now, I'm afraid it's just my good opinion, but at least it's an opinion based on experience and knowledge, if that's any consolation. Which, I acknowledge, it may not be.'

'Stephen, you must have lost track of what you were originally going to tell me by now. I certainly have.'

'I'm trying to let you know it's not *just* because I want something. I'm sincerely interested in your work.' Stephen gestured to the various pieces of sculpture in the yard. 'It intrigues me.'

Agnete had walked over to one of the taller works, the school of fish, and fingered a small piece of metal slightly darker than the others, its shape not quite as symmetrical as the rest of the pieces swimming through the air in swirling, upward drifts. Upon closer scrutiny, Stephen saw she had changed the spacing of this one piece of metal in relation to the others, as well as the weight of it. When the wind blew, it did not move in the same pattern as the rest; instead, it twitched and wavered in a way that suggested it was swimming harder, against the tide, in an effort to catch up.

'I'm that fish,' she said. 'I grew up in this house. It's the only place I've ever lived, and I love it here. But everyone in town knew that Therese, even though she raised me, wasn't my mother. Everyone knew that whoever my father was, he wasn't around. I survived adolescence by convincing myself I didn't care; I told myself being different didn't make me any less.' She pulled her hair away from her face, and Stephen was struck by her resemblance to her father. He could feel Bayber's hand, an iron clamp squeezing his wrist. Her father, had he been around, would likely have scared away anyone brave enough to come within five feet of Agnete.

'I made this piece because I've always had a feeling of being separate from everyone else, which I was fine with, but at the same time, a fear of being left behind. Does that make sense?'

Her explanation resonated with him, though he'd have been hard-pressed to articulate it as clearly. He'd stared at the ground, scowling in concentration, unable to say more than 'Yes, I understand what you mean. Maybe I'm that fish, as well.'

'Then there are two of us. We'll be our own school.'

'Agnete, what did Natalie tell you about your mother? About Alice, I mean.'

'That's a rather insensitive question.'

Stephen bit his lip, but couldn't stop from smiling.

'Something funny?'

'No. You sound like Finch, is all. He likes to remind me that I'm a rather insensitive person, so your conclusion seems reasonable.'

Agnete looked up at the sky and squeezed her eyes shut. 'Alice is exactly the way I imagined her.'

'From your dreams?'

'From everything Natalie told me. She talked about Alice whenever we were together. She said she wanted me to know her the way she did.' She shook her head, then opened her eyes wide, as if the world might have changed during those few brief seconds. She held up a hand and ticked qualities off on her fingers. 'Smart. Tenacious. Driven. Honest. Too cautious. Loyal to a fault. Natalie said she could always count on Alice to take her side when they were growing up; that Alice was like her other, better self.'

'But . . .'

'She told me that my mother died during childbirth.'

Stephen's image of Natalie as the fascinating, beguiling outsider dissipated. Agnete looked up at the sky again, blinking rapidly.

'Something in your eye?'

She looked at him in disbelief before breaking out with a laugh that was as bright as Lydia's but more resonant, warmer. 'I'm trying not to cry.'

'Right. Good.' He slapped his hand against his knee, adding an exclamation point. 'So, you hate your aunt. Perfectly understandable.'

Agnete dug the toe of her boot into the ground. 'What would be the point?' She reached out and touched the sleeve of his jacket. 'You don't have permission to judge her, Stephen. That's reserved for me. And for Alice. Anyway, I'm trying very hard to believe that, for whatever reason, Natalie made a decision in the spur of the moment to tell me something that wasn't true. She just couldn't figure out how to take it back once she'd said it.'

'You're defending her?'

'Of course not. But people always do things they hadn't intended to do. You're angry. You allow yourself the luxury of considering a horrible thought. You don't have any intention of acting on it, of course, but you've given it a home in your head. It burrows in, pays attention, waits for an opportunity. And in the moment when something requires a decision, it's right there, seeming just as viable as the saner option, the morally correct response. So you choose. And with one decision, you've become a different person, capable of doing something so reprehensible, you convince yourself it's completely justified. Because why else would you be doing it? And if, no, when you start to doubt, you can't see your way back to making it right, so you just keep moving forward, making it wrong over and over again.'

He stared at her fingers, imagining them coaxing life into a piece of clay. 'I find it curious you can be so kind.'

'Kindness doesn't have anything to do with it. I want to give her some peace. Natalie was haunted.'

'By her guilt?'

'Regret, I think. But more than that, by a fear of being alone. I could feel it in her, whenever we said good-bye; the way she'd hold on to me, with this sort of fierceness. It was an odd embrace, hungry, almost like she thought she could weave us into one person. And that, I can understand. It's so dreadful to think you're alone in the world.'

It was a thought Stephen preferred not to consider. 'But what about the painting? Natalie never told you anything about it? Or mentioned the other pieces?'

'Therese told me it'd been done by a friend of the family. I never asked about it. I never liked it, really. My aunt must have brought it with her when she bought the house or else sent it with Therese. I remember being afraid to look at it when I was little; Natalie's expression was so intense. At some point I must have gotten used to it. Now I forget it's there.'

'But you can see there's something special about it, can't you? Your father is a genius. I could look at that painting every day for the rest of my life and never get tired of seeing it.' He pulled a piece of paper from the sketch pad he'd been taking notes on and roughed out the main panel of the triptych for her. 'If you could see the two pieces together, you'd be amazed by the transition of color. It's seamless, from one panel to the next, brighter in the center, darker on each end, as if to convey something about the uncertainty of the future. The shadows in this panel, the light bleeding in from the window Natalie's standing in front of, the strokes he used to paint her skirt—you can almost feel the suede fabric between your fingers when you look at it. It's probably worth millions of dollars, Agnete. Even without the other panel.'

'I'd have traded that money to have my family without a second thought.' Agnete turned her head away from his sketch. 'You're just looking at layers of paint, Stephen. I'm looking at my life. All I see when I look at that painting now are the people missing from it.'

***

After dinner, Stephen took great pains to pose the Kessler women beneath the painting. Chairs were moved, objects brought into the field to add balance, the positions of arms and legs adjusted, faces turned, chins tilted up. Finch was exhausted and rapidly losing patience, especially when he could see Alice fading. 'You're not Stieglitz, Stephen. Take the picture. We've overstayed our welcome.'

Stephen waved Finch away but took several shots in quick succession and then several more of the painting alone.

'Professor Finch, would you take a picture of Stephen and

me? I'm going to use it as blackmail to remind him he promised to buy one of my pieces.' Agnete favored him with a wide smile, and Finch felt his heart melt as he helped Alice from the hard chair where Stephen had deposited her. Bayber blood. Apparently he was powerless against it.

Stephen and Agnete struck a pose on the hearth, the two of them talking a blue streak. Their arms rested casually across each other's shoulders, their heads bent together, one mass of inky hair. Had he ever in his life had that much energy? It seemed unlikely. Finch peered through the viewfinder of Stephen's 35 mm, adjusting the lens, fiddling with the zoom, trying to bring Stephen and Agnete into focus. 'Something's wrong here,' he started, then pulled the camera away and looked at the two of them more closely, his heart in his throat. The identical shape of their faces, the aquiline noses, the high cheekbones—how had he not noticed it earlier? He peered into the viewfinder again, praying to see something other than the same high forehead on each of them. But there was nothing wrong with the camera. The picture was perfectly clear.

He sat down on the top step and held the camera out to Alice. 'Could you . . . ?'

'I'm afraid the buttons and dials are too small for my fingers.'

'No,' Finch said. 'Just look.' He handed her the camera and concentrated on a nick in the step tile, not wanting to see her expression. She stared through the viewfinder for a long minute before setting the camera down. Then her hand was on his sleeve, and he turned to see in her face the same disbelief that must be in his own: eyes wide with shock, mouth slightly agape. He shook his head and closed his eyes before cursing Thomas under his breath. And Dylan's wife, for good measure. So this was the reason he'd insisted on Stephen.

'You're going to have to tell him,' Alice whispered.

Finch felt a fist constricting around his heart. 'I don't think I can,' he said.

'Finch, he'll have to know. And soon.' She tilted her head toward the pair of them, chittering away in front of the fire.

Finch called for a cab, adamant that Agnete and Alice had done enough already and that everyone would benefit from a good night's sleep. Agnete finally acquiesced, throwing her arms around his neck in an unexpected hug and pecking Stephen on the cheek. They left, agreeing to meet at the hotel for a late breakfast the next day. He was quiet during the short ride back to the hotel, doing his best not to look at Stephen.

'Finch, have I done something?'

'Hmmm? No, no. You haven't done anything.' Finch gritted his teeth, grimacing at the truth of his words.

'Alice seemed a bit put off by me, I thought.'

'Really? I didn't notice that,' Finch said, and stared out the rear window of the cab at the lights woven through tree branches, haloed and sparking in the cold air. 'I imagine she's still trying to absorb the day's revelations. They seemed to be unending.'

At the hotel, Finch divvied up their correspondence before saying good night. He assigned Stephen the task of filling in Cranston and forwarding the photos he'd taken of the second triptych panel to the lab, while insisting he'd handle the update to Bayber himself. 'And I'm turning this damn thing off,' he said, waving his cell phone in Stephen's face. 'Lydia has my room number if she needs me, as do you.'

Safely behind the locked door of his room, he collapsed on the bed. It was one thing to contemplate causing pain to a total stranger, as he'd done with Agnete. But she'd been only two-dimensional to him then, a figment imagined, not wholly believed. Stephen was real, an oddly endearing, frenetic, brilliant mess, desperate for approval from the one person who could no longer give it to him—the man he knew as his father.

The thought that he might be forced to tell Stephen a truth that would likely upend him was more than Finch could stand. *Help me, Claire.* He closed his eyes and buried his face against the starch of the bedsheet in fervent prayer— that it would not be now her voice faded away from him for good, a star slipping out of the dark sky into a void of silence.

Her breath was on his cheek. *It pains me to see you like this. What do I do?*

There was silence, in which he could count every day she'd been gone from him as a dull strike against his heart. *What was it you said to Alice when she asked you about Natalie, earlier? I will say the same thing to you now. Stephen is an adult. He will come to his own conclusions regarding what you tell him, and make his own judgments of those involved.*

But he will be hurt.

Yes. But he will be healed, as well. He has more family than he imagined. A half sister, and her mother. And the man her mother loves, and that man's nephew, and the woman who cares for them all. And you, Denny. Aren't you his friend?

That's not the same thing.

She gave a derisive snort, and her hair tickled against his ear. *Oh, isn't it? Go to sleep now, you foolish gizzard. You've worn yourself down to the bone. You'll have to build up your strength if you expect to be toting any grandchild of mine around on the back of your stubborn neck.*

In his hotel room, too keyed up to sleep, Stephen down-loaded the photos from camera to laptop, then quickly forwarded them to the lab and knocked out the message to Cranston. Risking Finch's wrath, which had yet to be so severe he couldn't cajole him out of it, he e-mailed a few of the pictures to Mrs. Blankenship, instructing her to print them out and show them to Bayber as soon as possible: Agnete in the backyard standing next to one of her sculptures; Alice and Agnete seated under the painting; and then on a whim, and to show Bayber his daughter seemed fond enough of the men he'd tasked with finding her, the picture of himself sitting next to Agnete on the fireplace hearth. Having finished, he stretched out on the bed and folded his arms behind his head, staring at the low beams of the ceiling and trying to puzzle out where the third panel could be.

Both Alice and Agnete claimed never to have seen the remaining triptych panel, and there was little reason for them to lie. Now that he and Finch had found the second panel, Stephen felt confident the third would have as its subject a pregnant Alice, since the painting of Natalie and Agnete resembled the second photograph Natalie had sent to Bayber.

Everything turned back to Natalie. Stephen put a hand over his eyes and focused on her, trying to steal his way into Natalie's head. She was clever enough to have known the painting's value, so it was unlikely she would have disposed of it. That thought alone caused him to shudder, a ruined and slashed Bayber sitting atop a trash heap, or charred beyond recognition, the singed frame smoldering in an alley somewhere. No. She was smarter than that. Keeping it, and keeping it hidden, would have pleased her, thinking only she and Thomas knew of its existence. Another thing linking them. Another secret kept from Alice.

So if she hadn't gotten rid of it, it was stashed somewhere. She couldn't risk insuring it without revealing its existence. He could think of only two possibilities: George Reston, Jr., or the Edells. While he wished it would be in the hands of the oblivious and slightly dim-witted Edells, the far more likely scenario, also the more distasteful, was that Natalie had instructed George to hold on to the painting. If George knew Natalie was dead, Stephen was certain he would sell the painting as quickly as possible. The idea that another appraiser at another auction house might be working on the catalogue description at this minute was enough to sour Stephen's stomach and send bright screws of light spiraling into his brain. He and Finch had to find the painting before someone else did.

He squinted at the bedside lamp, fumbling to turn it off, then dragged himself into the bathroom, retrieving a cold cloth for his head. On his way back to bed, he turned down the thermostat and waited until the fan stopped whirring and blasting the room with hot air before crawling between the sheets. Morning would come soon enough, and he would have another chance to prompt Agnete into remembering some elusive but critical detail that would provide him with the answer.

The yolks ran across his plate in a river of yellow, into the soft mash of beans he'd pushed to the side. It was a mistake eating eggs after eleven-thirty in the morning, Stephen decided. They'd outlived their appeal by that hour, and he eyed Finch's untouched sandwich enviously, the flagrant red of a charred pepper peeking out between toasted bread and a glob of pale, milky cheese. Ordering poorly was always a disappointment. He gulped his latte instead, and considered ordering churros, a food that could be enjoyed regardless of the hour.

In spite of what Finch had claimed the night before, Alice was definitely avoiding him, scarcely able to look him in the eye. She was sitting behind a plate of blue cornmeal pancakes, and he felt sure she'd rather be in her own kitchen, eating Saisee's grits. Finch kept his coffee cup to his mouth, and even Agnete was subdued, pushing pieces of food around her plate as if excavating something. Evidently the responsibility of starting the conversation was going to fall to him. He was about to tackle the subject of auctioning the triptych, providing the missing panel could be found, when his phone buzzed in his pocket. Ignoring Finch's glare, he pulled it out and checked the number. Mrs. Blankenship. He excused himself from the table, due to Finch's vigorous nod in the direction of the lobby more than a sudden glut of manners, and sank into one of the deep leather chairs to check his messages. There were three from Mrs. Blankenship, beginning at six o'clock that morning Santa Fe time. Eight o'clock in New York. She likely hadn't been able to reach Finch, with his phone off. It was early for her to be calling, unless she'd had a problem downloading the file he'd sent. She'd finally left a message with the third call, a little more than an hour ago, and just before it played, Stephen was gripped by something awful and familiar, a memory he had desperately tried to keep at the far back of his brain: his mother's calls while he was in Rome.

He didn't remember walking back into the dining room, or sitting down again in his chair, or putting his napkin in his lap. He only remembered that there was something he should definitely not say in front of Alice. In front of Agnete. He looked at Finch and realized it would hurt Finch just as much, in a different kind of way. If no one asked him, he wouldn't have to say anything, and until he said it, it didn't have to be true.

'Stephen?' Finch said, suddenly alarmed.

He was crying. He couldn't remember crying before, in

Rome, with his mother's quavering voice on the other end of the line; or at his father's wake, while waiting for the never-ending procession of mourners to snake past him in the receiving line. He couldn't even remember crying at the funeral, standing outside in the rain, with his face already frozen and wet. But he didn't have to say anything to Finch after all; Finch, who somehow knew him so well, and knew exactly what had happened without Stephen having to say a word.

Everything after—the decisions, the plans, the phone calls, the flights—was a blizzard. All the information fell around him in a blanket; he waited for someone to point him in a direction and give him a shove. Go here, do this, pack that. Finch collected the details from Mrs. Blankenship: Thomas had been improving; then he hadn't. Thomas saw the photos Stephen had sent and seemed to rally, but when she went in a little later with his breakfast, he had a fever and his coloring looked off. She called the doctor, and then on the recommendation of the day nurse called for an ambulance. He'd died with the pictures clutched in his hand.

'I let him down,' Stephen told Finch, while they were waiting for Alice and Agnete to return to the hotel with their own luggage.

'Stephen, you gave him his reunion, even if he wasn't there to see it.' Finch seemed to choose his words carefully, speaking to him slowly, as if he was a child. 'He was very ill. Liver failure, the doctor said, among other things. He wasn't going to get better. You know that, don't you?' Finch's voice floated over him, a cloud of comfort. 'If you can, you'll need to help Agnete. Try to remember, she never had the chance to meet her father. Not once.'

Finch had spent more than an hour on the phone trying to get a direct flight to New York for the two of them, but it was too close to the holiday and everything was booked or involved convoluted routes, hours in the air and on the ground. It was decided they would keep their existing reservations and go back to Tennessee with Alice and Agnete for a couple of days, all of them making their way to New York from there.

'I need to go home first,' Alice said, and Stephen noted her tentative emphasis on the word *home,* as though trying it on for size. 'I have to see Phinneaus.' She said it the same way she might have said *I have to have air.*

She was more shaken than Stephen would have thought, considering she hadn't seen Thomas for over thirty-five years. It was the compression of too many surprises, he assumed, everything spring-loaded like a jack-in-the-box, jumping out at her with flailing arms when she hadn't expected it. They huddled together in lines, and at points of departure, and sat next to each other on the airplane, four ashen, grim-looking people who periodically cried but rarely at the same time or for the same reason. Phinneaus picked them up in Memphis.

'You should drive,' Stephen said to him, his voice dulled from breathing in the recycled air of transit.

'Stephen, it's my car,' Phinneaus said.

'Right. Just don't give the keys to Finch. He's a lunatic behind the wheel.'

'Get in the backseat, Stephen.'

At least when he was riding with Finch, Stephen could claim shotgun. Now, instead, he was crammed into the back with Agnete and Finch, Finch sitting between the two of them since his legs were shortest. On the drive to Orion, Stephen dozed in fits and starts, jerking awake in a state of disorientation, unsure of where he was. Alice sat so close to Phinneaus in the front seat that in the dimming light it was hard for Stephen to tell where one stopped and the other started. He realized he would soon be alone again. After the funeral Alice and Phinneaus would come back to Tennessee and Agnete would eventually end up back in Santa Fe. Finch would no doubt be consumed with his impending grandfatherhood and his teaching. The professor snorted in his sleep; his head lolled to the side. Who was going to watch out for the man after all this was over? Not Lydia—she and *the Kelvin* would soon be otherwise occupied. Stephen managed to extricate himself from his coat and wedge it against Finch's neck. Who would caution him about his reckless driving? Who would understand his misguided and, ultimately, mistaken arguments regarding the importance of American Regionalism? With or without the final panel, whether in a slightly larger office or in the same dank square he currently inhabited, Stephen was the only one going back to the same life. Bayber was gone, and the thing Stephen had most wanted to achieve, bringing back the two panels, had eluded him.

In Orion, he fell through the front door of the house he'd seen only once before, grateful for the familiarity of something—the sound of Saisee's voice, the smell of her cooking, the warm, fragrant air of the kitchen. There was Frankie, who after lightly hugging Alice, astonished Stephen by wrapping his arms around his knees, locking him to the spot where he stood, a more enthusiastic welcome than the one he'd received previously.

'Your eye's much better now,' Frankie said.

How long had it been, in child days, since he'd been here? In adult time, it seemed eons. Saisee bustled about, busy and happy to have a house full of people who needed her, to have mouths to feed and clothes to wash and rooms to assign. She'd never known Thomas and had no connection with him save for Agnete, whom she treated like a long-lost doll, smoothing her hair and fingering the fabric of her coat while she clucked and hovered over her.

Stumbling into the living room the next morning, Stephen looked around and took in the peculiar assortment they made. Agnete sat on the floor next to Frankie, watching as he marched a carved horned toad back and forth over her shin. Alice's eyes never left Agnete's face, but she was glued to Phinneaus's side, her fingers tracing the veins on the back of his hand. Saisee wore a path between the kitchen and the living room, bringing out mugs of coffee, and plates barely visible beneath clouds of spoon bread, ambrosia dotted with maraschino cherries—the cheerful red of them an affront to his eyes—and rosy slices of ham. And Finch, in spite of his drawn appearance, tapped away on his laptop, occasionally giving Stephen an uneasy glance. *No doubt ordering multiple copies of Pat the Bunny,* Stephen thought.

Luggage had been dropped everywhere, as if their plane had disgorged its contents over the house, and there were boxes of papers stacked high in the room's corners. When Stephen asked about them, it was Phinneaus who answered.

'Natalie's papers. At some point, Alice and Agnete may need to go through them. Saisee brought them all down from upstairs.'

'From the attic, you mean?'

'Lord, no,' Saisee said. 'From Miss Natalie's rooms on the second floor. No one ever goes up to the attic. Those stairs are so steep they'd likely kill a person.'

No one ever goes up to the attic.

Stephen leapt from the sofa and ran to the front hall, starting up the stairs. He turned around a third of the way up, running into Agnete, who had followed him, and said, 'Grab my case, can you? It's at the bottom of the stairs with everyone else's things.' He raced up to the second floor and then to the attic, taking the stairs two at a time. Having no luck with the knob, he threw the weight of his body against the swollen attic door, jubilant when it yielded and swung open.

Agnete was right behind him; he could hear her breath just over his shoulder. It took no more than a second of scanning the room before he found it, a large crate propped up against the wall in the corner. There was a trunk in front of it, some moving boxes of sweaters with the lingering scents of mothballs and lavender sachet, and paper bags full of magazines: *Art in America, ARTnews, Art & Antiques*. The dog-eared pages in each were mentions of Thomas Bayber.

'Someone was a fan,' he said, thumbing rapidly through back issues, a cloud of dust coating the inside of his nose and making him sneeze. 'Help me move these.'

'Whose is all of this?' Agnete asked. 'My mother's?'

'I don't think so. I doubt she even knew this was here. It looks like it was all Natalie's.' He pointed to a yellowed address label on one of the magazine covers. He pushed the clothes and bags of magazines away with the side of his foot, then he and Agnete each took an end of the trunk and pulled it toward the center of the attic. The crate stood alone against the wall, its corners opaque with webs and the carcasses of small insects.

'Stephen, we should ask Alice before we do anything else. All of these things are hers or Natalie's. Maybe she'd prefer to be there when they're opened.'

Stephen tried to control his pulse, his breathing. The hairs on his arms were standing up; he could feel a spark of static at the back of his throat that refused to be swallowed. His mouth was almost too dry to form the necessary words. 'Alice has been through a lot. Don't you think it would be better if we knew what was inside before we dragged the crate downstairs? If it's not the painting, we can tell her it's not here. Save her the disappointment.'

'Oh, but I haven't been through anything at all,' she said, her voice heavy with sarcasm. She rubbed her hands together; he could see she was as anxious as he was. 'Really, Stephen. Does anyone believe you when you say things like that? You're the one who would be disappointed, not my mother.'

'Agnete, please.'

She hesitated before nodding. 'All right. Do you have anything we can use to . . .'

Stephen had opened his case and was thumping a small pry bar against his palm. He wedged the end of the bar into the sliver of space where the crate's frame met the top slat and pushed up until the nails screeched out and the top of the crate loosened from the front panel. He motioned for Agnete to help, and the two of them pulled the crate to the middle of the attic floor, laying it flat. Stephen handed her the pry bar, then got on his knees and reached inside.

'Whatever is in here, it's well-wrapped.'

Agnete was looking at the bottom corner of the crate, at a shipping label. 'It's addressed to Alice,' she said. 'Stephen, look. Do you recognize this handwriting?'

He stopped pulling at the bundle and scooted over next to her. 'Yes,' he said. 'That's Bayber's writing.'

'My father,' she said, looking at him.

Her father. He hadn't thought a thing about that, about the way she and Bayber were connected, what both of the paintings might mean to her. He'd thought only of their value in a broader sense—the thrill of the discovery, rare additions to a known and supposedly finite body of work. Now he stopped, remembering the cuff links he kept with him at all times. How would he feel, unexpectedly coming across something of Dylan's? Agnete was right. That would be worth more than all the Pollocks and Mangolds, the Klees and Gormleys put together.

Agnete's skin was stretched thin over the bones of her face, a filament of blue visible along the side of her neck, appearing again at her temple. He could see the even ledge of her teeth pressing down against her bottom lip.

'You should be the one to open it,' he said.

She shook her head. 'No. Both of us. You were the one who brought us all together, Stephen. You and Professor Finch.'

He hesitated, then nodded, and they turned the crate so its open end faced them. They stuck their arms inside and grabbed hold of what felt like a moving blanket, shimmying it back and forth until it was free of the crate. Stephen pulled the covering aside, and Agnete gasped.

'That's my mother. That's Alice. She's beautiful.'

He stood the third panel of the triptych up against the wall. The oil was in a large but simple gilt frame. He thought of the other two pieces as he studied this one, mentally arranging them in their proper order, seeing the way the backgrounds would bleed into each other; the girls in the outer panels each pulling their younger selves away from Bayber and into the future; the past, present, and future joined. But where Natalie clutched at an infant Agnete and looked solemnly at the viewer, Alice, in her panel, was facing sideways and looking up to the sky, her face radiant with joy, her hair free and floating around her in an aura of pale gold. One arm encircled the swell of her belly while the other reached behind her for the hand of the younger Alice. The blue grosbeak that was missing from the cage in the center panel was here, perched on Alice's shoulder, looking like it was whispering in her ear.

Agnete was crying. Stephen rested his arm awkwardly across her shoulder, and she turned in to him, burying her face against his chest. He could feel the front of his shirt getting damp. He attempted to nudge the crate out of the way with his shoe, but it was too heavy.

'Agnete, there's something else in here.'

She wiped her face with the palms of her hands and watched as he lifted a smaller painting, covered in a piece of flannel sheet, from the crate and unwrapped it: a medium unframed canvas.

'What is it?' she asked him.

'I've been here,' Stephen said, tracing the painting lightly with his fingers. 'I know this place. It's your father's summer house. Where he and Alice first met.' The view was from the lake, in the middle of a storm. Stephen could approximate the vantage point; he could almost feel the waves pitching beneath him while he stood in a small boat, looking toward land. The foreground was a miasma of froth and foam, swells charging across the water, a wet sheen reflected from the rocks onshore and from the roof of the cabin. The windows were illuminated by a murky glow, and smoke curling from one of the chimneys hinted at a fire burning. He looked more closely. Watery smears across the top of the painting were actually the shallow Vs of birds, several flocks flying in the same direction, but the strokes did not look quite like Bayber's. Stephen turned the painting over and handed it to Agnete, who read out loud what was written in strong cursive on the back:

Alice,
Do not let grief be the only map you carry,
lest you lose your way back to happiness.
T.

EPILOGUE

Finch stopped at Thomas's apartment—his apartment—the morning after they got back to the city. Mrs. Blankenship was settled on the edge of a chair in the living room waiting for him, her coat buttoned up to the neck in the chill air, a piece of paper folded in her gloved hand. The heat must have gone off again. That, or Cranston's largesse had come to an abrupt end. Finch would have to call someone.

'I can't go into the back rooms anymore,' she said. 'It makes me so sad.' She pressed the paper into his hand. 'It was in the drawer of the nightstand. I found it when I was gathering his things: medicines, eyeglasses, his hairbrush. There isn't much.'

Common vanities, hidden away. Finch couldn't recall ever seeing Thomas in glasses. He took the paper she held out to him.

'I didn't read it.' She wouldn't meet his gaze, which suggested otherwise.

'I'll see you at the service tomorrow,' he said.

Mrs. Blankenship nodded. 'Do you want me to stay?'

'You go ahead. I'll lock up.' Finch squeezed her hand,

realizing the woman was bereft. She and Thomas had had their own relationship after all; so many years of fussing and sorting, clucking and picking up after. What had they talked about, the two of them? He shook his head when she offered him her keys to the apartment. 'We'll sort everything out later.' He wondered if Stephen might not be interested in living here, or perhaps Agnete.

After Mrs. Blankenship left, the room settled with the same thick quiet he'd felt months ago at the cabin. He went into Thomas's bedroom and pulled the drapes open before sitting down in the chair by the window and unfolding the piece of paper. It was a letter.

Mr. Stephen Jameson
c/o Murchison & Dunne, 22nd floor

October 1, 2007

Stephen,
I understand from others you are a man who
appreciates directness and has little patience for the
meandering discourse that passes these days for
conversation. So be it. I do not yet know whether
you and I will have the pleasure of meeting. I agreed
years ago never to contact you at the behest of your
mother, and out of respect for her husband, I have
abided by that agreement until now. But as the years
in front of me grow fewer, I would like the
opportunity to at least once see my own son.

I did not love your mother, and she quickly
realized she did not love me. I make no attempt to
justify my behavior, past or present. I have lived my
life in service only to myself, and now I am left with

the deserved remains of such a life. Your father—the man who raised you—was a good man, though that word does not do justice to his character. He was a far better parent than I had the inclination to be.

You have a sister, Stephen; a half sister if you prefer. I do not know her whereabouts, but my hope is that you are able to find her, and that she is more of her mother than of me, although to imagine two on this earth drawn from the same hand seems more than God would allow. If you are in need of counsel, seek out Dennis Finch. He is a principled man, and compassionate, someone who will remind himself of your best qualities while struggling to forgive your worst. In short, he is a friend. You can trust him to do what he says, a trait which becomes increasingly rare.

It is hard to know what to wish for someone who should not be a stranger, yet is. So I will say only this. The estimation of an artist's talent is often based on his ability to render both light and shadow. If you have any choice in the matter, spend your time seeking the former.

Thomas Bayber

Finch folded the piece of paper and stuffed it into his pocket as he heard again Bayber's words on that October afternoon. *Would it be so strange I would want back what I once had, just as you do?* It was never the triptych Thomas wanted to reclaim. Finch looked out the window and watched the sun paint a wide swath of light on the buildings across the street. There was not nearly enough time after all.

ACKNOWLEDGMENTS

I have been incredibly fortunate to have as my agent the wonderful Sally Wofford-Girand and her team at Union Literary. My editor at Simon & Schuster, Trish Todd, has been a gracious navigator, helping me see what was in my head but not yet on the page, and Thalia Suzuma at HarperFiction U.K. gently encouraged me to uncover parts of the story I hadn't realized were hidden. I could not have asked for more supportive guidance and enthusiasm than I received from the three of them. Thanks, as well, go to the team at Simon & Schuster for all of their efforts on my behalf.

To my readers: Ellen Sussman, teacher, mentor and friend, whose generosity has been unparalleled, thanks are not enough; and Christine Chua, my extraordinary tiger writing buddy, who always helped me find a way out of the weeds, your encouragement, keen insights, and thoughtful suggestions were invaluable. Calvin Klein has been a constant supporter from before the beginning, and I am grateful to have him, and the extended Klein family, in my life. To Gabriela Cosio-Avilla; John DeMartini; Anne Ferril; Nancy

Hoefig; Philip McCaffrey; Lori Petrucelli; and Jean, Mike, and Tony Valentine, your enthusiasm and support have been sustaining. For all of my writing friends who have pushed me and celebrated with me, I have been blessed to have both your feedback and your gracious support.

To my family—I could not have done this without you: my father, who found the missing words; my sisters, who believed this was possible before I did; and my nephews, Conor, Cody, and Kyle, whose love of reading is inspirational. And most important to my mother—first reader, best reader, always.

the
gravity
of birds

Tracy Guzeman lives and works in the San Francisco
Bay Area. A Pushcart Prize nominee, her fiction has
been published in *Gulf Coast*, *Vestal Review* and
Glimmer Train Stories, and performed as part of the
New Short Fiction Series Emerging Voices Group
Show. *The Gravity of Birds* is her first novel.

'*The Gravity of Birds* is part mystery, part psychological
drama and intriguing love story. This is a stunning debut'
Ellen Sussman, author of *New York Times*
bestselling *French Lessons*

'*The Gravity of Birds* is one of those rare, exquisitely
written novels that haunt you long after you've finished
the page'
Alyson Richman, author of the bestselling *The Lost Wife*

'A warmhearted, assured and haunting debut. Always
graceful and often breathtaking'
Meg Waite Clayton, author of the bestselling
The Wednesday Sisters